HOUSE OF GIRAL

Mark Laurence Latowsky

HOUSE OF GIRAL

iUniverse books may be ordered through booksellers or by contacting:

iUniverse
1663 Liberty Drive
Bloomington, IN 47403
www.iuniverse.com
844-349-9409

ISBN: 978-1-6632-5048-3 (sc)
ISBN: 978-1-6632-5050-6 (hc)
ISBN: 978-1-6632-5049-0 (e)

Library of Congress Control Number: 2023902296

Print information available on the last page.

iUniverse rev. date: 02/17/2023

Dedicated to: Rob and Trish MacGregor.

For Jessica, whose name is blessed of wealth;
Issac, her first born child, of laughter and promise.
And Jasper, her richly blessed treasure holder.

In memory of my late mother Evelyn
Kallen and father Albert Latowsky.

The quickest road to easy street runs through the sewer
— John Madden

Prologue

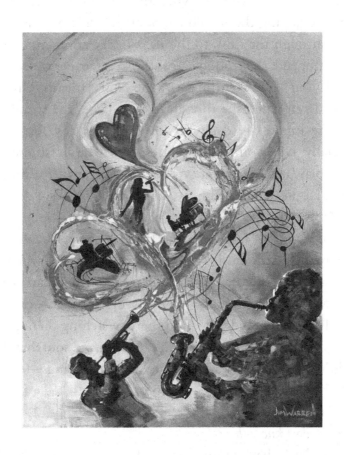

March 9, 2022

The music drifted around her, a jazz piece she recognized from the 1920s. It boomed from the open doors of a bar or restaurant on Fort Lauderdale Beach and drew Jennifer "Jo" Hart like metal to a magnet.

She jogged here five evenings a week but never had done so on a Saturday evening, when the snowbirds were out in droves, enjoying the incredible South Florida weather. She loped through the dusk to the next intersection, and when traffic stopped, she trotted across the street, eager to see who was playing "Farewell Blues" by the New Orleans Rhythm Kings. Even when she thought of the name, she wondered how she knew. She'd always loved jazz in any form, but especially jazz from the twenties. She'd never studied it, didn't play an instrument, yet for some strange reason this particular piece haunted her.

Midway down the street, the music got louder. She followed it into a large bar, the Bourbon Street Club. The place rocked with music that came from the stage, where an ethnically diverse band of seven men and one woman played "Farewell Blues." She made her way up to the bar, ordered a bottle of water, and just stood there, watching them play a variety of instruments with such precision and soul that they could've been the New Orleans Rhythm Kings—except that the group from the twenties had consisted of eight white men.

How do I know that?

She didn't have an answer, and that bothered her. But the longer she listened, the less the answer mattered. Her foot tapped to the rhythm, her body swayed, the music transported her.

She is fourteen, like Santiago Garcia, and they hurry through town, eager to hear the music. They aren't allowed to be here without an adult, but who will know? Their nannies are napping. They probably haven't heard that the Rhythm Kings are playing near the Las Olas drawbridge. It isn't like the city fathers or anyone else announced it. All word of mouth, from one neighbor to another.

She can hear the music now, and she and Santiago glance at each other and walk faster, faster. Pretty soon they are running, clutching each other's hands, and suddenly, she sees them, the eight musicians on a makeshift stage. Sunlight spills over them, their instruments glint in the light, and "Farewell Blues" fills the sea air.

"Beautiful." Santiago throws his arms out to his sides. "The music, the place, the smell of the air ..."

Then someone comes up behind them. "What the hell are you doing here, young lady?"

She and Santiago spin around, and her father stands there, his cheeks puffed out with rage, his eyes dark and large, his hands fisted at his sides. Her younger brother, Raul, is slightly behind him. She steps back, and Santiago steps forward. "Sir, we heard the band was going to be here and ..."

"I don't give a goddamn what you heard, boy."

"The fastest way to easy street runs through the gutter." - John Madden

Jo wrenched back, deeply shaken, and glanced around wildly. Several people stood on either side of her now, and it seemed they stared at her like they knew she was struggling. The band played on. Jennifer made her way through the crowd, murmuring, "Excuse me, excuse me." She made it to the front door and hurried out into the evening.

She ran. It didn't matter where or in what direction, as long as she got away from here, from the music that had triggered the memory or flashback or whatever the hell it was. *Run, run as fast as you can, away from that music, away.* She didn't know how far she had gone when her legs cramped up, she could barely breathe, and suddenly she just couldn't run anymore. Her knees buckled, and she sank to the ground, her body shaking with sobs.

What's wrong with me?

"Nothing, nothing's wrong with me," she whispered, barely able to catch her breath.

She pressed her hands against her thighs and rocked back on her heels, glancing around to get her bearings. She didn't have any idea where she was. Nothing looked familiar. When had it gotten so dark?

She pushed to her feet and glanced up and down the street, panic clawing in her chest, making its way into her throat. She knew where she was—on that country road outside her parents' home, and her father was behind her, pushing her up the sidewalk, toward the front door, which

Raul opened with a sweeping gesture of his arm, as though their father were a king.

"*No!*" she shrieked, and tore away from all of it, running with her arms tucked in tightly at her sides, her breath exploding from her chest, terror whipping her forward faster. "Help me!" she shrieked. "Help me, he's going to ..." And she tripped and pitched forward, and her arms shot out to break her fall. Someone ran over to her, a woman in jeans and a sweater. "Hey, are you okay? Should I call 911?"

"Are you real?" Jennifer asked. "You look real." Curly brown hair, a cute face, a quick smile. "Please be real."

"Yeah, I'm real." She came over, touched Jennifer's arm. "Listen, why don't you just sit down right here." She patted a section of wall behind her that marked the boundary of someone's yard. "Tell me who to call. Husband? Boyfriend? Family? And what's your name, anyway? I'm Annette. I live just down the block."

Her name. What the hell was her name?

Where was her brutal father? Her sniveling brother? Her fiancé? No, no this was all mixed up. It was as if her brain had collapsed and was now rewiring itself a piece at a time, but the pieces didn't fit. "I ... I ... don't know my name." She slumped to the wall, pressed her hands over her face, and wept.

She heard Annette on the phone, saying, "Yes, yes, that's right. She's melting down right here on the street." Jennifer struggled to contain her sobs.

Humans don't melt. Psyches do.

She burst into hysterical laughter and rocked back and forth, back and forth, her arms locked at her waist. When she couldn't laugh anymore, when it hurt to laugh, she slapped the pocket in her running pants and brought out her cell phone. Stared at it. "What's my name?"

"Your name is Jennifer Hart. People call you Jo. Close friends call you JoJo."

"And who are you?"

"I'm Siri. And I—"

"You're a piece of shit!" she screamed, and she hurled the cell over her shoulder and into the yard behind her.

She heard sirens now, shrieks and squeals that sounded like a herd of wild animals. The air thundered with their approach. Jennifer grabbed onto the railing that sectioned off the yard, vaulted over it and ran until she was tackled from behind and struck the ground. "Alert Broward Mental Health," said the man who now handcuffed her and pulled her to her feet. "We've got a wild one."

Bet your ass. She slammed her knee into his groin, and he grunted and fell back. But another man grabbed her around the waist, lifted her up as though she weighed nothing at all, and carried her to an ambulance. She screamed and struggled to free herself, but now she was on a bed, and another man restrained her ankles, then strapped something around her middle.

"Please," she sobbed. "I didn't do it."

He sank a needle deep into her neck, and darkness seized her.

Part 1

Discovery

Mistakes are the portals of discovery.
—James Joyce

Chapter 1

WHEN ALBERT ANDREW YOUNG ENTERED THE ER EARLY Thursday morning March 10, 2022, it was nearly empty. What a difference from the last couple of years, when COVID was running rampant through South Florida with more than twenty thousand cases a day and ERs were so jammed care had to be rationed.

Millie, the receptionist at the front desk, waved him over. "Morning, Dr. Young. The patient who was in ER 7 got moved an hour ago when a room opened up on the psych ward. Room 137."

"Is Dr. House already with her?"

She nodded. "He arrived about ten minutes ago."

"Thanks, Millie."

Young swept past the front desk and pushed through the double doors to the first floor. The psychiatric ward was at the end of the hall and included a thirteen-bed locked ward, conference room, visiting area, courtyard, library, rec room, several offices, and a bloodletting room. The treatment area was the largest. It was here where patients in his psychedelic program received one of various hallucinogens as part of their treatment. His program was the only one of its kind in South Florida, and with it he'd had excellent success. It worked particularly well with traumatized patients.

He went through another set of double doors and entered the psych ward. Four patients were in the rec room, either watching TV or reading, and two others stood at the floor-to-ceiling windows, staring out into the courtyard. A pair of black-and-white cats, Bob and Betty, strolled around, rubbing up against patients, purring. The woman at the window, a rape victim, glanced down at Bob and picked him up, loving on him. Sometimes when a patient was on the brink of mania, the cats sensed it, and one of them would stick to the person like Velcro.

Young had adopted the cats for the ward after reading about Oscar, the nursing home cat at a facility in Rhode Island who allegedly identified which patients were near death. In his first five years at the facility, he had accurately forecast fifty deaths. In the two years Bob and Betty had been living here, they had accurately predicted twenty-two instances where patients were approaching a manic state.

Room 137 was at the end of the hall. It was a prime number, divisible only by one or by itself, and was also the value of the fine structure constant, one of the unsolved mysteries of modern physics. It was a number that stood at the root of the universe and all matter. It wasn't just the DNA of light, as author Arthur I. Miller once wrote, the death card followed by the Chariot in Tarot card readings, but the sum of the Hebrew letters of the word "Kabbalah," marking the path a life takes accross the Sephirot of conscious life.

The number at some point in time had become so puzzling to physicists that the famed Richard Feynman, who won the Nobel Prize in 1965 for his contribution to the development of quantum electrodynamics, had said physicists should put a sign on their doors to remind them of what they didn't know. The sign would be simple: 137.

For most of his life, Nobel laureate Wolfgang Pauli was equally confounded by the number. In fact, when he entered the hospital at age fifty-eight for routine surgery and saw that his room number was 137, he remarked that he wouldn't get out alive. And he didn't.

Young felt that any patient assigned to this room would be as challenging to him as 137 was to Feynman and Pauli.

As he walked into the room, Laurence House, head of the ER, glanced up from the iPad he held. "Hey, Andy. We've got ourselves a sleeping beauty."

"Christ, Larry, not so loud. She might hear us. What do you think?"

House was a ridiculously tall man, nearly six and a half feet, and towered over Young. He was also a few years younger, maybe forty, with the kind of handsome face that left women swooning. He rubbed his chin. "So you need a bottom-line diagnosis?"

"Yeah. How did she present?" inquired Young. In truth he already knew.

"Ms. Hart came in by ambulance three days ago, wildly agitated, combative and out of control. In the ER, she seemed to get drowsier by the minute, then crashed, falling rapidly into a stuporous coma. She was swiftly taken to the ICU and spent the greater part of that day and subsequent night under observation. The next day, she was alert, conscious, and talkative, and orders were made to transfer her to the medical ward. She was under the care and direction of my medical team until early this morning, when a psych ward bed opened up. I didn't see her again after that until I arrived ten minutes ago."

"Right, and what've you done for her, Dr. House?"

"Well, Andy, you can see she's pink and warm and breathing on her own. All Supplemental oxygen discontinued prior to transfer. Her IV is patent, running D5W, TKVO."

"Did she need ER resuscitation?"

"Not according to paramedic records," House replied. "What about the nursing notes? Were interventions necessary in the IUC?"

Young picked up the chart from the foot of the bed and began rummaging through it. "Here we are—nursing notes dated March 10, 2022, 1:15 AM. Jennifer "Jo" Hart picked up off the street. No contact information. Apparently some woman reported seeing her raving and rolling on the ground outside her condo. On arrival, vital signs: BP one forty over ninety-five, HR one ten, RR sixteen, afebrile. Observations: appeared confused, thrashing about, disoriented not to person but to place and time. Restrained, IV placed, supplemental oxygen given, four liters per minute, administered by nasal prongs. ER physician requested. Responded promptly at 1:17 A.M. Preliminary exam, looked pale, diaphoretic. No cyanosis, no scleral icterus or petechial hemorrhages noted. Glasgow Coma Scale fluctuating between eleven to fifteen. Peripheral pulses easily palpable. Thyroid normal. Chest sounds equal and bilateral. Cardiovascular examination: systolic ejection murmur, grade II/IV, heard maximally over the lower left sternal border, no respiratory variation. No clicks, S3 or S4. Abdominal exam benign. GU deferred. No skin or head bruising."

"Did the admitting doc who initially examined her perform a neurological exam?"

Young shrugged. "Who knows? I wasn't there. If this actually was done, I can't find documentation of it anywhere in these notes." Between the two, a spaceless sense of incredulity that had existed from time zero, aways seeming fiercely prominent between them, was now significantly widened. "What tests were done in the ER, Herr Doctor?"

House handed Young the chart. "Take a look for yourself, Sherlock."

Young slowly turned over the multicolored coded plastic binder tabs, revealing the laboratory section near the end of Jenny's chart. "Here we are. Results of initial ER studies. Sugar nine point zero. Creatinine sixty, BUN ten. Electrolytes: sodium one forty-nine, potassium three point six, chloride one hundred. Alkaline phosphatase, AST, amylase and bilirubin all normal. UDS results pending." Young turned the chart over, opening up another section under the green tab. "Portable CXR result: Normal. Twelve-lead EKG: Sinus tachycardia, rate one twenty per minute. No extra beats. Axis, PR interval, QRS complex, normal. No ST elevations or depressions. No evidence of LVH or Strain."

House combed his long fingers through thick strands of his dark hair, pressing them steadily across the lines of his scalp. "Were blood gasses done in the ER?"

Young began to flip the chart tabs and noticed that House watched him carefully.

"Hey, slow down, Sherlock. What's on that note pinned to the front of the chart?"

Hey, asshole. It didn't take much to intensify Young's dislike of House. Young snapped the yellow Post-it note off the chart and relayed its message with a marked tone of bland indifference: "Blood Gasses: paO2 ninety-seven, paCO2 thirty-two, HCO3 twenty-one. Ketones, lactate normal. cardiac enzymes negative."

A weird epiphany-like expression seized House's face— the kind Young had seen many times before,

"So, Sherlock, shall we have a look-see at sleeping beauty?"

As Broward Hospital, ER staff physician and chief of medicine, Dr. House was expected to initiate Ms. Hart's physical examination. Just how he chose to begin this sequence of discovery, Young found particularly odd. House pressed his nose right up against hers, giving it a good, hard audible sniff.

"WTAF, Larry?

Lawrence quickly pulled back. "Ah, the sweet smell of success!"

"What does that even mean?" Young glanced over at House's blue-speckled eyes, which fired and flickered bright, brilliant scintillations. His blue crystalline Ariens emitted an immediacy whose prolonged effect seemed to recede and elongate like a Doppler. Young sensed that inside House, it was like mind over matter, as if mind and matter were suddenly unified of liquid remembrance. Time seemed to diffuse out of his cranial vault, clearing a working space, pouring back two long nights of image and sound over empty falx and fault, the two of them becoming one past and present picture.

House felt for Jennifer's pulse. "Still regular and one ten. Respiratory rate sixteen."

Young closely watched as House pulled the loose flesh of

Jennifer's eye back in order to see and reveal the state of her conjunctiva. Nothing seemed significant. House then picked up her pale diaphoretic hand, pinching her right thumbnail between his index finger and thumb. He pressed down hard. Reflexively, she withdrew her hand.

"Nice," House mumbled.

"What's nice?" Young asked.

"So far, all of it."

Jennifer's eyes were still shut. To continue his examination, House had to literally pry her lids open. Then he slowly dragged a piece of cotton across her cornea until she blinked. "Excellent," said House. "Now let's take a quick look at the back of her throat."

"Why?" Young asked.

"Signs have their importance."

Which explains exactly nothing, Young thought, growing more irritable with him by the minute.

House now used a tongue depressor, pressing down on her lingua until her mouth opened reflexively. Young watched as her arms flailed a bit under her restraints, but this didn't seem to matter much to House, who made a quick, firm jab towards the back of Jennifer's throat. She gagged hard and seemed to swallow the entire thing whole. House tried to withdraw the instrument, but Jennifer's teeth were clamped shut so firmly he was forced to manually hold open her jaw, from which he extracted a somewhat mangled tongue depressor with teeth marks all over it. House tossed the used item clear across the room. The two of them, eyes glued to the arc, watched it rise and fall, they both heard the same sharp metallic twang as it bounced up and off the edge of the silver garbage can.

Young disliked the way House didn't ease up on the depressor when she'd started gagging. He felt Larry seemed to enjoy hearing her gag.

House brought out a penlight and began to shine it back and forth, first in one eye and then the other, looking to gauge separately each pupillary reflex. Then narrowing his focus upon one eye, Larry shone the penlight into the other. Cover and uncover. First one eye, and then the other.

"So, Larry, what do you think is going on?" Young asked.

The sound of his voice seemed to snap House back into the present.

House gave him back a firm look of disdain.

"Look, all I need House is medical clearance. Just give me your damn stamp of approval, officially sign off the case, and I'll be on my way."

"Not so fast, Sherlock. Have you considered PE? Jo's vital signs and blood gasses certainly support it."

"That's your area. Not mine."

Young sensed House was at once fully consumed. As if he were reaching back accross wide banks of his eidetic memory, seeing and integrating into one moment the entire picture of Jenny's medical chart.

"Here's something curious," House's eyes sparked with insistence. "The admitting physician took photos. Take a look Albert. Actual track marks recorded on her arms."

He held out the iPad, and Young took a look. They were track marks there, all right. Yet in the here and now her arms were clean; there were no marks or shadows, nothing. *How odd.* He quickly emailed the photos to himself. Clicked the SEND button after which a faint whooshing sound was heard. House's eyes dropped. "Nothing to be done." Young was utterly stumped. "What do you make of this, Larry?"

House shrugged. "Damned if I know. An allergic reaction to something? An idiosyncratic anomaly? The admitting physician had noted that although Jo had the track marks at that time no other physical or laboratory sign of drug abuse was identified, to lend credible support either to a notion of past or recent IV drug use. Her UDS came back clean; nothing of significance detected—no opiates, no cocaine, no benzodiazepines, no alcohol. For purposes of better etiological clarification, 2D echocardiography was performed in the ER and three sets of blood cultures were drawn. No positive evidence came forth to enhance or support a diagnosis of subacute bacterial endocarditis—or, for that matter, anything else..

"We'll just have to wait and see. When she comes to we'll ask about allergies. Is there anything you know, Albert? Any pertinent documentation in the chart? Have you spoken to her family doctor?"

Nope. We don't know if she even has one, Young replied.

I'll order a V/Q scan, said House, and check on the UDS this time around."

"Fine. I'll take over from here."

With that, Young left the room.

Chapter

2

Jo came to conscious awareness. She was in a hospital room connected to IVs, lethargic and deeply alarmed. She didn't know why or how she came to hospital, how long she had been residing here, or even where this hospital was. The last thing she remembered was taking her usual evening jog along Lauderdale Beach.

She struggled to sit up, looked around the room for her cell phone, wallet, and whatever else she was carrying with her on her jog. She spotted her cell on the bedside table, plugged into an outlet. There was no sign of her wallet or clothes.

She scooped up her phone and found dozens of text messages from Chris Laker, her fiancé, dated March 10th. The only recent text said, "Call me when you can. I'm not permitted to see you because I'm not family."

"What the hell," she murmured.

Jenny got out of bed and made a beeline for the bathroom. She wasn't catheterized, so she reckoned she must've used the bathroom at some point before. Or a bedpan. Her head felt as though it were filled with brain fog, a sign that she'd been heavily drugged. But why?

Once she'd emptied her bladder, she washed her face, then looked at herself in the mirror. She looked like shit. Her hair was a gargantuan mess, and her dark eyes seemed, haunted, so she thought, even though she wasn't sure what she meant by that. *Haunted by what? Why?*

As she came out of the bathroom, a man entered her room with a broom, bucket, and mop. He looked in his late twenties and vaguely familiar. "Hey," she said. "Where am I?"

He glanced up, obviously startled. "Broward Mental Health Hospital, Señora."

"Why?"

"I don't know. You should ring the service bell and talk to one of the nurses."

"Where? Where is it?"

He hurried over to the bed, untangled the cord, set the bell on the pillow.

"There you go."

"Thanks. What's your name?"

"Diego. Diego Guzman."

Again he looked oddly familiar to her. "Have we met before?"

"I don't think so. I'm sure I'd remember. Go ahead and call the nurse." Diego quickly mopped up her room, then left.

Outside in the hall, he was deeply shaken. Diego felt as if he knew this Jennifer Hart, yet he was sure they'd never met. She was brought in three days ago, and yesterday, when he was mopping up Dr. Young's empty office, he had managed to gain a peek at her medical record—a huge breach of confidentiality. He could be fired for it. But he knew some things were worth taking the risk.

She was a Jungian psychologist who was Baker Acted by ER hospital staff after being found in a semi delirious state in a neighborhood on Lauderdale beach. Dr. Albert Young had been assigned as her shrink, and that made Diego feel strange and uneasy. He didn't trust him. Dr. Young headed a medical program here at Broward County Hospital that used psychedelics in the treatment of traumatized patients. But Diego's unease was due to something more than that.

He headed to the employee break room and, relieved that it was empty, sat quietly by himself, breathing deeply and rhythmically, eyes shut, until images began floating through him. A therapist had taught him this visualization technique in 2018, after a near-death experience in which he recalled snippets of a past life in the 1920s. But those memories returned incomplete.

His sister in that life had a name that had started with a *P. Patti? Pam? Pretty Penny? Something like that.* If this was her—and he wasn't sure it was—then he owed her. In that life, he had never stood up for her against their abusive, alcoholic father; never helped her; never attempted to get her away from him. As his psychotherapist had explained, this past regret had imprinted itself upon his genome. It were as if this highly charged memory were passed forward as he came into this life. If she was that woman, his sister from a former life, then she was here for him especially to remember that life, in all its terrifying ugliness, for now he had a second chance to right the karmic wrongs of that life.

If.

Diego bolted to his feet, so disturbed by the suddenness of all this that he told his supervisor he had to leave early, giving the feeble   excuse that he had an exam at college that evening, and needed time to study for it. The center paid for his college classes, a grand perk of the job, and so his supervisor was more than happy to let him go early.

Two years ago, he'd decided to major in political science as a solid background for his ultimate goal—becoming a lawyer.

Diego drove to his grandmother's place in the Latino area of Lauderdale, where he'd grown up and where his parents had had a wildly popular Cuban café. It like many others had gone under during the COVID pandemic.

His grandmother, Abuelita Adele Cantera, came over in the Mariel boat lift in 1981, when she was twenty-eight years old and already a renowned *Santeria* in Havana. She had continued her Santeria practices in the neighborhood where she lived, and helped raise Diego when his parents were busy with their flourishing café. He had always confided in her first. Whenever she went into a trance, her "*santo*," Isabella came through.

He parked in front of Adele's house, the front yard filled with bougainvilleas and fruit trees—papayas, figs, mangos, avocados—and a garden of herbs that she used in her work. Before he reached the front door, it opened and his grandmother stood there, her long arms thrown out, threaded hair tumbling to her shoulders. "Diego, mi amor!"

He hugged her hello. "Hope it's okay that I didn't call first."

"You never have to call. Come in, come in."

They went inside the house, where the rooms were

fragrant with a variety of scents from the numerous fresh flowers and the incense she often burned when doing readings for her clients. On their way through the brightly colored kitchen, she grabbed a couple of bottles of water from the fridge.

"*Tienes hambre, Diego?*"

He shook his head, took the bottle of water she held out. "I'm not hungry just need your advice on something, Adele."

"My advice or Isabella's?"

"Both."

Together they entered her large workroom. Under a window that overlooked the backyard, an altar was set up with statues of the various Yoruba Gods in Santeria, with Elegua as the most prominent. Elegua was the Orisha Saint who governed crossroads and opened doors. A pair of vases held freshly cut sunflowers and roses. An ornate dish between the vases held a small chocolate chip cookie and loose pocket change. Elegua supposedly enjoyed cookies and other sweets, as well as money.

Adele lit a cigar and picked up a bottle of Florida water—items she used in her *limpiezas*, or cleansings—and walked around him, blowing smoke and flicking Florida water at him. She then swept her hands down either side of his body without touching him. An energy cleansing. "Let's hear Isabella's take on things, Diego."

"Shouldn't I explain first?"

"Unnecessary."

She sat in her usual high chair near the altar, the cigar burning in a nearby ashtray, and Diego settled on the colorful couch across from her. She removed her shoes, placed her bare feet flat against the floor, and began an incantation in the ancient Yoruba language. Her eyes rolled back in her head, and she flicked her hair off her shoulder—a gesture that meant Isabella had arrived.

Isabella had been a Santeria in Havana in the 1800s, and her spirit had been with Adele since she was a kid. "Buenos tardes, Diego." Such a soft, beautiful voice. Almost melodious.

"Un placer, Isabella."

Her English was good, slightly accented, and she didn't waste any time getting to the point. "This woman. Her name, I believe it's … Josephine … no, Jo. There are things she needs to remember and see before she can heal, and in some way you will be a catalyst for all this remembering."

"How can I be a catalyst?"

"Your presence. The journey you're about to take is one of self-discovery, for you and for her. When you drowned, aspects of this story were available to you. For her, the story comes in horrifying bits of fractured pieces, and concern over the father. It's important for you to realize this journey is not without risk. You will encounter both good and evil. The time has come to put the past to rest, but that happens only by exposing the evil for what it is, and for what it was."

"So I knew her in that life in the 1920s?"

"You don't need validation from me, Diego. You sense these connections yourself. You have met her this time around to make amends for what you failed to do before. You will be her protector or her undoing. The choice is yours."

Shit. Why hadn't she said that he would be the hero who swept in and made things right? Either/or could mean another failure. "What else should I know?"

"In this facility, you will encounter others from that life. Adele will be helpful. And I am always here, Diego, to clarify and guide."

He thanked her. Adele's head dropped down toward her chest, her breathing changed, and she seamlessly came out of her trance. "Well?"

"She helped. She always does."

"Excellent." She stood, turned to the altar, picked up the cigar and blew smoke over it and over him, then handed him a small metal medallion. "Elegua. He's my *Santo*. He governs the crossroads and opens doors. He will be your protector. Always carry it with you."

"I will." He slipped it inside a zippered compartment of his wallet.

As she walked with him to the door, she smiled, "When you Diego become an *Abogado*, you will try to right the wrongs in this world. One of the things you'll do is mediate and defend patients like Jo from abuse and neglect"

He didn't know what to think about that. "Well, right now I have an exam to study for. I need to get going." He hugged her good-bye and glanced back once as he drove off. Adele stood there on the porch, silently watching him .

In her dream, she heard the music, a jazz piece from another era, and then Jo was on a sidewalk, and the man behind her—she couldn't see his face—was pushing her toward the front door. She started screaming. The man grabbed onto the back of her hair and jerked her toward him, then Jo bolted out of the dream. She came to covered in sweat, the inside of her mouth tasted foul, and her heart was slamming hard against her ribs, as if she'd been running.

The time on her cell showed 3:14 AM., the darkest pocket of a perfect night, that time when nightmares leaped into life. She rolled over and tried to go back to sleep, but the music haunted and followed her. She recognized it now: "Farewell Blues" by the New Orleans Rhythm Kings. That music was connected to something bad, something painful, but she couldn't remember just what that *bad* was.

She couldn't sleep. She needed to get outside and jog. The jogging always helped. But she was in a hospital gown and didn't know where her clothes or running shoes were. She threw off the covers, pulled off the oxygen gizmo connected to her index finger, slowly making her way toward the bathroom. But just then, a nurse hurried in. Her name tag read, "Abby."

"Everything okay here, Jennifer? Your pulse just went through the roof."

"I'm fine. Gotta pee, that's all."

"Go ahead. Then I need to take your blood pressure."

In the bathroom, she emptied her bladder and washed her face, then glanced up at the mirror. For just a moment, the reflection in the mirror wasn't her own, but that of a young woman, a teen, with curly dark hair and deep haunted eyes.

Who the fuck are you? Was this some kind of emerging archetype?

Jung himself experienced something like this when he and Freud had met in Vienna in 1909 and Jung first asked Freud about his views on precognition and parapsychology. Freud dismissed all such questions as nonsensical, and Jung barely held back a sharp retort. Suddenly Jung felt as though his diaphragm were made of glowing red hot metal, and apparently that energy leaped away from him and hit the bookcase. Jung called it a "catalytic exteriorization phenomenon." Freud thought it was bullshit until Jung told him it would happen again—and it did.

This incident pretty much ended their cordial friendship and left Jung feeling disoriented and uncertain. It eventually led to confrontation with his own unconscious. Was that what was happening to her? Was that why she couldn't remember? Why she forgot what had happened that evening on Lauderdale beach?

Jo reached out to touch the image of that young girl in the mirror, but something took shape behind her: a tall heavyset man with muscular shoulders and arms, and a mean face. He raised a fist, and Jo spun around, arms thrown up to defend herself. But no one was there. When she turned back to the mirror, her own narcissus reflection stared back at her, face pale, eyes terrified. The fierce abyss had sent back a sly reflected smile.

Enough, enough.

She hurried out of the bathroom, where the nurse was waiting for her, blood pressure cuff open and ready.

"I was just having a bad dream, not a heart attack," Jo remarked.

"Be sure dear to share the dream with Dr. Young."

"I haven't even met the man yet."

"He's been exceptionally busy. You're on his schedule for tomorrow. And your BP is excellent. A lab tech will see you in a bit to draw some blood, get a urine sample—stuff like that."

"Is there somewhere on the hospital grounds where I can go jogging?"

"We have a gym."

"No, I mean a place to jog outside."

"You'll have to talk to Dr. Young about that."

Once the nurse left, Jo went over to the window and peered outside. The grounds were lit. She saw a clear path that curved through the trees. An escape route? How the hell could she get out of here? She rang the service bell, and the same nurse returned. "Is there a problem, miss Jennifer?"

"I'd like to check myself out of the hospital."

"Oh, honey. But only Dr. Young can sign the release papers, and he hasn't seen you yet."

"You said he'll be in to see me sometime tomorrow?"

"Yes, that's right."

"And if I demand to be released, he'll sign the papers, right? I mean, I've got a psychology practice I really need to get back to."

Abby now looked uncomfortable. "Well, I ... uh, guess no one told you ... that you were Baker Acted."

WTF? "For *what reason?*"

"You'll have to talk to Dr. Young about that."

Why couldn't she recall what had happened? "But a Baker Act is good for only three days. This is my fourth day here."

"You were sedated until this morning. And that's when the three days begin."

She felt like screaming but knew that if she did, she would be sedated once again.

"Oh. Okay," she said calmly in her best phony "got my shit together" voice.

"Try to get some sleep," Abby said, and left.

Jo marched over to the bedside table, unplugged her phone, and texted Chris. His cell was off, but he would see the text in the morning. "Please get in here tomorrow. Even mental patients are allowed to see their lawyers."

She pressed SEND and was shocked when he replied in less than a minute.

"I spoke to your shrink today. He asked me to come by in the morning. He wants to talk with both of us together. I miss you!"

She hurried into the bathroom and called his cell. He answered on the first ring. "My God, Jo. Are you okay?"

She could almost see him, propped up in bed on an elbow, the bedside lamp on. He would be wearing just boxers and maybe a t-shirt, if the air conditioning was on. His dark hair would be sort of wild, as if he hadn't combed it in a week. "Yes, except that I can't remember any of what happened, why I'm here. The shrink hasn't yet even been in to see me."

"He said he wanted to give you a day to acclimate."

"Acclimate to what? Being in a psycho ward? C'mon, Chris. Do you know why I was Baker Acted? Did this ER doc tell you?"

"He said you were reported to have had a meltdown of sorts. You were found writhing and muttering senselessly on the ground in some neighborhood of Lauderdale Beach."

"I went jogging on the beach, that's ..." Then she remembered hearing music, jazz, something familiar. "That's not a fucking meltdown."

"Look, we'll talk about it tomorrow. I'll be there around nine, okay?"

"Okay."

"Love you, Jojo."

"Love you too."

They disconnected, and she sat there at the edge of the bed, puzzled that he hadn't called or texted earlier today, to tell her that he'd spoken to Young, that he would be here tomorrow. Why all the secrecy? On the other hand, maybe she was just imagining it. Chris was a prosecutor who worked long hours and juggled multiple tasks in his firm. Maybe it had slipped his mind.

Fuck that.

If their situations had been reversed, she would have found a way to see him as soon as she'd learned where he was and what had happened. Chris was too calm, too willing to go along with whatever Young the shrink told him. He was an attorney, for Christ's sake. Why wasn't he acting like one?

Her adopted parents were dead; she'd never had siblings. Chris and her buddy Marina were the closest things she had to family. She hoped Marina, a flight attendant, wasn't somewhere in South America—or, if she was, that she would be home by tomorrow. If Chris didn't step up to the task, Marina surely would. Since they were kids, they had always had each other's backs.

Jo slipped under the covers, unplugged her cell, tucked it under the pillow, volume high so she wouldn't miss a text or a call or an email.

Young didn't want to be in the hospital cafeteria at seven that morning. But he hadn't slept well, hadn't had time to go shopping, and his fridge was a Mother Hubbard's cupboard.

So here he was, not quite all with it, his head sort of foggy, and he had a full schedule ahead of him.

As he ate, he went through his email. His ex-wife, Amy, noted that he hadn't sent her alimony check yet this month and was asking whether he could please hurry up and do that. She had bills to pay that included their son's rent for the month. Bill had been laid off from his part-time job and didn't have the money. "And just in case you'd like to pitch in for once, Andy," the message read, "his rent is $1800. You can Venmo it to him."

Bill, twenty-one, was in his last year of college at the University of Florida, living off campus. They hadn't spoken since the divorce six years ago, when he'd told the judge he preferred to live with his mother. Amy's sarcasm pissed him off, so he sent Bill the rent via Venmo and decided his ex could wait another week or two for her goddamn alimony.

When he approached his office a while later, a really tall, good-looking man was sitting in a chair in the hall, scrolling through his phone. He wore khaki pants with a skull shirt and tie. "May I help you with something?" Young asked.

The man glanced up. He had eerie blue eyes like those of a husky; they were deeply unsettling. "Are you Dr. Young?"

"Yes."

The man stood, extended his hand. "Chris Laker. I'm Jo's fiancé."

Young grasped his hand. He had a strong, definitive grip. "And you're more than an hour early, Mr. Laker."

"I have to be in court by ten. I didn't want to cut it too short."

Young motioned him toward his office, and they stepped inside. "What kind of law do you practice?"

"Right now, I'm a prosecutor."

Young thought it sounded vaguely threatening. "Have a seat, Mr. Laker. Let me give you a rundown on Jennifer's condition."

"Just give me the bottom line, Dr. Young. Why was she Baker Acted?"

"As I explained over the phone ..."

"She had a meltdown in front of a condo in a neighborhood near Lauderdale Beach."

"What does that mean exactly?"

This guy was definitely a lawyer. *Spare me the medical bullshit; just give me the facts.* So Young laid it out for him. "The woman who called the police subsequently gave a statement about what she'd witnessed and why she'd called the cops. The arresting officer emailed me a recording of her statement." He brought out his cell and clicked the recording.

"My name is Annette Long. Around 10:30 PM. on the evening of March 9, 2022, I left my condo to drive over to my sister's place. I saw this woman jogging toward me, shrieking, 'Help me! He's going to—' Then she tripped and fell, sprawling onto the sidewalk. I ran over to her to see if she was all right, but she was still shrieking for help. When she finally became aware of me, she asked if I was real and practically begged me to be real. When I asked her name, she said she didn't know then she got wildly hysterical, totally melted down, sobbing."

Young paused the recording. "Has she ever done anything like this before?"

Laker looked troubled. "Not since she and I have been together for the last two years. But sometimes at night she wakes up screaming that he's going to find her, catch her, and beat her, and then she can't fall back asleep."

"Who is the *he*?"

"No idea." He paused. "But she's a Jungian psychologist, Dr. Young. She's been through therapy."

"Is she still in therapy?"

"No. Can you finish playing that recording?"

"Sure."

Young clicked Play. Annette Long continued. "I got her to sit on a nearby wall and called the cops. She alternately cried and laughed hysterically. And then, in a fit of rage, she shouted that Siri was a piece of shit and hurled her phone into the distance. When she heard the sirens and then the police cars, she took off running. One of the cops tackled her and handcuffed her, and someone jabbed a syringe into her neck."

"Jesus," Laker murmured. "What's your diagnosis?"

"I haven't spoken to her yet. But given how traumatized she apparently was, I thought it best to have you here as well initially. Is she presently taking any meds that you know of?"

"No. She takes a lot of vitamins, jogs at least ten miles a week, she's physically fit."

"Then let's go and see her."

"I'd like to have some time alone with her, Dr. Young."

That idea bothered Young, and he didn't know why. "Well, I, uh …"

"Let me put it this way. I *insist* on having time alone with her."

Young offered what he hoped was his most charming smile. "That sounds very lawyerly, Mr. Laker."

Laker's smile didn't touch his eerie eyes. "It's intended

to. Truth be told, I've never liked this goddamn Baker Act. In 1972 it was initially intended as a first bill of rights for the mentally ill in Florida, to keep them out of state hospitals, where they were in the not too distant past strapped to beds, drugged, and basically abused. But in the half century since it was authorized, it has become an abomination, at times used on school aged kids."

"Jo isn't a kid."

"No, but now she's caught in a vicious cycle in which for three days of examination she remains subject to whatever treatment you prescribe."

Young felt his resentment toward this man swelling.

"I haven't prescribed anything yet, since I haven't seen her."

"Then let's get *that* show on the road. I'll see her alone first. What's her room number?"

WTF, Andy thought. Laker now acted like he was in charge. "One thirty-seven. I'll be along shortly."

But before Young could add anything more, Laker got up and took leave of the office. And this left Young fuming mad.

Chapter

3

THE RECREATIONAL AREA WAS EMPTY WHEN JENNIFER WALKED in. Two women were sitting in front of the TV, which was tuned to a cooking channel, and both of them looked heavily drugged. They both wore hospital gowns, and Jo was grateful she'd found her jogging clothes in the closet, washed and ironed. It felt good to be out of that stupid hospital gown. Neither of the women seemed to notice her as she passed them and headed for the library. It wasn't massive by any means, but she probably would be able to find something engaging to read. She desperately needed a distraction.

She moved from shelf to shelf, disappointed to see that most of the books were romance novels. In nonfiction, the choices weren't much of an improvement: memoirs and a lot of self-help books with titles like *How to Love Yourself, 30 Days to Deeper Happiness, It Is What It Is.* Most of them seemed to indicate that human beings were psychically broken and screaming for repair.

Then she found Jung's autobiography, *Memories, Dreams and Reflections,* and two books she'd heard of but had never read: Carol Bowman's *Children's Past Lives* and *Return from Heaven.* She selected all three and carried them over to a table. She'd read Jung's bio before, so she took a look at the back covers of the Bowman books. She read the inside flaps and the openings of both. Her head started pounding—a white, blinding pain—and she saw herself as a young girl of four or five, snapping upright on a bed or couch and shrieking, *He's coming for me, coming to beat me, do bad things to me* ...

Jennifer bolted to her feet, hands pressed to the sides of her head, eyes squeezed shut as if to keep the memory from leaping away from her and into her waking life.

"Jo?"

She spun around, and there stood Chris. *Are you real?* Of course he was real. She threw open her arms, and they rushed toward each other. With his arms around her, she felt as if she were home. She filled her lungs with the scent of him—his skin, hair—and then the taste of him, when he kissed her.

"I thought you'd be here later."

"Got to be in court, so I came early. Let's sit down."

"Chris, can you get me the hell outta here?"

They sat across from each other, but he kept her hand swallowed up in his. "I spoke with Young already. He's going to be in here shortly. I could tell he didn't want me to be alone with you, but I insisted. I think I can get you out, but it won't be quickly. Let's just listen to what he says, and then we can decide what to do, how to approach this. Jo, can you remember what happened?"

She didn't remember much of anything. She only wanted to sit with him, touch him, talk with him. They were going to get married. They loved each other. On Sunday mornings, he made blueberry pancakes for her. That was what she remembered. "No, not really. I need to get out of here. My clients—"

"Don't worry about your clients. I contacted everyone in your appointment book and told them you'd been called out of town on an emergency. They've all rescheduled."

"Thanks, but shit, I should've done that."

"You did. I sent the emails from your computer, as you."

"So what the hell do I have to do to get outta here?"

Just then, a tall man with thick, graying hair entered the room, iPad in hand. "All you have to do, Jennifer, is talk with me." He smiled as he said it, and he approached them, his hand extended. They shook.

"I'm Dr. Young."

His touch creeped her out. Why? She slipped her hand out of his grasp. "You're the shrink," she said.

"Right."

"Just so you understand, Dr. Young, Chris and I are engaged and living together. He's the closest thing I have to blood family. He has to be included in all this."

"Yes, I understand." Young sat down beside Chris.

She didn't like the seating arrangement. It felt as if she were present at a tribunal, a pair of judges sitting across from her, looking at her as though she were an alien who had just landed her craft on the front lawn of the hospital. Apparently Chris didn't like the arrangement either. He moved to the chair next to her and sat down, draping his arm across the back of it.

"So, Jennifer, have you now remembered what happened the night you were brought in?" Young asked.

"I was jogging on Lauderdale beach. I'd never jogged

there on a Saturday evening, and people were out in droves. Beyond that, I don't recall much of anything else."

She disliked the way Young looked at her as she spoke. His dark eyes dominated her, his face intense, his look icy cold, and penetrating. She felt strange, scared, as if he were a nine-foot giant and she his pet turtle, and if she didn't say the right things, he'd step onto her and grind her to the ground.

"I'd like you to listen to the statement given to the police by the woman who called them. Maybe it will jar your memory, Jenny."

"I've heard it," Chris said. "For now, that's enough. I'd like you to forward that to me, Dr. Young. Summary, Jo, you were shrieking for help, someone was after you, you didn't know your name, and when Siri told you your name, you hurled your cell away. You freaked the fuck out."

"What concerns me is that she had track marks on her arms," Young said.

Jennifer glared at him. "Track marks on my arms? I don't use illicit drugs. I've never used any kind of drug." She held her arms out against the table, palms upward. "Do you see track marks there, Dr. Young?"

"No, I don't. But the admitting doc in the ER took photos of the marks." Young brought up the photos and turned his iPad so Jennifer and Chris could see it.

Chris slipped the iPad closer to them. Jennifer studied the pictures. The arms definitely looked like hers. There was a birthmark near her right elbow, shaped erratically. She often wondered why it reminded her of a scar, not a birthmark. But the photos clearly showed needle marks up and down both of her arms. "They're my arms, but like I said, Dr.

Young, I don't use drugs. I definitely don't *shoot* drugs." She glanced up. "Did I test positive for any kind of drug?"

"Nope." Young raked his fingers back through his hair. "And that's the most puzzling part of it."

She felt Chris's discomfort and restlessness and wasn't surprised when he blurted out, "Your point, Dr. Young?"

"Jennifer was traumatized by something that may have triggered a response in her body—the track marks. This paranormal kind of phenomenon has been known to happen with what was once called multiple personality disorder, now reclassified and known to be part of a spectrum of dissociative disorders. With the multiple type, which is now called fragmented dissociative identity disorder, one self can be in perfect health, but another self may have diabetes, impaired hearing, immunodeficiency. This other self may at times display odd or uncharacteristic behaviors, such as injection drug use."

She disliked where this conversation was headed. "I don't have a multiple personality disorder."

"Not yet that we've observed."

"Hey, talk to *me* about that," Chris said. "I live with her. And no, she's never acted like someone else."

"You've clearly been traumatized, though, and I think you'd benefit from a program I head up here at the clinic, Ms. Hart."

"What's the program?" she asked as her eyes darkened.

"The use of psychedelics to help traumatized residents remember what it was that traumatized them."

"Like I said, Dr. Young, I don't do drugs."

"As long as you're here under the Baker Act, you don't have a choice about your treatment, Jennifer."

A well of panic opened in the pit of her stomach. She glanced quickly at Chris. "Is that legal?"

"Of course it's legal," Young said quickly.

"What types of psychedelics?" Chris asked.

Jennifer noticed he hadn't answered her question about legalities, a white lie of omission, and speculated that he didn't want to offer a legal opinion about it with Young here.

"We've used DMT, LSD, Ketamine, Psilocybin, MDMA, Ibogaine and Ayahuasca, It just depends on the patient. In fact, a group of patients in the program are meeting this afternoon for a chat session. You can sit in, Jennifer, and listen to their stories about how they're healing from trauma."

"If they're healing, why are they still in the program?" she asked.

"Because they aren't fully healed yet," Young replied.

"Is her attendance mandatory?" Chris asked.

"Not for this. But it might ease your fear, Jennifer."

"I'm not *afraid*. I just don't want to do drugs. I'm a psychologist with a PhD, Dr. Young. A Jungian one. In my profession, there are other methods for treating trauma. Like therapy."

He looked more interested now. "Are you in therapy?"

"Not now. But I was for several years."

"And it helped?"

"Yeah, it did."

"What was the issue?"

She disliked the way his dark eyes bored into hers, as if he was peering inside of her—or thought he could. "The issue was abandonment. I was adopted. They were good people, but I really had a need to know who my birth parents were … why they gave me up for adoption."

"And did you come to terms with that?"

"Does anyone who's adopted? I finally realized it didn't matter. Their reasons were their reasons. I started practicing gratitude that I had wonderful adoptive parents who could afford to send me through college and grad school. Unfortunately, they're both now dead."

"In other words, Dr. Young, Jo doesn't need to be here," Chris said. "She has clients she'd like to see. She has—"

"Right now she's Baker Acted, and at the end of the third day, my panel and I will decide whether she needs to stay longer or is fit enough to leave."

Right then, Jennifer detested this man with such passion it shocked her. He enjoyed having this power over her. She could see it in his eyes, hear it in his voice. "I'd like to speak privately with Chris now, Dr. Young."

"Of course." Young gathered up his phone and iPad, got to his feet. "If you want to go to the gathering this afternoon, Jennifer, it starts at 1:00 PM. sharp. Your first treatment will be tomorrow. Nice meeting you, Chris."

As soon as he left, Jennifer grabbed hold of Laker's arm. "Is this legal? Can I be forced to do this?"

"Legally, I don't know. I need to look into it. I may be able to at least get a delay on this treatment."

A delay? That's it? "I really need to get the fuck outta here."

Chris slipped his arms around her, hugging her. "I know. I'll see what I can do, Jo. Right now, though, I have to get to court. I'll text you later." Then he leaned back, cupped her face in his hands, and kissed her. "You should go to that group thing this afternoon; listen to what the others have to say about the treatment. Love you."

With that, they both got up, Jennifer grabbed the three books she'd selected and walked to the end of the ward with him. He kissed her again, and she nearly wept when he walked through those doors that would be locked to her and moved out into the free world.

She stood there for long moments, struggling with the realization that she was ·a ward of the state. She promised herself that if Chris couldn't get her out, she would escape on her own.

Somehow.

Someway.

Albert Andrew Young sat back in his office chair, brooding, poring over Jennifer's medical records, which had been forwarded to him by her primary care physician. Something about her bothered him—something deep that bumped up against his own unconscious, those pockets of darkness within himself where evil lurked.

Amy had divorced him because of that darkness, what she called his *rage*. Afterward, his sons refused any contact with him. Yet he did good things for this community, gave freely of his services at a local mental health clinic, offered pro bono counseling to the divorced, the bereaved, the poor. Even when his sons were young kids, they'd never seen his rage. But they'd seen the bruises on Amy's arms, the black eyes she'd tried to cover with makeup.

I'm not a bad man.

But he knew that was a bald-faced lie. Sometimes when he emerged from these periods of blackness, he felt he'd done wicked things and had covered them up as quickly as possible. Guilt haunted him relentlessly.

Don't think about it. You have nothing to feel guilty about.

He finished typing out his notes on his conversation with Jennifer, his subjective impressions and observations. And, of course, he had the objective recording, which would provide more detailed particularized specifics.

Amy had been into astrology, and now he remembered that on one of their early dates, she'd asked whether he knew his birth data because she wanted to take a look at his natal chart. He thought she was joking and started laughing.

"What's so amusing?"

"Astrology, Amy."

She smiled in that oddly wry way she had, just the right corner of her mouth curving upward, as if maybe she was thinking, *Oh yeah, dude? Think again.* Out came her cell phone. She clicked on the image. "Birth data."

So he'd given it to her. In seconds, she had his natal chart. Stared at it. Burst out laughing. "A double Scorpio—sun and rising—and two other planets together in the same constellation, Mr. Ultra Secretive. And then there's this picky Virgo moon. Jesus, did you know Ted Bundy had four natal planets in Scorpio, too?"

He didn't have any idea what that meant or why that could be significant, but he listened closely nonetheless as she began talking about his chart. Nearly everything she said seemed true enough, and he began feeling deeply uncomfortable. Finally he leaned forward, softly touching her hand. "Hey, Amy. They say destiny is written in the stars. Consider me a convert!"

Even after their worst arguments, when he couldn't help

himself and had hit her badly, she would later look at the astrological transits for the incident and tell him why he'd acted as he had. After their divorce, he'd studied astrology, learned its strange symbolic language, and sometimes even did natal charts on his patients. He'd gotten Jennifer's birth data from her primary physician. He had somehow obtained a certified copy of her birth certificate from the office of the registrar, which had her official time of birth stamped upon it. He erected her natal chart, studied its particulars, and then brought up his own chart alongside it, and what he saw deeply disturbed him.

Their charts were like dead mirror images. He had Scorpio rising; she had the opposite—Taurus. He was born on November 14, and she was born on May 14, so their sun signs—Scorpio and Taurus—were also inverted mirror images. His Virgo and her Pisces moon—direct polar opposites. It all meant she was as stubborn as he was, and probably just as secretive. It meant she was deeply intuitive and compassionate, her destiny often torn between the head and heart.

He suddenly wished Amy were here so he could show her the charts and ask for her expert interpretation. But these days, they barely spoke. When they did, it was always about money.

He exited the open astrology app on his phone, wolfed down a sandwich, tested the recorder on his cell, and then gathered up his stuff to head over to the rec room, where he would meet with the residents. He hoped Jennifer would put in an appearance.

Just outside his office door, he ran into Diego Guzman, the janitor.

"Morning, Dr. Young. Okay if I mop up your office?"

"Sure. And hey, I'd appreciate it if you dusted off the window blinds and the bookcase, Diego."

"That's technically a housekeeping chore, sir."

"You do it better than housekeeping." He handed Diego a crisp fifty-dollar bill. "Thanks much, Diego."

Diego silently stood in the doorway of Young's office, staring after him, until he looked down the at the fifty-dollar note, which featured subtle background colors of blue and red. Apparently this note included an embedded security thread that glowed pale yellow when illuminated by UV light. When held to this light, an invisible portrait watermark of President Grant would become visible from both sides of the note. He noted the color-shifting numeral fifty in the lower right corner. *Blood money.* Those were the first words that sprang into his head.

Why?

He crumpled up the bill and tossed it away from him.

But he quickly scooped it up. He couldn't throw away money. He would give it to his *abuelita.* She would know how to cleanse it. He brought out the Elegua medallion she'd given him and wrapped it tightly inside the bill.

As he mopped up the room, he was tempted to take a look at Young's computer. But he was afraid someone might pass in the hall and see him do it. Instead he pulled a feather duster off his cart and started moving around the room— blinds, bookcase ... and desk. He raised the computer's lid. The screen saver shocked him. It was a sketch of the plantation home where he'd lived as Raul in the 1920s.

He quickly snapped a photo of it with his cell, shut the lid, and moved back into the room, dusting, his heart slamming around, pounding out notes of minor keys in his chest.

The group was small—two men and three women, including Jennifer. They sat at a large, round table in a room painted in soft-colored yellows. Sunlight spilled through the huge window that looked out into a beautifully tended garden with a fountain, benches, and what looked like a jogging path that ran deep into the thickness of the trees. Jennifer wondered whether there was a fence beyond the residential forest.

Young got up from his seat in the circle. "Thank you all for coming. We have a new member of our group today, Jennifer Hart. Let's all go round the circle, and each of you give your name and some information about yourself." He glanced at the man to his right—a tall, good-looking black kid with the stubble of a beard. "You first, Bob."

"Name's Bob Parker. I'm twenty-five and in grad school at the University of Miami. I've been in Dr. Young's program for six months. I … was sexually abused by my uncle."

The middle-aged woman next to him wore jeans and a black silk blouse that set off her wild tumble of red auburn hair. She drummed her thin fingers nervously against her thigh. "Lynette Garwood, my name. Mom to two teenage daughters and CEO of Garwood Cosmetics. I'm forty-three, and for fifteen years I was married to a longstanding abusive fucker. Eighteen months ago, he beat me up so badly I ended up in the hospital with amnesia and multiple bodily fractures. I filed charges against and divorced him. He's now in prison. I've been in this program for just over a year. It has helped me tremendously."

Jennifer knew the Garwood brand. She used the cosmetics.

"Oh, and we always trade cell numbers," Lynette added, and promptly provided hers.

Jennifer entered Lynette's info and gave her own number.

Lynette gently elbowed the woman next to her. "Hey, kiddo. Your turn."

"Margarita Hernandez," she said, with a slight accent. "I'm thirty-three." She gathered her thick dark hair behind her head and secured it in place with a barrette. "I'm from Puerto Rico, and when Hurricane Maria devastated the island in 2017, I was, uh, abducted by, uh, aliens. This program has helped me remember some of what happened. Piece by piece by piece, this program is helping me to heal that trauma."

Abducted by aliens. Jennifer had once treated a man who claimed that when he was in his teens, he and a friend had seen a UFO land in a remote area in New Mexico while they were camping. They were both abducted on the spot, but only her patient had returned. In the aftermath, her patient was grilled by detectives who believed he'd murdered his friend. They just hadn't been able to definitively prove it.

"I have a question, Margarita," Jennifer said. "Has anyone else in your family been abducted?"

She looked surprised, her dark eyes widening. "Wow, yes. My grandmother. How ... how did you know?"

"Abductions often happen in families."

Young held up his hands. "Please reserve your interpretive

commentaries for later, after I leave you to talk among yourselves. Hank, your turn."

Hank Everett was an older man who looked like an aging hippie. He spoke in a halting voice that might indicate he disliked speaking publicly. "I've got ... PTSD. I'm an Iraqi war vet, fifty-two. I don't know if the program has helped me as of yet. I've only been here for a month."

Now they all looked at Jennifer. "Jennifer Hart. I'm here because I was ... Baker Acted. And I don't have any conscious memory of what actually happened."

Young smiled, but it was a phony smile, Jennifer thought, and didn't touch the rest of his face. "Okay, a good start. I'll get out of here so you can talk freely amongst yourselves."

Lynette laughed. "But you'll be videotaping and recording us, right?"

Now Young looked pissed. "No, Lynette." He swept his hands toward the camera in a corner near the ceiling. "This camera's been off this entire time. And it will stay off."

"I'll take you straight up at your word, Doc."

Then Young left, shutting the door behind him, and Lynette immediately dug inside her voluminous bag for a sweater. She pulled her chair over to the corner where the camera was, rolled onto the balls of her feet, and covered the camera with the sweater. "There you go, Doc."

"What about audio?" Bob Parker asked.

Hank Everett fiddled with his phone. "Not a problem. A little music should do the trick."

And then a familiar rhythm filled the room as Mick Jagger belted out "I Can't Get No Satisfaction."

Hank smiled. "Volume good?"

"Maybe tone it down, just a little," Lynette said.

He did. "How's that?"

Lynette grinned. "Perfect."

"You don't trust him," Jennifer remarked.

Hank looked amused. "Never, ever, trust a shrink."

Margarita leaned forward, hands folded on the table. "Please, Jennifer, don't get us wrong. The doc is good at what he does. His program works. But all of us here have been spied on and watched at one time or another, and we don't like it, not a bit."

Bob snickered. "Does being spied on by aliens count?"

Margarita rolled her eyes. "Carajo, hombre. Of course it does."

"Are you all residents here?" Jennifer asked.

No one immediately spoke—not even Lynette, who seemed to be their de facto leader.

Jennifer tried again. "Well?"

"I am," said Bob. "by choice."

Hank got up from the table and lit a cigarette, walked over to the window, and sat on the sill. "This is my third stay here. First time, I got Baker Acted." He glanced at Jennifer. "But I remember what happened. The wife and I were bowling. We were winning. That really pissed off the captain of the other team. So when it was my turn and the final round, he accidentally but intentionally fell into me, and my ball thundered down the gutter. He made some sarcastic snide remark and I … I saw red. I grabbed another bowling ball and shot it toward him, with such fury that he … he never saw it coming. It slammed bare into his ankles. Broke the right one, fractured the left into pieces— and down the fucker went."

"And that got you Baker Acted?" Jennifer asked.

"Yup. My first treatment in the doc's program was with ayahuasca. It usually makes you sick, so I took some papaya enzymes beforehand and was fine. Then I relived what I'd done through the other guy's perspective. I mean, I was *him*. I felt the pain of his ankles when the bowling ball hit him. The doc released me after three days, and about a month later, I headed over to this dude's house and apologized. He was on crutches by then. But you know what he did? He just dropped his crutches, hobbled over to me, and gave me a great big hug."

"Tell her why you're here now, Hank." This came from young Bob Parker.

He scratched at his beard and shrugged. "I got Timothy Leary–quality acid. I mean, this shit was *strong stuff*. I saw myself and my uncle in a life, both together in, like, the Renaissance. I was an art critic, he was a budding artist, and I panned his art. He ..." Bob's voice constricted, then he cleared his throat. "He killed himself. For him, this life seemed all about revenge. For me, I think it's more about understanding and asking for forgiveness. These days, I criticize nothing and no one."

"I ... I sometimes experience memories that don't seem to belong to me," Jennifer said.

Bob's eyes lit up. "That happened to me, too! Tell Young that you want the Leary treatment."

Margarita piped up again. "Not so fast, Bob. DMT really worked well for me. I relived my abduction, but within a nonthreatening environment."

"I can't get out of here until Young and his panel, whoever they truly are, determine that I won't be ... what? A dire threat to the community? To myself? What the actual fuck. I just want out. If I have to take LSD or DMT to get out, then fine.

Bring it on, Young. Bring it on, universe. Jo thought. Unless she could find a way to escape before tomorrow morning came round. Then she crossed her fingers tight.

YOUNG WAS IN THE MIDST OF LEADING A GROUP OF INTERNS through the clinic's facility when his cell beeped, signaling that the discussion group was dispersing nearly two hours after he'd left them to talk among themselves. He ended the hospital tour early, in the meditation garden, had moved away from the others, eager to access the videotape and audio from that discussion.

He stopped at the far end of the garden, where the trees started, the old banyans with their labyrinthian root system, where the only thing he could hear was the wind whispering through the primeval forest. He clicked on the icon for his remote camera, ran it for fifteen seconds, then nearly tossed his phone clear away from him.

One of them had covered the camera, probably distrustful Lynette. And he couldn't hear a damn thing because Mick Jagger was singing about getting no satisfaction. *It had to be that fucker Hank Everett who did that.* Hank, who looked like he hailed from a bygone hippie era but was actually about twenty years too young. Hank, who held the same free, rebellious spirit of his hippie counterparts.

Young kept listening, hoping, for another few minutes

that something would change, but nothing did. They'd tricked him. His own patients, they'd fucking deluded him good.

He pocketed his cell and returned to his group of interns, directing them to the hospital cafeteria. He headed to the clinic reception area and spotted Lynette on her way out the front door. Young hurried after her, falling into step alongside her. "Hey, Lynette. How'd the group discussion go?"

She stopped and flashed that winning smile of hers. "Great. I like Jennifer. We all do. After listening to our stories, I think she's ready to try something. What're you considering for her?"

"I haven't decided yet. Even if I had, I couldn't discuss it with you. You know that."

"Yet you weren't entirely honest with us, Doc." She poked him gently in the chest. "You had intended to tape and record our discussions, but we nipped that in the bud."

He laughed and hoped it didn't sound phony. "C'mon, Lynette. I don't lie."

She rolled her eyes. "Yeah, right. House says everyone lies. Have a pleasant evening, Herr Dokor."

She wagged her middle finger high up in the air as she continued out to the parking lot. He stared after her, wondering whether the group had planned some kind of revolt against him. But what evil could they possibly pull off? Except for Lynette, Hank, and Margarita, they were all in-house patients. Each had health insurance that paid for their psychedelic treatments.

Thanks to the program's past successes, the hospital and Broward County had been funding this program for more than four years. It had started with a paradigm shift in US government's attitude toward the therapeutic use of psychedelics, initiated by a grassroots renaissance on college campuses. Harvard had a renowned active psychedelic research program, their present prototype, whose research publications were grounded in well-designed and controlled experimental study conditions. Some had shown positive results. Yet most of the knowledge gained and gleaned from their exemplary studies was simply a repetition, a rehashing of what was well known inside a small psychedelic community. But the fact it was Harvard had proven helpful in establishing his program and getting his boss, Eleanor Raskin, on board. She was an Harvard alum.

However, if patients started complaining or began to create a social media backlash against the program, the hospital might very well pull their funding. Then the whole thing would collapse faster than a power line in a hurricane. It would permanently taint his reputation. Word would leak out into the professional community, his speaking invitations would instantly dry up, soon enough his medical articles would be blacklisted and rejected.

"Hey, Andy, what's up?"

Shit. Not now, House. He glanced back. House had changed into street clothes, jeans, a blue print shirt, and a light sweater. "You off for the day, Andy?"

"Yeah, thank God. Been here since seven this morning. Heading for dinner with the wife."

The wife. As though she were an object, like a table, a car. "Where?"

"Kaluz. Love its location, out there upon the water."

"Pretty spot, for sure."

"So, make any headway in regard to those track marks found on Sleeping Beauty?"

"Sleeping Beauty is now fully conscious. She attended a discussion group today with some of the other patients in my program. I showed her the photos you took of those track marks. She says she has never used drugs of any kind, and her fiancé backs that up."

"So no explanation."

"Well, maybe. When I first saw her, she was in the library and I saw that she had selected a couple of books: Jung's autobiography and two books on reincarnation by a woman named Bowman. I downloaded Bowman's ebooks, had a chance to browse through them while I was waiting for the new group of interns to arrive."

"Jung's a dear old friend, but who's this Bowman woman?"

"Apparently quite well known. She worked for a time with Ian Stevenson, the psychiatrist from UVA who investigated several thousand cases of past lives in India. Anyway, in her second book, *Return from Heaven*, one of the cases she investigated supposedly involved a boy being reborn into the same family several years after he'd died."

"C'mon man." House smirked. "Reincarnation? You can't be serious, Andy."

"I am. Just listen. The kid's first time around, as James, he was diagnosed with metastatic neuroblastoma before he was two. Radiation and chemo quickly followed, but the kid's body was so fragile they had to insert an IV port into his right jugular vein just to sustain him. That incision left a scar on James's neck. A couple months later, he was readmitted for bleeding tumors in his mouth. The doctors found a large one somewhere behind his left eye that had blinded him and left that side of his face distorted. Anyway, he died nearly a year later."

"Jesus. How tragic."

"Several years later, she got pregnant with another son. When he was born, he was blind in his left eye and had a birthmark on his neck that resembled a scar. He apparently also had snippets of memory from his past life as James; he wanted to see the apartment where he and his mom had lived before, that kind of thing. But the incredulous part of this story is most definitely the physical evidence."

They were still standing outside the front door in the fading afternoon light. It struck one side of House's face, rendering a perfect profile. House rubbed the back of his neck and looked at Young. His expression this time wasn't skepticism; it was disbelief. "So let me get this straight. In the midst of her meltdown, these track marks appeared, then as quick as they appeared, they vanished. And your theory is that she was ... what? Reliving an event or remembering something from a past life? What was this, a somatic memory?"

"It's a real life possibility—one I want to explore more tomorrow during her first treatment with DMT." Actually, Young intended to use PCP, which, though illegal in the program, he felt provided better results. "You want to assist?"

"Absolutely. What time?"

"Nine AM"

"I'll be there." He stuck out this hand. "Thanks, Andy. This should be interesting."

Young grasped his agreeable hand, and they shook on it.

℘

Jennifer paced frantically around the meditation garden, her substitute for a jog, then dropped to the ground and did fifty quick pushups. After that it was fifty jumping jacks, then running in place, knees high. Gradually, her panic started ebbing, and she paused at the window that looked out into the woods. The trees beckoned her. But unless she wanted to slam through the picture window and risk getting cut to shreds, there wasn't any way out. And that was if the window broke, which probably wouldn't happen.

Jennifer sat by the fountain, texting her closest friend, Marina Bruce, the flight attendant. Just in case she was elsewhere in the world, or on a flight, she used WhatsApp. "I need help. Are you traveling?" She sent the same message in triplicate, also as a text and on Facebook.

She stared at her phone, willing Marina to answer. *Please, please answer.* Until finally, she did.

"Just landed in Miami. Help with what?"

Jennifer worded her message concisely and carefully: "I was Baker Acted. Am presently at Broward Mental Health Hospital. Tomorrow morning I'm mandated to take part in a psychedelic treatment program. You know me, I don't do drugs. I just need to get the fuck outta here."

"Give me 5 minutes. I'll call you."

Less than two minutes later, her cell vibrated. Marina's number came up, and Jennifer took the call. "Hey, I—"

"What the fuck is going on?" Marina exclaimed. "Has Chris been there? Can he pull some legal strings to get you out?"

Jennifer gave her a quick recap about what had happened today. "So the bottom line is that he isn't sure about the law and has to do some research."

A brief silence ensued, then Marina snapped, "Jo, that's bullshit. Chris knows the law. Is he aware of the treatment they're going to use?"

"Yes."

"Where's he now?"

"He and his team are huddled for another appearance in court tomorrow."

"So you haven't heard from him?"

"Not since he was here this morning."

"Okay, let me get home and call Sam," she said, referring to her brother. "He'll know exactly what to do. I'll be in touch. In the meantime, text Chris. Call him. Make it crystal clear he needs to do something by early tomorrow morning."

"Very early. My treatment is scheduled for 9:00 AM. sharp."

"We'll talk soon, Jo. Hang in there."

Marina had disliked Chris Laker long before he and Jennifer had moved in together. In early 2021, during the pandemic, he was boarding one of her flights from Miami to Costa Rica, and one of the other flight attendants barred him from entering the plane without a mask. He made such a scene that he was escorted off the plane by a pair of air marshals.

When Jennifer introduced them several months later, Marina recognized him, the entitled attorney. He'd never seen her the day he tried to board flight, so the recognition wasn't mutual. Marina had debated about whether she should tell Jennifer what she'd witnessed that day, but she decided that if he really was the shit he appeared to be that day, she'd learn it soon enough on her own.

She and Laker had never been on anything like friendly terms. They barely tolerated each other. His lie about not knowing what legal recourse Jennifer might have was entirely laughable. Christopher was a renowned prosecutor in Florida. Even if he actually didn't know, a single call to one of his prosecutor brothers would obtain the answer in less than five minutes. So what was Laker's game? Did he suddenly regard Jennifer as a stain on his impeccable reputation?

It was nearly 8:00 PM. when she walked into her townhouse a block north of Las Olas Boulevard. She already had exchanged her heels for flats, but now she made a beeline for her bedroom, shedding her flight uniform piece by piece. She badly needed sleep, a shower, and food, and it didn't matter what order they came in.

Marina caught sight of herself in the full-length mirror on her bedroom wall: a tall, slender woman with thick, chocolate-colored hair that fell to her shoulders. She was thirty-four, Peruvian, and her belly was still as flat as a pancake, in part because she'd never had kids, never been pregnant; and in part because, like Jennifer, she was a runner.

Thanks to the open windows, the room was cool. She grabbed an oversized shirt from a closet hanger and shrugged it on. As she hurried on out into the kitchen to fix herself a bite to eat, she called her brother. Sam, two years older, lived locally with his wife and two young kids and, of course, was still up.

"Sam, puedes hablar? Necesito tu consejo."

He laughed out loud. "Well, hello to you too, Marina. Advice on what?"

She explained the situation. "What legal recourse does she have?"

He didn't answer immediately. Marina heard his couch squeak as he got up. "Going out onto the porch. We can talk privately there. Shit, I wish you'd asked me something easy."

In the background, she heard one of his kids shouting, "Daddyyyy! Hey, Daddy-o!"

"Hey, Barb," Sam called. "Can you see what Tommy wants?"

Marina chopped up veggies, tossed them in a pool of oil, turned on the burner, and got a couple of eggs from the fridge.

"Okay, out on the porch now. Has the clinic filed with the court yet?"

"I don't have any idea. But she's been there four days, so my guess is yes."

"It'd be a hell of a lot easier if they haven't. But I can still file a writ of habeas corpus tomorrow morning and request a hearing concerning her release. Or I could try to get a court order. She's a psychologist with a huge ongoing practice. We might have a chance. Why hasn't Chris handled this?"

"Because he's a senseless asshole. How soon do you think you can get on this? Her first psychedelic treatment is scheduled for tomorrow morning."

"I'll do my best, *chica*. We'll be in touch. Love you."

"Ditto." She finished making her omelet and gobbled it down. If they came for Jennifer really early like 7:00 A.M., then Sam wouldn't be able to do anything. The courts in Broward County operated from 8:00 AM. to 3:30 PM. If they picked her up a little later that morning, she might have a chance. She started to punch out Jennifer's number, but her phone rang first.

"Jo, I was just about to call you," Marina said, and she told her what Sam had said.

"Fuck," Jennifer murmured. "I've been calling and texting Chris. He doesn't answer. And he's not at home. The security cams he installed haven't registered anything."

"Forget Chris. He wouldn't be able to do anything tonight anyway. Look, Sam and I will be there first thing in the morning."

There were soft, barely controlled sobs heard on the other end. "You … you always have my back, Marina. Thank you so much my friend."

"Get some sleep, Jo."

When they disconnected, Jennifer's words echoed in Marina's head. *You always have my back.* These were words from that other life, where she was a boy, Santiago, whose closest friend was Penny, the teenage daughter in a neighborhood up the road from where he lived with his family. As Santiago, she'd helped Penny escape a horrific situation with her abusive father, and those words were what Penny had uttered on the night of the escape. In some of her dreams and meditations, she'd seen snippets of that other life in the 1920s but hadn't understood it until now. This instant.

You always have my back.

Marina rinsed her dishes, put them in the dishwasher, and carried those words with her into the shower. For a long time, such words had haunted her. She'd been startled awake from nightmares she couldn't remember, as soon as she'd opened her eyes, but those words had remained behind, sounds attached to shadowy figures. When she'd had a past regression to that life as Santiago the neighbor, it had opened with his death from a gunshot wound. Santiago had been shot by Penny's old man, Pablo Giral, a sadistic fuck who had done horrifically unspeakable things to her.

She was sure Penny was Jennifer this time around but was clueless about who Penny's father might be in this life. Maybe he hadn't come back yet. And what about Penny's brothers? She remembered them as a pack, like wolves. Had any of them yet returned?

You always have my back.

But I might be too late this time, she thought, and she let the hot water pound over her. Then she pressed her hands into her face and softly wept.

Diego hated days like this, when he had to check into the hospital by 5:00 AM, before the sun had risen. The Acid Room, his name for where they did these treatments, had to be cleaned meticulously—the floor, windows, and counter surfaces; the chairs, electrodes, computer screens— everything. And not just cleaned, but fully sterilized, in accordance with post-COVID regulations.

The place was so quiet at this hour that Diego thought he could hear the dead walking around. They probably liked the twilit halls and rooms. The large cart he pushed up the hall was as silent as the dead, with not a squeak or creak heard in any hinge or wheel. He braked outside the room, removing the smaller items he would need. The sweeping and mopping would be last.

He unlocked the door and walked in. Always in here, the odor of Clorox and vinegar lingered. Two years ago, when COVID was in full swing and the clinic had to take in COVID patients, that odor had infused the air of the facility, not just in here. Still, he wore a mask.

The room itself was spacious and colorful, with two murals of pastoral scenes in mountains, along the ocean. Four specialized reclinable chairs stood in the center. Here patients were connected to electrodes and instruments that measured and recorded everything from brain waves to blood pressure, heartbeat, perspiration, along with other pertinent bodily functions. Counters and sinks, video cameras and recorders, computers and testing instruments occupied the rest of the area.

Diego started with the counter surfaces and the chairs. As he cleaned, he recalled the Abuelita medallion Adele had given him for Jennifer. The image on it was that of the Orisha Yemaya, a patron saint of women—pregnant, abused, undervalued, neglected. She was the mother of all earthly things. He planned to give it to her after he cleaned her room sometime later this morning.

He honestly didn't know whether these medallions and statues Adele gave him held any power to protect the recipients or to make them more psychic, receptive, immune to disease, or anything else. But he trusted and believed in Adele, and so he accepted and disbursed them.

Once or twice a week, he was asked to disinfect this room. He made it a habit to find out who the unfortunate patient would be. He knew that Young had had the entire room videotaped and recorded 24–7, so the first thing he did was bring out his iPad and fuck with the main computer. He sure wasn't any master hacker, but the clinic's security sucked big time, and he knew more than enough to find the patient's name.

When he discovered it would be Jennifer Hart, he installed two video cameras in the room that he would be able to discreetly monitor from his phone. They would show and tell him all that they did, what they asked her, and her responses and reactions. He cleansed and disinfected, and when he was done, he lit a stalk of sage and a cigar, performing his own ritual of protection.

He opened a drawer in the cabinet and lifted out a thin bound document. It was dedicated to Dr. Eleanor Raskin, sealed on September 17, 2017—the exact date Young's psychedelic program had begun operation. Towards the far bottom edge of its black cover, Diego saw written in gold vintage typeface, "Broward Manual of Psychedelic Operations." He opened its black binding and read.

> Eleanor, so great to hear from you and your kind desire for dedication and suggestions. Effecting what this manual contains is strictly up to you. My good intent preconditions are to initiate Broward County Psychedelic Program as a Harvard University satellite. Your personal ties with Harvard and Professor Raskin, your formal education and training, and your work and teachings over two decades at our university have guided us all to where we are now. To say that your Broward manual should contain fully transparent sections would express nothing more than expectation.

Of course, we expect a listing of the specific medical conditions where psychedelic use is deemed appropriate in your program, relatively inappropriate, and those that are contraindicated, along with a section outlining your program's policies and procedures, staff and patient expectations, a subsection clarifying what are considered appropriate, inappropriate, and unacceptable behaviors, together with a listing of consequences outlined thereof.

We suggest a section reserved for quality practice guidelines, program drug and dosing protocols, how your program best chooses set and setting, general acceptable standards of program care. We suggest a section clarifying what your program requires of its physicians, orderlies, and associate staff. Another section should provide clear and acceptable forms of documentation; copy and transmission; the giving of informed consent; legal and medical confidentiality; with end and quality-of-life considerations. We wish you would include an appendix of your personal best references. All my love and warmest wishes. I know your endeavors will be successful and great! RA

Under Richard's signature, in Eleanor's handwriting, were the following references:

Alfred Huang. The Complete I Ching. 1998. Vermont: Inner Traditions.

Aldous Huxley. *Doors to Perception*. 1954. New York: Harper and Row.

Carl Gustaf Jung. *Liber Novus*. 2009. NY: WW Norton and Company.

Herman Hesse. *Steppenwolf.* 1927 Frankfurt am Main: S. Fischer Verlag.

Julia Kristiva. *The Black Sun*. 1989. NY: Columbia University Press.

Lao Tzu. *Tao Ti Ching*. 2021. London, United Kingdom: Arcturus Pub.

Louis Carroll. *Alice's Adventures in Wonderland*. 1845. London: MacMillan.

Padmasambhava. *Tibetan Book of the Dead*. 2007. Penguin Classics.

Sigmund Freud. *Psychopathology of Everyday Life*. 1914 NY: Macmillan.

Sylvia Plath. *Ariel*. 1965. London, United Kingdom: Faber and Faber.

Timothy Leary. *The Psychedelic Experience*. 1964 New York: Citadel.

Diego dropped it in his bag.

Then, at 6:25 AM. he headed straight for the nut ward, to room 137. Jennifer was up already, dressed, eating breakfast. She smiled when he poked his head into the room.

"You're up early, Jennifer."

"Call me Jo or JoJo. I've got some tests. You're here early too, Diego."

He thought "Jojo" sounded like a little kid name, not well suited for her. "Jo" was more dignified. "Once a week, I have to disinfect the treatment room. I have something for you." He walked over to the table where she was eating and brought the Yemaya medallion out, now hanging from a silver chain. "My grandmother is a Santera. She insisted that I give this to you."

He dropped it into her outstretched hand. Her thumb slipped over it, exploring it. "Wow. Yemaya, right ?"

"Yes." He tried to contain his excitement. "You know about the Orishas?"

"Way back when I dated a Cuban guy who was studying to become a Santero." She slipped the chain over her head, and the medallion rested against her shirt, just about the area where her heart was. "Please thank your grandmother for me, Diego."

"Are you going to have the treatment?" he asked.

"I can't refuse it, since right now I'm technically a ward of the state. But between you and me, Diego, I may get a last-minute legal reprieve. Treatment is scheduled for 9:00 AM."

No, he thought. When he'd found her name in the computer, he'd seen the time for her treatment. "Uh, no it's scheduled for seven thirty."

Horror filled her eyes. "How do you know that?"

"I found it on the computer, in the treatment room."

"Shit." She scooped up her cell and texted someone. "Diego, if you were a patient here, how would you escape?"

"I ... I can't help you. I'd lose my job, and they'd probably press criminal charges."

"I don't want you to help me. Just tell me how you would get out of here."

He thought a moment, then grabbed a napkin, brought out a pen, and sketched a possible escape route. "But you'd have to be dressed like a nurse or technician or like someone on the cleaning crew. You'd have to get from your room to this hallway"—he showed her on the sketch—"where the supply area is. There's an exit that leads out into the parking lot."

"Awesome." She folded the napkin and slipped it inside one of the books on the table.

Diego noted the title: *Return from Heaven* by Carol Bowman. "I loved this book. For me it explained a lot of things.."

"Like what?"

"About a past life I had in the 1920s." *I think I was one of your clueless brothers.*

Her cell dinged just then. Her eyes filled with tears. "My ... my legal reprieve won't happen before 7:30 AM. The courts don't even open till eight."

"Who's trying to get you this legal reprieve?"

"The attorney brother of my friend Marina Bruce. They're advising me to go through with the treatment and—"

"Morning, Ms. Hart," said a cheerful nurse as she swept into the room with a smiling wheelchair. "Off to the treatment area." She glanced around the room then turned to Diego.

"You can go ahead and mop up, Diego"

Jennifer didn't get up. "I prefer not to go."

"Sorry, hon, that's not even a choice. Hop into the chair, please and thank you."

Jo's eyes met Diego's, and he felt her growing panic. He grasped her arm, helping her into the chair, and gave it a quick squeeze just to show her he was on her side.

"You'll be coming back to a room that's sparkling clean, ma'am."

"Thanks. Can you make sure my books don't get returned to the library?"

"Sure thing."

Then she was in the wheelchair with the cheerful nurse whisking her away. Diego realized her cell phone was still on the table. He scooped it up and started to go after them but worried that Young might have a chance to look at her phone. So he pocketed it. Then he proceeded to mop her room. When no one else came in, he paused by the window and looked at her phone, at the text messages. He noted Marina's number, got out his own i-phone, and texted her. "Hi, my name is Diego Guzman. I work in janitorial at the clinic. Jo & I were talking about her obtaining legal reprieve, right before the nurse came to get her for the treatment. They moved the treatment up to 7:30 AM. She left her phone in the room & I didn't want any of the staff to see it, read the texts or emails. She asked me how she might be able to escape this facility. I'll hold onto her cell until she returns from treatment."

Marina's response was quick: "Thank you, Diego. Please

tell her to just stay put. My brother and I will be there early this afternoon to get her released. Can you make sure she gets her cell back? She'll be lost without it."

"Sure, no problem. I think the time for the treatment was moved up intentionally. I gave her a medallion for protection—Yemaya. It came from my grandmother, a Santera."

"I am familiar with Yemaya. Many thanks to you and your abuelita, Diego. I hope to meet you this afternoon, when we get her out of there."

THE ROOM WHERE SHE WAS TAKEN WAS BRIGHTLY COLORED and cheerful. The morning light streamed through the huge crystalline window and struck the murals in such a way that they seemed to come alive.

"Morning, Jennifer," said the pretty young nurse. "Have a seat over there." She pointed at the partially reclining chair closest to the window. "Kick off your shoes if you want, and empty your pockets."

Jennifer patted the pocket of her jeans and realized she'd left her cell phone in the room. She hoped Diego had stuck it in a drawer. Just the text messages between her and Marina were probably sufficient for them to keep her here even longer. "Pockets empty, shoes off. Do you know what's being used for my treatment?"

"Since this is your first treatment, I suspect it will be Ketamine or maybe a small dose of DMT. It's usually administered through an IV."

She sat in the chair, her hands already sweating. "I thought it was used primarily for suicidal thoughts and depression. I don't experience either of these."

The nurse glanced at her, smiling. "Well, since you're

here and were Baker Acted, you've experienced trauma, which is something that ketamine or DMT can treat." The nurse pulled down the plain white screens that covered the colorful murals. "For either one, we try to keep the possible visual distractions at a minimal level."

"Why?"

"The drug works more efficiently in this setting."

She swabbed the inside of Jennifer's right elbow and attached an IV and bottle to the pole. Just then, Young hurried in with House. "Good to see you, Jo," said Young. "You've met Dr. House, I believe. He's going to assist me today."

She felt like telling Young that only friends could call her Jo.

"Morning, Ms. Hart," said House. "I trust you've eaten a small breakfast? We don't administer these treatments on a full or empty stomach."

"Yes, I've eaten."

"So here's what's going to happen," Young said, approaching the chair. "The infusion will be a slow drip. You'll start experiencing something almost immediately."

"What kind of something?" she asked.

"That differs from person to person," House said. "But generally, colors will become brighter, you'll feel lighter. The doors to your perceptions will open up."

"Aldous Huxley," she said.

"We'll be asking you questions along the way about what you're experiencing," Young added. "Don't worry if you don't feel like talking."

"Once today's treatment is finished, you'll be using a nasal spray twice a week," House explained. "It's called

Esketamine. You'll receive it here or alternatively at your primary physician's office, that is if you're no longer a resident here the clinic."

I won't be here. Trust me. "What's its purpose?"

"A backup and solidifier," House replied. "Patients get the nasal spray in a tapering regime, twice a week for one to four weeks, then once a week for five to nine weeks."

"Okay, let's get started," she said.

"We'll be recording and taping this," Young added, nodding at the nurse.

She then inserted the needle into Jennifer's arm, and the drip began.

The visuals of Young and House moving around, checking the IV, and hovering over her distracted her, so she shut her eyes. She could still hear their whispered voices, the hum of a machine, the nurse asking a question. But suddenly those sounds seemed to fade further and further away, now she was floating in a sea of color that swirled and danced all around her.

Within the swirl of color, she glimpsed an opening, a kind of tunnel through the color which now beckoned to her. She hurled her arms into the air and shot through the tunnel at the speed of light, somersaulting through the color, flying closer and closer to the stars—so close to them she saw the magnificent conjunction of Jupiter and Saturn. She knew that this happened on December 21-22, 2020, so did that mean she was moving backward through time?

"What are you experiencing?" Young asked.

"The ... conjunction." She found it difficult to form words. "Saturn, Jupiter."

He asked something else, but his question was swallowed by time, consumed by color.

She kept flying higher and higher, until she was near the sun. A voice whispered, "Don't be like Icarus. You'll get burnt. Fly lower. Touch down."

And just like that, her feet splayed out as she touched down upon the earth. The colors faded into the clear blue sky with lush green trees sprouting up all around her. She was standing out in front of a plantation house she recognized, but no one was rushing out the door, screaming at her, threatening her. She ran over to the bike outside the house, hopped on, and took off up the road. Santiago pedaled toward her, waving.

He motioned toward a road that veered away from her house, and up that road they went, laughing. The wind whipped through her hair; they both were laughing and loving this youthful freedom. Then a car turned onto their road, a Nash Touring that belonged to her father. The top was down; and she saw her father and brothers in the car.

And they saw her and Santiago.

The Nash abruptly stopped, and her father leapt out and trotted toward them, shouting, "Get over here, both of you!"

She and Santiago took off, pedaling madly, faster, faster, outpacing him. Trees ahead, woods. Somewhere in all that green, they knew there was a barn. They could hide there, in the hay. She glanced back just once. Her father was back in the car, behind the wheel, and the Nash was gaining on them.

Suddenly her older brother, Sebastian, leapt out of the car and raced toward them. He was a powerful athlete, a runner, and as he neared her, she panicked and jerked on the handlebars, and the bike fell to the side of the road, throwing her off. She scrambled to get up, but he was already on top of her, grabbing hold of her hair, her arm, hissing at her like a snake.

He jerked her to her feet and pushed her forward, toward her other two brothers, Raul and Carlos, and ultimately toward their father. He was irate, his face blood red. He had removed his belt, doubled it over, and now was slapping it against an open palm.

"Ay, chica," Sebastian laughed. "Vas a desear que estas muerto." She knew what it meant—that she was going to wish she were dead.

Then Sebastian pushed her forward, toward the monster. She stood there trembling in fear, shaking and struggling not to cry. "You know you aren't supposed to be seeing him."

The belt slapped his palm so hard a welt appeared.

"Ever."

Another slap to his bleeding palm.

"He's ... he's my ... friend."

"No, Santiago only wants to fuck you."

An abject horror filled her, and she felt the ghastly words slice up her throat. She tried to hold them back but they were too powerful, and spewed out of her. "You mean he wants to fuck me like you do, *Papi*? Huh? Is that it? Like you and Carlos and ..."

The belt lashed across her chest and arms, and she leapt back, screaming for help. But Sebastian and Carlos grabbed her by the arms and started tearing off her clothes, touching her all over, everywhere. Raul, her youngest brother, screamed, "Stop! Stop it! You're hurting her!"

Then the belt lashed him twice across his back and he

stumbled away oozing blood. Carlos and Sebastian shoved her down onto the back seat, and her father beat her with the belt as one of her brothers kept a hand over her mouth so that her screams couldn't travel far. She heard that haunting music again—"Farewell Blues," by the New Orleans Rhythm Kings—and ...

Jennifer bolted to her feet so fast the needle jerked out of her arm, the IV pole toppled, and the bottle that held the infusion shattered. She looked around wildly, backing away from the nurse, House and Young, and screamed, "No, no! I'm not doing this! Stay away from me! I want to see my lawyer! This is wrong, wrong! It's evil!"

"Calm down, Ms. Hart," said House, moving slowly and rhythmically toward her, patting the air with his hands. "We're only here to help you."

"Here, hon," said the nurse, holding out a large bottle. "Drink some water. Let's get this stuff washed out of your system."

Jo's fingers closed around the bottle, gripping it tight. She kept backing away from them until her back was against the wall, where she could see and observe each one of them. Young was to her left, just entering her peripheral vision, but for moments, that was all. In just the space between one heartbeat and the next, she saw that monster who had beaten her. She saw him in Young's dark eyes, and she threw her arms up into the air, shrieking, "Don't come near me!"

A woman hurried into the room—not a nurse. This woman wore street clothes but she had a stethoscope around her neck. "What the hell's going on here?" she demanded.

"The patient had a bad reaction to the DMT treatment," Young said. "We're trying to calm her down."

"For Chrissakes, Dr. Young. You and Dr. House get out of here."

"B-but ..." Young stammered.

"I said *leave!*"

And both men did. The woman looked at the nurse and stabbed her thumb over her shoulder. "I'll take care of things now, Denny."

"I'll be outside in the hall if you need me, Dr. Raskin."

Then it was just her and this woman, Dr. Raskin, inside the room. The bad men were gone, the monster and the laughing brothers. Not a memory trace remained. Jo groped behind her for a chair and fell full force into it, breathing hard, stifling back her sobs. Dr. Raskin scooped the water bottle off the floor and held it out. "It's okay to drink. Go ahead, Jennifer. I'm Eleanor."

"This is wrong," Jo whispered. "He ... he didn't give me a choice. He ..."

"You mean for your treatment?" The woman doctor came closer and gestured at her arms, the track marks. "Sit tight, Jennifer." Raskin then hurried to the door to speak with Denny, the nurse assigned to Jenny.

Moments later, Young and House came in, both frowning. Raskin began, "Jennifer, can you hold out your arms for me?"

So she did. Raskin gestured. "Gentlemen, those look like track marks to me. How many times did you poke her, anyway?"

They both looked shocked. "Jesus," Young murmured. "Just like the photos, Larry."

"What the fuck," House muttered. His face filled full of incredulicity.

Jennifer quickly tucked her arms in at her sides.

Denny, the nurse, spoke up. "I inserted just one needle, for the IV, Dr. Raskin."

Raskin looked at Young. "What photos are you referring to?"

"I'd, uh, rather talk about this in private," House replied.

Why?" Jennifer suddenly blurted. "I've already seen the photos. Those arms were my arms." She extended her arms again, palms up. "These arms. Same track marks that are in the pictures. Those photos came from when I was admitted. But when I finally came to, there weren't any tracks left on my arms. I … I'm pretty sure these ones will have disappeared by tomorrow."

"So you're saying that whatever you were experiencing triggered their appearance?"

"It's the only thing … that makes any sense to me."

"Uh-huh," Raskin murmured. "Right now, Jennifer, let's get you safely back into your room."

"Thanks, that would be fine."

"And gentlemen, I'd like to see you both tomorrow morning in my office. Now, if you'll excuse us."

Raskin pushed the wheelchair straight between them, then she and Jenny left the room and entered the hall. For a few minutes, neither of them spoke. Then Jo broke the silence. "What kind of physician are you?"

"Psychiatrist. I'm the head of this unit. I've never been crazy about Dr. Young's version of our psychedelic program, but I agreed to it because it's viable and integrated, well founded and funded, at present supported through a variety of well-intended sources. He has had some amazing successes, but obviously you aren't a good candidate set for this kind of program."

"So I don't have to go through this again?"

"Absolutely not."

Jennifer squeezed back tears of joy. When she spoke, her voice choked. "Thanks."

Raskin patted her shoulder. "I'll assign you a different doctor. But I'd like you to do something for me as well. Write a detailed report on what you experienced and email it to me."

"I don't have my computer with me here. And that's really difficult on a cell phone."

"I'll get my assistant to leave a laptop in your room. What's your email, Jennifer?"

"Johart22@gmail.com."

"I'll email you first so then you'll have my address. Be as precise as you can. I'm admittedly curious, especially about those track marks appearing on your arms."

Me too.

Raskin took her to the door of her room. Jennifer gingerly rose from the wheelchair and for the first time got a clear look at this woman who had rescued her. Late forties, dark hair with threaded blond highlights, slender and fit. She wore dark-colored slacks that fit her well, and a pale yellow print shirt that set off the blonde streaks in her hair. Her shoes were NOBULL sneakers, reported to be among the most comfortable on the market.

"I'll get started on that report as soon as I take a shower, Dr. Raskin. Thanks so much for your help and concern."

Jennifer extended her hand, and Raskin grasped it with

both of her own. "This Baker Act law needs to be revised if not tossed. Writing out your experience will help you both recall and process the finer details. I'll text you so you'll have on record my email address and cell number, so that you can get in touch with me any time."

"I appreciate that. And Eleanor, please call me Jo."

When Young entered the treatment area to clean up from the shattered IV bottle, Diego was already there with his mop and bucket. "I've got this mess, Dr. Young," he said.

"Thanks, Diego. Much appreciated."

"What happened, anyway?"

"Patient freaked out. It doesn't happen often, but when it does—he threw open his arms—this is what you get."

He went over to the computer, downloaded the video record of the treatment, then emailed it to himself. When it popped up on his phone, he then deleted it from the computer. Just in case Raskin returned looking for evidence about what had happened, she wouldn't find squat. He thanked Diego again and returned to his office.

He loaded the video and recording onto his personal computer, turned on Bluetooth, and started watching the video of the treatment. She hadn't said much during the forty-seven minutes before she'd leapt to her feet, but what she had said highly intrigued him.

The reference she made to the conjunction of Jupiter and Saturn on the winter solstice of 2020 was curious. Did she have an idea to what the true message was about that conjunction?

Jupiter–Saturn conjunctions happened every twenty odd

years. The last one occurred in 2000, but this one in 2020 was the closest seen on record since 1623, the closest observable conjoint since 1226. The two giant planets appeared almost fully conjoined, separated by less than half a degree of arc. Young's extensive research had led him to understand this same conjunction had happened on the very day Christ was born. That one was dead on, with zero degrees of separation. It appeared in Pisces on El Risha as the brightest star in the heavens. It was so brightly lit that three wise sages followed it to the place of Christ's birth. That was why it was called the Star of Bethlehem.

Did that mean Jennifer Hart had lived a life during that era? Not necessarily. But this same conjunctive thing had happened with another female patient of Young's several years ago. She'd seen the star of Christ, and parts of her life in that era, during which she was raped and killed. But Jennifer had gone back into a life in the 1920s. She had specifically mentioned that time repeatedly. *1920s, monster father, spineless brothers in a Nash, headed toward Santiago and me ...* Now Young's head fiercely pounded, he felt that inner darkness rise to swallow him and again take him away. House's voice broke Young away from the darkness.

"Andy." He shut the door, came over, and plopped down in one of the chairs in front of his desk. "Shit's going to fly tomorrow morning with Raskin. How're we gonna handle it?"

"Same way we handle anything else in this place. Tell her the truth. She got DMT and after forty-five minutes freaked out. Denny was there, saw it all. She'll fully back us up."

House gestured at the laptop. "The video and recording?"

Young nodded. "And you can see the track marks on her arm."

He turned on the computer and started the video again. House leaned forward, staring at the track marks. "I've never seen anything remotely like this before."

"Me either."

"How're you going to proceed with her treatment from this point forward?"

Young wasn't sure. He felt the darkness crouch down deep inside him, as though it was trying to hide itself from House. "Try to ease her back into that life, I guess, to see what kind of trauma was involved."

"Her old man was beating her, assaulting her. And it sounded like he'd raped her before. Jesus. What kind of monster would do that?"

Young rubbed his hands over his face and shook his head.

"So you really think she was reliving something from a past life?" House asked.

Young's hand dropped to his desk. "Yeah, I do." He stopped the video. "It sure as hell wasn't this life. Her adoption report was sent over from HRS. She was given up when she was but an infant. The couple who adopted her were well off, and by all I read in her record, they were spiritual pillars of their community."

"Even community pillars can be evil fallen spirits."

"Yeah, but her records include multiple testimonies from neighbors, friends, relatives. They paid her way through college and grad school, helped her get set up in her counseling practice."

"So are you going to explain your theory to Raskin?"

"It seems like the best course."

"Truth and all that. Her adoptive parents still alive?"

He shook his head. "They died several years ago, car crash."

"Well." He rapped his knuckles against the desk and stood up. "I'll bring those admission photos that I took. For now it's back to the ER."

"Thanks for helping today, Larry. Sorry it turned into such a shit show."

"Not your fault."

But it *was* his fault. He'd used PCP.

Instead of writing a report about her experience, Jennifer turned on her phone's recorder and talked, fast, like a stream of consciousness. She moved around the room, gathering up stuff that she might need when she fled this place. The one thing she didn't have was her phone. Had Diego taken it? Put it somewhere?

She brought up the Find My Phone app, pressed the bell icon, and heard the sound—a loud, clear ringing. It was in the drawer on the other side of the room, with a Post-it stuck to it: "Found it, stashed it away. Text me when you get this. Diego."

Jennifer paused the recording and texted Diego. "Found it. Muchas gracias."

Several minutes later, he pushed his huge cleaning cart into the room. "Marina and I were texting. She'll be over this afternoon with her brother. They're going to get you out, Jo."

"I'm not sticking around another three or four hours, Diego. I need to get outta here now."

"I kinda figured you'd say that." He hurried over to his cart, brought out a bag, and handed it to her. "Take this. Janitorial clothes. Just slip them on over your own clothes. Follow the route I showed you. Keep on pushing this cart, and don't look up as long as you see people around."

"Now? I should do this now?"

"Yeah. The rotating lunch hours just started; fewer employees will be around."

Jennifer just stood there, clutching the bag, her eyes burning with tears. Then she hugged him. "Thank you for helping."

She quickly donned the hospital's green janitorial clothes. Once she was outside, they would be easy to strip off. She slipped on her running shoes. Diego got her handbag from the closet. "I'm putting a charger and a battery backup in your bag."

In minutes, she was ready to leave, her handbag on the cart with the cleaning supplies. Diego poked his head out the door, checking the hallway. "On second thought, I'm walking with you."

He handed her a broom and a cap. She wound her hair around her hand, pulled the cap over it, and tugged it down lower over her face. "How do I look?"

"Perfect." He brought out an ID badge. "Clip that to your collar and we're good to go."

She did, and they pushed the cart out into the hall. Her heart pounded. She kept her eyes lowered and fussed with stuff on the cart. "I'm going to grab an Uber, go home first, get my car. Chris should be at work, so that's ideal."

"Did you tell him what you're doing?"

"Nope. He stopped texting me after his visit. I think he feels like I've put him in legal jeopardy or something."

A pair of nurses came toward them. Jennifer kept her head down. *Please keep going, ladies.*

"They didn't even glance at you," Diego whispered.

Thank God!

"Nearly there," Diego said.

They turned right into a hallway, and when she glanced up, she saw the sign for the janitorial supply area; it was just ahead. They picked up their pace, and moments later, Diego pushed the door open and they entered the supply room. Jennifer glanced around at the shelves of cleaning supplies and the dozen or so large yellow cleaning carts.

"Exit's back here." Diego touched her elbow, and they turned down a narrow corridor with more shelves of supplies on either side. Now she saw the exit sign. "It comes out into the employee parking lot on the south side of the clinic. There're security cams out there, so at some point they'll go through the footage and see that you've left. As long as you keep your face down and turned away from the cameras, they'll think it's just someone from the janitorial department."

Jennifer brought out her cell and tapped in her home address. A map came up. Two blocks away on the other side of the wooded area was Las Olas Boulevard, where she could call an Uber. They paused at the exit. Diego held up a set of keys.

"The other option is that you take my car. It's a white Mazda SUV parked in the back corner of the lot closest to the trees. We're about the same height, and as long as your hair doesn't show and you wear sunglasses, they'll think it's me.

I can Uber to your place later and pick it up. I've got extra keys, so you can just leave these in the glove compartment."

"You sure about this, Diego? I don't want to put your job at risk."

"It'll be fine." He pressed the keys into her hand. "Put your bag in the backpack."

"Why ... why're you doing this?"

"Because ... because once I had a chance to help someone but didn't. Now I am."

She hugged him again, made sure her hair was tucked way up under the cap, slipped on sunglasses, and slung the strap on the pack over her shoulder. "I'll text you when I get home."

"Good. Now go ... go!"

She pushed open the door and inhaled the smells of South Florida on a chipper March afternoon—that scent of salt and green and hope. Then she stepped out into freedom and walked quickly, but not too quickly, toward the white Mazda SUV at the back corner of the lot.

Chapter

6

Marina drove by Jo's place to pick up clothes and anything else she might need, and was relieved that Chris's car wasn't in the driveway.

She retrieved the spare key from under one of the many flower pots on the front porch and let herself into the house. In the living room, she saw two large suitcases, one packed and ready to go, the other open, with Chris's clothes inside. On her way through the kitchen, she noticed that most of the cupboards were strung open and that a set of dishes was stacked on the counter. In the bedroom, Chris's closet was nearly empty. It looked as if he'd moved out. *Good riddance,* she thought.

Marina found a large backpack on the closet floor and used it for some of Jo's clothes. She added several pairs of running shoes and a pair of sandals. With Chris gone, Jo could stay with her.

As she was leaving, Chris pulled up and got out of his car. She marched toward him. "Hey, Chris, just curious. Why didn't you get Jo out of the nuthouse?"

"Not that easy. She was Baker Acted and legally, there isn't much I can do."

"Really? My brother says otherwise. We're heading over there to spring her. Does she know you've moved out?"

"No. I, uh, didn't want to add to her stress."

"Yeah. Sure. So she'll come back here and see for herself, and her stress levels will go through the fucking roof."

"I've got my own reasons for moving out."

Mr. Ego Narcissist. "So let me guess. Her commitment makes you look bad."

"Fuck off, Marina." He stormed past her into the house.

Marina waited until he left, carrying the rest of his stuff, then called a locksmith to come over and change the locks. It didn't take long, and the locksmith made two keys on the spot. Satisfied that Chris wouldn't be able to get in, she texted her brother that she was on her way to his office.

Sam was outside, pacing, his cell plastered to his ear. When he saw her, he ended his call, hurried over, and got in. "Thanks for picking me up. Barb's car is in the shop, and she needed a car today."

"Glad to do it. Are we set for getting her out?"

He patted his leather briefcase. "Everything's in here. I've got a court order."

Broward County Hospital looked more like a hotel than a clinic—six stories, an emergency entrance, beautiful grounds, several brand-new shining ambulances parked out front. The place had an excellent reputation, but thanks to *One Flew Over the Cuckoo's Nest*, it gave her the creeps.

"When I go to a place like this, all I can think about is the Kesey classic," Sam remarked.

"Yeah, I was just thinking the same thing."

She parked in the front lot, and she and Sam went inside. The lobby didn't smell antiseptic like so many hospital waiting rooms. Large potted plants stood near the windows, where sunlight spilled through the glass. Bouquets of freshly cut flowers on the front desk scented the air. But the nurse sitting at the front desk looked like a Nurse Ratched. Sam elbowed Marina and tilted his head toward the nurse. "Uncanny resemblance?" he whispered.

"No kidding. Be your best bossy lawyerly self, okay?"

They went up to the desk, Sam a few steps ahead of her. The Nurse Ratched clone glanced up. "May I help you with something?"

"Yes. I have a court order for Jennifer Hart's release."

She peered at him over the rim of her glasses. "And you are?"

"Sam Bruce, with Bruce & Logan law firm."

"I'll check if Dr. Raskin is still in the building."

"And who is she?"

"Head of the Psychiatric Department." The Ratched clone swiveled in her chair so her back was to them and spoke to someone on her cell.

Sam glanced at Marina and rolled his eyes. He set his briefcase on the counter and removed the paperwork. A tall woman came through the double doors, reading something on her phone, then she glanced up and Marina saw her face. She had elegant cheekbones, thick hair that fell to her jaw, a broad forehead, a generous mouth. But it was her eyes that triggered a tightening in Marina's chest—eyes a Mediterranean blue that seemed to reflect everything.

I know you. But from where?

The woman paused to speak to the desk nurse, glanced back, and headed toward her and Sam.

"Hi, I'm Dr. Raskin." She shook hands with both of them, and they introduced themselves.

Up close, her eyes revealed the story. *The connection,* Marina thought, and a tremor of recognition rippled through her.

"I understand you have a court order for Jennifer Hart's release?"

"Right here." Sam held out a thin folder.

Raskin glanced at it. "Well, I'm not going to argue with the court. Are you related to Jo?"

The way she used the special nickname indicated that Jennifer liked her, had invited her to call her Jo. It meant she was an ally. "We're close friends," Marina said. "Sam is my brother."

"Will you be taking her home?" Raskin asked.

"To my place," Marina said. "The man she was living with—engaged to—moved out of their home, and she doesn't know it yet. I don't want her to be alone."

"That's good. The treatment she had today may have brought up issues for her, so I'm delighted she'll have a friend to talk to."

"What kind of treatment?" Sam asked.

"DMT. If she experiences anymore trauma from today's treatment, please give me a call."

She repeated her cell number twice, and Marina copied it into her address book. "Are you her psychiatrist, Dr. Raskin?"

"No. Dr. Young was. But she'll be assigned a new psychiatrist from here on in."

The man who strolled over to them, hands in the pockets of his white hospital coat, was handsome in a movie star way. A fake smile stuck to his face like Velcro. "Hi, I'm Dr. Young." He looked at Marina and extended his hand. "Jennifer is my patient."

Marina grasped his outstretched hand and then quickly slipped her hand away. It felt soiled, dirty.

"*Was* your patient, " Raskin said. "I'm taking over your treatment program."

Young's expression tightened with barely subdued fury. What had been just a tightening in her chest earlier now exploded into full-blown recognition.

I know you.

Several years ago, when she was hospitalized for an intestinal problem, Marina had a series of vivid dreams about what she believed was a past life in Florida in the 1920s. She was a young kid, Santiago, whose closest friend was Penny Giral, the daughter of monstrous Pablo Giral, a Cuban American land mogul—an abusive alcoholic.

Marina had gone to a craniosacral therapist and then a past-life therapist in the hopes that a regression would pinpoint a reason for her intestinal problems. The regression had opened with her death as Santiago. He'd been shot in the stomach by Pablo Giral, who had learned that Santiago had helped Penny escape her messed-up family by joining a circus. Now this brute of a man stood in front of her.

"Good to meet you, Ms. Bruce," Young said.

You killed me, fucker. Once she'd remembered during the regression how she'd died, she no longer had intestinal problems. So she had learned an important karmic lesson.

Sam showed him the court order. Young looked

astonished. "I really advise against this, Dr. Raskin. She's deeply traumatized."

"I'm overruling you on this one, Dr. Young. I think part of her trauma is due to the treatment you and Dr. House administered."

"And she sure as hell isn't going to improve with you as her shrink, Señor Giral," Marina spat.

Sam and Dr. Raskin both looked at her. "Giral? Who's that?" Sam asked.

"I was just about to ask the same thing," Raskin remarked.

Marina instantly regretted blurting out the Giral name. Young looked shocked and stammered, "I ... I really advise against this."

"You made your position clear," Raskin snapped. "It'll be duly noted in her records. We'll discuss this tomorrow when I meet with you and Dr. House."

Young looked pissed. "Be sure your notes include my objections." Then he hurried away.

She turned back to Marina and Sam. "I'll need a copy of the court order, Mr. Bruce. If you can give it to the nurse at the desk, she'll make a copy."

"Will do."

"C'mon, Marina, I'll take you to Jo's room."

"Thanks."

When they were far enough from the front desk that they wouldn't be overheard, Raskin said, "What do you know about that name—Giral?"

The question surprised Marina, and she wasn't sure how much to say. "Research mostly." That seemed like a safe answer. "Pablo Giral was a Cuban American land mogul in the 1920s. Owned a huge spread west of Lauderdale.

Had four kids: three sons and a daughter, Penny. He was an abusive alcoholic."

Raskin didn't answer immediately. "Let's step out into the courtyard, Marina. It's more private."

"Okay, sure."

The courtyard was lushly beautiful, with a fountain in the middle and a couple of benches where they settled. "Just curious. Why were you doing research on Giral?" Raskin asked.

Truth time. "Well, this may sound odd, but here goes. Several years ago, I ended up in the hospital with digestive problems. I had a series of extremely vivid dreams ..." She went on to tell Raskin the rest of it: what she'd experienced in the regression, and how her health issue had cleared up after she'd seen herself, as Santiago, shot in the stomach by Giral.

"Good God," Raskin said, her voice shocked, soft. "I was Pablo Giral's wife, Carmen."

Marina just stared at her. "But ... how ..."

"Oh my God." She rubbed her hands over her face. "How did we all come to be here, now, in a psychiatric unit?" Her hands dropped to her thighs. "Back in the early 2000s, when I was doing my psychiatric residency, I developed problems with my vocal cords. No one could find the cause. One of my doctors suggested a past-life regression and recommended Carol Bowman, whose focus is on healing through regressions. Just like you, I relived my death as Carmen Giral. After Pablo killed Santiago—you— he shot me and our three sons and then shot himself. In that life, I didn't speak out against his abuse. Anyway, once

I understood that, the problem with my vocal cords slowly cleared up."

This revelation rendered Marina temporarily mute. She coughed, cleared her throat. "Today, when you first came over to Sam and me, I felt this tremor of recognition. That's usually my best indicator—a sign that there's a past-life connection. I just didn't know which life. Dr. Young ... you know who he was, right?"

She rolled her lower lip between her teeth and looked uncomfortable. "Either one of my sons or ... Pablo Giral." Tears pooled in the corners of her eyes. "From the day I met him, I've had my suspicions because of my visceral reactions to him."

"And Jo was Penny, his daughter. I'm pretty sure those memories are the source of her meltdown."

"I'm meeting with Young and the ER doc, Larry House, tomorrow morning. I'd like to end Young's psychedelic treatment program version, but I don't have the power to do that unless I can demonstrate malignant intent or fraud. But right now, I do have the authority to take it over."

"It wouldn't surprise me if, at some level, Young knows who Jo was. Did you meet Chris Laker, the man she was living with?"

Raskin shook her head. "Not yet. Why?"

"My sense is that he was in that life as well, but I'm not sure in what capacity. And just so you're aware, I've never spoken to Jo about any of this."

"Maybe you should."

"I'd like to get her out of here first and settled at my place before I open that door."

"That's smart." She stood. "Let's get her released. And

please stay in touch, Marina. I mean, the odds of all this happening here are ..."

"Yeah. Astronomical." Marina slung her arm around Raskin's shoulders. "Thank you for being so honest with me."

"Had to." She smiled. "The thing about fate and destiny is that odds don't apply, karma does. Found my voice this time around. And now I understand these track marks that appeared on Jo's arms. In the other life, as Penny, she injected drugs to dull the pain of Pablo's abuse."

"Wow. And in this life, she has never even smoked a joint. Are you sure he administered the correct drug to Jo?"

"No, I'm not sure at all. He's supposedly a professional and knows what he's doing, and so I haven't inferred such malice of intent behind his actions. But you can be damn sure I'm going to nose around now."

They headed down the hall to room 137. The door was open; Jo wasn't inside. Marina glanced in the closet—it was empty—and then went into the bathroom. Not a single personal item. As she turned to tell Raskin, the doctor said, "Just got a voice recording from her. The report on her treatment that I'd asked for. She said she took off."

"Shit."

"Where do you think she went?"

"Home, first. I'd better get going. I'll be in touch."

"I'm here to help however I can."

Marina hugged her. "Thank you for providing me a lot of the missing pieces."

Young returned to the clinic late that night. House had long since gone home, so there wouldn't be anyone around to interfere. Tonight the darkness had swallowed him, and there were several hours he couldn't account for. He knew what he had to do.

The darkness had been moving in closer and closer since the incident with Raskin the previous afternoon, when she'd humiliated him by stripping him of his authority over his own patient. He fully expected that tomorrow morning, when she met with him and House, she would inform them she was now in charge of the treatment program and they would be required to answer directly to her.

And, worse, Jennifer had escaped the clinic. The darkness had swallowed him so completely Young couldn't account for several hours.

He went into the lab, turned on the video recorder, connected it to his computer, and hooked himself up to an IV of PCP, the same thing he'd given Jennifer. It was time for him to explore this blackness and its source. In a sense, the psychiatric experience showed you who you were in this life as well who you had been in lives past. He stretched out and in minutes was gone.

Once Diego had picked up his car, he plugged in his cell phone, navigated to the recording of Jo's treatment that he'd retrieved from the treatment room, and headed to his grand mother's place. He had a sample of what had been in that IV bottle but didn't have any idea who might be able to test it, to find out what it was. But his abuelita would know.

He desperately wanted to watch the video he'd captured from the treatment room, but not while he was driving. So he satisfied himself with just the recoding for now. But before he was able to start it, a second recording showed up in his email with a message at the top that read, "Recording in progress." In other words, someone was in the treatment room now.

Diego let that recording proceed and brought out the one made during Jo's treatment.

For the first five or ten minutes, it was just Young and House talking, with occasional responses from the nurse. They were using DMT. Jo didn't have to answer their questions, as it might be difficult to talk. Then he heard rage, vitriol, rants about what Penny and Santiago had done, rants about what he would do to her. And all of it was in Jo's voice as she relived a horrifying past event in her life as Penny Giral.

Diego had never heard anything like it—except that he had, when he had been Raul, Penny's brother. And he recalled parts of this same incident, recalled being in the Nash with his monstrous father and brothers, watching as Penny and Santiago pedaled madly away from Pablo Giral, as Penny fell off her bike, as she was dragged and carried back into the car and was brutally beaten. He remembered shouting at his father and brothers to stop, just stop, recalled Penny's shrieks and screams, and remembered his father turning that belt on him and demanding that he shut up.

He swerved off the interstate and into the first neighborhood he reached, and he stopped. He was shaking. He felt what he'd felt then—the shame and guilt and remorse that he hadn't more forcefully intervened, that he didn't do squat to stop the horror that followed.

He turned off the recording, and waves of disgust and regret, mistrust and shame washed through him. He'd helped her escape, but she hadn't texted him, hadn't contacted him at all. Why not? Had he failed to help her now, in this life, too?

Diego pressed his forehead against the steering wheel and sobbed.

Part 2

The Long Way Home

Whether or not we believe in survival of
consciousness after death, reincarnation and karma
hold certain implications for our behavior.
—Stanislav Grof

Chapter

7

EVAN FUENTES DROVE WEST OUT OF LAUDERDALE, FOLLOWING the directions on his cell's GPS. Used to be there wasn't much out here. But since the late sixties to early seventies, the area had undergone the same massive development as the rest of South Florida: Plantation, Sunrise, Lauderhill, Lauderdale Lake. But this address, 137 High Road, was beyond those towns.

It stood at the edge of what was now the Everglades. But a century ago, it had been a sparsely populated farming community dominated by a group of super-rich men. They had been part of a massive land rush that had resulted in Florida's first real estate bubble—and its first real estate meltdown.

He left the highway when the GPS voice told him to, and the road turned to potholes, pebbles, and dirt. Huge, graceful trees rose on either side of him, two species of cypress—bald and pond types. In the nearby swamps, these types had huge root systems that enabled the giant trees to flourish.

He didn't see any turnoffs or street signs coming up, but the GPS told him to turn in two hundred feet. Then he saw a slight indentation in the trees just ahead and a mangled street sign where the GPS said to turn. Cypress roots had taken over the sides of the dirt road and encroached on the boundaries of the old, decaying properties. But he found 137 easily enough. The rusted metal numbers were still on the front of the place, with the three in the numbers hanging upside down.

He pulled his Bureau van into the overgrown driveway and stopped next to a dusty truck. A bearded old man in jeans and suspenders was leaning against it, smoking a cigar.

"I'm guessin' you're Agent Fuentes, right, boy?"

"I am." Fuentes extended his hand, and they shook. "Good to meet you, Mr. Chandler."

"Amos. Call me Amos."

"I'm Evan." Fuentes gestured at the house. "It's seen better days."

"Sure has, boy."

In its glory, it had been a southern plantation. Now its grand old front columns looked thin and tired, covered with green mold and old vines that wrapped around as if to smother them in their embrace. The federal government had bought up all this land several years ago to turn the area into a national park; this house and the others were slated for demolition.

Chandler dropped his head back, blew a couple of smoke rings, then leaned over and stubbed out the cigar. "Body's over here, boy. Weeds are hidin' it." He motioned for Fuentes to follow him.

The weeds in the yard were at least a foot and a half tall. Chandler stomped his way through them until he reached the woman's body, nestled in the high grass as if she'd found a new home. Middle aged. Her body broken and bruised.

Fuentes crouched and patted her down. No cell, no wallet, no loose change, nothing. He texted the coroner.

"Need you at 137 High Road way, west of town."

"Leaving in 5."

Fuentes started snapping photos. "Any idea who she is, Amos?"

"Not a clue, boy. I was out walking the dog earlier this morn, and she musta caught the scent. Tore straight away from me; came right over here."

Fuentes moved around the body, taking more photos. The woman lay on her back, feet bound together, arms thrown out to her sides. She'd been shot through the back. The bullet had exited the body through a point on her lower left chest, right about where her heart was. He got a good snapshot of her face, took her fingerprints. "The house has been vacant how long, would you say?"

"For decades, same as the rest of these places."

"You know about this house, right?"

"Know what, boy?"

Fuentes knew his Florida history well, especially its vast and weird criminal history. This place was the Giral family mansion, the site of multiple murders and a suicide. Back in the early 1920s, Pablo Giral, a rich Cuban American, had been charged with shooting a teenaged neighbor boy who had helped his fifteen-year-old daughter, Penelope—Penny—escape the horrors of her father's abuses. On the day Giral was to be arrested, he shot his three sons, his wife, and then himself.

The case always had intrigued Fuentes because there were so many gaps in the story. How had Giral made so much money in Cuba that he was able to move to the United States and become a real estate mogul? What was the relationship between the neighbor and Giral's daughter? Who was Giral's wife?

Some of these questions had been answered in 2017, after Obama opened Cuba to American tourism and Fuentes, his wife, and his daughter had spent two weeks in Havana. His primary goal was research—finding out what he could about Giral's history. But his first destination was the place where his parents had lived before they'd fled in the Mariel boat lift in May 1980. His mother, then thirty-seven, had been pregnant with him. He'd been born in Miami five months later, on Halloween Eve 1980. An American. For that he was eternally grateful.

He and Concha had wanted their parents to join them on the trip, but they were certain the Cuban government would detain and imprison them for having fled. He remembered they had walked for blocks to find the house and that walking through Havana was like walking back through time, from one century into another. The house was in what he thought of as the seventeenth century but had been presently contemporized as an Airbnb.

They'd gone inside, and he'd snapped tons of photos to show his parents, found out from the clerk that the place was now owned by a Canadian couple. Fuentes explained that his parents had lived here before escaping during the Mariel, and the clerk offered to show them around. Concha wanted to return the next day with her sketchpad, but Fuentes had seen enough. He'd explained he had other research to do and urged her and their daughter to enjoy the city on their own.

The next day, he'd hit the Havana library and a museum. He'd learned that Giral was a charmer who could talk anyone into anything. Cuban investors, riding high on the prosperity of the twenties, had bought into Giral's lies, his prospects about investment opportunities in the interior. He'd absconded with their millions. It was the same thing that con men had pulled off throughout history, but Giral was so slick he constantly got away with it.

By 1921, Pablo Giral owned this place, then a grand plantation, and lived here with his wife, Carmen; his three sons, Raul, Carlos, and Sebastian; and his daughter, Penelope. Rumors about his abuse of Penelope were rampant and well documented.

Fuentes noted that the woman's body was positioned in the same area where a teen, Santiago, had been found in 1923. Both bodies were arranged like Christ on the cross, arms thrown out, feet bound together.

He gave Chandler the short historical version, and the old man frowned and relit his cigar. "You're FBI, right, boy?

"Technically, yes."

"What's that mean?"

"I'm a special homicide investigator—cold cases. I'm a local history buff. These old crimes intrigue me. This poor woman? She's positioned just like a kid Giral shot. So do we have a copycat killer?"

"Seriously? Back, what, a century?"

"You never know, Amos. The coroner will be here in a little while. I'm going to walk down the road a ways. I'm curious about where this teenaged kid who Giral shot lived."

"I'll walk with you. Cigar smoke bother you? I can put it out."

"I love the smell of cigar smoke. My grandfather used to have one after dinner every night. Real Cuban cigars. He'd sit out on the back porch in our house in Little Havana, blow smoke rings, and watch the stars."

"So who was this kid Giral killed?"

They turned right out of the driveway and walked up the road. "Santiago Garcia. He lived around here somewhere. From what I've read, he and Giral's daughter were friends, went to the same school, used to ride bikes around here in the afternoons. But it was the twenties, right? Women didn't yet have the right to vote. Neither did blacks. Underage daughters were kept on tight leashes. Penny was barely fifteen."

"Them times were barbaric, boy."

"Yup. And it seems our politicians are trying to take us back there. Anyway, a couple years after Santiago was murdered, his mother wrote a book about it, about the Girals, about the horrors. A lot of our information about them comes from her book *The House of Giral*."

As he talked, Fuentes kept looking at the houses they passed, all of them as horrific and decrepit as the Giral place. Then they reached a smaller house with no great columns out front, just two plain stories with big open windows and a pair of small balconies. Fuentes stopped, pointed. "I think this is where Santiago lived. Modest compared to those other places."

"What'd his old man do, boy?"

"Teacher, I think."

Chandler snorted. "Hardly a rich man's profession, I reckon, boy."

Fuentes walked up to the front porch. No Trespassing signs were plastered across the door and windows, and door had a padlock on it. Fuentes peered through one of the windows, but the glass was filthy and he couldn't see anything. From his pack, he brought out a glass cutter and cut a hole midway up the glass. He stuck his hand inside and felt for the window lever, pushed it to the right, unlocked the window, then used a screwdriver along the bottom edge, opening it enough to get three fingers under it.

The thing creaked and complained as he pushed upward. Dust flew; ants scattered. Once it jammed open, he stuck his forehead inside. The front room held a couple of pieces of old furniture: a ripped couch, an ancient wooden rocking chair, several hand-carved wooden pieces. Chandler came up alongside him. "Gonna take a look inside, boy?"

"Yeah." He climbed inside the window, Chandler right behind him.

The floors were scuffed brown wood, the walls a faded sand color. They crossed through the front room, their footsteps creaking, until they reached a small kitchen. Light spilled through the dusty window above the sink, exposing stuff strewn across the floor: slabs of wood, nails, and a green Dumpster jammed full with garbage bags.

"Weird," Chandler remarked. "Looks like someone's been renovating the place, but it was s'posed to get levelled along with these other houses."

Maybe not so weird, Fuentes thought, and he pulled a garbage bag out of the Dumpster. "Let's see if any of these bags can tell us a story."

He opened one bag and pulled out bloodstained towels. Four of them. "Jesus."

Chandler grabbed another bag, tore it open. "More towels."

"This Dumpster's going with us." Fuentes dropped the bags back into it.

"How're ya gonna get this sucker through the window, boy?"

"I'm not. There has to be another door in this place. Let's split up and check the rest of the house. I'll take the second floor."

"I'll look 'bout the rest of the first, boy," Chandler said, and walked on through the kitchen toward a hallway. Fuentes headed for the stairs, taking them two at a time. The second floor had three bedrooms and a bathroom. Only one room had furniture: a bed that looked fairly new, a bureau that held several men's T-shirts and underwear, and a small closet that held two pairs of jeans. Men's jeans. All the clothes looked brand spanking new. He snapped photos here and there, then pulled back the lightweight quilt. The sheets were heavily bloodstained.

"Fuck."

He stripped the bed, rolled the sheets into the quilt, and carried the bundle into the hall. He continued into the bathroom. Nothing there immediately stood out. He opened the cabinet under the sink and saw some sponges, cleaning supplies, and two rolls of soiled paper towels. In the closet were three clothing items, two bottles of unopened wine, and twin containers of cannabis edibles. There was no label on the front of the container indicating a physician's prescription or dispensary. He snapped more photos.

Fuentes went back to the cupboard under the sink and, using a large sponge, picked up the weed containers. The sponge was bone dry but held a tinge of pink. He dropped it together with the containers into the bundle of sheets.

"Hey boy!" Chandler shouted from downstairs. "You gotta see this shit!"

Fuentes scooped up the bundle and made his way back down the stairs. In the kitchen, Chandler had emptied all the garbage bags onto the floor and had started arranging similar items together. The most intriguing pile contained women's bras and panties in every conceivable color, size, shape, and fabric. Some of the clothes were bloodstained; some were torn. "Shit," Fuentes murmured. "So we have a guy with a sex fetish for women's lingerie and murder."

Chandler gave his cigar another puff then stubbed it out against the dusty floor and slipped it into his shirt pocket. "Seems to me, boy, you got a major sick fuck on your hands."

His phone belted out Jimi Hendrix's version of *All Along the Watchtower*, the stanza where two riders are approaching and the winds begin to howl, when all of a sudden the number for the coroner, Tom Pearson, popped up. Fuentes took the call.

"Hey, Evan," said Pearson. "My GPS just quit. How do I get to where you are?"

Fuentes talked him to the mangled street sign. "I'll be there shortly. We've got a Dumpster worth of evidence."

"We?"

"Amos Chandler, who found the body, is with me."

They then put everything back in the Dumpster, and Fuentes followed Chandler to the door he'd located at the back of the house. It was unlocked. They tilted the Dumpster back upon its two rear wheels and pulled it backward to the Giral house.

Pearson was already out front, leaning against the forensics van. He was a short, muscular black man in his mid-fifties who had been coroner in Broward County for the last dozen or so years. Give him a corpse and he'd tell you everything you wanted or needed to know about it. Fuentes trusted him implicitly. But Pearson had zero sense of direction. Without his GPS, he got as lost as a millennial in the city, where he'd lived long enough to raise a son and a daughter.

"What the actual fuck, man. I never woulda found this place. Good to see you, Evan."

"You too. This is Amos Chandler. He found the body. Where's the rest of your team?"

"On their way. But probably got lost." He gestured at the Dumpster. "Where'd you find all that stuff?"

"House just up the road." Fuentes gave him the condensed version of the story.

"Christ. We'll load this crap into the van after I look at the body." He glanced at Chandler. "Do you live around here? On High Road? I mean, there's not much around."

"I live over a barn about two miles from here. When the feds bought the land and turned it into a park, they hired me to get everything rolling."

"I won't even guess what that means," Pearson said. "But thank you for calling us about the body. May I see it now?"

Chandler led the way, and Pearson fell in step with Fuentes. "Am I going to puke?" Pearson asked.

"Maybe." Fuentes paused. "Probably."

Pearson quickly unzipped the fanny pack attached to his waist. "Time for my papaya enzymes."

He brought out a small container, shook three white pills into his hand, popped them into his mouth, and chewed. "The real papaya would be more effective, especially those black seeds. But hey, these should do fine."

Then they reached the body. Pearson walked around the woman once, started to cough and gag, then hurried off to puke. Fuentes and Chandler just stood where they were.

"Christ, he wasn't kiddin', was he," Chandler remarked.

"Nope."

"Weed's good for that."

"If you have some on you, could you give him a hit?"

"Got a vape. That okay?"

"Sure. Whatever works."

Chandler hurried over to Pearson, but Fuentes stayed where he was, staring at the woman. Her hair was pretty. Dark glossy strands wrapped around her neck, some plastered up against her cheeks. He was no expert on women's clothing sizes but guessed this woman wore small in everything.

With Pearson's sensitive stomach tamed, he hurried back to Fuentes and Chandler. "She was killed elsewhere and brought out here, displayed like this. The scene has been deliberately arranged, Evan, intended to mislead you. But"—he gestured at the Dumpster—"if any of that stuff has her blood type on it, then she may have been murdered right back where you found the Dumpster. I'll have my team go through both that house and this one." He pointed at the Giral house. "And just in case this fuck comes back, I think we should install some security cams. I've got some extras in the van." With that he proceeded to move around the body, snapping photos. Then he cordoned off the area.

"Can you get me an autopsy report fast, in a day or two?" Fuentes asked.

"I can try." He giggled, an odd sound coming from a grown man. "The weed must have done the trick. For my stomach. Thanks, Amos."

"Got more if you need it. Have an official weed card, so I'm legit."

Two black SUVs with tinted windows pulled up in unison, and three of his team members got out: two men, a woman. Pearson went over to them and took them to the body, and the three went to work doing what forensics do.

Fuentes turned to Chandler. "Let's take a look inside the Giral place."

"I've always wanted to get inside there, boy. Now that you told me the Giral story, I'm wondering if the place is haunted."

"Wouldn't surprise me."

"Hey, Tom, holler when you all need help getting those bags into the van. We're going to take a look inside the Giral house."

"Hold on, I'm coming with you."

Fuentes tapped a note to himself to run the prints of the dead woman as soon as he got back to the office.

Jo had spent the night in a motel and now drove aimlessly, with no particular destination in mind. She felt as if her life were unraveling at the seams. Chris had moved out without explanation; she was now a fugitive from a mental hospital, and what she'd experienced during her so-called treatment had terrified her. She'd been horrifically immersed in a past life, but when and where? And she'd heard "Farewell Blues" by the New Orleans Rhythm Kings. Considering that Chris had moved out, the name of the piece certainly qualified as a synchronicity—even specifically a precognition, like a glimpse into the future.

But the music also hinted at something deeper. Had it been pivotal to that past life?

She finally pulled into a park, picked up the Bowman books, and walked over to a picnic table near a pond—a peaceful spot, surrounded by huge banyan trees dripping with Spanish moss, and the weather was ideal. Several joggers were pounding out their miles on a running path, a few people were walking their dogs, and two women with a couple of kids were having a picnic by the pond. Nothing threatening here.

She reached into her bag for a sandwich and her cell phone. She had multiple text messages from Marina, and several from Diego, asking where she was and whether she was all right. She answered Marina first: "Am okay. May I stay at your place? Chris moved out and I really don't want to stay at the house alone."

"Your room is always ready. Christ, Jojo, you took off just a few hours before Sam and I arrived. He delivered a court order for your immediate release."

"I had to get outta there. I'll be by later, Marina. Thanks! And please thank Sam for me."

She replied to Diego next. "Am fine. Thank you so much for your help. Am sitting in a peaceful park right now, grateful to be out of the hospital. Anyone mention anything about your car?"

Less than a minute later, her cell rang. It was Diego. "Listen, I didn't want to put this in a text message, but I cleaned up the treatment area after your session. The IV bottle had shattered, and as I cleaned up the floor, I got some of the stuff into a container and took it to my grand mother. A chemist friend of hers analyzed it. Jo, Dr. Young didn't treat you with DMT. It was PCP. I've got the chemist's report right here. Want me to email it to you?"

"*PCP? That's illegal!*"

"Yeah, I did some additional research on it."

"Email it to me, Diego." She debated sending it to Dr. Raskin but decided not to. Not yet. She wanted to know what else this Dr. Young might be willing to do. "Keep this to yourself, Diego. I'm going to do the same. For now."

"Don't worry about me, Jo. I'll keep you posted on stuff around here. I know that the doctors were supposed to meet with Dr. Raskin this morning, but the meeting got postponed."

"We'll talk soon. I can't thank you enough for what you did."

"Like I said before, I'm trying to make up for not helping someone when I could have."

She remembered that comment of his and wondered again what it meant. "Karmic debt, huh?"

He chuckled. "I guess so."

They disconnected, and she bit into her sandwich and set the two Bowman books in front of her. *Which one?* She chose *Return from Heaven*, placed both her hands on top of it. "What in this book do I need to know about?" She shut her eyes and asked the question again, then she at random opened the book. *Chapter 2: A Child Reborn.*

She started reading. The story was about a young mother, Kathy, and her son, James, who was diagnosed with neuroblastoma with metastases before he was two. He went through a course of radiation and chemo but was so fragile that an IV access port had to be placed in his right jugular vein just to keep him alive. It left a pronounced scar on his neck. He subsequently developed a tumor behind his left eye that blinded him. He died before his third birthday. Four years later, Kathy got pregnant again with another son, Chad. He was born with a birthmark on his neck that looked like a scar, and he was blind in his left eye.

Shudders tore through Jennifer. She rubbed her hands over the inside of her arms, which were smooth and normal. Those track marks in the photos Young and House had shown her—were they evidence of a traumatic past life? Was that the trauma she'd seen during the treatment? Did this triggered the track marks? From some past life, when she'd been shot up?

Which life? Why? Had she done it to escape that horrible man who had beat her in the scene she'd seen during her treatment?

Young and House met with Eleanor Raskin that afternoon. As soon as they entered her office, Young felt the tenseness, the distinct divisions—that she was the boss and he and House were the employees, not colleagues. He hated that.

Raskin was at her desk computer, typing away, and didn't take even a peek at them until she had completed whatever she was doing. "So, gentlemen, sorry I had to delay this morning's meeting. As I'm sure you know by now, even if Jennifer Hart hadn't escaped, she wouldn't be here, because there was a court order for her release."

"B-but—" Young stammered.

"Let me finish, Dr. Young. Her escape really makes us look bad. But probably worse is that we were served with a court order for her release. Yes, that happens occasionally, but if it gets out to the media, that she was part of your psychedelic program, shit's going to hit the fan."

"The shit already hit the fan," House said.

"No, I mean big time. Dr. House, when you were helping Dr. Young prepare for the treatment yesterday, did you check that the IV bottle was labeled 'DMT' and not something else?"

What the fuck. Her question, Young thought, implied that she suspected something.

"Of course not," House snapped. "Dr. Young is a professional. He knows what he's doing."

"And are you absolutely sure, Dr. Young, that the bottle was labeled correctly?"

"Yes, I am."

Now House spoke up. "Dr. Raskin, allow me some brevity before extending this line of thinking any further. A moment of digression to reflect upon the particular contextual aspects of this case and to outline the specific sequence of events that first brought Ms. Hart to Hospital."

Young nearly groaned out loud. House looked calm and cool on the outside, but Young sensed that his insides churned like a port wine pickle, green and bilious. He looked blankly at Young, winked at Eleanor as though they were coconspirators, then began to articulate what would sound more than credible to most. House proceeded to give a full account of Jo's March 10th early morning ER visit, followed by case details from his own examination. Young could see that House was ever so proud of his creed. His attention to minutiae was both a beast and a blessing, the best and worst of his burden.

"Our patient, Jennifer Hart, is a thirty-two-year-old

Jungian psychologist of Cuban descent, charming and competent, with active practice in the Fort Lauderdale area. The initial history siphoned from the field was rather vague. Indications were of some sort of altercation, a psychic event, a physical fight or temporal struggle. Paramedics found her on the street near an open bar. She was reportedly on the ground, glancing wildly around, rocking back and forth on all fours. She seemed deeply shaken. Suddenly she broke into a fit of hysterical laughter, screaming 'You're a piece of shit!' Screeching nonsense at the world ... as if her brain had collapsed. For some unspeakable reason, she then bolted up and fled. She ran for miles before ambulances arrived. A scuffle ensued. Paramedics caught up with her and, after having taken her to the ground, needed to sedate this wild one against her will before bringing her by ambulance to our Broward County Hospital ER, where she was promptly seen, assessed, and Baker Acted."

House, to Young's chagrin, was only getting started. Ms. Hart was alert upon arrival, panic stricken, a faraway look in her eyes, he said. Her faculty of self-orientation, between field and hospital assessments, having returned to working order. Delirious to notions of place and time, wildly combative and highly disorganized of thought, Jenny had to be forcefully restrained, save for the coming of incidental harm to herself or other hospital staff. Raskin only listened. An irate reddish purple color subsumed Young's face.

"Such a delirious state of mind, as you might expect, would soon begin to unravel. Her GCS scores marked a precariously low level of consciousness, which, after tending briefly upwards, plummeted over a matter of minutes from thirteen to ten and then seven. Her vitals—hypertensive, tachycardic and tachypneic—a perfect trifecta, matching a unified situation of psychic and bodily urgency."

House paused to take a deep breath before continuing.

"Ms. Hart, over the next hour or two, showed fluctuating unresponsiveness." House looked, with eyes darting around the room, then grabbed hold of the chart. "Something like bruises were noted in the nursing notes," he said, flipping through sections. "It's documented somewhere. Here it is. 'Tracking down the volar aspects of her arms with scratches on her legs.'"

House now recounted the minutiae of his own neurological examination, detailing how he had held his nose and mouth up close to hers, then pulled back, sensing upon her breath "nothing but the sweet smell of success."

Young remembered that. Then, like now, Young hadn't a clue what that even meant, the implication was clear to Dr. Raskin, that on her breath House discerned no scent of ammonia.

"Ms. Hart's eyes were closed. I couldn't elicit any response to question or command. Because I saw no spontaneous movement, I pulled out a silver bobby pin from my coat pocket to test whatever magnitude of workings had been left to her sensorimotor apparatus. I began at the soles of her feet and inched up the sides of her legs to her groin, torso, and chest. I then turned back to her feet, dotting the sides of each toe, making sure nothing was missed. Then I crossed over, tested her hands and chin, cheeks, brows, and earlobes."

House then painfully recalled, to Young's annoyance, the minutiae of each cranial nerve he examined.

For a moment Dr. Raskin said nothing. House abruptly turned the medical conversation onto Pulmonary

Embolism (PE) probing Young and Raskin for any signs of acknowledgment. Eleanor then picked up Jennifer's chart. "I see you made a provisional diagnosis of stress, Dr. Young."

"I did no such thing," Young snapped back. "If you'd read her chart carefully, you would've seen my detailed psychiatric diagnoses." Then he ticked off the particulars. Axis I: bipolar illness, not active. Axis 2: complex PTSD, not active. Substance abuse, designation pending results of UDS. Axis 3: borderline personality, predisposing factor. Axis 4: Reason for current admission: adjustment disorder with mixed mood. Inciting factors, interpersonal.

Axis 5: GAF 25. Outpatient plan: office follow up.

House, of course, immediately leaped in. " Had you considered drawing blood cultures, had you followed up her UDS report—or any other test, for that matter—then—"

"Her UDS returned crystal clean," Young shot back. "No opiates. No cocaine. No alcohol. No benzos. Nothing of particular interest detected."

House was quick to retaliate. "Nothing on EMIT, but did you check her UDS quantitatively, for drug metabolites?"

Young moved on further to discuss Jo's investigations, ignoring this apparently relevant question. "2D echo showed no evidence of endocarditis, and blood cultures were negative. Ms. Hart—Jenny, that is—showed no signs of respiratory distress, so it didn't seem necessary for us to rush in and do a V/Q scan to rule out PE, moreover—"

Raskin threw up her hands. "Gentlemen, this isn't about who can outwit the other in medical talk. Something went very wrong with Ms. Hart's treatment. So for now, I'm taking over the program. Before any patient is assigned a psychedelic treatment, it has to be cleared through me. I'll administer the drug. You can still question the patients, Andy, and Larry can still assist you. But I'll be in charge. Questions?"

Young didn't have any. It was obvious Raskin was usurping the program, his authority, his success—all of it. The beast of his rage suddenly rolled over inside him. He hated her. Since she first interviewed him, he'd found her fundamentally repulsive. Now that repulsion only deepened.

"An observation," Young said. "This program has never been one of your favorites, Eleanor. But that doesn't give you the right to take it over."

She cocked her head and looked shocked, then amused. "I'm taking it over because one of your patients, supposedly under your care, completely lost it, Dr. Young. If you've got a problem with that, take it to the administrator."

Young stood up, shoved his chair back. "Fine, I will."

Then he spun round and marched straight out of her office, battle lines drawn.

Chapter

8

MARINA SAW JO'S CAR PULL INTO HER DRIVEWAY AROUND SIX that evening. She hurled open the front door, threw her arms open, and shouted, "Bienvenido, amiga! Mi casa es tu casa."

Jo laughed and hurried up the sidewalk with a large pack hanging from her shoulder, thumping against her slender hip. When she reached Marina, they stood there for a moment, just looking at each other, and then Jo's eyes brimmed with tears. She wrapped her arms around Marina.

"Gracias, amiga, for letting me stay here."

Marina stepped back, her hands on Jo's shoulders. "Are you fucking kidding me, Jojo? *Letting* you stay here? C'mon. Get your ass inside. Dinner's ready. Your room's ready."

As they stepped inside the house, Jo lifted her head and sniffed noisily at the air like a dog. "I smell some kind of delicious casserole and ... apple pie?"

"Fifty percent. The pie is pecan. I've got a couple of bottles of wine. Red or white?"

"Red."

They walked into the kitchen, and Jo set her pack on the floor and claimed a metal seat at the island in the center. Two places were set. A fruit salad and basket of warm rolls

113

were already on the table, and Jo helped herself to both. *A good sign*, Marina thought. She was hungry. Marina scooped casserole into a couple of bowls, set them on the table.

"Why didn't you come over here last night, Jo?"

"I … I just needed some time to process things. I should've texted you. I'm sorry. I got a stinking motel room."

Marina popped open the bottle of merlot, filled two glasses, and picked hers up. "Salud, amiga."

"Salud." They clinked glasses, sipped.

"How'd you get out of there?" Marina asked. She already knew the answer, of course. She'd traded emails with Diego Guzman.

"I had an ally. Diego Guzman, the janitor. That stays between us, Marina. I don't want to jeopardize his job."

Marina didn't know how much to tell her about what Raskin had shared, about what she had pieced together over the years, so she decided to say nothing for the time being. "I stopped by your place and ran into Chris as he was moving out."

The pain in Jo's eyes said it all. "Yeah … as soon as I walked into the house … to pick up my car and other stuff, I knew he'd left. The place felt … empty." She knuckled her eyes, her voice broke. "Fuck. I … don't know … what's happening to my life, Marina."

Marina reached across the table and covered Jo's hand with her own. She spoke gently, softly. "Hey, let's go a step at a time. And right now, the step is eat and drink."

And for the longest time, that was what they did: ate, drank, and chatted about the trip they'd taken to Cuba in 2017. They'd spent a lot of time at La Florida, a bar and restaurant in old town Havana where Hemingway had hung out with wife number four, Mary. His image was everywhere—a statue, photos on the walls, the covers of his books.

Marina got out her phone and showed Jo photos of her latest excursion in Peru, when she'd gone to visit her parents in Lima. "My parents are in their seventies, but they'd been eager to see Markawasi, so that's where we went."

"It just looks like a plateau with incredible animal statues."

"No one knows who or what created those statues. They look to be sculpted by sand and wind. There's nothing up there—no McDonald's, no Trader Joe's, no neighborhood, no gas stations, not even a goddamn toilet. We took camping gear and hired a team to bring a Jiffy John, food, supplies. We spent two nights there. I'm convinced it's a place that straddles dimensions."

"What's the altitude?"

"Twelve five. We took a chopper. Most people go up on mules."

Jo ate the last bite of her casserole, set the spoon in the bowl, and looked at Marina. "I ... want to go. But right now ... I feel like the only thing I can do is ... is figure out what I'm experiencing. And why."

Marina refilled her wine glass. "What happened during your treatment, Jo?"

She took her time describing it. But Marina recognized the people she mentioned: the abusive father, the complacent and intimidated brothers, the passive mother. The disturbing part for her was that she now understood how the pieces fit—or, at least, how some of the pieces fit.

As Jo talked, her eyes sometimes welled with tears. Other times, those tears coursed down her cheeks. But now and then, her voice was steady and clear; she didn't cry. And it was during one of those moments when Marina nearly told her what she knew, suspected, and had stitched together.

But she was afraid that truth might send Jo over the edge into another meltdown, leaving her unable to function and with tracks appearing on her arms. So she held off. She made a mental note about certain details Jo mentioned: "Farewell Blues," the bar on Lauderdale Beach where she claimed she'd heard the music, and her feelings toward Young.

Around 9:30 PM. with a bottle of wine now empty, she suggested they continue talking in the morning. "Right now we both need sleep."

"Want to go running in the morning, Marina? I feel really out of shape."

"Sure. I grabbed some of your clothes from your place. Everything's in your room." They got up and started clearing the table. "I'd love to meet Diego. How about if I text him and arrange something for tomorrow?"

Jo's face lit up. "Great. His grandmother is a Santera. I wouldn't mind getting a reading from her. She gave Diego an Elegua medallion that he insisted I keep on me. For protection."

"Well, it worked. Want me to do the cards for you before we hit the sack?"

"Fantastic. Let me take a shower first."

"Go on. I'll finish loading the dishwasher."

She headed down the hall, and Marina loaded the dishwasher and started it. She had a hunch that Diego had been involved in that Giral life but wouldn't know for sure until she met him in person. The people in that life were beginning to fill in: Raskin as Giral's wife, Carmen; Young as Pablo Giral; herself as Santiago; Jo as Penny; and Diego as—who? One of the brothers? The performer who had brought her into the circus, enabling her to escape Giral? Someone else? And who had Chris Laker been? Was it he who had snatched her away under the grips of Giral?

It struck Marina that if these people had been players in that life, then Jo being admitted to the Broward County Hospital clinic meant that place was the confrontation she needed to have with her unconscious, the potential point of rebirth out of a traumatic past life.

Marina got out her round deck of cards, the Tarot of the Cloisters, her favorite deck. In her life as Santiago, his mother had been the neighborhood seer and reader of cards. She had a few specific memories of his mother teaching him the Tarot, and of Brisca Guzman, a Cuban card oracle. It was, in fact, their twinned genomic visulospacial motor tracking capacities, which, having taken on generations of adaptations accross divisive familial lines to acquire, and perfect, needing to merge and vest over vastly obscure contexts. It was this particular Afro-Cuban way of the Saintly, whose destiny would be passed forward, perpetually earmarked as it were, fated by the souls higher conception at the birth of Santiago into that past life, yet whose genomic imprint must still accrue further unknown developments, until it could be passed forward unto Marina, expressed through her life, in the here and now.

The first time she'd seen a deck of tarot cards she was maybe nine or ten, in a New Age bookstore in Miami with her mother, when they were on a family vacation. She noticed a display of various decks and picked up one and carried it up to the register where her mother was talking with the clerk. "May I get these, Mom?"

Her mother glanced at her, and then at the deck. "You know what they are?"

"Tarot cards."

The clerk, a plump, jovial red haired woman wearing multiple bracelets with clasps that clacked together like castanets when she moved, opened the box, removed the deck of cards, and shuffled them. "What's your question, girl?"

She thought a moment, a warm look of fascination and wonder striking high points of her now glowing face. "How do I know about the cards?"

"Hmm. I was wondering the exact same thing," her mother remarked.

"Interesting question." The woman spread out the deck on the counter and told Marina to draw three cards. Marina didn't recall which cards she chose, but she clearly remembered the woman's words: "Well, hon, it looks to me like this interest of yours started in a past life. Pretty cool, non?"

"A past life of what?" Marina asked.

The woman looked at Marina's mother. "This curiosity. Nurture that capacity in her."

"I already am."

"So, a past life as what?"

The woman gave no indication, shuffled the cards, and spread them out again, facedown. "My dear girl, please if you would, choose another three."

Marina chose three cards and turned them over. The woman pointed at the Page of Wands. "You were a boy."

Then her fingers moved over to the Empress. "Your mother was a seer and card reader." She touched the third card, the Sun. "You lived in a warm, or hot climate."

"Where?"

The woman smiled. "The cards don't tell me that. Maybe it was here in Florida?"

Marina's mother took a keen interest in the reading. "Can you recommend an expert book so that she can better learn the cards, their meanings, and how to lay them out?"

The woman recommended a couple, and her mother bought them, along with the deck. And in this temporal life, that's where Marina's study in earnest of divination systems had begun.

Jo returned to the kitchen with a towel wrapped around her wet hair, wearing running shorts and a T-shirt. Her feet were bare. She sat down across from Marina at the kitchen table.

"So should I ask something specific?"

"Let's just see what the general flow is." She spread out the cards. "Pick six. Right here let us be as perfectly clear as we possibly can, should this 'Pick Six' gaming reference later be interpreted merely as a timely interception. For Jenny had already decided on one of her favorites, the Ladle Spread. She'd found it in *Power Tarot*, which contained more than a hundred different manifests. Jo selected her cards, but Marina laid them out and started from the left, turning them over one at a time. *How strange*, she thought, in a flash of uncanny recall, as she realized that Tarot readings proceed like a majority of musical languages, with each line of a stanza beginning far left and moving far right, that this Cuban fortune-telling formulaic rite and mechanism would've been set against its own primal essences, those of Kabbalistic Hebrew and Yoruba Amharic origin, which, like all the Semitic languages run directionally opposite, from right to left.

"This position represents the situation as it is *now*. The Tower, a major arcana card." It depicted people leaping out of a burning tower. "This should be, my dear little giral, a real live 911 wake-up call. For some if not most of us, have not even now, eleven years hence, fully recognized what brightly shone of salient meaning amidst the fiery signs of September 11 2011, its sound referent dialing out the universal phone number of all human urgent panic: 911. A violent psychic upheaval destined, like that which happened on that fated day of Twin Tower burnings, that is what repeats in the offing. It portends uniquely significant unpleasant surprises." Jo, at the same time, appeared to be frantically searching high and low, accross and through the banks of her sage-like memory, for the right or best way to express this. *Potential for great personal ...* But before she could come up with what amounted to change, Marina's mother interceded, speaking under an eerily omnipresent voice, which seemed to have a wider — I Ching like, set of conditional interpretations: *"Nothing, my dear, so common as the wish one has to be remarkable. Life only understood backwards. The knowledge of truth awakened in 20/20 visions, always only seen in retrospect. The sign found in the conjunction of 2020, is that of a passed warning, which, along with its twinned blessing, must yet bare fruit in a new life of yours lived forward."*

Jo snorted. "Yeah. I'd say that's more or less accurate." She pointed at the second position. "This position is what's hidden, right?"

"Yup. You remembered. Pray that thee who once allowed her saintly prayer to pass unabated and unbeknownst of formative ways, those of forgotten childhood memory, let grace yet descend upon yours and mine, rock and roll a child's soul akin and anew, again." *Lest we forget belief is not merely an idea the mind possesses but rather an idea that possesses the mind—the compelling irrationality of a thing — not an argument against its existence, but a condition of it. Belief in a supernatural source of evil is no way a necessity. Men alone are quite capable of every known wickedness."*

Marina turned the card over. "King of Swords. Him. Young." *Or Pablo Giral,* Marina thought. Her eery omnipresent like voice, deeply resonated through the spread.

A healthy man does not torture others. Generally speaking it is the tortured who turn into torturers. Marina said as her mom smiled.

Carl Gustav Jung spoke those words." She gasped. The farther backwards one can look the further forward one will see. Where exactly this quote came from, and why it had seemingly for no apparent reason appeared now in her mind she did not know.

To know thyself is the beginning of wisdom.

She flipped over the third card. "What's emerging. The Queen of Cups. Help from a woman. I think that's me."

"You've always had my back," Jo said.

Then came the fourth card. "Three of swords." *"That which does not kill you makes you stronger,"* said the woman. *"But ye, who by man so sheddeth a man's blood shall his blood be shed."* Marina's mom, as before, smiled once again.

"Ugh," Jo said. "Disappointment, loss, heartbreak. That's Chris walking out."

Marina turned over the fifth card and the sixth. "This is what you pull out, the final resolution. The Hanged Man indicates that you need to urgently change your perspective in some way, but if you do that, the Chariot is the outcome. That's the go-for-it card—victory through willpower and determination." The bitterest tears shed over graves for words left unsaid and deeds left ever undone. *You must never forget nor forgo the past. You have learned as a young child that in Tarot readings 13 is the Death Card and 7 is the Chariot. Do not forget 137 itself is a numerical sequence: 1 God, 3 Christ 7 Heaven. So that 13 the card of Death followed by 7 The Heavenly Chariot, is equivalently 137, temporal death and eternal rebirth. This then is all your destiny.*

"Can you open up the Chariot?"

"Sure." Marina gestured at the deck. "Pick a card.

She did and turned over the Magician. "Okay, you're victorious by capitalizing on the seemingly magical things that come into your life and by following their synchronicity."

Jo nodded slowly. "I understand the Hanged Man. I can't cower and run away, Marina. I need to lure this fucker out."

"How?"

"I'm not sure yet. But I think it begins with our meeting up with Diego."

Marina picked up her cell and checked for text messages. "Okay then. Here we go. Diego can meet up with us tomorrow afternoon at three at his grandmother's place."

When Fuentes had returned to the office yesterday, he'd run the dead woman's prints. Carmen Collier, forty-four, had a record. She'd been arrested several times for shoplifting while she was living out on the streets. During one shoplifting incident, she'd assaulted the cop who tried to arrest her and had become so violent she was Baker Acted and admitted to the psyche ward at Broward County Hospital. There, she was diagnosed as having bipolar illness. It gave him a place to start.

He thought it most interesting that the Collier woman had the same first name as Giral's wife had. Coincidence? Not a chance.

His first stop that morning was the local police department, where he spoke with Lt. Luke Nelson, who had emailed Fuentes the department's records on Carmen Collier. "What's sad about this case is that she'd never been reported missing," Nelson remarked, "not by no one."

They were sitting in his spacious, sunlit office that looked out into a small park. Out there, people were doing ordinary things: walking dogs, jogging, enjoying the gorgeous weather. "That's not just sad," Fuentes remarked. "It's tragic. You'd hope there was at least one person, somewhere, anyone, who gave a shit whether she was dead or alive."

Nelson, a muscular man who probably hit the gym for a couple of hours on a daily basis, shrugged. "Yeah, you'd hope. But this world is nuts. Apparently when the store manager confronted her about what she'd shoplifted, she got so violent she slugged the manager, then assaulted the arresting officer."

"I'm not familiar with this mental health facility where she ended up," Fuentes said. "What do you really know about it?"

"It's the only facility in South Florida that utilizes psychedelics in the treatment of bipolar disorder or with traumatized patients. Dr. Albert Young is in charge of the program. Psychedelics seem like an extreme treatment, but what the hell do I know?" Nelson motioned to his heart.

"I'll talk to him." Fuentes nodded, rapped his knuckles against the desk, and got up. "Thanks for the info, Lieutenant."

"Keep me in the loop."

"I definitely will."

The hospital was about eight miles from the Broward Police Department, but that eight miles was jammed with traffic. It was dead time. Eminem's final rap game battles, all those songs of redemption, suddenly came flurrying across his brain: "Lose Yourself." "Spit Shine." "Love Me." "Adrenaline Rush." Fuentes had places to go and people to meet. Eight miles high and running, but who was his mind featuring? 50 Cent or Xzibit? Eminem or Jay-Z?

You don't see me in the hood, dude, but I'm still grinding. Still getting chased by those lights. Still hearing those sirens.

Released from lockdown and the rampant contagion that had plagued the country for the last three years, snowbirds had returned in droves this winter. Nearly every other license plate he saw was out of mind and out of state. The eight miles took him nearly one half hour, and when he pulled into the hospital's back lot, he couldn't find a parking space. He finally found a spot on a street two blocks away, and there he parked his dark unmarked Explorer.

When he entered the spacious lobby, it looked somewhat like the waiting room of any hospital, except that the walls were covered with colorful art: vibrant oils and acrylics of local beach scenes, palm trees—the usual Florida trademarks. He went over to the desk, where a nurse—Abby, according to her name tag—smiled politely. "What can I do for you, sir?"

"I'd like to see Dr. Young."

"Do you have an appointment?"

He set his badge in front of her. "I don't need an appointment."

"Oh my." She eyed the badge nervously. "Let me make sure he's in, Agent Fuentes."

While she was on the phone, Fuentes checked his text messages and email. The coroner, Tom Pearson, had texted him: "First, thanks for the info on the dead woman. Turns out that Carmen Collier has AB negative blood, and the bloody sheets and towels you collected from the house, they also tested AB negative. So I think that's where she was killed. I'm also typing any lingerie with blood on it. The sponges didn't have much blood in them, enough to type."

Fuentes wondered whether the killer had been living in that old house with Carmen Collier. If so, for how long? Or maybe she had, as a homeless person, heard through the grape vine about that old abandoned neighborhood west of Lauderdale and had moved into the house.

He texted in reply, "When you and your team were out there yesterday, Tom, did you work the house for prints? We dusted that bedroom thoroughly. But the prints we found in there were smudged and basically useless. However, some viable ones were lifted from the bathroom and kitchen."

"Did you run them?" came the response.

"Doing it now. I'll text you when we've got some solid leads."

"Agent Fuentes?" Abby asked.

He glanced up at the nurse. "Yes?"

"I'll take you to Dr. Young's office now."

"Thanks."

They headed towards the double doors, which opened when she held up her badge. *A locked ward*, he thought.

"So what's this all about?" she asked.

"Homicide investigation."

Her carefully plucked brows shot up. "Of one of our ex-patients?"

"Yes." He hesitated to say anything more to her. *Then again, why not? Maybe she knows something.* "Carmen Collier. She was Baker Acted. Or, as Canadian snowbirds say, formed."

Her curious blue eyes widened. "Unlikely she'd be forgotten round here. She was a maniac. If memory serves correctly, I think she was eventually diagnosed as bipolar."

"How long was she here?"

"Couple of months. Dr. Young believed the psychedelic treatment had worked and so later she was released, to her own wayward cognizance."

"When was this? Do you remember?"

"Within the last year."

They stopped outside an open door with Young's name plaque on it. "Go on in, Agent Fuentes; he won't bite."

"I appreciate your help, Abby. Thanks."

Even seated at a laptop, Young looked as tall and thin as a scarecrow. He had an oddly handsome face, intense skeletal eyes, threads of gray cutting across his dark hair. His smile was polite and phony. "Agent Fuentes, please, take a seat. How can I help you?"

"I'm looking for information on the homicide of a patient who spent some time here. Carmen Collier. I understand she was a resident in your psychedelic treatment program."

"*Homicide?* My God. I just can't recall. Let me look her up."

Interesting, Fuentes thought, *that Abby the nurse clearly remembered Carmen and that Young has to consult his computer files.* Was it his imagination, or did Young look uneasy?

While Young's fingers danced across the keypad, Fuentes turned on the recorder, tapping twice the app icon on his cell.

"Here she is," Young said. "Initial admittance came through a Baker Act after she assaulted a police officer during an arrest for shoplifting."

"What was the date of her admittance?"

"April 16, 2021. Was retained for more than a month. Released on May 21."

"How long was she in your psychedelic program, Dr. Young?"

He looked at the screen. "Four weeks, four treatments. I used DMT."

"And it cured her?"

Young looked amused. "Bipolar disorder isn't something that can be cured, Agent Fuentes. However, it can be handled, with proper meds and therapy—put under control. At the time Carmen was released from Broward County Hospital, her illness had stabilized. To that extent, she had an excellent grasp of the reality of her condition. "Where ... was her body found?"

"On the front lawn of an old place way west of Lauderdale." He brought up one of his photos of how Carmen's body was arranged. "Like this."

"Jesus." He drew back in terror of the sight.

But Fuentes thought his horror seemed as phony as his earlier smile. "Did she have family? Relatives?"

Young glanced at the screen, then shook his head. "None reported. And while she was here, she never had a single visitor ... that I remember."

"So when she was released, where did she go, Dr. Young?"

"No idea. We don't have jurisdiction over where patients go upon release."

"Did she have friends? A boyfriend? Anyone?"

"Not that I know of. What can you do without leads?"

"Her photo is being released today. We're hoping someone will come forward."

"Well, please let me know what happens, Agent Fuentes."

"I certainly will." *Will not*, he thought.

Once Agent Fuentes left the office, Young shakily got to his feet and shut the door. Then he turned, pressed back against it, and knuckled his eyes. He resented the intrusion of federal law enforcement into his professional life. *First that court order to release Jennifer Hart, now this federal homicide specialist with his petty inferences, about my psychedelic treatment program.*

And Carmen Collier.

After the janitor had found him in the lab several days ago, he'd gone home with the recording and audio, listened and watched, and descended into a dark consummate sea so black and singular that not a burst of light could squeak through. He didn't emerge from it for hours. And when he did come to, he'd been sobbing in his car, his hands tightly gripped upon the steering wheel, murmuring, "Carmen,

Carmen." Bloody gloves rested on the passenger seat beside him. He hadn't a clue where he'd been or what had happened. He still didn't. But even now, as before, he'd experienced those flashes of confusing images that felt like puzzle pieces of a dimly remembered dream. He'd written them off as detritus his unconscious had randomly coughed up: unresolved issues with his ex-wife and son, with his work here at the hospital, with Eleanor Raskin. But now he wasn't so sure.

He glanced at his watch, grabbed his laptop, and headed upstairs to talk to the hospital administrator, Dr. Jack Gordon. He'd been the administrator here for over a decade, supported Young's psychedelic program, believed these treatments needed to be tailored to the particular wants and wishes of the patient. *One size doesn't fit all.*

When Young rapped at Gordon's open door, he was on the phone, legs elevated, feet resting on the corner of his desk. His wildly dark ungroomed hair looked even wilder today, as if he'd rolled out of bed and forgotten to brush it. He motioned Young into the office. His feet dropped to the floor as he swiveled around in his chair to face him.

"Sure, that's fine," he said to his caller. "We'll talk soon." He disconnected, rolled up his eyes. "So, Andy. I'm assuming this is about your disagreement with Eleanor?"

"It wasn't a disagreement, Jack. She pulled a power play and put herself in charge — in charge of *my* program." This emphasis was playing havoc with his mind.

"But I understand she did it with good reason—because of what happened to your patient Jennifer Hart during her treatment, under your care."

"Every patient has a different reaction. All depends how deep the trauma is."

"Well, hers apparently was quite deep, Andy, since she fled our facility and we were presented with an official court order for her release. That court order really makes us look bad."

Young felt his coiled red anger unfurl through him, forced himself to remain calm, civil. "C'mon, Jack. It's not the first time we've been served with a court order for a patient's release. Whenever people are mandated to do something they don't want to do, the court is always the first place they go."

"An attorney is the first place they go."

"Yeah, well, okay. You know what I mean. Dr. Raskin isn't familiar with how the program works, what's involved."

"Which is why you'll still be running it and she'll be overseeing it."

Pissed and irate at Gordon's cavalier attitude, Young leaned forward. "How can she oversee something about which she's basically clueless?"

He spoke a bit too forcefully, and Gordon's demeanor abruptly changed from "We're colleagues" to "I'm your boss and what I say is law."

"For now, let's leave things as they are, slow it down. In a few months, I promise, we'll revisit the issue."

Fuck that. "I think it's a big mistake, Jack."

"Duly noted. Now, if you'll excuse me, Andy, I've got a shitload of calls to return."

Dismissed and within moments—their conversation, he thought, would be forgotten.

DIEGO AND HIS ABUELITA HAD WHIPPED UP SOME CUBAN goodies for their guests: chicken and spinach empanadas, arepas, black beans and rice, baked plantains smothered in butter, and, of course, plenty of Cuban coffee. Adele had set the table in the spacious kitchen, which looked out into the trees and gardens of the front yard.

"If Isabella comes through spontaneously, Diego, will they, uh, you know, get spooked?"

"I doubt it."

"Good. Because I think Isabella's got stuff to tell them."

The doorbell rang, and Diego answered it, welcoming Jenny and Marina into Adele's beautiful home. He thought Jo looked more rested, more relaxed, more *normal*, and he was so grateful he'd been able to help her escape the hospital. But his help was only beginning. He had a lot to compensate for from his life as Raul Giral.

When he introduced Jo to his grandmother, Diego noticed how her expression changed, her eyes brightening as if Isabella were peering through them. Her mouth swung into a wide smile. "Un placer." Adele ignored their outstretched hands and gave them both an *abrqzo*, the Cuban version of a hug. "Diego has told me much about you both. Now, please, sit, and help yourselves to a late lunch ... or an early dinner."

"Wow, this is a beautiful spread of food," Marina said in flawless Spanish.

"I don't know many Americans who speak Spanish as well as you do," Adele remarked.

"I'm Peruvian."

They started passing around the platters and bowls of food, chatting about the beautiful weather, inflation, the high price of gas—usual stuff—as though they were all regular people just getting together for a bite to eat. Diego knew, though, that Jo and Marina had specifics on their minds. It didn't take long for Jo to get to one or two of those specifics.

"What's new at the clinic, Diego?"

He and his grandmother exchanged a glance. "Tell her," Adele said.

"A federal homicide detective dropped by today to see Dr. Young. Apparently one of his former patients was murdered."

"*What? Who?*" Marina asked.

"Her name was Carmen Collier. She was bipolar."

"There hasn't been anything in the news about it," Jo said. "Not that I've seen or heard."

"One of the nurses told me the feds haven't yet released any information about it, but they're going to, in the next day or two," Diego explained.

"Where was this woman killed?" Marina asked.

Diego had no idea just how much Jo remembered of the Giral life or whether she consciously remembered anything about it at all. But at some level, the narrative of that life breathed in her soul, her cells, her bones. So he was hesitant about how much to say or even how to say it. He suspected that Marina, staring intently at him, was wrestling with the exact same thing.

"She was found in the front yard of a place in that old abandoned neighborhood west of Lauderdale that's been slated for a national park."

"The Giral neighborhood?" Marina asked.

Diego didn't know the area had been named after the Giral family. "Is that what it's called?"

Marina nodded. Diego noticed that Jo listened carefully but didn't show any obvious signs of distress—at least none that were apparent to him.

Adele spoke up. "In the 1920s, that Giral neighborhood was a place of extremes. You had the very rich, like the Girals; you had ordinary farming families; and then there were the eccentrics, like the famous seer who lived there. She read for everyone from locals to celebrities and government people. After her son was shot by Pablo Giral, she became a political activist."

"I've never heard this," Marina said. "Where did you get this information, Adele?"

"I'll show you." Adele pushed her chair back from the table and walked over to an old cabinet against the wall. She pulled open one of the many drawers, withdrew a folder, and returned to the table. "Some years ago, a history professor came to me for a reading." She opened the folder, spreading the pamphlets across the table. "He brought me these. Political pamphlets that Margarita Garcia wrote, had printed, and handed out wherever she could."

It was all news to Diego. He, Jo, and Marina each reached for a pamphlet.

> My name is Margarita Garcia. On March 17, 1923, my 15-year-old son, Santiago, was shot by Pablo Giral. That was two months ago. As of yet, he has not been arrested. Why not? Because he's rich and I am not. Therefore my son's life isn't as important as ... Pablo Giral's freedom? What kind of justice is that?
>
> You will hear there weren't any witnesses. That's a lie. I was a witness. Me, his mother. Santiago was on his bike, passing by the Giral home, when Pablo Giral himself ran out of his house, came at Santiago with a rifle, shouting at him to get off his land. Only a week earlier, Santiago had helped Penny Giral escape her father's abusive household. I screamed at Santiago to run, to get out of there, but he paused just long enough for Giral to shoot him.
>
> No mother should outlive her child. No mother should see her child killed.
>
> Five weeks later, police arrived to arrest him. Giral held them off for a time with gunfire, then he ran back into his house, killed his wife and sons, and then himself.
>
> NEVER BE SILENT ABOUT INJUSTICES. NEVER.

The pamphlet was signed "Margarita Garcia" and dated May 16, 1923—eleven days before the Ku Klux Klan would defy a US court law requiring full publication of its membership.

Marina gasped, and her hands flew to her chest as she suddenly fell forward, sobbing uncontrollably. Jo leaped to her feet, putting her arms around Marina, and talked softly to her, calming her down. But her bright eyes were drawn, mired in swirls of panic.

Adele got up again, hurried into the kitchen, and brought out a teapot that Diego knew held a special tea that Isabella had instructed her to make for situations just like this. She poured a cup and held it out to Jo as if an offering. She took it and coaxed Marina to sip at it. She sipped on it repeatedly, and within a few minutes, Marina sat back, blowing her nose and rubbing at her eyes. "I … I …"

"It's okay, Marina," Diego said. "You don't have to explain anything."

"Unless you want to," Adele added. "The tea often widens space between the memory and now."

"Space," Marina repeated, and laughed. "There's no space for me here." She sat up straight, holding the teacup firmly with both hands. Steam curled upward toward her nostrils. She looked pointedly at Jo. "There's stuff you need to know. About all of this."

Jo sat down again. "Christ, just get it out, Marina. I'm already fucked up. What's happening?"

Diego touched the app that turned his cell recorder on.

The odd and terrible truth about what Marina said was that Jo had already seen much of this in her dreams, in her meltdowns, in those moments of relaxation she got during yoga or through meditation. She knew it was an awful past life that influenced many of her decisions in this life. But every time she got closer to the specifics, some old memory would take over and swallow her; then she could be hurled back upon the dirt road that led to the Giral house. In the Giral neighborhood. Facing the Giral men: father and three brothers.

Those events usually ended the same way—with beatings and rape, mostly by her father, but sometimes, too, by her brothers. Meanwhile, her mother stood by so passively, occasionally wincing, sobbing, and always turning her head away. The walls between some of these memories were huge, seemingly impenetrable, but now Jo saw cracks appearing in them—small apertures through which she could peer. But could she see?

There stood Santiago Garcia, her buddy, her best and closest friend, telling her how she could escape with the circus: "It'll be easy, they want women, you'll fit right in. Friend of mine can teach you the tightrope …"

And so she had fled. And because of it, her monstrous father had killed Santiago.

Who was Marina this time round?

That single thought slammed her conscience into a cascade of buried cellular memories, all essence blown wide open, and now threw jaded fragmentary shrapnel across her wounded brain.

Jo pressed her hands hard over her eyes that they would not see as her body eased back against the chair. Her hands then slipped off her face and onto the table. She sat there, feeling both empty and whole, fractured and healed. Plenty of people had written about how Jung had reacted to his split with Freud. But how had Freud felt?

Like this. Perhaps. She glanced at Marina, then at Diego.

"You were Raul," she finally said. "my youngest, cutest, loveliest brother."

"Your spineless younger brother. I was terrified of and terrorized by Giral too."

"Who is now Dr. Young."

Diego nodded.

"And Dr. Raskin was Carmen Giral," Marina added.

"How do you know that?" Jo asked.

"She told me."

That fits, Jo thought. It was why she'd intervened in the treatment room, why she'd told Young and House to leave. It struck her as proper karmic fate that in this life, Raskin should become Young's boss. "The big question remains: how much immediacy does Young realize about himself?"

"I think he recognizes you at some level, Jo, and that's why he insisted on treatment."

"Why? To confirm something he already suspected?"

"My understanding of Pablo Giral is that he was a veritable psychopath, a control freak," Marina said. "So if he had a visceral reaction to you, Jo, that need to control you—maybe to control everyone and everything around him—this still remains a dominant personality trait for him."

"It definitely is," Diego remarked. "I've seen it in how he treats others' employees."

Adele touched her grandson's arm. "Tell them the rest of it, Diego. It's important for everyone here to have the same exhaustive information."

"Marina, what do you think?" Diego asked.

"I agree with Adele."

Jo looked at each of them. "C'mon. I'm obviously the only one here who doesn't know what you're talking about."

"You were told that your treatment was with DMT, right?"

"Yeah."

"It was PCP."

"Which is illegal!" Jo exclaimed.

Diego added, "I cleaned up the lab after Dr. Raskin took you back to your room. Since the IV bottle shattered, I collected some of the liquid, and Adele contacted a chemist friend, and he analyzed it and identified it as PCP."

Marina picked up her cell. "I did some research. Here's what Google returned." She started reading aloud. "'PCP has different effects on different people. It causes some people to feel joyful, leaving others to feel nothing but anxiety and panic. Sometimes this particular psychedelic will generate a mixed state, wherein one's horizon is seen laced of ecstatic and delirious parts. If this kind of phenomenon takes hold, it can easily lead one to feel the need to escape or lash out, which more often than not occurs in fits of violent behavior. Under tightening grip, symptoms of mental illness emerge, like believing things that aren't true (delusions), seeing things that aren't real (hallucinations), or feeling like someone is out to get them (paranoia) examples such as these hardly unheard or uncommon. Users feel detached from others, separate in their environment, strangely disassociated, even from themselves.'"

"That sounds like any hallucinogen."

"Too much PCP can be fatal," Marina said. "It isn't approved, too dangerous for treatment. So he broke the law."

"Good," Jo said. "Then we've got something on him. But I think we'd better keep it to ourselves, hush hush for now."

Suddenly, Adele's eyes rolled back in their sockets so that only their whites showed, then she raised up her hands. "Amigos," she said, her voice much softer. "Bienvenidos. Soy Isabella."

"Hola, Isabella," Diego said. "She's the spirit Adele channels."

"Wow," Marina breathed. "Mucho gusto, Isabella."

"Un placer," Jo said.

"My English, not as fluent as my Spanish," she said. "But it's good you're all gathered together. There shall be a federal detective who is drawn into all this. He'll benefit from what you four know, and you will benefit from what he knows. He's the detective who visited Dr. Young, who did not like that visit at all."

"What's his name?" Diego asked. "Can you tell us that?"

She waved her arm at their phones. "You have news on your phones. I believe you will find his name there now."

Jo quickly tapped the *Sun Sentinel* app on her phone and, sure enough, it was there, the headline reading, "Body of Murdered Woman Found on Front Lawn of Old Giral Mansion."

Jo scanned the article for the name of the investigator and found it easily enough. Evan Fuentes. A federal homicide investigator. "Why federal?" Jo asked.

Marina glanced up from her phone. "Because the government bought the whole area up. The feds want to turn it into a national park. The body was found in their jurisdiction."

At the end of the article was a photo of the old Giral mansion—run down, neglected, a gigantic eyesore. But she suddenly knew this was the place she'd seen in dreams, visions, and during her meltdown. A chill raced up her spine. "Jesus. This is the place where we lived, Diego. He ... chased me ... and Santiago ... up that road when we were on bikes. He ..."

"I remember," Marina whispered.

"And the neighborhood seer"—Jo looked at Marina— "was Santiago's mother."

Marina bit at her lower lip, nodded. "Isabella, was Fuentes in that life?"

She didn't immediately answer. Adele's eyes, just the sclera still showing, flicked back and forth, tracked from one side to the other, as though she were looking, searching for information, trying to bring the picture of memory back, whole and intact.

"Perhaps. But he knows his local history and has had a special interest in the Giral family sages for as long as I can remember."

"Should we contact him?" Jo asked.

Again Adele's eyes flicked and rolled from side to side as if she were unconsciously imitating the REM stage of dream sleep. "There are at least two possibilities that I see now. If you don't contact him, he may not find the killer, and then there will be other deaths. If you do contact him, all of you will be released from the horror of that life—but not without great risk to yourselves."

"What do you know that the investigators aren't releasing to the public?" Marina asked.

Adele's eyes stopped flicking. "The woman, Carmen Collier, was living in the house where you lived as Santiago. It's where she was murdered. This fact hasn't yet been released to the public. She was an ex-patient of Young's. That isn't public knowledge either. If you contact Fuentes and reveal you know that, he should be more open to talking with all of us. And with me."

"If you know all this, Isabella, then you must know who killed her," Jenny said.

"As do you, Jo."

She sat with that statement for a few moments. "*Young? Is that what you're saying? He* killed this woman?"

But Isabella was gone. Adele's head rested in the curve of her arms and stilled there; she softly snored. "This happens sometimes when the session is long," Diego said as he pushed away from the table. He went over to a couch in the living room, grabbed a throw. Then he returned to the table and slipped it around his grandmother's shoulders. "She'll be out for quite a while."

"What do you and Marina think about what she said?" Jo asked.

"That we should talk to Fuentes," Marina said.

Diego nodded. "And that we keep the PCP findings to ourselves, for now."

"So that we can in some way set Young up," Jo added.

"I think that at some point we need to bring Raskin into this group," Marina said.

"Yes," Jo and Diego said simultaneously.

Then Diego added, "I'm pretty sure Adele would be an *agreed* on this."

Jo sat back, her head racing. For the first time in years, she felt as if she was finally beginning to close in on the source of her nightmares and visions.

Fuentes had hoped release of the info on the homicide in news outlets and on social media would go viral. But within ten hours, it had gone wildly viral. The story was featured on all the morning news shows, it was plastered over Facebook, Instagram, and Twitter. Kindle sales of Margarita Garcia's memoir, *House of Giral*, went so far through the roof it hit number two on Amazon's bestseller list.

Calls and emails poured into his office faster than he and his assistant could answer them. He finally contacted Lt. Luke Nelson at the Broward County Sheriff's office and asked whether he and his people could help assist with the mountainous mass of responses. Nelson was delighted to.

In the first flood of emails, he and Nelson weeded out three good leads—people who had known Carmen when she lived on the streets before she was Baker Acted, and then again after she was released. The leads were a bartender, a woman in recovery, and one off-the-cuff woman who claimed she was the reincarnation of Penny Giral. His initial response when he'd read her email was that homicides like this brought the nutcases out of the proverbial walls.

They opted to start with the bartender, who worked at Hector's Cantina on Las Olas Boulevard. The place was a local watering hole, and at noon, the lunch crowd had claimed it. Fuentes and Nelson, neither of them in uniform, went up to the bar. The bartender, a strapping kid, with muscular tattooed arms and a winning smile came over.

"What can I get you guys?"

"We're looking for Rick Baker," Fuentes said.

"I'm Rick."

"You called our tip line about Carmen Collier," Nelson said.

His smile instantly vanished. "Man, poor Carmen. It's so sad—but not surprising. Let's sit out back in the patio, more private there."

He asked the other guy behind the bar to cover for him, and Fuentes and Nelson followed him to the patio out back. They sat at a wooden table with flower boxes on two sides, which gave them a lot of privacy. "You mind if we record this?" Fuentes asked.

"Nope, not one bit."

He and Nelson turned on their recorders. "So how well did you know Carmen?" Nelson asked.

"For four or five years, she was a regular. When I first met her, she was living with some guy here in town. She had a great job as a chef at one of the high-end restaurants. Made a ton of money. Then her boyfriend left her. The dude evicted her from his apartment, after which things, well … sort of fell apart."

"What restaurant?" Fuentes asked.

"I honestly can't remember the name. Anyway, she couldn't afford the outrageous rents in Lauderdale and started living out on the streets. She didn't have any family that I knew of. I felt sorry for her and told her she was welcome to stay in my spare room. That lasted about two months, while she looked for a job. She did her chef thing here for maybe six weeks or so, then stopped coming in, moved out of my place. Then I didn't see her for a while."

"When was the last time you saw her?"

"About a year ago. She came in one night, got pretty drunk, met some guy, and left with him. The next night, again, she came in, and left with another guy. Not long after that, I heard about her shoplifting inside a women's clothing store just up the block—and, of course, her arrest."

"She was Baker Acted," Nelson said.

"Yeah, I heard that. She came in one night after she was released, told me she had secured a place to live and was celebrating."

"Did she say where she was living?" Nelson asked. "Or with whom?"

"Somewhere west of Lauderdale. And this I remember: she was living with a guy."

Bingo, Fuentes thought. "Any idea where west? There're a lot of towns out that way."

He thought a moment, frowning. "She never mentioned a town, but my sense was that it was *really* west." Yet all that Fuentes could picture was the Wild West.

"You've been really helpful, Rick. We appreciate it. If anything else comes to mind, text or call me." He ticked off his cell number, and Rick tapped it straight into his phone.

As they got up, Nelson said, "Just curious, Rick. Did she say anything about her treatment at the mental health hospital? Anything about what treatments were prescribed?"

"She said she was taking a bunch of meds and that they'd treated her with hallucinogens. Weird, right? I mean, you're bipolar and they give you ayahuasca or DMT or some shit like that? It makes no sense. Is it even legal to do that?"

Fuentes shrugged. "My understanding is that the Broward County Clinic has the only psychedelic treatment program accredited in the state and has enjoyed some highly impressive successes with traumatized patients." *And some tragic failures.*

"She did say she really liked her shrink," Rick added.

"Who was he? Did she say?" Nelson asked.

"She just referred to him as ... Andy."

Andy. Not Dr. Young. Fuentes wondered if that might imply something more than just a simple patient–doctor relationship.

They walked back inside the bar. "We'll be in touch, Rick. Thanks again for your help."

He and Nelson walked up Las Olas boulevard, where Fuentes had parked. "What do you think, Evan?"

"That we should as soon as possible speak to the woman in recovery and to the nutcase who says she's the reincarnated soul of Penny Giral."

"I've got one woman's house and work address. That reincarnated Giral girl"—he laughed as he said it—"left just her number."

"You ever been to the Giral place?"

"Nope, never."

"Then I'll take you out there after we talk to these two women."

Leila Thompkins, the woman in recovery who had called in a tip, worked at a treatment center in south Lauderdale. She was a thirty something black woman with a quick smile and haunted eyes. She took Fuentes and Nelson into a small, pleasant library and sat them down at one of the tables off the stacks.

"This is where I met Carmen." She rapped her knuckles against the wood. "At this here table. We were both in recovery and trying to read our way back into the normal world."

"What had she been using?" Nelson asked.

"Mostly coke and crack. She told me she was in treatment because her boyfriend had recommended it. She was tryin' to keep the peace with him."

"Did she have a family? Kids? Parents?" Fuentes asked.

"Nope. No siblings. Parents were long dead and gone. Had a kid when she was sixteen. Gave it up for adoption. That's about it. I liked her. She had a weird, twisted, wonderful sense of humor and really helped me get through my recovery here. We used to blast Amy through the speakers, you know, how the man in rehab said, 'Why you think you here?' She'd just laugh as she said, 'I got no idea.'

"We stayed with friends once we both were out of recovery. Then the BF fucking flipped her fast; that's when things really fell apart. I last saw her maybe two weeks ago. We had coffee. She seemed a lot happier, said she was living in a cool old place near the Everglades with some guy who worked a lot."

"Did she tell you where?" Nelson was busily scribbling notes now instead of recording.

"Yeah. The old Giral neighborhood. Famous back in the twenties. Has a history, I guess …"

There it is, Fuentes thought. *Confirmation of what the coroner found through blood type.* "Any idea who the guy was that she was living with?"

"No, she never said."

As soon as he and Nelson left the recovery center, Fuentes called the other woman's number. She or someone else answered on the first ring, as if she'd been waiting for the call. "Hello?" a quiet but steady voice said.

"I'm Agent Fuentes with the FBI. Are you the woman who called in a tip about Carmen Collier and said"—he coughed twice—"you're the reincarnated Penny Giral?" It sounded so absurd when he said it aloud.

"Uh, yes. I'm Jennifer."

He and Nelson got into the car. "So, uh, what can you tell me about Carmen?"

"Quite a bit. I'd like to meet at the old Giral place in an hour. Is that doable for you?"

"Sure thing. See you there in an hour."

As he disconnected, Nelson chuckled. "Weird, isn't it, how things work out? We were going over there anyway. It's both what she wanted and where she intended us to meet."

"Synchronicity."

"I rather like to call it fate"

Chapter

10

MARINA DROVE HER SUV WEST OF THE CITY, THE SUNROOF
open to the mid-afternoon light. Her GPS faithfully provided
directions: "Turn here," "Turn in three hundred feet," "Take
a left," "Take a right," and, finally, "You have arrived."

She pulled to a stop in front of the neglected house, and
no one spoke. They all stared. "This is the place?" Adele
asked.

"Yes," Marina replied, and she got out.

As she walked toward the crumbling sidewalk, she heard
the SUV's doors open and shut. She heard Adele, Jo, and
Diego behind her, their shoes crunching over branches and
the broken sidewalk. And in her mind, she saw the place as
it once had looked when she, as Santiago, had pedaled past
on a bike.

Jo came up alongside her. "Wow," she said softly. "Eerie."

"I look forward to the day this fucking place is levelled."

"Me too," Diego said.

"I'm going inside," Jo said.

"Lots of No Trespassing signs on the place."

"So what."

Jo headed toward the front door of the old Giral mansion.

Marina and Diego exchanged a glance. "Let's go, Diego. Maybe it'll jog our memories."

"It may rip our memories open completely," he remarked, and he fell into step alongside her, both of them following Jo.

In spite of the No Trespassing signs, the front door was unlocked, and Jo walked into the front room. It was bare now, with dust covering the floor, one of the windows broken, the walls faded and cracked here and there. But against that far wall, she remembered, there had been a pair of couches placed at ninety-degree angles to each other, and sometimes after the monster had beaten Penny, he had tossed her over there like a bag of garbage.

And a table had been in the center of the room—wooden, large enough for the family to eat together. Her mother would be hustling around, bringing platters of food, her eyes red from crying over what the monster had done. The monster and Penny's brothers would be drinking at the table, pleased with what they'd made her succumb to.

She moved slowly from room to room, her consciousness divided between that girl Penny she had once been and the woman she was now, who was slowly beginning to recall the details of the horror. She stopped, shut her eyes, and thought of Abuelita, "Show me what I need to know." Nothing happened; she didn't feel anything in particular—no nudge, no hunch, *nada.*

She continued into the bathroom. She remembered colorful walls, ornate mirrors, sinks, and toilets. All of that was gone. The room had obviously been rebuilt somewhere along the way. There was a larger toilet, a larger sink, a shower. The room now looked like something from the 1960s. But here she saw herself as Penny, trying to cleanse herself of trauma and rape, valiantly trying to hide something she valued.

Penny was on her knees at the side of the sink, struggling to shove something into the wall.

Jo dropped to her knees in the same spot and moved her hands over the tiles, looking for any that were loose. Then she sat down, scooted back, and slammed her feet against the wall. A couple of tiles gave way. She snapped forward, dug her nails into the loose ends, pulled a small space out of the wall.

The hole wasn't large, but then again, neither were her hands. She thrust her right hand inside, moved it around, felt the sharp corner edge of something that felt metallic, began working it out and through the opening. The metal box was rusted in a few spots, but with little effort she was able to pry it open. She remove a thin dusty notebook.

Jo scooted back against the wall and opened it.

August 12, 1922

> My first entry. Santiago and I met at the town fair this afternoon on our freedom bikes. That's how we've come to think of them. His mom had some clients, and monster dad and brothers were out doing their usual bullshitting with investors. So Santiago and I were free ...

Jo flicked through the pages to another entry, her mouth now bone dry, her eyes aching, her mind racing, her heart . . .

September 7, 1922

*I just started 9ᵗʰ grade today. Monster doesn't want
me to go to school, but this one time my mother
stood up for me, arguing with him about why I
have every right to education, just like my brothers
do. Tomorrow, of course, my mother may have two
black eyes. So it is in the Giral home ...*

"Jo?

She slapped the diary shut and looked up at Marina,
who was standing in the doorway. "He was a fucking horror
show, Marina. I found a diary that Penny kept." She held it
up like a pointer to the sky, then at once dropped it in her
bag. "Did you remember any stuff?" In her head something
brightened, her empty darkness lit up and scattered, like tiny
little firecracker bursts. The stars of Hiroshima were falling.

She nodded. "Yeah, a kind of weird thing. Apparently
Carmen Giral was at one time friends with Santiago's mom,
Margarita. She sometimes came over here to do readings
when the kids were in school and Pablo and the sons were
at work. But a couple of times, when the men were out of
town, Santiago came over with her, and he, Penny, and
their moms would sit around in the kitchen having a psychic
pillow party. And then—"

"Let me guess. Giral and the boys came home
unexpectedly, and all hell broke loose."

"Yeah. The—"

"It's okay. I can imagine what happened."

"Hey, ladies," Diego called from the front room. "I think
the cops are here. Adele and I will meet you on the porch."

Jo hurriedly replaced the tiles in the wall, and she and Marina met up with Diego and his grandmother on the porch. "What do we tell them?" Diego asked.

"The truth," Jo replied.

As they started up the crumbling sidewalk to meet the three women and young man who exited the old mansion, Nelson said, "Hey, Evan. You believe in past lives?"

Fuentes shrugged. "I suppose it's possible. But I don't have any proof. Who really knows, right? It's best we just listen to what she—they—have to say. No judgment."

But as they neared the porch, Fuentes realized he recognized the older woman—Adele Cantera, a renowned Santera in the Latino community.

The truth shall set you free.

His mother had gotten many readings over a lifetime from her, and during one of those readings he'd been present, having tagged along for the ride. He was at the time just about to graduate from college, that he remembered. Adele had told him he would go to law school, then work for the feds as a homicide investigator. She had also correctly described the woman he would marry and where he would meet her. Everything she'd said then had happened later, just the way she said it would.

"I'm Agent Evan Fuentes; this is Lieutenant Luke Nelson. And Señora Cantera, you used to read for my mother."

She smiled and her eyes twinkled. " I thought you looked familiar, Señor Fuentes. This is my grandson Diego, Marina Bruce, and Jennifer Hart."

"Friends call me Jo," she said. "I've got some canvas

chairs in the back of my car. We can set them up on the porch and talk there. Let me get them."

"I'll help you," Nelson said.

"Thanks."

They walked off, and Fuentes looked at Marina. "Why did Jo want to meet here?"

"Because we have information about the murder that may help you," she replied.

"You mean that she claims she was Penny Giral?"

"It's not a claim, Señor Fuentes," said Adele. "Let us show you."

Before Fuentes could ask her to explain this certain oddity, Nelson and Jo returned with the chairs. They set them down in a semicircle arrangement on the old porch, where a pleasant cross breeze kept them cool. *The archetypal shapes had been set.* Nelson had also grabbed a cooler, and passed out cold bottles of water .

"So Adele seems quite certain you were once Penny Giral, Jo."

"Adele's certain because it's true," Diego said. "And I was Penny Giral's younger brother, Raul."

"And I was Santiago, Penny's closest friend," added Marina. "And we've identified the woman who was Giral's wife, whom he shot along with his sons and himself on the day he was going to be arrested for shooting Santiago."

Yeah, sure. All together here. A group fantasy held at the old homestead. "That's interesting, but what does it have to do with the murder of Carmen Collier?"

"First off, her name," Jo said. Pablo Giral's wife was also named Carmen."

So? What? "That's it?"

"And she was found here in the front yard." Jo gestured at the area in front of the house.

Marina got up and trotted down into the yard. "Bet her body was found right about here."

She stood in the high grass where old man Chandler had found the Collier woman's body covered in tall weeds. He had released this fact about where Carmen Collier had been found—the front yard—but not with photos of the exact location of the body or its position.

Marina went on. "And I'm betting the woman's body was found flat on her back, arms extended out at her sides, her feet tied, stakes through her palms."

"Why do you think that?"

"Because it's how Giral arranged Santiago's body after he had shot him."

All except the stakes.

Now Nelson spoke up. "Am I missing something here? Historically, it's known that Pablo Giral killed Santiago, but he wasn't charged for the crime until weeks later. On the day the police came to arrest him, he held them briefly off with gunfire, but then retreated back into the house, where he shot his wife, sons, and himself. Nothing left to solve, there."

"We're not asking you to solve the Giral murders," Jo said. "We're trying to explain how this past-life drama is playing itself out now, a century later, both of them showing the same exacting criminal mind signature."

"And I think we're doing a lousy job of explaining it," Marina replied. "Diego works at the Broward Mental Health Hospital as a janitor. Jo also ended up there, as did the woman who was Giral's wife, in that past life."

"Who is she?"

"Eleanor Raskin. She heads up the psychiatric department," Jo replied. "And we also believe that, the reincarnated headmaster of the House, Giral himself works there."

Fuentes leaned forward, eyes bulging, wearing a frown. "Let me get this straight … he's acting out what happened a century ago? Is that what you're saying?"

Jo nodded. "Yes, but I don't know how much, if anything, he consciously remembers."

"What's his name this time around?" Nelson asked.

"Dr. Albert Andrew Young, the shrink who treated me in his psychedelic program."

Well, well, Fuentes thought. Young had impressed him as an odd sort of guy, but not as a psychopath. Yet only a deeply disturbed, asocial and indifferent, psychopathic fucker like that, could have murdered Carmen Collier in the way he had. Then moved the body to the Giral lawn, and arranged it to signify, perhaps that, "our lord Jesus Christ had forgiven his sins."

"We know Carmen Collier was an ex-patient of his."

"Wow," Jo murmured.

"Fine, yet this is mere conjecture. What tangible proof, if any, do you have on this Young?" Fuentes asked.

"If he was remembering who I really was, at least at some level, then it does make sense that he would attempt to harm me. He would be compelled, now as then, by the same predisposed images and thoughts, that of a criminal mind ever ready and able to execute the same sadistic drive. More to the point, one should see a close similarity, of behavioral patterning, forensic clues left at the scene, manifestations of the same criminal signature."

Jo looked at Diego. "Now its time to tell him what you found."

Diego rubbed his palms against his jeans as if to cleanse them of their dirt. "The morning of Jo's treatment, I got to work around 5:30 AM. She freaked out, from whatever it was he gave her, and the IV bottle got knocked loose, hit the floor, and shattered. Later that morning, when I cleaned up the fractured mess inside the lab, I scooped a sample off the floor of what had been administered in the IV, brought it over to Adele, and she had a close chemist friend of hers analyze it."

Adele held up her phone. "I have his report right here and can email it to you, Evan. He said it was definitely PCP, not DMT."

Now it was getting most interesting. Fuentes ticked off his phone number. "Text it, Adele, please and thanks. If memory serves correctly, PCP is illegal, whether its use is recreational or in treatment."

And without patient consent, if not abusive, entirely unethical. Fuentes thought.

Jo nodded. "Yes. It's an over the top hallucinogenic. A small dose might be seriously harmful, or at certain times, even prove fatal."

"Have any of you alerted Broward County Hospital administration about this?"

"No, not yet," Jo replied. "You're the first people that we've told."

"I have real-time video and a recording of her treatment," Diego said. "And of Young when, at some later time that week, he gave himself the very same supposed treatment."

"You have them with you?" Nelson asked.

"On my phone. If you like i'll text them to you."

"Thing is, we'd like to keep this among ourselves right now," Jo interceded. "If he did kill Carmen Collier, I doubt he consciously remembers it. Most likely he'll just flatly deny it. He'll probably have, or make up, as he would an alibi."

"That's a super sweeping supposition on your part, Ms. Hart," Nelson remarked.

"You'll see what she really means, Agent Fuentes, when you listen to the tapes," Adele said, with a long ranging faraway look in her eyes. It was, at the same time the look and call, of her manifest destiny.

"I'm not only a Santeria medium but work as a licensed psychologist, lieutenant. I've treated and cared for many traumatized people. My sense is that the Giral life damaged … all of us. But if Young killed this Collier woman in this life, then the trauma of that life may have been substantially worse—and still is, for him now. Believe you me when I say karma pays good deeds forward, just as she places despair upon evil ones. It's the price a soul must pay for passing or failing … their temporal earthly trials. This dichotomy applies to him as it does alike for any and all of us."

Adele leaned forward, forearms for a second resting on her knees, then her eyes suddenly rolled back in their sockets until only the whites showed. "Me llamo Isabella …"

"Holy shit," Nelson muttered. "She's in full trance."

Fuentes had seen this strange transformation occur many times throughout the years. He saw it most recently when he'd gone to Cuba. But it was happening in the here and now, and that startled him. His heart hadn't expected it. "She's a Santera, Luke. This is what they do. They listen, and the dead speak back, through them."

Adele glanced at him, but her wild eyes were no longer the color of dark chocolate. They were bright aryan blue and belonged to Isabella. "It's a pleasure to meet you, Evan Fuentes. When your mother first consulted me, you were but a young ten-year-old boy, squirming in your chair the entire time. But even back then, this juncture upon us looked possible if not probable. When you returned years later, before you went to law school, this juncture became almost certain. And now, here we are."

"What can you tell me? Us?"

"You could arrest the doctor right now on the spot. But I don't think there'd likely be a conviction. He needs to be ..." She hesitated, perhaps hunting for the right descriptive words or phrase, to spill from the silence of her mind. "Tiene que ser configurado."

Literally, it meant Young would have to be configured—in other words, set up. "Why?"

"So that he incriminates himself. *Unconsciously he knows all of this, is his doing.* Now, please take the others to the place where this lady, Carmen Collier, was actually killed."

"Yeah," said Jo. "I was wondering about that, why you hadn't said anything."

"That fact hasn't yet been released to the public."

"We're not the fucking public, agent Fuentes." Marina spat. *Blood red splatter.*

Fuentes glanced around at Adele; her eyes were dark dark Café Noir brown. She had returned to this life just as Isabella had left the dead, and it gave off an eery impression. It were or it seemed, over this brief interval of time, that nothing other than a deepening of iris tint had changed."Okay, let's take a drive over there."

"Over where?" Jo asked.

"To the place where Santiago and his mother once lived."

Jo knew what lay ahead. She had seen and realized it once before, saw its fist first knuckle upon her birth horizon. Now it was crunch time. This unconscious confrontation was her destiny and fate, a litmus test whose smiling acids awaited in darkened earnest.

When their SUV pulled up in front of the old neighborhood place where she'd lived as Santiago, Marina felt that now eerily familiar inner shudder return. It started in her solar plexus chakra, and whipped its synergy up through her body.

"Looks empty and haunted."

"We found the room, where she was murdered," Fuentes said.

"You and Lieutenant Nelson?" Marina asked.

"Nope. Me and the old man who found the body, initially."

They went inside, and Adele brought a bottle of Florida water out of her bag, poured out a few drips of its clear crystalline substance into the palm of her hand, then flicked it around, murmuring a pious gospel-like prayer. She was in fact doing a limpieza, cleansing the evil spirits of the place. Marina now felt the shadow of that life pushing up against her. She again envisioned that pallid yellow fog which once rubbed its muzzle and licked its smoky tongue accross pristine window panes, that diabolical thing which nestled in pools and lingered in drains, demanding to be acknowledged. She pushed right back at it. For Marina needed to know the deepest depths, of Giral's evil ways in *this* life

They followed Fuentes as he walked upstairs and halted at the open doorway of a room, crisscrossed with yellow crime tape. "We left it just as we found it, except for the bloody sheets and towels that we took so the blood could be typed." He ducked under the tape and held it up so that the others could enter. "We found women's lingerie in the chest of drawers—bras, panties—but also men's clothing in the closet. The AB negative blood on the sheets and towels is the same blood type Carmen Collier had. She was living here, all right, no doubt about it."

Marina moved slowly round the room and saw the shiny brown wooden table where Santiago's mother had often done her readings. She ran her hand over the surface of the table, the walls, the bricks, and the woodwork, and occasionally she saw a story, a quick narrative of his life, as Santiago with his mother. Compared to Penny Giral's living hell, his had been deeply and preciously peaceful—except when it came to the Girals.

She ran her fingertips across the dusty glass of the windowpane, knowing this had been Santiago's room. He'd often peered out of this window, in a dreamlike state or fully awake, hoping to catch a glimpse of Penny riding the dirt road on her bike, smiling and waving at him to join her. "Was she living here with her killer?" Jo asked, breaking the thick deadened silence.

"Given the men's clothing in the closet, yes, I think so," Fuentes said.

"But you found lots of lingerie," Diego said. "So probably Carmen wasn't the only woman who lived out here with him."

"Probably not the only one." He paused, possibilities rolling through his head. " Do we know? Is Young married?"

"Divorced," Diego said. "I've heard rumors at the clinic that he's estranged from his wife and son, too."

"Does he have a home? Condo? Flat? What?"

"Let me check." Nelson tapped away at his phone. "Home on the intracoastal. Zillow says it's worth a million and a half. Three thousand square feet, four bedrooms, two baths, a full theater and pool."

"Address?"

Nelson provided it. "We'll have to take a look, Evan. Invite ourselves in for coffee."

"Yucky," Jo said. "Coffee with Young. I'd vomit with projectile disgust."

"For right now, can we install security cameras here and at the Giral place?" Marina asked.

Agent Fuentes's ears curled up like a copycat. "Excellent idea," he said.

Lieutenant Nelson strode out to the unmarked black SUV, and when he returned ten minutes later, he had three security cameras in hand. *Nothing fancy*, Marina thought, until she recognized the three cameras as Amazon products. She had seen them earlier that day as she scrolled across the website. They were DJI Pocket 2 Combo vlogging cameras, pocket-sized, exclusive, gimbal motorized, sunset white triaxial 4K video recorders. She recalled the particular details: 64 megapixel photoset, ActiveTrack 3.0, YouTube and TikTok video capacity, meant for Android smart or iPhone usage.

Are they solar powered?"

"Yup," Nelson replied, "green as emeralds."

"I think all of us need app access to these video cameras," Marina said, interceding.

"And to the ones you install in the Giral place," Jo added.

"But then what?" Marina threw her hands in the air. "We really don't yet have a clear 'set him up' plan."

"A sting," Fuentes said, with a wry curled up smile.

"Look," Jo snapped. "I don't give a hoot if you give this prick the shit show of a bumblebee or the undying stings of a scorpion. The bottom line for us is that Dr. Albert Young may be a killer and not even consciously know it. Perhaps what he knows, at convenient times, is forgotten. Or he may not be a killer at all. There may be someone else out there, lurking around. Bottom line, we need a fucking *plan*."

Nelson went quiet. So did everyone else. Thirty seconds passed, then fifty. It was more than a minute before Marina finally burst out. "How do we lure him here?"

"Not yet," Fuentes said, backtracking. "I want to talk to this Raskin woman first. Why does she think she was Carmen Giral? Let's take things one step at a time. First we need to install these high-end cameras, hiding them so they aren't visible. Then do the same with the Giral house. Do we have any more security cams in the car, Luke?"

"Got a loaded box. I carry it around with me in the trunk of my van."

"Great. Then let's do a look-see, find the spots best suited for these cameras."

Under the darkening twilight sky, they all hovered for a time as a large group—Luke and Fuentes, Carmen, Marina and Diego, all of whom, of course, centered around Jo. The scene appeared as if it came straight out of a renascence painting, but not a single soul could recall which, whose it was, when or, even if it was drawn, why it took place. It was a spatial oddity, a monumental parapraxis of sorts, akin to that HAL computer in 2001 A Space Odyssey, it pressed its mechanical state of refusal down and about, smothering Jo.

Yet in the light of the morning, after the caw of the crow bird has sounded a new day's dawning, it were as if a spiritual shift came of that Peter A. Barelkowski untitled image, that would, from unconscious memory, be ushered back to her in return.

ON THEIR WAY BACK INTO TOWN, JO TEXTED ELEANOR Raskin. "Can we meet somewhere for coffee? A bite to eat? There have been some interesting developments I'd like to discuss with you."

Raskin answered within a few minutes. "Wonderful to hear from you, Jo. Your escape and subsequent court order for release really threw a wrench into Young's program. I'm now in charge of it. I have the day off tomorrow. Where should we meet? What time?"

"How about Havana Cafe on the beach? At noon."

"Great. See you then."

They dropped off Diego and his grandmother, then continued on to Marina's place. When she pulled into the driveway, Jo said, "I've got to pick up some stuff from my place. And I'm meeting with Eleanor Raskin tomorrow at noon at Havana Cafe for a bite to eat on the beach. You game?"

"Absolutely. Wait. I had the locks changed so Chris couldn't get in." She removed a brand new shiny key from her key ring. "Here's the newest key."

"Thanks. I'll be back in less than an hour."

Jo hurried down to the curb, where her car was parked, and within a few minutes walked into her house. The place felt eerie—empty, quiet, as if the rooms were waiting to exhale. She hurried hard into her bedroom, brought a suitcase out of the closet, opened it on her bed, and started yanking shirts and jeans off the hangers, tossing them all in the suitcase.

"Jo?" A man was calling to her from the front of the house.

Chris.

She hurried out into the living room, and there he stood, Chris Laker, in jeans, sandals, and a T-shirt that said, "Don't forget to call your attorney." And as she stared at him, his features seemed to melt away and rearrange themselves into a face that seemed vaguely familiar.

"I ... knew you. The ... the circus tightrope walker. In that life ... you also left."

"You're talking crazy shit, Jennifer."

"Yeah? I guess that's why all the blood just drained out of your face."

"You changed the fucking locks."

"It's my house, and you moved out. So yeah, the locks were changed."

"I hadn't gotten all my stuff out, Jo."

"Go ahead." She stabbed her thumb toward the spare bedroom, where, at some point, Marina had stashed the rest of his belongings. "Make it snappy. I need to be somewhere."

He looked shocked that she'd spoken to him that way. "Wow, I think I liked the other you much better. This one—"

"Doesn't need you anymore. Chris, you could've gotten a court order to get me out of that clinic, but you couldn't even be bothered. Why? Because it might make you look bad amongst your peers? So Marina's brother got the court order. And something interesting, Chris. I have this vague memory that you tossed me out of the fucking circus when my attempt at tightrope walking embarrassed you. Weird, huh, how patterns tend to repeat themselves from life to life." *COPY.*

Then she turned and went back into her bedroom to finish packing. She heard him in the next room, moving his belongings out. *Good riddance,* she thought.

She retrieved toiletries from the bathroom, then carried her bag into the living room, where Chris had stacked a couple of boxes. When he came out with the rest of his stuff, he quipped, "This past-life stuff is bullshit, Jo. You really need to get professional help."

She looked at a him, wondering why or how she could have ever loved this guy, and laughed. "Look who's talking, dude. So which former girlfriend have you moved in with?"

"How could you … never mind."

He picked up the boxes and carried them down the sidewalk to his car. She just stood there in the doorway, watching, as he loaded the boxes into the trunk and then got in and drove off. Jo felt nothing—not anger or remorse, not guilt, only indifference. She wondered, though, how many patterns of her past life had been carried forward into this one. Not the drugs Penny had used. Not the shame and humiliation she'd endured. But perhaps that desperate need to escape, what she'd felt in that life, had carried over. This time around, she didn't just want to flee those horrifying memories; she needed to make sure Young himself remembered who he had been and what cruelties he had perpetrated.

She went back inside the house, made herself an espresso, then returned to the living room to read more of Penny's diary.

September 9, 1922

There are so many times I feel unworthy and to blame. I tell myself it's because of how Monster treats me, how my brothers ignore me, how my mother pretends none of these horrors are happening. But why should any of that make me feel unworthy? I'm a pretty girl. When Santiago and I talk about these things, I feel differently about myself. His friendship makes me feel worthy.

Today, for instance, we met in our favorite part of the woods, deep in the forest, where no one can see us. We sat together in the deep shade of the cypress trees. He had his sketchpad with him and sketched the me he sees.

I think that when he draws, he sees inside of me, the me of me, the real me. To Santiago, I am worthy, I'm beautiful, I can grow up to become whatever I want. But only if I can escape these people to whom I am related by blood. I don't consider them my family. Santiago and his mom are my real family.

Jo wondered whether she might see the whole of herself through Santiago's drawings, Penny's diary, a dose of Santeria wisdom, all of it catalyzed by psychedelics. Maybe then she would realize, and maybe even come to terms with, all that had happened to her.

> Today I packed us a lunch and we had a picnic out there in the woods. The birds were singing, squirrels were chattering in the trees, and Santiago and I tossed them bits of bread and cheese. It was so peaceful we both wanted to stay there ... forever.
>
> But as the afternoon melted away, I began feeling anxious and scared that my mother had returned from town, that Monster and my brothers had come home early from work to discover I was absent. Now they may be out hunting for me, like I'm prey they intend to catch and consume.
>
> "I'd better get going, Santiago."
>
> "Maybe you can live with mom and me," he said, getting to his feet. "My mom could adopt you."
>
> I laughed. I couldn't help it. "I doubt that Monster would allow it. He'd probably start tying me up on weekends so I couldn't even go to the bathroom."
>
> We walked through the woods slowly, holding hands, and I relished this small bit of freedom. Out here, I could breathe, I could run and dance and shout with joy—as long as no one was around. We paused at the edge of the trees, watching the house carefully. No vehicles out front. No sign that anyone was home.

"Coast looks clear," Santiago said.

"Hope it's not a trick." I looked back at him, and suddenly he kissed me. His arms went around me. My heart pounded. "I'm going to get you outta here, Jo. Somehow. Someway."

I stepped back, squeezed his hand, then tore myself away through the trees, and across the road.

October 1, 1922

He got drunk earlier tonight and came after me, shouting, slapping his belt against the palm of his hand. I backed away from him, screaming. "Child abuse is a crime, Papa!"

My mother came running in from the kitchen, yelling at the monster to stop, just stop, but he turned worse on her. His belt lashed out and struck her hard across the chest. She grabbed the belt out of his hands and smote him across the face.

He stumbled back, blood pouring from the welt across his cheeks and nose. Such rage erupted from him that I outraced everyone to the front door, where my mother, brothers, and I trembling in fear, tore through it. But Raul held back, and as Monster came after us, he stuck out his leg, and my father tripped and went flying. He landed facedown, flat on the sidewalk, and didn't move.

We stood there for a moment, staring. Finally, my mother crouched over the top of him.

"Pablo?"

No response.

"Hospital. We need to get him to the hospital. Sebastian, get the car, bring it around."

Sebastian seemed paralyzed. "But ... but ..."

"Get the fucking car, now!" shouted my mother.

Carlos snapped, "I'll get it."

"Just let him die," I said.

My mother looked up at me, eyes filled with tears. "*Mi amor*, I'm sorry I never stood up to him before. But we need him. All the money is ... in his name."

"He deserves to die," Raul said. "You haven't seen half of what he does to her, to Penny."

Carlos then pulled up in the Nash. My mother stood and wrapped her arms around me. "I'll help you escape," she whispered. Then she snapped her fingers at Sebastian. "Help me get Father into the car."

Raul and I watched mother and Sebastian carry Monster out to the Nash. I looked at Raul. "Thank you. For what you did, tripping him. He might well have killed me and Mom."

"And me," Raul said quietly, then turned his face away and went into the house.

I hurried after him. Neither of us spoke. We immediately went to the liquor cabinet and started removing the bottles of Scotch and Gin and everything else the monster drank, draining them all down the sink. We didn't know what to do with all the empty glass bottles that remained.

"Let's put them in bags and carry them out to the road where the construction crews leave their garbage," Raul suggested.

We put them in a pair of old wagons we'd used as kids, attached ropes, hopped on our bikes, and pedaled probably a mile to the construction site, where a couple of homes were being built. When we arrived and spotted two huge garbage bins that held broken bricks and wood, paper bags and empty cans of soda, then dumped everything we had.

Once the wagons were empty, we stood there, staring blankly. Then Raul touched my shoulder. "I'm sorry I've been such a shit to you, Penny."

And for the first time I can ever remember, we hugged.

October 31, 1922

Halloween. Monster was released from hospital today. His nose and right shoulder were broken, his face was a scraped-up mess, and he had a monumental concussion. He obviously wasn't a happy camper and didn't say very much. When we got home, after lunch, he limped back to his room and took a nap. The house was strangely peaceful.

The ding of Jo's cell phone interrupted her reading. It was a text from Marina. "Hey, I made dinner. You hungry? It's already seven."

"On my way."

Jo dropped the diary into her handbag, picked up her bag, and locked the front door as she left. During the drive, she thought about the incident Penny had written about, where both her mother and Raul had been her allies. The others needed to read these entries, too.

Marina and Diego had agreed to meet Jo at the Havana Cafe at noon. She'd gone by Office Depot first and made four copies of Penny's journal for Marina, Diego, Eleanor, and Evan Fuentes.

Traffic on the beach was a nightmare, and as Jo drove around looking for a parking spot, out of the corner of her eye she spotted the Bourbon Street Pub. She suddenly realized she remembered it from the night of her meltdown.

She'd heard music; that had prompted her to go inside the place, where she'd watched seven men and a woman play "Farewell Blues" by the New Orleans Rhythm Kings. She picked up her phone and said, "Siri, play 'Farewell Blues' by the New Orleans Rhythm Kings."

"Here it is, girl."

She listened until she'd found a parking space. Initially the music made her feel weirdly uncomfortable, but soon she started enjoying it again. The difference between now and the night of her meltdown was that she had recalled significant pieces of the life that had haunted her. Many parts were still missing, but she felt fairly certain the rest of Penny's journal would fill in what's left of the details. She hadn't remembered, for instance, when Raul and mother had intervened when Monster had intended to beat her silly. She hadn't remembered the warm hug that Penny described.

Jo got out of the car and walked the two blocks to the beach. Havana Cafe was one of the few places that was right on the beach instead of across the street from it, where most of the concrete lay. It looked crowded, but as she approached the place, she spotted Eleanor already seated at a table on the porch. Jo waved at her, then made her way to the table.

"Great spot. How'd you get this one?"

Eleanor grinned. "They know me here. Whenever I came home from med school, this cafe was my first stop."

Jo sat down. "Marina and Diego are going to join us. You okay?"

"Wonderful. So what's been going on, Jo? You look a hell of a lot better than you did the day you took off."

"Been busy," she said. She then caught Eleanor up on what had been happening.

Eleanor just sat there, listening closely, sipping at her coffee. She didn't say a thing. Then the server came over, and Marina and Diego arrived. They all ordered. When the server had left, Eleanor got right to the point. "Jo explained what's been going on. This Agent Fuentes you mentioned,

Jo, he called me, and we're meeting tomorrow—but not at the clinic. So I have to ask ... When you three were at the old Giral place, did it seem familiar? Did it stir up memories?"

"It did, for us all," Diego said.

"I also found Penny's diary there, hidden in the bathroom wall." Jo brought out the three copies she'd made and handed them out. "Take a look at the entry for October 31."

They got so engrossed in the diary that when the server came over and set a basket of warm buttery biscuits on the table, none of them even bothered to glance up, in spite of the delicious scent. Eleanor was the first to speak. "Well, I'm glad to know that Carmen and Raul did the right thing for once. How'd you find this treasure chest of memoirs, Jo?"

"I don't know. I went into the bathroom to look around, and for no good reason just felt I should check for loose wall tiles. So that's what I did."

"Jesus, did you read the Thanksgiving entry?" Marina asked.

"I didn't get that far yet," Jo replied.

Marina started reading. "'Thanksgiving Day, 1922. Santiago and I met up at his place this morning, when everyone in the Giral house was sleeping in. I had breakfast with him and his mom. Margarita told me she spoke to a cop friend at the local PD and made a formal complaint about the way Monster abuses me. She doubts that anything will come of it because Monster is so rich he just buys off the police. But at least now there will be a record.

"'Before I left, Margarita gave me some fresh eggs so I'd have an excuse about where I was. But when I came into the house, Monster was up, sitting at the breakfast table, Mom was cooking, and the brothers were just coming downstairs.

Monster looked at me with such hatred and subdued rage I nearly spun around and fled the house. But every time I run from him, I'm caught and humiliated, degraded, beaten, raped.

"So this time when he got to his feet and came toward me, slapping his folded belt against the palm of his hand, shouting about how I stole his liquor, how I knew my prettiness seduced him, that I needed to be taught a real life lesson, I grabbed the heavy Hearth whisk broom Mom uses to sweep around here. Clutching it like a weapon in both hands, with firm grip on the stick, I swung it wildly in the air, hard and fast, barely missing the tip of his nose. I reset then came at him violently again, screaming, "Stay back, you fucking monster!"

"He lashed out with his fisted belt, but I leaped to the side and swung the broom even harder back. The force at his wrist jerked the belt out of his hand. I swung around, quickly settling on a flat planar attack, and leaned with the blunt handle of the broom, which slammed into the side of his ribs. Monster then stumbled backward with a grunt, reached behind him, and pulled out what looked like a Glock 22. It was a Norinco 1911.

"Panicked beyond recognition, Mom grabbed the boiling pot of water off the stove and shrieked, "No more!" Then she hurled the contents of water and pot at him. He shrieked as the stream of steaming water struck havoc across his red stinging face.

"He lost grip of the gun, and as it fell, Raul swept in and scooped it up. Sebastian came up behind the monster and, with vigor, shoved him forward. Monster's shoes slipped, his feet slid water to air. Next thing I knew, his body went down to the ground, his ass slamming sharply on the hardwood floor.

"My mother hurried over to Raul, grabbed the gun from his hand, then fired off two shots in rapid succession. The bursts of gunfire shocked the room into stillness. Mother marched right over to Monster and, pointing the gun straight at him, its six-inch barrel inched ever close to his temple, said, "Let's here get something straight, Pablo. If you ever pull this shit again, I'll shoot you straight through the face!"

"Giral hard-knuckled his eyes and scooted backwards on his ass. I could tell he was livid. In this blanked vortex spun of ravished, reddened, righteous rage, Monster somehow climbed up to his feet, sneering, "Woman, you'll regret this." As he lunged for her neck, the front door flew open and two policemen barreled in, with Santiago and Margarita close behind."

"Holy shit," Diego murmured.

"They arrested him on the spot," Eleanor said softly. "That I remember."

Jo paged through the diary. "Looks like he was gone till right around Christmas. In between, at the suggestion of the police, I moved in with Santiago and his mom." She glanced at Marina. "Do you remember any of that?"

"Some," she replied. "As you were talking about it. How long did this episode last?"

Jo shrugged. She didn't have any idea. "Diego? How much of this do you remember?"

"Some of it. With Penny living elsewhere, Pablo's rage didn't have an outlet until one day he went apeshit. Incensed of spirit, he sprang at my throat, got me in a headlock. I was stunned and momentarily couldn't speak. It was all I could do just to breathe. Carlos and Sebastian had to actively intervene. I can still feel the grip of his sharp-tipped pearly white incisors and those fanged leeches of spit, which struck and stuck to me like sticky pearls of venomous glue.

"They had to peel him off of me, and his poisons off my skin and body, after which we began making plans to take leave of the Giral home. We knew what he would do to Carmen if it was left just the two of them. So I think we stayed a bit. Or maybe we left for a while and came back. I'm not sure. What do you remember, Eleanor?"

Raskin glanced up from the journal, frowning slightly. "How miserable I was. I recall being envious of Santiago's mother because she didn't have to answer to anyone, and I was deeply grateful to her for ... for keeping my daughter Penny safe."

The scantily dressed server at the Havana Cafe had suddenly arrived with their meals, so they tucked away their copies of Penny's diary. Diego decided it was about time to take this to the next level.

"I'd like you all to hear the audio I have of Dr. Young when he gave himself a treatment."

Eleanor frowned. "You have audio of *him? How?*"

She could fire him on the spot for such unruly behaviour, but of course, he didn't think she would. "I made a point of installing it in the treatment room when I was cleaning up the shattered IV bottle from Jo's treatment. I also scooped up some of what it held, and my grandmother had it tested at a lab. It was PCP, not DMT. I have the report on my phone. I'm texting it to you."

With this confession completed Raskin's eyes lit up, and

she leaned forward, speaking quietly. "If that's true, I can indeed fire him."

"Listen to the audio first," Diego said.

Eleanor looked around at the crowded porch. "Too many people. No privacy. Let's go to my place. I don't live too far from here."

They followed Eleanor in their own cars, and in less than half an hour, all were settled inside Raskin's impeccable kitchen. They listened to the audio of Albert Young, in the grips of whatever he'd given himself, speaking in the low, gruff voice of Pablo Giral. The first time Diego had listened to this, it had horrified him. Now it only pissed him off. When it was done, Eleanor was the first to speak. "It sounds like some of his memories came alive. So it seems he's not completely clueless about his life as Pablo Giral."

"Do you think he has conscious memories of that life?" Jo asked.

"Probably not. It's more likely they are, at best, subconscious. At issue here are his emotional patterns, repetitive loops of urge, motive, and desire from that other life, cast forward into this one. His temporal mindset reflects the expression of a soul whose latent genomic imprint and sequence of codons were remnants of past insatiable desires, inherited down the familial line. His anger and rage come from the uncontrolled hard wired need to harm and control others. It's possible that at some level he recognizes who we were. This is especially relevant for you, Jo. That would explain why he used PCP. An overdose of that could have maimed, even killed, you."

"I imagine he didn't react well to your taking over his treatment program," Marina remarked.

Raskin laughed. "I know he went to the hospital administrator about my taking over *his* treatment program. That didn't go over, either."

Jo chuckled. "Given the way he treated you as Carmen Giral, that probably had him pissed off big time. The past life wife now in charge."

"No doubt that enraged him. Did you tell Fuentes about the PCP?"

"Yes," Jo replied. "He agreed to keep it to himself for now. It's the one thing we've got over Young."

"I'd like to see this house where Carmen Collier was killed," Eleanor said.

Marina nodded. "It was where Santiago and Margarita lived. And yes, being in that place, for me, stirred up a lot of forgotten memories."

"If Young was involved in her murder, then it's a significant synchronicity, in that her name was, and presently still is, Carmen." Eleanor tapped Diego's phone. "Can you send me a copy of that recording?"

"Sending it to all of you now," Diego said.

Jo sat forward. "So what's our next step?"

"Tomorrow I'll meet with Fuentes, and we'll go from there," Eleanor said.

"Go where, though?" Diego asked.

"That depends on what Young does, from this point forward."

Chapter

12

YOUNG HAD ARRIVED AT THE CLINIC BY FIVE THIRTY THAT morning and was already in the cafeteria when House set his breakfast tray down at the spot across from him. "You're helping out today with the treatment?" Young asked.

"Can't. Got a ton of work to catch up on. Not my area of expertise. " He buttered his toast and slapped strawberry jam on it. "Besides, you've got Eleanor to help out." He smirked as he said that.

"Yeah, don't remind me. Abby isn't on duty today, so I need another nurse, too."

"Plenty of them around."

"Yeah, but Abby has worked in treatment the longest. She knows the routine."

"Have Eleanor do the scut work."

They both snickered at that.

Young didn't have any doubt that he could administer the treatment to his new patient. But it would have to be one of the approved psychedelics. In the report he'd written for Eleanor about this treatment and the patient, he said he favored DMT. Eleanor had already seen the patient—a woman of twenty-nine with a history of depression—and had given her permission for one treatment. She wanted to see how the patient was after this before approving any more. That irritated him. It all irritated him. He hadn't taken the issue to the hospital board—yet. He intended to collect data first on how Raskin conducted her oversight of the treatment. So his first stop when he left the cafeteria was the treatment room. He made sure the security cam and recorder were working, and he started wiping down everything.

Diego, the janitor, arrived before he'd finished. "Morning, Dr. Young. I'm supposed to clean up in here before the morning's treatment. Okay if I get started?"

"Hey, Diego. You saved me. I'll just turn all this over to you. The treatment won't be till nine."

"Great. I'll be finished long before then." He went over to the door and pushed his massive janitorial cart into the office. "Is Dr. House going to be here too?"

"Not this morning. But Dr. Raskin will. And Diego, could you dust those blinds again?"

"Sure."

Again Young brought a fifty-dollar bill out of his wallet and set it on the desk. "Many thanks, Diego."

As he left the treatment room, he saw House at the other end of the hall, making his usual 6:00 AM. rounds with his group. He noticed that all the interns were studying their phones. Young walked over to him.

"Don't they look studious today, Larry."

"Yeah. I asked them to define CIPPES. That was their homework. Hail, ye future doctors," he said to the interns. "Anyone find the answer?"

An intern whose name tag read "Ed Pullman" spoke up. "No clue, Dr. House."

Laughter rippled through the group.

"You wanna be docs, gather round for a game of show-and-tell. The rules are quite simple: I show, you tell. Who wants to begin?"

Six hands simultaneously shot into the air. House glanced at Young. "So much hope it kills. We're headed to the radiology suite. Want to join us?"

"Sure. Diego is cleaning the treatment room."

The interns followed them into the radiology area, where the man in charge, Dr. Nap, rolled his eyes. "You're back, Dr. House?"

"I am."

"I understand Ms. Hart is no longer an active patient of yours." Nap smiled.

House nodded. "Yes, I transferred her case to Dr. Young late last week. After that, she, uh, took off. Medical ethics and due diligence require proper follow up of all initiated investigations. Besides being in her best interest, her case poses a unique and valuable opportunity for purposes of resident education, training and ... treating."

"But sort of beside the point, don't you think?" Young quipped, his voice low. "Since she's no longer a patient of yours."

House smiled. "Dr. Nap, the results, please, on Ms. Hart."

Nap scooped up an iPad, scrolled, went over to one of the mainframe computers, and brought up the results of Jennifer's scans. The interns gathered around. "You'll want a look-see at the reports, House, no?"

House nodded. Two typed reports came through the printer. Young picked up one; House picked up the other and began to read the first report out loud to the group.

"'Procedure V/Q scan: 99Tc aerosol 1,000 MBq given by nebulizer, ventilation scan performed. Patient instructed to cough, take two deep breaths, 99mTc-MAA 75 MBq was then injected intravenously, and a perfusion scan of the lung completed.' As you see on the computer screen, the technique involved a photon-emission computerized tomography with gamma cameras that generated multiple 3D images of the lungs. Result? V/Q level zero point eight. A small non segmental perfusion defect is noted. Summary: low probability V/Q scan."

The interns, Young thought, looked intrigued. House continued without delay. "The technique—CT head without contrast. Findings: No mass noted. No evidence of intracerebral hemorrhage. Basal cisterns appear patent, normal shape and size. Ventricles of normal caliber. No suggestion of hydrocephalus. Cerebral parenchyma normal shape, density, and appearance. Basal ganglia, posterior fossa structures unremarkable. No suggestion of major vessel vascular territory infarct. No intra- or extra-axial lesions. Basal skull, petrous temporal bones intact, air cells patent. No fracture identified."

House paused and sounded frustrated when he spoke to Nap. "Where are the Thoracic and Chest CT's I ordered?"

"Better late than never, right?" Young remarked, needling House in the same way he often needled Young.

Dr. Nap just smiled. "Those films are still being processed. All you've got to do is ask and I can tell you what you want to know."

House nodded. Dr. Nap proceeded. "In typical cases of crack lung, radiological findings clear almost immediately after drug cessation. We're talking hours, not days. You were quite right, Dr. House, in ordering the CT when you did. If you had waited even a couple hours longer, we might not have caught anything of value."

Young thought House looked delighted with what Nap had said. "So, Dr. Nap, are you saying that you see *positive* radiological evidence of CIPPES?

His bright blue eyes matched his sarcastic grin when he began to speak. "But what you really mean, Dr. Nap, is you've found evidence supporting your *bias* towards CIPPES.

Nap shook his head. "No, not that, exactly." He reached for a stack of large manila envelopes that rested on the desk in front of him, pulled out two plain films, and snapped them vertically under the view-box. "These are the plain CXR films we took of Ms. Hart. The first is a portable one taken in the ER, the second a repeat film with PA and lateral views."

As much as House annoyed Young, he felt the man was almost a mind reader, at times far ahead of everyone. With uncanny anticipation and a fine attention to detail, his certain prospect had been proven right again and again, many times over.

House turned to the group of interns. "Are any of you *Herr Doktors* willing to take a stab at the etiological and radiological manifestations of cocaine toxicity?"

A waving hand shot up. A nod followed. A small, barely audible voice sounded its rite of passage. "Pulmonary edema or hemorrhage."

Then multiple voices rose in the group.

"X-ray attenuation."

"Consolidation."

"Opacification."

House gestured at Nap for his expert interpretation. "What does Ms. Hart's X-ray reveal?"

Nap nodded. "Lung hemorrhages due to drug intoxication, manifest on plain X-ray films as perihilar areas of increased opacity, whereas fluid leakages arrive by the way of perihilar attenuation, with or without septal thickening. Unless something else is at work, such findings typically occur alone, without signs of pleural effusion or cardiomegaly."

"Go on," House said.

"High-resolution Thoracic and Chest CT's were performed. Most X-ray positive cases of lung hemorrhage show themselves multi-focally on CT scan as ground-glass areas of increased perihilar opacity, while X-ray cases of fluid leakage rather show attenuated areas of consolidation and septal thickening."

Young heard House's murmur of exasperation. "That's all fine, Dr. Nap, for you to talk up the theoretical line, but now how about we walk the real? Give me what positive findings you actually identified, on Ms. Hart's CT."

Young thought Nap displayed nary a sign nor smidgin of irritation, which was to his enormous credit. Young wondered what House's real intent was with all this bravado.

"Ms. Hart's CXR ... suggested the presence of small pleural effusions. Thoracic CT confirmed these and a small pericardial effusion, but with normal heart size. Our CT also suggested the presence of ... cocaine-induced lung hemorrhages."

Wrong, Young thought. Jennifer Hart hadn't done cocaine. House hadn't yet mentioned the track marks he'd seen on Jennifer's arms, which had vanished in a day.

House looked out at his awestruck audience. "So, Herr Doktors, let's now talk differential diagnosis. Is this the typical CT picture one sees of a drug abuser? Or could this be something else, more sinister, like a dissecting thoracic aneurysm?"

"Neither," boasted one intern, self confidently "but it brings up the prospect of SBE."

Nap shook his head in agreement. "Yes, it does—speaking, of course, in the theoretical. Our diagnostic radiological investigations have, I believe, produced a picture fairly consistent with that line of thinking. This make the etiological inference reasonable. Nevertheless, I fail to find *specific* radiological evidence on Ms. Harts CT that confirm this suspected diagnosis. Typically, with subacute bacterial endocarditis, we see peripherally distributed lung nodules bent in various phases of cavitation. Such classic marks of septic embolism were *not* identified on Ms. Hart's Thoracic or Chest CTs."

House's brows shot up and his eyes widened. Two large circles taking everything in. "You haven't mentioned Dr. Nap, about Ms. Hart's mediastinum, its magnitude and form.

Young thought Nap now appeared far beyond irritated, he looked highly offended and with good reason, House was trying to belittle and humiliate Nap, just as he'd done many times over with him. *Motherfucker House.*

"What the f*ck, Laurence? Nap snapped back. Do you really think I nap on the job? Just go through the motions?" House smiled at the pun.

"My dear Dr. Nap, no offence intended," House's blue eyes beginning to recede while his demeanor recanted. "We know, everyone lies." Young's fiery mind was about to fume.

You've got to be kidding me. This asshole is calling Dr. Nap a professional liar. To his credit Young held his ire at bay, kept these thoughts about House and Nap private, for now.

"We're done here, Dr. House, Nap fumed. I've explained more than enough, and frankly, other than your trying to instruct the interns, I don't see the point of all of this. If you'd like, we can talk about it later in private, just the two of us. For the meantime ..." He slapped a thick folder down in front of House. "There're the facts."

House began to object, but Young touched his arm. "Save it, Larry."

Nap then stormed over to the door and flung it open. "Have a great day, gentlemen."

The group left, and as soon as they were out in the hall, House griped, "That fucker can't take his own criticism, constructive or not."

Look who's talking, Young thought.

"Dr. Nap had most conveniently forgotten our last conversation," House continued. "Freud was the first to define forgetfulness as psychic parapraxis, 'para' being Latin for 'beside' or 'along with'; 'praxis' meaning 'action.' This *parapraxis* is a forgetfulness of action—that which in psyche appears along with or beside the act, which is nothing but a normal gauge of what was once conscious memory. Subconscious parapraxis in dream memory pictures and conscious forgetfulness here in waking life represented to Freud the common cardinal symptom of a psychopathology of everyday life. Meaning you and I and everybody else, lies and forgets.

Young felt as though that last remark was directed most

precisely to incriminate him, and he suddenly wondered what that something was, that House believed he knew.

As soon as Young had left, Diego pocketed the fifty dollars he'd later give to Adele, then checked the security camera. It was on. So the first thing he did was throw the circuit switch for this room, knocking out the electricity. Then he threw the switch down again and went over to Young's computer. He quickly but not too quickly began to configure the camera so that it would automatically email him the visual and audio recordings. Then he installed his own security cam, placing it at another angle.

Next he scrolled around through the computer, looking for the newest files. There were several. He stuck a USB drive into a port on its side and copied the files. Then he shut the lid on the computer, turned the cameras back on, and went to work cleaning the room.

He paused by the windows to text Eleanor that he was cleaning the treatment room and that Young had turned on the security cam. "Thanks for letting me know, Diego. I'll be meeting Fuentes this afternoon at the Habana Cafe. Guess it's our go-to place for Giral discussions. Does Adele have more any insights left for us?"

"I'm seeing her later today. I'll ask. Keep us posted about your meeting with Fuentes."

"I sure will."

Fifteen minutes later, the treatment patient of the day, Pam Leonard, arrived with Eleanor. Dr. Raskin parked her wheelchair adjacent to the treatment chair, then Pam shuffled herself out from one, settling in the other. Diego started loading up his cart so he could, when the time was ripe, quickly get himself out of here.

"Diego, make sure Pam is comfortable, will you?" Eleanor asked. "I need to get the IV bottle from the fridge."

She headed for the refrigerated area, and Diego brought Pam a bottle of cold water from the mini fridge, which was set a ways back against the wall. She was a petite soft little thing, pretty in an offbeat kinky sore of way, but her trembling bodily told Eleanor another story, that in her mind she was scared shitless. "Here you go," Diego said, and held out the water bottle. Artificial refreshment to cool and prepare the mind.

"Thanks. Listen, you don't have to tell me but, have you done this treatment?"

"I just work here."

"Well, Pam continued, I've done small doses of ayahuasca before, but never DMT. Am I going to freak out? I mean, I read about that woman who fled this place after she was Baker Acted."

"You should ask Dr. Raskin about that, Pam. I've known her for many years. She's a terrific and caring professional and would be more than happy to answer your questions."

When Raskin returned to the room, Diego said, "Pam has some questions, Dr. Raskin."

"Ask away, Pam." She set up the IV pole and bottle.

Diego didn't stick around. This was his cue to make exit. He gently pushed the cart out the door and into the hall just as Young was headed in. "All cleaned up, Dr. Young. Dr. Raskin and the patient are already inside." Not a glance was exchanged between the two.

"Thanks, Diego."

Diego wondered who this Pam woman was. Whether she was someone from the Giral life. He hadn't got any conscious sense of recognition when they'd spoken, but that might not mean anything in particular. Besides, it seemed that as Raul Giral, his life back then, had been fairly limited in terms of other people: family, Santiago and his mother, people with whom he and his brothers worked, store clerks, common folk.

He suspected she was simply a depressed and anxious young millennial woman who had no special connection to the Giral life. But what about Fuentes? Isabella, the spirit his grandmother channeled, had said she didn't know whether Fuentes had been a part of that life. But she wasn't always right, and over the years Diego had learned to listen first and foremost to his own instinctive hunches.

Young resented Raskin's presence in *his* treatment room. He resented that she'd taken over *his* program, *his* patients, *his* procedures. She had already set up the IV and noted the bright red sticker on the IV bottle, with "DMT" printed neatly and clearly on it. That meant she'd gone through *his* supplies in the refrigerator, and that deceptive and distasteful fact of betrayal pissed him off many magnitudes more.

The audacious nerve of this so called Raskin woman. Explaining to Pam Leonard how the process would unfold, but she really fucked up on a couple of pertinent details, so he interrupted.

"Actually, Pam, Dr. Raskin is relatively new at this. Initially, you'll feel—"

"Excuse me, Dr. Young. I was speaking." *You narcissistic queen bitch.*

His dark temper seized him of all thought and he reflexively blurted, "You don't know what the hell you're talking about."

The fire that blazed in Raskin's eyes struck a chord so deep inside Young that it shocked him. His heart nearly arrested on the spot of this discovery. He'd seen that fire before, but when? Where? In whose eyes? He could not consciously recall. "I think we're done here, Dr. Young." Raskin softly touched Pam's shoulder. "You're under no obligation to receive this treatment, Pam." She shot a glance at Young. We need her informed consent.

The naive wide eyed patient scanned the treatment room for advisement, her wild saccades passing first from Raskin to Young the over to House, where they momentarily ceased. Now infused of greater purpose they swung into accord to land squarely on Raskin.

"I prefer not to."

"Now just a goddamn minute!" Young burst out.

Raskin simply ignored him, held the wheelchair steady as Pam set herself down. Raskin pushed the chair to the door, handed Pam off into the hands of a capable nurse, then came back into the treatment room, slamming the door behind her.

"You apparently don't have a good grasp of the English language, Dr. Young. *I'm* now in charge of this treatment program. You don't interrupt me while I'm explaining something to a patient. You don't get to behave like a spoiled narcissist child who doesn't get his way. So as of right now, you"—she wanted to add asshole—" officially are no longer part of this mental health program."

Red poured across Young's vision like a torrent of blood,

and when she turned to open the door, he lunged straight at her. But Raskin must have sensed it, because she leaped off to the side, waited and watched, as Albert crashed into the door, stumbled backwards then tripped and fell, slamming his face rather hard upon the cold tiled floor. She sprung up to shut the door, then walking over to him, looked down at him with incredulous purpose of amusement. "You've got some major anger issues to deal with, Dr. Young. Your ego is most certainly in charge, so I'm going to recommend intensive therapy—preferably psychedelic." "I can conduct psychedelic therapy quite effectively on my own, Eleanore. Young quipped back with a wry painted smile pasted on his face. I don't need a goddamn therapist."

"Oh, right. Of course you don't. But I'll recommend it just the same, along with a leave of absence. I'll be submitting my report to the hospital administrator, tout de suite."

He felt the dark chaotic beast of his rage scrambling around inside of him and could already feel the darkness sneaking up on him like a thief, ready to swallow him whole.

"The treatment room is now and in the near future off limits to you," Raskin added, for what seemed emphatic purpose . "As for your information, Andy, I was lucky enough to have once studied under Stanislav Grof, a man who knows as much about psychedelic treatment as anyone else on the planet. You violated several ethical protocols: for example you did not recommend an eye covering to eliminate visual distractions, nor did you instill soft music to drown out white noise. You failed miserably to document your observations give reasonable account of your thoughts, provide objective evidence which if not confirms strongly suggests that your patient had a treatable rather than contraindicated condition.

I found no documentation whatsoever of her mindset. In your notes, you provided neither empirical evidence that the setting you chose was subjectively comfortable, nor that our patient was fully informed *a priori* of the untoward potentialities of this treatment you administered. All these errors preceded you Albert being brought in here."

"That's a … lie. I always explain everything to the patient."

"Yeah, sure you do. How much informed discussion did you have with Jennifer Hart? Here it seems we have an intriguing postscript. That this is all happening under a present Saturn-Pluto square. Saturn is the disciplinarian, the ruler of structure, responsibility, karma. Pluto is the unseen underworld, everything that's hidden, secret, what represents dramatic and irrevocable transformational change. And the square, Dr. Young, is that karmic challenge which has just been hurled at your face. *"When, will you remember?"*

She opened the door, and without a back glance, silently walked out.

Young stood there for what seemed the longest of time, her words echoing back and forth, over and again inside his head. *When are* you *going to remember … it all?*

He felt anxious as the black hole of a fugue state, which swirled wildly inside of him, whispering, teasing, demanding. All he knew was this compulsion to get out of there, fast.

Jo waited in a rental car parked at the back of the clinic's parking lot, eying her phone. It was nearly 10:00 AM. By now Eleanor had humiliated and enraged Young enough, that Jo fully expected he should soon take leave the clinic.

The plan was that she would follow him and that Diego and Marina, her backups, would be close behind them.

She had well disguised herself. An expensive wig transformed her into a brunette.

She wore large rosy plasticine sunglasses, garish earrings, a tee, leggings, running shoes, and a lightweight jacket that held her concealed Glock 22 weapon.

Her phone dinged. A text from Eleanor. "Young left the treatment room. Diego saw him hurrying through the lobby. I slapped a GPS chip on his car earlier this morning and am texting you and Diego the link so you'll able to track him without getting too close."

"I'm more than ready."

But was she really? Her terror of Giral was just as deep and pervasive as it ever was, only that she was now more conscious of it. In some ways, she almost preferred how it had been tucked away in her unconscious mind for years: that overwhelming horror of visions, snippets of cellular memory seeping into dream triggered nightmares, leading her to that iconic delirious meltdown of 09 03 2022 which had later gotten her Baker Acted.

At least in the years before, she'd been able to live a fairly normal life in between the nightmares and the creeping horror of something she didn't consciously understand. But now? Christ, now her entire life seemed to have a singular all or nothing direction—solve the riddle of the house of Giral. Period, or give it up. She had chosen to eat and breath Giral. But her obsession to know was driven by an intense unconscious desire that Pablo Giral be held fully accountable for what he'd done, that which she believed could happen only by Albert Young becoming conscious . . . of himself.

Her phone dinged, the link to the GPS appeared in her text messages. She clicked it.

She glanced up, scanning the parking lot, and saw Young come out of the building.

He walked quickly, but not so quickly that he would draw attention to himself. "Got him in sight," she texted to Diego and Eleanor.

Diego: "Me, too. Am in my car."

Eleanor: "Keep me in the loop. Am writing my report for our hospital administrator.

As Young pulled out, Jo snapped a photo of his gray Lincoln Navigator so the time, date and place would be officially noted. She didn't pull out until he was on the street, in the right-hand turn lane. She glanced into her rear view mirror and spotted Diego pulling out as well in the SUV she'd driven the day she'd fled this clinic.

Jo followed Young to I-95, staying five or six car lengths behind him. The GPS signal—a moving, flowing red dot—made that easy. After a seamless twenty minutes or so, he exited the interstate and headed west on I-75. Unless he was headed to Naples on the west coast, she guessed that his destination was the old Giral neighborhood.

She turned onto I-75 and was surprised when the GPS indicated another turn ten minutes later, which brought him into the town of Davie. Even though its population was now over a hundred thousand, Davie maintained its roots as a rural farming and equestrian community, just as it were back in the 1920s. Hitching posts stood along outside stores and restaurants, set of times virtually untouched; she saw several people on horseback, trotting along one of the riding paths through town. A group of men dressed like urban cowboys were tying up their horses outside a breakfast place. Several of them wore sidearms. The good ole Florida governor had made it legal to carry openly, as if this were the Wild West. The GPS showed a left turn onto a side street and a stop. Jo didn't follow. She pulled into a Target parking lot and brought up a map of Davie on her i-phone to see whether she could determine his exact location. *Store? House? Apartment building?* The scene looked like a neighborhood of homes. She took a screen shot of the GPS, fit it over the map of Davie, then enlarged the map until she could see the address: 137 Fountain Road. *Hmm.*

That, she recalled, had coincidentally been her room number on the psyche ward. And there had been that same strange 137 High Road place, belonging to . . . whom?

On Google Earth, she entered the address and zoomed in on the house. The place looked large—built around a swimming pool, with a barn in the back. It probably sat on a couple of acres. Armed with the correct address, she went to the Broward County Public Record site and entered it into their computer banks to find out who owned it. The site wasn't particularly easy to navigate on her phone, so she brought out her iPad and went online. On her phone, she returned to the GPS signal. Still beeping motionless.

She returned to the iPad and entered the address into the public records site. The name that came up surprised her: Amy Young. Was she Young's ex-wife? A sibling? A daughter? *Ex-wife*, she guessed.

The house had been transferred into her name six years prior, most probably in a divorce settlement. According to Zillow, the value of the house had gone up more than thirty percent over the last year, and was now worth between $700,000 and $850,000.

Not too bad, she thought, and she glanced at the phone again. The signal hadn't moved. Had he dropped by for a visit to chill with his ex?

Jo decided to take a look.

She started the engine, raised the windows, and texted Marina and Diego not to follow her. "Wait for me in the Target parking lot."

She turned onto Fountainhead Road, a wide, tree-lined street with large, gracious homes. A couple of teens were shooting baskets in the driveway of one place. Then, farther down the street, she spotted Young in the driveway of 137, arguing with a blonde bomb shell she assumed was his ex. As she approached, she snapped a photo, then drove on past.

Jo returned to the Target lot, where Marina and Diego were each parked in their respective cars. She pulled in and got out, and so did they. "So what's he doing?" Marina asked.

"Standing in the driveway arguing with the ex."

"So should we wait?" Diego asked. "See where he goes next?"

"I'm going to wait; you two don't have to."

"We're a team," Diego said.

"Exactly," Marina agreed.

"Then let's wait alone in separate areas."

Her phone jingled. She glanced at the screen and saw that Young was again on the move. "Here he comes."

They hurried back into their cars, and Marina and Diego

drove off to opposite sides of the lot. Jo waited until Young's car was headed toward I-75, then pulled back onto the road.

Fuentes met Dr. Raskin at a restaurant on Las Olas, where she had a table outside on the rear patio. She was scrolling through her phone when he approached. "Dr. Raskin?"

She glanced up. "Agent Fuentes?"

"Evan," he said.

"Eleanor," she replied.

They both laughed, and he sat down opposite her. She immediately slipped a thick folder across the table. "In there is everything I know about the Giral family; my past life as Carmen Giral, mother to Penny, Carlos, Raul, and Sebastian; how and why I think it all fits together now."

He flipped open the folder. "Wow."

"This looks extensive. Okay with you if I record our conversation?"

"Sure."

He brought out his cell, turned on the recorder. "Okay."

"I've been putting this together for quite a number of years. Like I told Marina, back in 2000 when I was doing my psychiatric residency, I developed problems with my vocal cords. No one could find an exact cause. One of my doctors suggested a past-life regression and recommended an expert, Carol Bowman. Her specialty focuses on healing through regressions. I relived my death as Carmen Giral, re-experienced scenes from that awful life. After that, the problem with my vocal cords, completely vanished."

Fuentes was impressed. "Can you email me this material as well?"

"Sure. Any leads on Carmen Collier's killer?"

"I've been following several. She was one of Dr. Young's patients. I'm assuming you knew that?"

"Yes. And that she lived on the street, and so on. Here's my theory, Evan, from a psychological point of view. I think that the murderous impulses and rage of Pablo Giral are the unconscious imprinting of a genomic pattern, a nominal tendency that manifests itself, under the proper circumstances from life to life, one to the next. I believe that's what we're seeing here. Synchronicity points the way. First, the woman's name was Carmen. This in itself is of course intriguing."

"Why?" Fuentes asked.

"It comes from the Hebrew word 'Karmel,' meaning 'guard,' 'garden,' and 'vineyard,' the biblical garden of God. In Latin, it means 'song.' Through the Spanish Marian epithet "María del Carmen", Lady of Carmel, it comes as a reference to Mount Carmel, an orchard and mountain range located in the Holy Land of Canaan, populated in early Christian times by hermits. Carmen was the name of the main character in George Bizet's opera *Carmen*, the same as Giral's wife. She was killed somewhere in the Giral neighborhood, her body displayed like Christ upon the cross, arranged on the front lawn of the old Giral mansion, just as Santiago's body had been arranged after he shot the kid."

Eleanor took in a deep breath before her final exhalation. "As if it were a subconscious criminal mind signature. There are all those synchronicities to boot, involving my past-life connections with Jo, Marina, and Diego, more to the point and fact that the three of us just happened to be connected a the time we met in some fated way to the same mental hospital. What are the odds of that?" *Fate has no odds.*

"I'm no math expert, but it's gotta be off the charts. The problem I have with all this rational conjecture is that I can't bring an actual case against Pablo Giral, dead now for … what? More than a century?"

"But you can bring a factual case against a psychiatrist who knowingly gave a patient an illegal drug treatment, willfully choosing PCP."

Jesus. "Do you have proof of that?"

She nodded, brought out her cell. "I'm texting it to you, Evan. Diego collected it from an IV bottle that shattered during Jo's treatment. His grandmother gave it to a chemist friend, who wrote up the report. I think that House may know or suspect this too. But you'll have to approach him yourself."

His phone beeped twice, and he read through the chemist's report. "Too much of this stuff can neurologically maim, if not kill you. Why would Young want to kill Jo?"

"Well, think about it. In the Giral life, when she was his daughter, he abused her—and me, mostly because we were women, and it was considered his right as a man, at the time, to do whatever he wanted to his wife and daughter. At some level, this time around, I think he recognizes her and me. Fortunately, in this life I've found my karmic voice, and I'm now his immediate boss."

Fuentes struggled to take in all this and was glad he had a recording that he could listen to later. "The act is not good enough, I have to prove intent, Eleanor. A good lawyer could quite easily argue to the jury that the PCP might've been a mistake. It happens—patients who go in for surgery are operated on for the wrong ailment, or the left leg is amputated instead of the right. I need *proof of intent*.

I mean, imagine it. He's now at trial. Twelve jurors. If the prosecuting attorney's argument is that Young is acting out of some thing as fictional and irrational as past-life impulses and rage, Young will certainly walk."

"Yeah, I know. But I've got a plan."

"Then let's hear it."

He shut off the recorder.

They followed Young, who made a straight beeline to the Hard Rock Cafe in Hollywood. It had a full casino of slot machines, poker tables, sports wagering, and just about anything else a gambler like Young might covet. They parked in different areas, then got out and met by Marina's car at the far back.

"Well?" Jo said.

"I'm ready." Marina ran her soft hands over her tight black skirt and silk blouse. She, too, wore a stylishly seductive wig that transformed her from a brunette to a blond.

All in all she looked nothing like the Marina Jo knew.

"Me too." Even Diego had presently disguised himself in a pair of dark shades and expensive but casual clothes, had slicked his hair back so that he looked more like a young Mafia don Juan than that *guy ordinaire* who worked his life in janitorial services.

"He may still recognize us," Jo warned.

"I doubt it," Marina said. "It'll be dimly lit, crowded, loud, plenty of distractions."

Diego nodded. "We'll just keep an eye on him."

Then the three of them, before they went inside the Hard Rock Cafe, paused for a moment at the entrance. There they stood, as if struck together by fate or destiny, save for one last look behind them. Above the rock-hard door they saw the silvery steel of the club's cut-off guitar, flashing its brilliant signature, greens and blues that suddenly morphed into bursts of purples and pinks. These light images cut a wildly penetrant reflection across the entire Fort Lauderdale district.

Somewhere in the far northwest periphery of their view, Broward County Hospital could be seen, beaming off multicolored hues, its breath of continence blown like a laser beam show, lighting up miles and miles of area for all to see.

Noisy and jammed with people, it was just the atmosphere Young craved. He bought a beer, got twenty bucks' worth of coins, and found an empty slot machine next to an attractive middle-aged MILF who laughed every time her machine rang with winning coins.

She's lucky. Now I need some of that funk'n luck.

By the time he'd played his twenty bucks' worth of coins, he'd won two hundred. He needed another beer and turned to the middle-aged woman.

"Might you hold onto my golden machine for me, while I get me a refill?"

She turned her head towards him and held up her empty wine glass.

"Would you?"

"Of course. What're you drinking?"

"Chilean merlot."

"Comin' right up."

He felt great as he made his way to the bar. A woman

and drinks and some gambling were the ideal antidotes to the depressing argument he'd had with Amy. About money. So when he ordered, it was for a bottle of Chilean Merlot, and two port glasses.

The woman's name was Helen Archer; she was a college professor who worked at the University of Miami and taught political science—divorced, had a daughter in law school. After she beat him badly at the poker table, they went hand in hand into the dining room, for food and more wine. By then it was nearly nine, and he was so shitfaced that he didn't care if he drove back to Lauderdale or not. As for Helen, she clearly didn't want to drive home in this condition. So they decided to hook up, stay and get a room together.

At the hotel's front desk, he asked for a room for the night. The clerk played the computer keyboard. "All we've got left is a regular double, not the deluxe. Its on the first floor. Room 137."

The moment Young heard that number, a shudder whipped its curse straight through him. He remembered, that Jo Hart had been in room 137. That that was the number on the house his ex now occupied. That she claimed he owed her $1,370,000 in back alimony. Now he and Helen had room 137. Nothing good ever seemingly came of that number. His mind seemed to snap. Do you have another room with a double bed?"

The clerk looked surprised, then amused. "Uh, well, let me look." Then she whispered, "A single room, yes, double bed."

"Number?"

"Eleven."

"Perfect, I'll take it."

Young left his credit card on the counter and slung his arm around Helen's shoulders, and they wove their intoxicated way, laughing, to the elevator.

Jo saw that Young's partner had left her cell phone at the dinner table. She hurried over, swept it up, and pocketed it. She made straightaway for the women's room, locked herself in a stall. The phone had no code on it, nothing to prevent someone from doing what she was doing.

Her name was Helen Archer. Judging from the emails and text messages, she was a U of M professor who taught political science in grad school—divorced, daughter at Yale, and an author to boot. This year, she'd published a book on how extremism in the Republican party could easily lead our fine country into the fictional world of Gilead, as depicted in Margaret Atwood's classic, *The Handmaid's Tale*. Jo liked her already. She copied Helen's number into her burner phone, then texted her: "Get out of there as quietly and quickly as possible. The man you're with is a killer."

When she saw that the text had gone through, she copied Helen into her Find My Phone app, then put Helen's cell to sleep and left the stall.

At the hotel's front desk, a pretty Asian woman greeted her, "Hi, what can I help you with?"

Jo set the cell phone on the counter. "A woman at the slot machine next to mine left with a man, and they recently came to the desk and checked in. She left her cell on the slot machine. I just want to make sure she gets it."

"They checked in just now?"

"A few minutes ago."

She looked at the computer. "Okay, let's see. Albert Young and Helen Archer checked in"—she glanced at the clock behind her, which read 10:17—"eleven minutes ago. Must be hers. I'll make sure she gets it right away. Thank you."

"Sure."

As Jo turned away to look for Marina and Diego, her mouth snapped a satisfied grin. Marina and Diego were there, moving toward her through the casino crowd. She motioned toward the door.

Once she was outside in the cool evening air, she felt vindicated. Well, almost. She hoped Young's bedmate would get the hell outta there and that when he came out of his drunken stupor in the morning, he would do or say ... what? Just what the hell did she want him to realize? That he was the reincarnation of a fucking monster whose impulses and rages had followed him? And prevailed unabated in this life? Not likely, not from this.

"What now?" Marina asked when she reached Jo.

"We go home to bed. I'm whipped."

"What were you doing at the hotel front desk?" Diego asked.

She told them as they walked toward their cars. Marina stopped, Diego and Jo stopped. They all stood motionless at the rear of the lot, where their cars were parked.

"Christ, Jo," Marina whispered. "You've got guts, girl."

Jo rocked forward onto the balls of her feet, then leaned in close to Marina and Diego.

"I want this fucker caught for something in *this* life."

"Jo, we're getting closer."

Marina slung her arms around Jo, hugging her; then Diego hugged them both.

"Let's do this."

But would they?

Here they were, 11:00 PM at night, nearly the witching hour, after twelve or thirteen hours of surveillance. She'd hoped today would expose Young in some way—that he would stumble and do something unthinkable or stupid. But it instead had ended with a pathetic whimper. Marina came up alongside Jo. "Go home, go to bed. They'll be busy for sometime up there fucking their brains out."

"What a waste," Diego said. "Yet we found out a lot. "He likes to gamble, he argued with his wife, he got drunk, picked up another gambler, secured a secret room with her here at the Hard Rock Cafe. Sooner or later, he'll fuck up. And I think it'll be sooner.

Chapter

13

WHEN YOUNG WOKE, HE DIDN'T HAVE A CLUE WHERE HE WAS. The sun cast an eerie orange glow through the blind on the window of his room. His head felt as if it had been stuffed with rotting food and had collapsed at some point in the late-night or early-morning hours.

He sat up, threw off the covers, and stumbled to the bathroom. As he showered, the hot water pounding against him, he started to remember. *The woman ... who was the woman I picked up?* He had a vague impression of her face. She'd been playing the slot machine next to his.

Her name, he recalled, had something to do with the zodiac sign Sagittarius, the archer. *That's it! Helen Archer. So where the hell is she?*

He felt marginally better after he'd showered, but he wished he had clean clothes. He scooped up his watch, noted the time—nearly ten in the morning. Albert tried to remember if had patients to see, anyone to treat, but nothing came to mind. Then it all rushed back: the way Eleanor Raskin had angered and humiliated him yesterday in front of Pam Leonard, told him he wasn't allowed in the treatment room, that he was officially on leave of absence now, and was supposed to enter treatment, preferably psychedelic therapy.

Fuck that.

Fuck her.

He put on yesterday's clothes, found a comb in the back pocket of his jeans, and stood in front of the bureau mirror, drawing it back and through his hair. As he did so, something weird happened to his reflection. His features started melting down like hot wax—his nose dripping first, then his eyes, chin, mouth, ears, even his hair. His whole face was a drooping, waxy, skeletal mess. *Who is this?*

Horrified, he wrenched back, but the image in the mirror morphed again, changing now into a face that looked much more familiar—still it wasn't his. The man in the mirror had a cruel face; dark, angry eyes; black hair; and a short, stubby neck. The longer Young stood there staring at this face, the greater clarity it assumed.

"I know you." He whispered these words, his voice hoarse. He reached out and drew his index finger across the man's forehead, down the right side of his face, across his chin and then his mouth, then up through the center of his face. "Who the fuck are you?"

The mirror suddenly exploded with fractured images of an angry madman waving a belt and racing after a stumbling young woman. The sun was blazing red in his eyes as he caught her by the hair, jerked her back, threw her to the ground, and started beating her with the belt. She shrieked and screamed and struggled to get to her feet. He threw himself onto her and started tearing off her clothes, stripped her down bare naked, against her feisty-fisted will.

Young gasped, rubbed the back of his hand across his

mouth, and backed away from the horrifying image. But it had already moved on past the deed. His eyes felt the sting of his prey as two younger men yanked the man to his feet and shoved him away from the woman. The man's pants were at his knees, and eerie clangs from the metallic parts of his belt buckle sounded, as he stumbled around like a wayward drunk, trying to pull them up until one of the young men grabbed his Icebreaker boxer briefs, the pouch tearing in a zigzag pattern, as he hoisted his sorry ass in the air and body-slammed him to the ground. Hard and down he went, but his indifferent continence left psychopathic traces, Cheshire cat smiles floating aimlessly in the wind. Another young man abruptly took charge. He ran over to the woman and helped her to her feet, pulling a warm shawl around her shoulders and hid the perky nipples of her perfectly shaped breasts.

The man pushed up from the ground, jerked his pants up, and got clumsily to his feet. He didn't catch sight of the woman who raced out of the house, swinging a broom as if it were a baseball bat. Before he even had glanced up, she struck him heavily across his shoulders with it.

Young's comb blackened, as the memory slipped from his hand, as he spun away from the mirror. He quickly looked about the room. No iPad case, no computer, just his cell, charging. He jerked the cord from the wall and yanked out the phone, pocketing both. Then swept up the room key from the bedside table and, in a state of frenzied panic, hurried out, anxious to get to his car, to a place where he felt comfortable and relatively safe.

Just outside the door was a pile of cups and dishes, two port wine glasses, an ice bucket.

He shared the elevator with a young, happy-looking couple he couldn't even look at for fear his face would reveal the incredulous horror of what he'd just witnessed. But was he actually a witness? Could this memory possibly belong to *him?*

No, fucker, no. I've never done nothing like that. Strange words for an educated psychiatrist to say, even to himself.

But as soon as these words had passed through his mind, another image flitted through, of the man, that man with the cruel eyes and the stubby neck, driving an old Nash convertible. But his car now looked brand spanking new. Its dark grey gloss shimmered cutting deep shadows against the twilight sun. He was chasing a man and woman on old-fashioned bikes, chasing them down a dirt road, dust flying up around the car. The woman turned her head and glanced back.

Same woman. Jesus.

Young knuckled his sordid eyes. The door of the elevator opened with a ding. He then stepped out into the hotel lobby, took a suspicious look around, then sped over to the front desk. A male clerk came over. "Checking out, sir?"

"Yes. Albert Young."

He tapped away at a computer. "You've already paid, sir."

"I ... need a receipt."

"Coming right up, sir." The printer spat out a receipt, and the clerk handed it to him.

Young glanced at the total figure—the charges for drinks, dinner, room service, the room itself. It was hard to fathom. Who would have thought it? But it added up to $1,037.37

"Fuck."

"Is there a problem, sir?" the clerk asked.

"Uh, yeah. The figures. That motherfucker number."

He stuffed the receipt in his shirt pocket and nearly ran outside.

Young was so rattled he couldn't find his car in the lot until he pressed his remote. Then he followed the irritating beep and blare of this white-noise path until he spotted his car at the far corner of the lot. He scrambled inside, into the familiar smells and comfort of the SUV, and sat there, shaking, shudders lashing through him, whipping its temporal aura round his god forsaken skull.

Meltdown. Freak-out. Cops. Baker Acted. He suddenly knew that if he kept silent sitting here, he would end up like Jennifer Hart, rendered unto a useless, sobbing mound of stale, pallid flesh and bones. A mind, heart, and soul nearly broken. With shaking hands, he started the car, his silver chrome tires screeching out of the lot, anxious to put miles upon miles of space between himself and that fucked-up mirror in room 137 of the Hard Rock Cafe.

His prospect had formulated a concrete practical plan. Homeward bound. He would go home and call House, ask him to oversee his own PCP treatment—one that Young knew he desperately needed.

The next morning came. It was Monday, March 15, 2022. Jo, Diego, and Marina were comfortably settled in Marina's living room with coffee and a platter of breakfast goodies, paging through the copies Jo had made of Penny Giral's diary. Jo tried to read the entries, as much as she could, sequentially. But now and then, she cheated and skipped forward to read a later entry, such as the one for December 25, 1922.

Christmas Day at the House of Giral.

We don't exchange gifts, per se, as a family. We do celebrate Christmas, but only as the birth of Christ, and that means church and the preacher's endless sermon. But for the Monster, it meant indifferently trotting all six of us to mass in the Nash, my brothers and I all jammed into the rear seat. A blackened odor of strangers filled the air, ripe fruit hung from southern trees, black bodies swung in the breeze, blood splattered on the poplar leaves, blood stains at the roots.

I hate rubbing arms with any of them, detest breathing the same air they breathe, hate smelling which of my brothers, after the act, badly needs a shower.

Ever since last Christmas, I feel less reluctant with Carlo and Sebastian, who came to my aid the last time Monster flipped out. Today they wear their Sunday best, look quite proper and gentlemanly, with their preppy ties and jackets and shiny shoes. While the working poor had just one good narrow-fitting dark grey jazz suit to wear to church on Sunday, Raul wore a kind of sausage-cased jacket preferred by younger men, one cinched by a raised waist, a military style seam, and a skirt flared at the back by a foot-long center vent. With deeply rolled shawl collars, four buttons set above the natural waist close together, this made for a double-breasted tight-pinched shoulder look, which, accented by a three-quarters back belt, conferred, against the bright striping of a flashy tie and shirt, a rather casual and conservative appearance. All the Girals wore Gentlemen's Emporium Vintage Victoria clothing, but only Pablo bore a classic bolo tie: cowboy silver cut, rhodite, gold saddle tan.

My mother sat in the passenger seat in a drab green rayon dress that Monster insisted she wear. No flashy flapper dress-up for her to expose her bare shoulders, her trim legs. Nope. Not for Carmen. The look of this Giral lady was likened to a plain-faced common folk pauper who should thank her lucky stars and forever be grateful that the handsome, famous Pablo Giral had married her.

It made me feel like puking.

Jo looked up. "Take a look at the entry on Christmas Day. Read down to the word emesis."

They all paged ahead and started reading. "Holy shit," Marina gasped.

"Christmas Day 1922." Diego glanced up. "A happening at the church. I remember reading something about it."

"Right, read it from Penny's point of view."

Jo picked up Penny's entry.

In fact, I vomited as soon as we parked and got out of the car. I suddenly bent over at the waist, and last night's dinner and this morning's breakfast splattered all over the front of the Nash. "My God," Monster snapped. "What the fuck's wrong with you, girl?"

The back of his hand thumped against the base of my skull, and I felt my mother move in close and grab his arm. "Enough, Pablo. The girl's sick on whatever you made the kids for breakfast."

For years, Monster cooked breakfast on Christmas morning. This had been the extent of his gift. My mother had just made a mockery of it. As I straightened up, I felt Monster's rage. But we were in a public place. People attending the church knew him; he couldn't make a scene.

We entered the church as a family, a scene as phony as what the church represented. The preacher and everyone else in there probably had heard about the horrors that went on in the Giral home. But here was the preacher, talking about how God loves all of us, blah, blah. I stopped listening. It was all lies.

People are always ruining things for you. It seems I'm always saying something like "glad to've met you" to someone I'm not glad I met at all. If you want to stay alive, you've gotta say that kind of stuff. But about certain ever-changing things, I believe they should stay the way they are. You ought to be able to stick them in one of those big glass cases and just leave them avatars alone.

I saw Santiago and his mom sitting a couple rows behind us, and as he caught my eye, Santiago tilted his head towards the front door behind us. I nodded and, after a few minutes, whispered to my mother that I had to use the restroom. I still felt nauseated.

"Go," she whispered. "Don't get sick here."

So I slipped out of the pew and hurried to the front of the church, where there was a bathroom. Sickly butterflies flitted around my stomach. I stood outside the restroom until Santiago loped toward me. We ducked out a side door in case Monster and my brothers were looking back.

The door creaked open into an alley. As soon as it closed behind us, Santiago gently hugged me. "I've missed you, Penny." We hadn't seen or been with each other since Thanksgiving. And that's much too long.

I rocked back, then planted onto him a fresh hello kiss. "I hate being here."

"My mom said that if the preacher knew she read cards and stuff, he'd probably want to burn her at the stake."

"That's scary shit, Santiago."

"Okay, but now I've got good news. Remember I told you I had a friend in the circus? He's a tightrope walker. He may be able to help you escape your sick family."

Just then, my mother opened the side door and stepped outside into the alley. She looked worried, not angry. "If your father—"

"Fuck him," I snapped.

My mother flinched. She didn't like that F-word, especially not when it was uttered under the yew tree outside a church or in a graveyard. She looked around nervously, glanced up at the sky. Maybe she expected lightning to strike us down?

"Mom, if there's a God in heaven who gives a shit, he'd have struck down monster by now. It's been a long time coming for what he's done to you, to me, to all of us."

Her red eyes blurred with tears. "Yes. Yes," she choked out her cries in a whisper. "Please go back inside before he realizes how long you've been gone."

"No. I'm sick. Is that all you've got to say, Mother?"

"My mother and I drove her home," Santiago interceded.

"Your mother's still inside the church." I replied.

"Yet I told her to leave ten minutes after I did."

Margarita did join us a little while later. She and my mother spoke in soft, hushed voices, while Santiago and I hurried up the

alley. "Tell me more about the circus. Is it
coming to town? When will it arrive here?"
I asked Santiago's mom.

"Sometime in March."

Jo glanced up from the diary. "What date was Santiago
shot?" She glanced at Marina.

"I think it was March 17, 1923. Yeah, St. Patty's Day."

"Was that celebrated back then?" Diego asked.

Marina shrugged. "No idea."

"March was the month the circus typically came to town,
right?" Jo asked.

"Yeah," Diego said, scrolling through his phone. "It
arrived March 9, that particular year, and it was at some point
between then and March 16, the day before Santiago was
shot, that Penny Giral ran away with the circus. Sometime
later that March, Margarita began printing her pamphlets,
but it took until June before the DA's office would issue a
warrant for Giral's arrest. On June 2, they came out to the
Giral mansion to arrest him, and that's when he killed his
wife, sons, and himself."

Jo again paged ahead in the diary. The dates of the last
two entries—March 15, 1923, and April 9, 1924— the
narrative language confused her.

March 15, 1923

Tomorrow I meet Santiago at the crossroad a
mile or two from here, and his circus friend
will pick me up. His name's Eddie.

My new life will begin.

I'm going to hide my diary in the bathroom wall.

Maybe Monster will find it, someday, or someone else.

April 9, 1924

She wasn't good at walking the tightrope, but she was popular with so many people at the circus, all of whom wanted their cards read. She made the circus a ton of money and kept enough of it for herself that she jumped train, one night in South Carolina. Maybe it was destiny, her fated cards telling her to do it. Maybe she was just ready. Nobody knew what happened, where she is, how she went. At least she's free of that awful family. But I miss her terribly. So I am going back to the Giral house to put her diary right back where she intended to hide it.

One other thing. Something else Jo learned about pretty Penny. She was two months pregnant after she fled. Back then she didn't know if it was Santiago's child or Pablo's. At any rate, the rumor floating around was she miscarried.

Yours sincerely,
Eddie

Jo had no certain conscious memory of being pregnant as Penny. Her memories had never gone much beyond her escape to the circus. She'd never thought about what Penny had done at the circus, except that she had embarrassed Eddie with her tightrope attempts. In her life as Giral's daughter, she had walked that thin line on a daily basis. Right now, she wasn't quite sure that what happened during the rest of Penny's life was even important. Wherever Penny's life had taken her after she escaped the circus—well, maybe that wasn't for her to know. Maybe she had, as the Vulcan Spock always said, lived long and prospered.

Jo hoped and wished this was so.

But before she could speak further to these latter entries, the doorbell rang. She got up to answer it, pausing long enough to peek through the peephole.

Eleanor?

Jo opened the door, and Raskin rushed in. "I ... I can't ... you aren't going to believe this. No, you will, you must believe it. I just got a call from Helen Archer. She said she'd gotten an email from you, Jo, that provided names and contact info—mine and Evan Fuentes's. She wants to meet us and tell her side of the casino story."

"Where?" Jo asked. "When does she want to meet?"

"When and wherever we say."

Marina got to her feet. "Now. Thirty minutes from now."

"Havana Cafe," Jo said. "We should let Evan know."

"I'll call him," Diego said, then he promptly got up and strolled out onto the porch, all along the way punching the skeleton keys of his phone, his face a gigantic smile.

Young knew exactly where Eleanor Raskin lived—on Lauderdale beach, two blocks inland from the ocean. You had to have money to live in this posh area—more money than he had, especially now that he was paying her alimony, and he apparently still owed so much in back pay, and had all the rest of his goddamn bills.

He had secured tight financial compensation during his leave of absence but wouldn't be out here driving through the dead streets of Lauderdale beach if it weren't for Raskin's interference. He slowly inched past her home but didn't see any cars in the drive way, went on around the block, parking his faded grey van two houses away, on the street.

Young walked with quick pace. Fortunately, the morning was cool, and so he was able to press the dark hood of his jacket down over his face without looking suspicious. The only person out and about was an elderly woman walking her poodle. She paid no attention to him. As he approached the Raskin house, he didn't see anyone—not a single nosy neighbor around, no one mowing the front lawn, no Amazon Prime van, no police. Did she have security cams set out front? He assumed she did. So he tugged the hoodie even more snugly around his head.

As he strolled up the driveway, he spotted the security cam perched at the corner of the house, kept his head bowed down, eyes pinned to the ground. He reached a side door, dug into his jacket pocket, and brought out his trusty, useful lock pick. He had bought it after his divorce from Amy, to get into the house she'd gotten in their settlement. She had promptly changed all the locks, he remembered, had absconded with some of his things—and he badly wanted them back.

So he had gotten into Amy's house, carried out what were *his* belongings, loading them into the trunk and back seat of his car. He didn't need to remove anything particular from the Raskin's place; he just wanted to poke about, see the goings-on inside the private sweet serenity of her safely locked home.

He stepped inside, smiling, thinking, *your cunningness is no match for me.*

It smelled just like a woman's home: the fragrant incense of fresh flowers, traces of perfume and scented soaps. That was all it took. The darkness gripped him, the ugly sex pockets of sadistic evil that had haunted him his entire life, now came alive, his will tightly locking while compelling, vibrant, masochistic fetishes exploded, dancing like a mushroom cloud of shrapnel, as if sparks of fallen stars had electrocuted a singular path in his head.

Young headed straight for her bedroom, following that trace of perfume, something expensive, something Amy had worn more than a couple of times before. He stopped at her bureau, opened the top drawer. Summer shorts, gym shorts, running shorts. Where were they?

Second drawer. Lingerie, appearing in every imaginable color and fabric. He leaned over, inhaling the smell of the clothes: a detergent and something else deeper, fresher—her skin.

Young dipped his fingers into the candy drawer, digging his hands in deeply from either side. Silks and cottons and nylons caressed his hands, his fingers, in sensuous scents. He felt each lace and frill. He brought out handfuls of pretty pink and black bow-laced panties, grabbed a bunch of her bare-skin-tight see-through bras and frilly white night gowns from the drawer, burying the scent of them all in his face.

He wanted all of these. As memoirs. Souvenirs. His own criminal signature.

He located a garbage bag underneath the bathroom sink and loaded it up with lingerie. He then went into the bathroom and added her soaps and shampoos, slipping them into the bag. He grabbed her royal bathrobe, which hung on a hook on the back of the door and stuffed it into the bag. A washcloth lay draped over the faucet; he snatched it up, and into the bag it went.

But before he left the house, he made sure he went to Raskin's desktop computer, where he accessed the security footage from the front cam and another behind the house. He deleted them both, then emptied the trash can contents in the lower right-hand corner of the screen.

"Bye-bye love. By bye sweet caress. Hello emptiness."

Then Young turned off both cams and he watched as the screen went black.

His head pounded and his mind ached as he made his way to the side door. When he stumbled outside, the fresh air startled him. And there he stood for a moment, taking deep, shuddering breaths. The blackness in his head had receded just a bit as he blinked hard and fast and glanced around, struggling to orient himself.

"Car ... SUV ... Van. Where the fuck is mine?"

Then he remembered, slung the bulging bag of lingerie over his shoulder, hurried up the driveway. All in all, it was a picture-poor Santa Claus imitation.

Many more people than those he recalled before were out on the sidewalk and road: joggers and riders, walkers compulsively working toward their daily ten thousand steps, kids with their dogs, cars, vans, a school bus, bicyclists, late risers and passersbys.

Young looked at no one. He just kept on moving toward his car, the blackness pounding its powerful migrainous fists against the nauseated insides of his bony skull.

When he was finally inside his car, the garbage and memoirs tightly secured in the back seat, he slammed his fist against the button on the glove compartment. Where upon command, the door flopped down. Young reached his hand inside and brought out a bottle that contained what he considered a foolproof remedy for his pounding head. He shook a quarter handful of perfect pills into his palm. He couldn't find the bottle of water he thought he placed in the cup holder earlier, so he tossed them all at once into his mouth, chewing on them hard and fast.

As Young pulled away from the curb, it felt like bits of pills remained sharply stuck in his throat. He chewed them down the side of his tongue until it bled and his mouth bore pink saliva, then swallowed the bitter chalked chunks of pills that remained. They slipped down his throat with the taste of iron. Albert then drove and drove. He drove like a bat out of hell and didn't stop 'til he pulled into his garage.

By then the pounding in his head had receded to a dull, constant thud. It made him feel as though tiny parts of his conscious brain were collapsing and fracturing beneath the heavy, unbearable weight of selectively old memories. He could barely reach the back seat to grab hold of the garbage bag, somehow successfully pressing the button to lower his garage door, after which he wove his way into the kitchen.

The room looked lopsided until it suddenly turned itself upside down. Everything started to fade. Nothing was where it belonged. The stove was stuffed in the pantry; the sink was hanging upside down, strung out of the window; the fridge lay on its side like some lazy whore, daring him with a wide-open door. Young rubbed his wild desiring eyes, desperately grabbed hold of the edge of the counter. *Couch*, he dizzily thought. He needed desperately to lie down. Nothing seemed calm or stilled. All was in motion.

He wasn't sure how he made it to the living room couch. Even it seemed off and didn't look right. The color and size were all wrong, and when he saw himself on top of it, his body was covered by that of a pretty peasant girl, yet her painted face was that a wild tribal woman, who screamed and sobbed.

Not me, not me, no.

He fell. The couch, gripping him tightly, transported his soul into another world.

He recognized that world. He recognized that house, the people around him, the Nash parked outside. He knew where he was. Who he was. He realized he'd known the truth of his life all along.

MARINA CALLED IN SICK FOR HER FLIGHT TOMORROW FROM Miami to Lima, and when her boss asked her what the problem was, she lied. "I tested positive for COVID."

"You've been vaxxed and boosted, right?" Her boss, a fifty-year-old woman who had been a flight attendant for nearly thirty years, sounded concerned.

"Of course. It's probably why I don't have any symptoms."

"Okay, take the five days they still recommend, test yourself daily, and let me know. But if you test negative before then, please come back to work. We're really short-staffed."

"I sure will." Another lie. "Thanks."

She was standing in the parking lot outside the FBI building, waiting for Evan Fuentes. He strode out minutes later, dressed in jeans and a cotton shirt, with an iPad bag slung over his shoulder. "Sorry, got a call from Lieutenant Nelson. He wanted to know if there have been new developments."

"Did you tell him about Eleanor's call?"

"Yeah. She's meeting us at her house, right?"

"Yes."

"Nelson says he wants a record of the break-in. I also

called the coroner and asked his team to dust the place for prints. How about if I follow you over there?"

"Okay."

The drive to Eleanor's entailed the usual traffic on A1A, tourists crowding the beaches, every parking space taken, kids and adults in bathing suits strolling through the warm sunshine. At the northern end of the beach, she turned into Eleanor's neighborhood and parked at the curb. Fuentes pulled in behind her. Eleanor's car was in the driveway, and as they got out, she stepped out onto the front porch.

"I haven't touched anything inside," she said. "I came home from work yesterday evening, realized someone had broken in, and stayed with my son and his wife last night."

"Was anything taken?" Fuentes asked.

"Uh, yeah. I'll show you."

Marina and Fuentes followed her inside. She paused at a side door in the utility room. "That's where the person got in. The lock was picked."

"How could you tell?" Marina asked.

Eleanor plucked tissue from a box of Kleenex and turned the knob with it. She gestured at the lock on the outside of the door. "It's a new lock. But look how scratched up it is."

"Security cams?" Fuentes asked.

"Yes, at the front and both sides of the house. This camera and the one at the front are disabled, and whatever they recorded was wiped off of my computer. Now to the bedroom."

Marina didn't know what she expected to see in here, but both she and Fuentes stopped in the doorway and stared.

The room looked as if it had been turned inside out. The mattress had been tossed onto the floor, sheets and covers tangled, pillows ripped apart. Feathers lay all over the place. The drawers in the bureau had been opened; lingerie left a scattered path to the bathroom. The closet door stood open; some of the clothes scattered on the floor were still on fallen hangers. The shoes were in disarray.

Fuentes walked over to the bed, flipped one of the pillows over. "Knife used on this."

Marina followed the trail of panties and bras into the bathroom, kneed open the door under the sink, saw a garbage bag container flipped on its side. "Looks like he helped himself to a trash bag, probably to put the lingerie in. Anything missing in here, Eleanor?"

"Yeah. Shampoo, soap, a couple bottles of my favorite perfume. A washcloth and a couple of towels."

Fuentes moved around, snapping photos. Before he'd finished, his cell rang. "Yeah, Dr. Pearson. C'mon upstairs. Is Luke Nelson with you? Uh-huh. Okay, bring everyone up here. The forensic team can start with the side door in the utility room. The lock was picked. Dust everything."

Marina looked at Eleanor. "You said he wiped out the security footage. Where's your computer?"

"Downstairs. C'mon, I'll show you."

"We want to be sure he didn't leave anything on it to track you when you're online."

"You know computers that well, Marina?"

"Diego does. He has been teaching me."

The computer, a MacBook Pro, was in a downstairs office. Marina sat down and proceeded to check it the way Diego had taught her. She kept in mind that if the intruder had been Young, she was dealing with the sign of the Scorpio, who wouldn't leave a single stone untouched. Nothing would be considered sacred.

As she worked, she was aware of the forensic crew moving into and throughout the house. She had to text Diego at one point, and he talked her into the root of the problem. The intruder had left a marker in her computer's code that could track her online. Diego explained how to delete it.

"Is it gone?" Eleanor asked. "Whatever you were doing?"

"I think so. But I'd like to keep your computer and turn it over to Diego."

"Fine with me. My work computer has the important files."

Marina shut down her home computer. She felt she and Eleanor were on the same page, thinking the same thing. At once she voiced it. "If Young is the guy who did this, then he might want to gain access to your work computer and track you in the same way he tried here."

"Fuck him," Eleanor muttered, and pulled up a chair next to Marina. "He's on a leave of absence. I recommended psychedelic therapy."

Marina stabbed her fingers through her hair. "Shit. So he has a motive. Did you enlighten Fuentes?"

"Yes."

Tom Pearson, the coroner, popped his head into the office. "You ladies should know that I got a call today from Dr. Laurence House. He and I have known each other for years. He said that Dr. Young asked him to oversee a psychedelic treatment he's giving himself. Personally, I think it's nothing short of madness and irresponsibility to self-administer this kind of treatment. But I advised House to go through with it and report the results to Evan, Luke, and me."

"Where are they conducting this experiment? Do you know?" Eleanor asked.

"At Larry's home, I think."

"And where does Larry intend to get the drugs?"

Tom rubbed his jaw. "He didn't, uh, say. But probably at the clinic."

"Nope," Eleanor said, and she began to text him, but Marina stopped her short of her first typo.

"Don't tip your hand, Eleanor."

"Hey, it's my department."

"Ask Diego to do an inventory and take photos," Marina advised. "I think he's working the night shift."

"Larry may have already taken what he needs."

Marina thought about it, but not for long. "True. So maybe the way to best approach this is explain to Dr. House what's going on and why it's vital he report all of it to you." Marina unplugged Eleanor's computer, picked it up, and set it by the door to take with them. When she returned to Raskin, the doctor kindly cradled her face in her hands.

"That other life ... when I was Carmen Giral ... my dear, it haunts me. It haunts my dreams. It haunts my waking life. It's been like that since ... since I was a kid, really. For most of that life, my fear of ... of Pablo Giral was so ... so extreme that I carried the gist of its genomic force forward. It's why I lost my voice at one point, why that past-life regression had healed me. Whenever I start to clam up about it all, my voice goes weird, all hoarse and scratchy, like I'm coming down with a cold."

At that moment, her voice *did* sound hoarse and scratchy. "Like now?" Marina asked.

Eleanor nodded. "I need to write all this up for the administrator. Then I'll go to Larry. I need to first have something ... *concrete* on him."

Diego got Marina's email at ten that evening while he was still at the clinic. Six hours earlier, he had gone through the supplies in the treatment room fridge, documenting the inventory with photos. He'd sent this to her. Before he clocked out at eleven that night, he went into the treatment room fridge again and took another, more detailed, inventory.

He discovered that three things were missing: an IV bottle of ketamine, one of LSD, and one of ayahuasca. No one had signed the takeout list. He emailed Eleanor.

Thirty minutes later, she arrived at the clinic, already looking exhausted. "Did you see Dr. House back here at any point today?" she asked.

"Nope. Usually I run into people as I'm cleaning rooms and offices, but I never saw him today, not once."

"So where are our missing IV bottles?"

"Let me take a look," he said.

Diego brought up images on his iPad that looked to be from a security cam. When he stitched the photos together into a video, House was clearly visible in the treatment's walk-in fridge, moving along the shelves, picking up this one, that one. The time stamp was 10:10 PM EST, March 15, 2022.

Eleanor looked pissed. "Poor Larry. He really incriminated himself here."

"Can you fire him?" Diego asked.

"Yes. I can also make his life miserable. Send me the photos and the video, Diego."

He did. "How can I help?"

"You've already helped enormously."

"Do you have somewhere to stay tonight?" he asked. "If not, you can stay at Adele's."

"Thank you, but I'm good. I'll stay with my son again."

"Where do you think Larry will do the treatment?"

"No idea. Maybe his place or Young's. Preferably, in their prospect interest, not at all. I'm texting him now."

She read the text out loud as her fingers tapped it out. "Larry, there's video that shows you removed three IV bottles from the treatment fridge at 10:10 tonight. I'm attaching the video. I'm assuming this is to treat your colleague, Dr. Young. I'm gifting you one hour to return the drugs to the clinic. Otherwise, this video is going straight to the hospital administrator, with you, House, out of a job."

Diego smiled. "That's *bare* forceful. Has he responded?"

"Not yet."

She sank herself back into the nearest chair. Diego went over to the small fridge tucked in the near the corner of the room to get her a bottle of cold water. "Can I get you something to eat, perhaps from the cafeteria, Eleanor?"

"That would be great. With everything that's been going on, I forgot to eat dinner."

"Salad? A sandwich?"

"Yeah, and a lemonade."

"Coming right up."

"Thanks, Diego. If I hear from him, I'll forward the text to you and the others tout de suite."

Diego took the stairs two at a time to the first floor. The cafeteria was pretty empty at this hour, just the late night-shifters getting coffee and sifting through snacks while he waited, a text came through from Eleanor that was addressed to everyone in their little gang of Jo compatriots. It was from House, and it read, "Just trying to accommodate a colleague, Dr. Raskin. Am on my way to the clinic to return the drugs now as we speak."

Eleanor had responded: "FYI: accommodation shouldn't include theft. And that's what this was. I can press charges for that, Larry. Are you willing to risk that … for Dr. Young?"

"I said I'm on my way to the hospital clinic. Just a few minutes out."

"Yeah, we'll see," Diego murmured.

He picked up the cafeteria order for Eleanor but, instead of taking the stairs, went into the lobby to take the elevator. There he saw House hurrying through the front door, a cold storage bag slung over his shoulder. House took a beeline to the front desk, opened the bag. "I'd like to leave this for Dr. Raskin." Then he showed the nurse on duty what was inside.

"She advised me that you should take it up to the treatment area and give it to her personally."

House rolled his eyes. "Christ almighty."

Way overly irritated, he tried to calm himself while walking to the elevator. Diego followed him. *Think positive thoughts*, an irate voice inside of him pleaded. When they were both comfortably set inside the elevator, he glanced at Diego. "You're working late, son."

Son? "Just tyin' up loose ends." He held up the takeout bag of cafeteria goodies.

"Mmm, me too."

The elevator dinged at the second floor and then opened. They both got out. House headed for the treatment room, while Diego tagged along behind, smiling to himself. He called Jo, told her to stay on the line, turning on his cell's recorder.

Jo, of course, had questions. "What's going on?"

"Maybe a setup with House. But it critically involves you, Diego. So you need to listen."

"I'm here. All ears."

Diego entered the room on cue. House, a minute or so later.

"So here're the *stolen* drugs, Dr. Raskin." House slapped the padded-shouldered cooler upon the table, extracting the three unharmed bottles, for her evidentiary review.

"And which one, House, may I ask, were you going to use on Dr. Young?"

"That was and still is up to him. I picked only the three drugs he requested."

Diego set her meal on the table where the IV bottles were. House looked at him. "Tying up loose ends too, Diego?"

"Yes sir."

"Thanks for the meal," Eleanor said with kind appreciation. "I'm famished."

"You bet. Want me to put these bottles back in the fridge?"

"No, not just yet."

"Just leave them where they are, Diego."

That voice belonged to Agent Fuentes, who stood in the doorway. Right then, he felt like an imposing official figure. Fuentes walked straight over to House. "You're under arrest, Dr. House, for absconding with three drugs from the hospital clinic. I can cuff you or you can walk out of here peacefully. Your choice."

House looked shocked. "Now just a goddamn minute. If anyone should be arrested here, it's Dr. Young."

"You're his facilitator."

"But he's at fault!"

"That's true. But here we are, for sure, with you and the drugs, Dr. House."

Diego caught the message in the glance Fuentes and Eleanor exchanged and knew she had texted him. Or maybe he had texted her as he had been following House. Whatever the truth, they had a common plan. And this was something Diego knew nothing about.

Fuentes really enjoyed seeing House squirm with discomfort. It seemed to please him to witness that pedantic wind balloon of arrogance being punctured. He could almost hear the air hissing away, see the blood flowing downward, pulling the color from House's face. It felt authentically gratifying.

"While it's true that you undoubtedly will be out on bond within an hour or two, it won't matter. You're now close on my radar. I'll get you for something. Like, hmm, I suspect you knew that Dr. Young didn't use DMT on Jennifer Hart."

"As far as I know, he most certainly did."

"Then you must have just taken him at his word. He actually used PCP."

The startled expression arriving on House's face told Fuentes he was telling the truth. But the smile beneath it suggested something more. House apparently hadn't known for sure about the PCP but most he likely had a suspicion. "Jesus, no wonder she flipped out." House tried to compose himself, raked his long fingers through his hair, shook his head. "This is all about that past-life crap, am I right?"

"Speculations, speculations. All of our lives ... fantastical speculations. All about genomic patterning and cellular memory, criminal signatures and forensic fingerprinting."

"Andy and I had spoken about it a couple of times before. Andy almost convinced me that Jo Hart's track marks came from trauma experienced in another past life, one in which she used injectable drugs to escape and forget. He *believed* this transmigration shit, okay? *He's* the one who needs psychotherapy. Not Jennifer Hart. For this and other reasons."

"It *is* true," Eleanor said. "The past-life material. Dr. Young is acting out unconscious compulsions and propensities which followed him from a life as Pablo Giral in the 1920s to this life as Albert Young, nearly a century later."

House stared intensely at her. His incredulous look pierced her to the soul. He apparently couldn't quite believe what Raskin was saying. This woman, who had risen to head administrator of the psychiatric unit, who had trained at such a prestigious clinic as Harvard, next in power here and subservient only to the county hospital administrator—it was she who was actually spouting this unverifiable, objectively unsubstantiated trash. Yet House knew she was a Sagittarian woman who had dug for the joy, love and song of truth.

House stood up, exclaiming, "In the name of science and medicine ... I mean ... c'mon. Reincarnation? Tall tales of hogwash. Give me the objective facts, Eleanor. Show me the money. Provide me some documented evidence, specific references from the medical and scientific literature. You and I both know you can't. More importantly, we've both taken the same Hippocratic oath: to do no harm. We share a common thread of teaching that has over and over, time and again, told us the same thing—that every open and sane common rational mind must, in the name of science, dismiss all subjective reports as holy biased heresy!"

"I think what you meant was 'hearsay,'" said Fuentes, putting on a sarcastic smile.

"Do you know who James Leinenger is, Dr. House?" asked Dr. Raskin.

"Yeah. I did my homework."

"Well?" She stabbed at her salad, bit into her sandwich. "Who is he?"

"When Leinenger was a kid, he was *reported* to have recalled a past life as a World War II pilot who was shot down. He *apparently* knew the exact type of plane he'd flown, the name of his copilot, even where he'd been shot down. In that life, his name was, oddly enough, James. His father in this life recently won twenty grand in Bigelow's contest for essays that prove consciousness survives death. But now we have a medical researcher earthly bent to tear his case apart, claiming his dates contradict those documented elsewhere ..."

Fuentes threw up his hands. "You'd be better off listening than arguing, Dr. House." He glanced at Eleanor. "Go ahead, enlighten him."

Eleanor polished off her sandwich and salad, and she dabbed at her mouth, settling on a stool across from House. "Here are the facts, Dr. House ... as outrageous as they may sound. I remember my past life as Carmen Giral, Pablo's wife. I remember being the mother of three sons, and one of them"—she pointed at Diego—"is here: Raul, my youngest. My only daughter Penny, was consistently beaten and raped by Pablo. Sometimes the older brothers joined in. None of us stood up for her until near the end. That girl, now, is Dr. Jennifer Hart."

Fuentes's heart almost leaped clear from his chest. He felt the moment close upon his mind. He could see the way House's body stiffened and seemed to pull into itself. Maybe it was the fact that it had all come, Fuentes thought, from an objective scientifically trained psychiatrist. Or maybe House had entertained these possibilities of prospect already. Eleanor's recitation, as it were, was confirmation in his own mind. The process really didn't matter as much as the result. He sensed House had now been sentenced by their court.

"Holy fuck," House gasped. "That explains ... a lot. Does Jennifer know all this?"

Nearly done, by their court, Fuentes thought. "Indeed, she does now."

House sent his crystalline bright blue Aryan stare straight at Diego. "And you can ... remember this life, too? No fucking way, dude."

"Yeah. Guilty as charged. I was the cowardly son. When I first saw Jo, I felt that inner connection. This then was confirmed by a number of synchronicities. I knew I had to make amends in this life for what I hadn't done in that life."

House pointed a wagging finger at Diego. "But you ... helped her escape?"

"Yup."

"What about Marina?"

"She was Penny's BFF, Santiago," Fuentes proudly replied.

"Whom Giral shot, right?" House speculated.

"Uh-huh," Eleanor replied.

House gazed at Fuentes. "And you, Detective? What was your role back then?"

Fuentes had wondered many times about that before. He had talked about it with Adele and her spiritual buddy, Isabella. He had discussed it with his own wife, with Eleanor and Diego, with Jo, and with Marina. Not one of them remembered him from that life. But since they all fit somehow in that complex narrative, he figured he probably did too. He just didn't know where, how or why.

"I've got no certain idea about that, Dr. House." House crossed his arms at his waist, looked down at the floor, then turned his sight to enclose each of them.

"Okay, I'm catching a definite positive vibe here that if I cooperate with whatever you guys've been cooking up, I can and will avoid arrest." He paused and turned his gaze to Fuentes. "Right? Am I right about this?"

Fuentes smiled; he couldn't help it. "Very good, Dr. House. I'm genuinely impressed with your keen and intelligent intuition. What have you heard about that Giral mansion west of town? Do you know it still exists and of—"

"In the Giral neighborhood, right?"

Fuentes nodded. "The recent murder of Carmen Collier? Her body was found on the front lawn of the Giral place."

"I know something about it. I listen to the news, you know."

And with that, Fuentes told him the rest—about the place where the kid Santiago had lived with his mother, the neighborhood seer, and what he'd found there. Then House really surprised him.

"I'd like to see both places. Hell, maybe I lived there, too!"

"Fine, I'll take you," Fuentes said. "Tomorrow."

"Wait. What about right now?" Eleanor asked, mediating. "What are you going to tell Young? About the treatment?"

"That I just can't do it."

"He'll want to know why," Fuentes said.

"No worries. I'll tell him that drugs were discovered missing and that I'm not going down for that, for him, for sure."

Fuentes nodded his approval. "Good place to start, Dr. House."

"Is it? I ... I just don't know. I believe, Agent Fuentes, you don't understand, can't possibly conceive how this guy thinks. He's a precise and detail-oriented fucker. He'll want to know who discovered them, who was present when they were found missing, and what's going to be done about it. A psychopath like Young will want, is compelled, to know shit like that."

"And that's exactly why your answers are going to be the ones we give you. Unless, of course, you rather prefer arrest and fingerprinting, putting your ass in stir as they say, spending an hour or two in our county jail, with a prospect of trial looming down the road, somewhere." His horizon appeared bleak.

House looked hard at each of them, then laughed. "In other words, I'm being recruited."

Fuentes smiled. "Yeah. Recruited to the good side of Jo's forensic gang of thieves.

Love and Theft. They'd heard it all before, who the hell knows?" House smiled.

"Bob Dylan wrote an album of the same name, I just can't for the life of me recall what date it was released." Raskin perked up.

"The date was September 11, 2001. Matching the emergency phone number, 911". It was wholeheartedly possible, even more so probable, that all in the room thought the same thing. Love and Theft had left, but what remained was this synchronicity, as pure as the sun and as natural as rainwater.

Jo met Helen Archer that same night at a coffee shop on Las Olas Boulevard. She looked much better than she had at the Hard Rock—sober now, her dark hair falling in graceful waves upon her soft shoulders. She wore khaki capri pants, a print silk blouse, and a lightweight sweater.

"First off, I want to thank you for sending that text message to me, Jo. I promptly got outta there while he was in the shower."

"I apologize if the text freaked you out, Helen. But I didn't want you to hang around and put yourself at risk. How'd you get home?"

"I called my daughter. She took an Uber to the Hard Rock, drove my car over to me."

The server came by and took their orders. Jo was starving and ordered a vegetarian omelet, biscuits, an OJ, and coffee. "Ditto for me," Helen told the server. When he'd left, she leaned forward, her expression intense. "So you're a cop?"

"Not exactly. I'm working with the FBI. Practically, I'm a Jungian psychologist."

"You said Andy's a killer. Is he your patient or something?"

Jo chuckled at that one. "I'm actually *his* patient."

Helen fell back in her chair, obviously bewildered. "I ... I don't understand."

Jo launched into the meat and potatoes of the story, beginning with the murder of Carmen Collier, then going farther back, to why she was Baker Acted, overwhelming Helen with background details of the Giral life. "Young was recently removed from the treatment program, placed on temporary leave, so I think this was an attempt to lose himself in booze and a one-night stand. Did you guys exchange phone numbers? Addresses?"

"No, thank God. But I'm easy to find through the University of Miami faculty."

"Did he talk at all about himself?" Did he reveal anything of personal value?

"The more he drank, the more he rambled: about his ugly divorce, how his estranged son still despises him, and, mostly, how successful his treatment program was, before that *bitch* Eleanor interfered and poked her nose into *my* business. When I asked him who Eleanor was, he said she was his *earlier* wife. But in spite of all the wine I drank, that remark struck me as weird. After everything you told me, I'm assuming Eleanor was Giral's wife in the 1920s?"

Jo nodded. "Correcto."

"So this is ... what? A past-life drama playing out some kind of karma in this life?"

"That pretty much describes it, in a nutshell."

"Wow. And the theory is that Giral's murderous rage was carried over into this life?"

"Yup, you got it."

The server, wearing a red-and-white-checkered dress, stood politely at the far edge of the table. She had been patiently waiting for who knows how long for this break in the conversation, and had brought their breakfasts and more coffee.

"Do you know what synchronicity is?" Helen asked.

"Sure. I'm a Jungian."

"Right, you would, of course. A while back, I myself wrote a book on synchronicities—the kinds that happen all the time in politics. But when you consider the staggering odds of so many players in the Giral life being all brought together at the same clinic at the same time, well ..." She shook her head. "It's mind-blowing."

"Yup. And as these synchronicities strikingly continue over time, their tendency is to magnify and multiply their effective power. Space-time exponentiation of the grid, of course."

"Did you follow him to the Hard Rock?"

"We did it: Me, Marina, and Diego."

"So that would be Penny and Raul Giral, and Santiago, the kid Pablo shot and whose body he arranged as Christ on the front lawn of the Giral place."

"That's right. You got it."

"This might be the most powerful cluster of synchronicity I've ever heard of."

"My question is, How the hell do I fit into this? Or do I?"

"You nearly became a victim."

"Back in the 1920s, were there any other Giral victims of horror?"

"None that we know of. But anything is possible."

"So if the FBI already knows that Young killed this Carmen Collier, why haven't they arrested him yet?"

"They need to have clear-cut proof."

Both of them finished off their breakfasts.

Helen broke the silence first. "Look, you possibly saved my life, Jo. How can I repay you?"

"Could you be our synchro expert? Take on the role of expert witness at his trial?"

"It would be my absolute pleasure. What I can do immediately is write up everything I can recall of that night. Have you ever seen the show *Criminal Minds*? It would be like a self-induced cognitive interview."

"Note down anything that might be helpful. Impressions. Conversations. Observations."

Suddenly she snapped her fingers and, as if magically, music filled the air. The music drifted around them both, a jazz piece from the 1920s. It boomed out of a past forgotten life, from the open doors of a bar, and drew Jo Hart like metal to a magnet as it did once before. Don't stop here. Don't take a look back. Don't try to glimpse forward. Let it be as it is. You can't think it out. Believe you me, you won't get your head around it. Leave destiny alone; just keep on keeping on. Synchronicities have their own ways of expression. It's as simple as that, and that's all there is to say.

"I just remembered another oddball thing. He doesn't like the number 137. That was the room the clerk assigned to us first, and he asked to change it. Later I mentioned it, and he said nothing good ever came from that number. That made me curious, so I kept asking questions. Apparently patients who end up in room 137 at the clinic are problematic for him. That number also figures into what his ex says he owes her in back alimony. And it's his former address, where his ex now lives."

Coincidental? Significant? Jo thought. Then it struck her. The old Giral place at 137 High Road. Had that tone and frequency followed Young into this life? Was such a thing genetically possible? It was. Of course, she'd been in room 137. Had Carmen Collier been in that room too? She texted Eleanor.

"Was Carmen Collier in room 137 when she was hospitalized at the clinic?"

"I think so, but let me confirm. Why?"

"Am with Helen Archer. Something she said about Young from that night at the Hard Rock."

"Checking … yes, she was. And so were you."

"Big synchronicity. The Giral place is at 137 High Road."

"Holy shit."

"Aha!" Helen remarked.

"You don't know the half of it," Jo said before explaining the half she knew.

Helen laughed. "Lady, this numeric thing is like a slickly oiled synchronicity machine." The truth is that neither of them—nor anyone else, for that matter—knew anything about the other half.

Chapter

15

Young got up early and went for a run—something he hadn't done for months. He kept to his Lauderdale neighborhood, and after a mile, his knees started complaining so he decided to walk. He hated not having a set schedule. Eleanor Raskin had taken that piece of his life away from him.

When he got back to the house, he threw open the closet in the bathroom and pulled out the trash bags he'd pilfered, which were filled to the brims with lingerie. Raskin's most personal lingerie. He didn't want to think too much about how he'd come into possession of all these wonderful items: colorful panties, slips, and bras. His memories of that were chopped up, coming to him in erratic, non sequential fragments. But he recalled enough to know he'd been in an altered state when he'd entered her home and made the rounds of the rooms. He had been, well, someone else—that was what House would tell him. That was the plan.

He started the shower and was about to step into the stall when his cell rang. It was House. "Hey, Larry. We on for today?" Young asked.

"Change in plans. I got the drugs you requested, but they were discovered missing, and there's a video showing me leaving the treatment fridge, carrying the IV bottles. I got arrested and spent the night in fucking jail. I'm only now out on bond."

"*Jail?* My God. Charged with what?"

"Theft of hallucinogenic drugs from the clinic."

"Was Raskin behind that?"

"Of course she was. And she figured out why I took them. Maybe it's time to make yourself scarce, Andy—get out of town for a while."

"Hey, she already came after me."

"Removing you from the treatment program was just her first step. Next, she may try to get you fired ... even arrested."

"How do you know that?"

"Heard it from the cop while I was in jail."

"Are they actually going to try you for this?" Young asked, incredulous that things had gone this far.

"Probably. Things are still in motion. I won't know for sure until my day comes up in court. Do you have somewhere to go for a few days?"

"Why the fuck should I have to get out of town? *She's* the one stirring things up."

"Hey, bro, I totally agree. But I know she's also dead serious."

"I hear you. Okay. I'll find a spot. Thanks for the tip, Larry."

"Stay in touch."

"I will."

Shit shit shit. None of this was supposed to happen. And it all started with that fucking Jennifer Hart being Baker Acted. That was when things began unraveling, he thought, *one pitiful thread at a time.*

But suddenly he knew it had been triggered long before Jennifer had entered his life. It had started when Amy told him she'd wanted a divorce. Why was it always the women who made his life miserable? *Amy, Jennifer, Eleanor … and Carmen*, he thought. Carmen had been the worst of them all, with her smug self-righteousness when he punished Penny, when he … wasn't to blame. She was the one at fault. She had seduced him.

"Penny? Who the hell is Penny?"

He quickly stepped into the shower, struggling to remember a woman named Penny, trying to block out the begrudged memory of Carmen's pretty face, her voluptuous body, her sexy little petite …

"No. Stop."

He turned the water up hotter, and it beat down against his head, driving out the names of these decrepit women as though they were devils being exorcised. Steam drifted up around him, and he inhaled it. The incestuous scent helped to clear his head. They were all devils, all these women—female Satans who hungered for his soul. He didn't need treatment to know that this was the truth.

Yet by cellular memory Young knew that *when* given the right set and setting, and *if* fed the right dose of psychedelic, a perfect storm of demonic ecstasy *might* very well befell his mind, being of greater conscious benefit … that or bereft. He sensed this eternal battle of the unconscious part of his id. And this fated part of his psyche Young loved to no end.

Young's ego hated this part of his psyche even more. Stilled of temporal time, Young knew, remembered, what his soul first saw upon the horizon of its birth—what his ego had, more or less, conveniently forgotten.

The karmic signs of his zodiac had set a fixed course back then; never was it fated in the here and now to be either/ or. His Scorpio sun and ascendant had come conjoined into this life double bonded, as if his conjunction were meant to prospect *both* blessing *and* curse. *The nerve of them,* he thought, *all those fucked-up ifs, whens, and entitled mights.*

In his mind a clear picture of Laurence House now emerged, the child prodigy under the pedantic grip of a practical life dedicated to science, and there he saw himself as an archangel, the minstrel of art and death.

Twilight time. Could he dream awhile under veils of deepening blue? Would he?

As fantasy strides over colorful skies with form disappearing from view, what benefits could be accrued from this ghastly line and life of wasted thought? What's in it for me?

"Speculations, speculations, dear Watson, our lives are full of fantastical speculations."

Perhaps. But those *ignorant* ifs and whens and mights seemed hell bent on ignoring his pleas of rationality, which for no rhyme or reason, kept on coming.

"What ifs are like a double edged sword. The other side of free will to believe. Live and evil are *litterally* mirror images of one another. The environment is always at play turning genes off in the present. A wide-open, turned-on human genome. This is what is needed."

This theory of being is much more than simple physical sound and light energy. As a matter of fact it's a decoded moral order known as DNA, shared amongst all living species. About this human morality Young never knew, knows nothing, sees nothing, and will hear nothing but his own defiant ego protests, laced heavily with delusive sadistic force.

Psychedelics hold this type of ambivalent power. Shalt thou take the risk? Draw fortune unto thine own hands and heart? What awaits Albert amounts to nothing less than seeing the greatest show on earth—a bludgeoning cellular sequence of regression. There'd be no turning back, no way home, fate hermetically sealed, lest his body be cast off like dust particles, blown and scattered at the wind's discretion.

This hyperbolic sequence would descend Young's psyche from adult to child, child to infant, infant to womb, present to past, human to animal to reptilian, until he reached bird, fly, and ant. Doors of perception wide open. He knew what needed to be done.

But would it be worth it?

He grabbed a bar of soap and began cleansing his body of those filthy blemishes he had, for some unknown reason, recently acquired. *That hooker skank I met in the Hard Rock*, he thought. *It must've been her.* He glanced at his torso and extremities. Sparsely scattered reddish purple patches were all screaming, for differential diagnosis. Where was fucking House now, when he could've used him the most? Then suddenly the next cascade of memory flashback came.

"Go to the ant, sluggard! Consider her ways and be wise. Ye of no no will man. Stick to the job. Been ye not sealed to work with helpers? All for one and one for all. Is this not what they say, of man? Look no further than the ant. She's got no captain, no overseer."

What the actual fuck is this crap? Under young's skin, something dark lurked and crept, nuzzled and waited.

"She knows her job and she does it well. She operates quietly, happily, efficiently, without much of any show. No female ant needs the watch of another. She gets the big jobs done. Believe ye not, man? Then cast thine eyes upon Google Earth. Sexist, ye say? Cast your gaze upon the binds of past periodicals. Google 'ant genomes.' Impressed not, my laddie? Google 'ant behavior."

"And what idiocy will I find there, man?" Young looked at his skin blemishes; they were clearly moving.

"Ants, like humans spend their days and nights amongst large social colonies numbering a few million members. Their group behavior, hardwired from the get-go, is not unlike that of humans.

"The typical ant genome is 361.8 Mb. Small, ye say, boy? Over time, two whole full genomic duplications have occurred. Have ye forgotten that girly queen mothers were fed magnitudes of sustenance as larvae. This is why they grew bigger and fatter than their male counterparts.

"Queens lay hundreds of thousands of eggs. Ye think this but a game of chance? Don't fool yourself, boy imbecile. Their singular gift of wings endowed them with a greater capacity, to fly and find a mate. Before forming a colony and raising their first offspring, queens must tear their wings off; this is the only time they do any kind of fieldwork, other than laying eggs."

Young could not reckon a singular reason let alone a lesson from all this crap. Were there bugs crawling beneath his skin?

"Forgotten your purpose, boy? Workers are wingless females, fed less as larvae. They can't reproduce. All colony jobs, including gathering food, building the nest, and taking care of the young, are done by females. Males have wings to fly and mate with queens yet they perform no chores back home. Their only job is sex. All die shortly after mating, meaning the only time you'll catch a glimpse of a male ant, is during the act of reproduction.

"Doth ye believe this crap, unimportant?"

Young had but a vague unspeakable inkling.

"Why, pray tell, is this cast upon ye now? Methodical ye are, boy. Ye and the ant are not so different but rather cast and wired, by the same genomic material."

Young slammed his fists hard against the faucet, the water turned off, and there he stood, for long moments, in the heat of the steam. Then he snapped the towel off the rack, wrapped it around himself, and picked up the trash bags filled with lingerie, setting them in the doorway to take with him. He packed a bag, put on fresh clothes—shirt, jeans, running shoes—and carried everything into the kitchen: Cooler. A bag of ice. Provisions.

Thirty minutes later, he loaded up his SUV, got on I-75, and headed west.

"Is that GPS still on the fender of Young's car?" Fuentes asked.

Eleanor shook her head. "It must've fallen off at some point after that special night he had at the Hard Rock."

"Too bad. So sad. House says he's on the move."

They stood in the middle of Eleanor's living room. She'd asked Fuentes to come with her to collect some clothes and other things so she could stay with Marina and Jo at Adele's.

252 | MARK LAURENCE LATOWSKY

"If he's on the move, my guess is that he's headed for the Giral neighborhood that he once ruled with such impunity."

"You going back to the clinic?" Fuentes asked.

"Not today. I can work remotely from Adele's."

She went into the bedroom to pack a bag, and Fuentes just stood there gazing out the window and into the street. He felt that he wasn't doing enough. Right now, Jo, Marina, and Eleanor felt threatened by this fucker enough that they weren't staying in their own homes. The story was one as old as humanity: women threatened by men—or, specifically, by one man.

He texted Lieutenant Nelson. "Luke, can you spare two of your best to keep watch outside of Adele's home? Just in case Young loses it completely and comes after them?"

"Seems more likely to me that if the unsub is Young, he'd go to one of their homes. I can assign three different patrol cars to those areas, and send two of my best to Adele's."

"As Kirk used to say, Make it so, amigo."

"I don't believe Kirk ever once called anyone an amigo, Evan."

Yeah, probably not. "I'm headed to the Giral place. Just in case."

"Count me in. Security cams there are still functioning."

"Meet me at Adele's. I'm going to follow Eleanor back there."

"See you in twenty."

Eleanor came out pulling a bag on wheels, her computer case slung over her shoulder. "I'll follow you over to Adele's."

"Thanks, Evan. I appreciate it. You know, I've dealt with strange wacko ideation, suicidal patients, and flat-out nut-cracking cases. But Young"—her voice caught, she shook her head—"he's a different kind of category altogether."

"You're talking as a shrink now, right?"

"Yeah, and it's not pretty. Young obeys his malicious conscience like a robot. His reptilian uncus, preset and automated, drives his essence without inhibitory ego resistance. His predatory nature, which is so cunning and deceptive, has essentially been given free rein. His executive state of entitlement seems like it's caught in a perpetual loop. His ego is able to activate and accomplish his fiendish bullshit, without a single conflicting psychic interruption."

"Wow." Fuentes didn't have any idea how to respond to that. The only time he'd been to a shrink was a month before he'd taken the Florida bar exam. His excessive anxiety that he wouldn't pass had been eating him alive, and he'd desperately needed something to calm him down. The shrink had provided several meditation techniques and breathing exercises that had done the trick. But the psychiatrist he'd seen hadn't spoken like Eleanor was talking now.

"I think it's psychopathic ego worship that compulsively drives Young to seek out, kill, and destroy everything he hates in himself. And it is this hate he projects upon other people."

Then, to his utter shock and horror, Eleanor covered her face with her hands and wept, softly, struggling to contain her tears, but failing. He went over to her, slipped his arms around her, held her, and whispered, "I won't let anything happen. Not to you, Eleanor, not now."

As he said these words, he suddenly saw himself holding Carmen Giral, just as he held Eleanor now, caressing and whispering the same things. He didn't know who he had been back then—a cop, friend, neighbor, lover—but he had failed her, miserably.

He would not fail her again, not this time around.

She stepped back, swiping at her bloodshot eyes, and looked straight at him. "I … you … once said those same words to me, Evan. And you knew … fuck this. Fuck all of it. I'm not going to hide again, from this fucker. I know you're going out to the Giral place. I'm going with you." She hurried back into her bedroom and returned with a weapon—a Glock 22 modified to carry fifteen rounds of .40 caliber ammunition. "I bought this after my divorce. And I know how to use it."

Shit. This will complicate things. Jo and Marina, and probably Diego, would insist on accompanying him and Nelson as well. "Let me think about this on the way to Adele's."

He turned toward the door, but Eleanor caught his arm. "You don't get it, Evan. Women are no longer part of that archetype, that collective paternal fiction where men protect them. HISTORY. His story. The Supreme Court took away our right to govern our own bodies, and hope to take us back to the time of Carmen Giral's world. But that's not going to happen. I refuse to lose my voice again, just because I didn't speak up then."

"Like I said, let's think about it a bit more on the way."

He opened the door, and they left the house. Eleanor paused long enough to lock the door and take hold of her own belongings.

⟡

Jo felt as though she were living in the matrix. Nothing was what it seemed. She had left her home and now shared a bedroom with Marina at Adele's place. And Isabella, a long dead spirit, also occupied the house, and she had quite a lot to say.

She and Marina sat across from Adele at her kitchen table, an old wooden table, scuffed, with a blunt family history. It held gouges here and there, scratches, even Diego's name was there, carved into a corner. Adele's eyes had rolled back into their sockets, only the whites of her eyes showed, and now Isabella spoke in her soft yet commanding voice.

"I grew up as a plantation slave in Cuba. I helped harvest sugar. My owners were Spanish despots, the man in charge very much like Pablo Giral. When I got pregnant with his child, he slit my throat. I was twenty-two years old. I can speak my truth now only because I'm in spirit."

Jo had no idea what to do with this confession, and that was what it felt like. It was like poetry by Plath or Anne Sexton. It seemed Isabella had been waiting for this exact moment to come, now for more than two centuries. "Well, I'm not in spirit," Jo said. "Neither is Marina. So what's *our* truth?"

Adele's mouth twitched into a soft smile. "Are you cowards or warriors?"

Jo and Marina glanced at each other. Marina's dark brows shot up. *Well, what are we?*

"Warriors," Jo said.

"Warriors must be ready to kill or be killed," Isabella said. "Are you prepared, or is your bravery in vain?"

Was she brave? Was she really ready to confront the ghosts of her Giral life? If not, then for the rest of this life, and even more likely the next one, Jo would be haunted by these same memories.

"Yes ... I ... I'm ready."

In this life everyone gets his or her own trial, she thought. And everyone has unique capacities and talents to successfully pass and get beyond themselves. Life learning comes in sequences of repeatable lessons. If the lesson of the trial is not learned, it just tends to repeat itself over and again, until it is. Signs come uniquely personalized, expressions of terms particular to the individual, yet at the same time, also universal for the species.

True knowledge arrives only in retrospect, destiny being after-the-fact knowledge, seen with 20/20 vision. Yet will, being ever contingent on belief and perspective, is what karma deems goodness for deeds paid forward, equivalently, evil of gilgul paid backward.

Failure to learn karmic lessons can be an unrecognized cost of prospect lost, signs of opportunity missed, or those falsely interpreted.

It is a strange paradox, but the trial *is* set against your essence. You are at war with yourself from the start, and as a warrior you must fight, by necessity, until its finality.

Marina grinned. "Me too. Count me in"

"Then your opportunity is about to arrive."

With that, Adele's eyes rolled back into place. She looked at them both, blinked hard and fast, then reached out and touched each of their faces with her hand. She made a sign of the cross on their foreheads, then pushed her chair back and went over to her altar. She lit a fresh candle and dropped pieces of chocolate into a platter of offerings. She seemed to study the gilded altar for several long minutes, then picked up two objects and returned to the table.

She set the two gorgeous pieces of amber down. "Amber is Oshun's stone, Oshun is the santo of femininity. The point is to carry the mother stone on your body."

Jo picked up one of the amber stones and rubbed her thumb over it. The surface was as smooth as infant skin. The stone itself was probably the most beautiful piece of amber she'd ever seen, its color the height of perfection, the stone itself pure, almost translucent. She slipped it into a back pocket of her jeans and zipped the pocket shut.

Marina zipped hers in her jacket pocket, then asked, "Now what?"

But the doorbell rang.

Adele got up to answer it. Jo touched Marina's arm. "I'm starting to feel like Trinity did in *The Matrix*."

"Then that makes me ... who? Laurence Fishburne as Morpheus?"

"Or Keanu Reeves as Neo."

"Adele and Isabella as the Oracle."

All this swirled in Jo's head. "Or we all may just be batshit nuts."

Fuentes, Eleanor, and Lieutenant Nelson now hurried into the kitchen, where both Jo and Marina stood. "We're going with you," Jo said. "Maybe it will just turn out to be another major fuckup like Hard Rock. Or maybe we'll actually get answers."

Fuentes looked stunned. "But maybe Young isn't our guy after all."

⁕

Young drove past the old Garcia place, moving slowly enough that he could check for security cams. He spotted one just below the eaves, opened the glove compartment, and brought out a gun, a Glock 17.

One shot shattered the whole thing to pieces. He smiled a sloppy one eighty then headed back up the road toward the old Garcia place. He didn't pull into the packed-dirt driveway. Instead he turned at the end of the block and found the entrance to what he guessed had been intended as an alleyway. But instead of more homes back here, there was a thickly wooded area that may have once been a mangrove. Old cedar trees leaned in over the alley—little more than a dirt path, covered with fallen leaves.

He parked behind the Garcia place and unlocked the door with the key he'd had made at some point, and it swung open. He snapped on gloves and quickly unloaded his car, carrying everything into the kitchen. There he stopped and looked slowly around. Someone had been here. *Cops, probably, Fuentes.*

Well, so what. He knew he hadn't left prints. He carried the box of lingerie upstairs. When he saw the bedlam in here, the box slipped out of his hands, thudding against the floor. The cops had upended everything. *Fuck them.* They had taken away all the lingerie. They had stripped the sheets off the bed. They had intruded, stolen, and taken from him.

So he picked up the box and hurled all the panties and bras and slips into the air. For seconds, all were airborne: a blue bra, rose-colored panties, a slip with polka dots covering it—all of it caught in suspended animation. Then he snapped back, went downstairs to his car and picked up the cans of kerosene. Three of them. He started on the second floor, pouring kerosene in every room, an erratic trail of it whose flames would soon follow. He made sure a few towels were nearby, and he doused them heavily too.

As he went downstairs, he poured a trail of kerosene alongside his side. The first can was empty midway down. He hurled it over the banister and opened the second can. On the first floor, he was much more liberal with the kerosene. This house, after all, would burn from the bottom floor up. Even though it was constructed of stone, everything inside was wood. And wood soaked in kerosene would burn as fast as money.

In the kitchen, he splashed the last can of kerosene everywhere—corners, stove, sink, counters, pantry—and brought the trail right up to the edge of the door.

He patted his jacket pocket for his keys. *Check*.

Phone. *Check*.

Gun. *Check*.

Lighter. *Check*.

He brought the last item out, poured the last of the kerosene across the threshold of this godly cursed and forsaken place. He went over to a cabinet, brought out a candle in a holder, and lit it with the lighter. Next, the stove. He turned on all the gas burners, then got the hell out of there. He sprinted to his car.

When he was a safe distance away, he stopped the car and got out. Less than two minutes later, the Garcia place blew, debris flying out in every direction—charred chunks of history that quickly set all the nearby woods on fire. For moments, he thought he could see the spirit of Santiago and his mother drifting and floating high above through the flames.

Young sped on through the neighborhood, wondering how long it would take the fire department and cops to show up. There were no fire hydrants in this old neighborhood.

He stopped at the Giral mansion, got out, and opened the gate to the backyard. He didn't know when this fence had gone up, or why a gate had been put in. Nevertheless he drove on through and parked in the backyard. Like the Garcia place, there were no other houses in the back, just the remnants of wetlands the Everglades had once claimed.

He would be safe here. It was home. It was where he belonged. But all the other houses must go, so that the neighborhood which was his, would always be Giral.

He could see it, the front lawn stretching out into the road, an arm of green, and pretty soon that goddamn kid would come riding by on his bike, gloating that he'd helped my pretty Penny escape—gloating proudly that she'd finally escaped this madhouse of Giral.

Pablo grabbed his shotgun and ran outside. "Pendejo!" he shouted. "Vayate!"

Santiago raised his middle finger up as he sped past on his bike and laughed.

Laughed like a mockingbird at Pablo Giral.

Pablo raised his rifle, aimed, fired. The kid toppled to the side; his bike slid out from under him, wheels spinning. Santiago struck the ground and didn't move. Pablo ran over to him, the kid was bleeding all over the fucking road, his bloodline seeping into the earth of this place. He just stared at him, at all the oozing blood, then brought the open end of his shotgun down hard against the base of the kid's skull, and fired.

"Adios, amigo" he said quietly.

A long time later, he grabbed onto Santiago's arms and pulled him from the road to the front lawn. He thought about how to arrange Santiago's body. Like Christ on the cross, he decided, this would be fitting. He bound the kid's feet with rope, flipped him onto his back, and made sure his arms were extended at either side. If he'd had stakes, he would have driven them through Santiago's hands. But all he had were a couple of short nails. He hammered them straight through Santiago's palms with his bare fist, but they were too short to hold in place, against the ground.

Shouting snapped him out of this memory, vision, hallucination—whatever it was. He found himself down on his knees, in the high weeds, on the front lawn. An old man was leaning out side the window of his truck, shouting, "Explosion at the old Garcia place! This whole damn fuckin' neighborhood's going up!"

Young struggled to his feet. He didn't know what the fuck he was actually doing, out here on the lawn. He didn't know this old guy—had no idea where he'd come from.

Did it matter? Not really. Right now, nothing mattered. *Need to get myself outta here.*

The old guy stuck out his hand as he approached. "I'm Amos. Amos Chandler. I found the body of that woman, Carmen Collier, out here, and you'd have thought the county and state cops would be out here in droves, right boy?"

Young shook his hand. "Sure. Yeah, of course. In droves. I'm Andy."

"But that's not what happened. One fed showed up, some guy named Fuentes, then, later on, a Broward County cop, and, finally, the coroner. Fuentes and I went to the Garcia place together, boy."

He gazed off at the flames that turned the air a muted orange.

"And we found that the killer had been living there, boy."

So that's what happened. "I'll be pushing off now, Amos. But before I go I'll make sure everyone finds their way here. Kinda strange it isn't showing up on GPS, right?"

"And you're here for what, boy?"

Young gestured at the Giral place. "Goin' to buy that house over there. Wanted to take a look around."

"Buy it? The feds own it. Are they selling it to you, boy?"

"If the price is right." Young grinned. "Anything can be bought and sold. South Florida real estate is hot right now." With that, Young thanked him, then hurried off toward the gate to retrieve his car. One hand in his jacket pocket, on his gun, just in case.

Before reaching the gate, Amos called, "Hey, hold on a second, boy."

Young glanced back. The old man now held a rifle pointed directly at him. "Uh, be mighty careful with that rifle, old man."

"Just spoke to Fuentes. He needs to talk with you, boy"

"Uh-huh." *Fuck*

"Take your hand outta that pocket, slowly boy... easy does it now."

"I am." But as he lifted his hand, Young fired the gun through the pocket.

The old man gasped, and fired his rifle as he stumbled back.

He was dead before he hit the ground.

Young ran over to him, checked for a carotid pulse in his neck. Nothing.

"Sorry, old man. Wrong time. Wrong place." Young quickly threw open the iron gate, rubbed the lock with a hanky then, without another look, raced to his car.

Jo saw the smoke before she reached the Giral house. Clouds of it drifted up and into the clear blue sky, marring it with gray. The smell and crackle of it infused the air. "Where's the fire department?"

"Out here?" Marian laughed. "The closest fire department is probably thirty miles away."

Her cell rang. *Fuentes.* "I just got a call from Amos Chandler, the old man who found Carmen Collier's body. He said that Young is at the Giral place, and he's about to grab his rifle to stop Young from leaving. He hung up before I could tell him that was serious insanity."

Fuentes raced past her, siren blaring, and through the back windshield Jo could just see Diego and Eleanor leaning forward. "Right about now, Evan is probably telling Eleanor and Diego to stay in the car until he and Luke have checked things out."

"Then we should too," Marina said.

Jo wasn't so sure about that. If Young was still in the vicinity, if Chandler had managed to keep him from leaving, she intended to confront him, face-to-face. "I'm betting that Young set fire to the old Garcia place."

Marina nodded. "Makes sense. Purge the ghosts of his past."

Jo swerved her car into the curve that brought her out onto High Road and raced after Fuentes. He soon screeched to a stop in front of the place, and Jo pulled in right behind him. She and Marina jumped out, but Lieutenant Nelson waved them back. "Stay in the car!" he shouted.

Marina ran back to the car, but Jo brought out her weapon and ran after Nelson and Fuentes. They tore across the yard to the open gate, with Jo reaching them seconds later. The old man lay in the high grass, hands still gripping his rifle, blood seeping into his shirt from a shot through the chest. His death seemed utterly senseless to Jo—one more instance of collateral damage in the seemingly endless saga of Giral. It outraged her that Young had gotten away with not only one but another homicide.

"Did the security video pick up anything?" Jo asked.

Nelson shook his head. "Nope." He pointed at the camera half-hidden under the eaves. "He shot it out."

Maria, Eleanor, and Diego joined them. "Shouldn't there be a team of cops out here because of the explosion? And the fire? All looking for Young?" Eleanor asked.

"I'm sure he's long gone." Fuentes pointed at the deep tire tracks in the grass closest to the fence that continued down the crumbled driveway and onto the street. "He got out of here fast."

"And went where?" Jo asked.

Nelson motioned at the smoke. "Not to the old Garcia place; that's for sure."

Jo finally heard the wail of sirens, and one of the vehicles appeared moments later—the coroner and his forensics team. And right behind them were three fire trucks. *This whole thing,* she thought, *turned out to be worse than I thought, considering what happened that night at the Hard Rock, because an innocent man lost his life to Young here. How many more lives have to end before this motherfucker is either caught or killed?*

Tom Pearson got out of the forensics van and came over to Fuentes and Nelson. "*This* place again? And meanwhile, the Garcia place has just blown up, setting the surrounding woods on fire." Then he cast a glance down at Amos Chandler's body. "Poor ole guy." Pearson ran his fingers through his hair. "At least this one isn't going to make me sick. I'll send the team inside the house. Again."

"Thanks," Fuentes said, and walked over to Jo's car. She was behind the wheel; Marina and Diego were getting in. "Where are the three of you staying tonight?"

"Probably Adele's place," Jo replied, and the other two nodded in agreement.

"We'll have a squad car keeping its eye on the neighborhood. If anything here changes, I'll let you know."

"How're you going to catch this pig, Evan?" asked Marina.

Right then, Fuentes felt as depressed as the three of them looked. "I really don't know. But we will. There's an APB out on him now. We've got people at his home, his ex's home, the clinic, your homes, and outside Adele's. If he makes a move on any of those locations, he's ours."

"He's outwitted us before," Jo said.

"His luck has run out," Fuentes said with a resolve he didn't entirely feel.

And what about her luck? The luck of the others? Had their luck run out as well?

On the way back to Adele's, Eleanor rode with them, in the back seat with Diego. No one spoke. Jo sensed the undercurrent of their collective mood—fear, yes, but also despair, the kind of terrible senseless ire which prospectively conveyed that this Giral saga would perpetually continue. She understood that the four of them were processing every thing that had happened, all that had gone wrong, and that any answers lay *within*, and *between*, each of them.

After all, she wasn't the only one who had suffered because of Pablo Giral. Of the four, Penny was the only one who hadn't been killed by Giral. Jo realized that *she* owed them even though some of *his* surplus believe it the the other way round. In her heart she knew it was because of her that each of them had been killed by Giral—Eleanor as Carmen, Maria as Santiago, and Diego as Raul. If Fuentes had been in that life, had Giral killed him too?

"What was Fuentes in that life?" Jo asked.

"No idea," Marina said.

"Ditto," echoed Diego.

Jo glanced at Eleanor, at her reflection in the rearview mirror, and saw the way she turned her head to the side, rubbed her hands over her face. "He was there in that life," Eleanor said. "He and Carmen Giral were lovers."

"How long have you known that, Eleanor?" asked Marina.

"Just today. When we were at my place."

"One more synchronicity for the lot of us," Jo said, "that

he just happened to be the man investigating all this. Any idea what happened to him back then?"

"Nope."

"So we're all looking for karmic closure," Marina said.

"Even Young, strangely enough." Jo's throat threatened to close up. "But you three died because of me. *I'm* the one with the greater karmic debt. *I* owe you all."

Marina turned in her seat and stared at Jo. "I know what that brain of yours is doing. I can see it twisting around and I realize what you're cooking up. You're trying to figure what trap you might lay for him, so you can take him down. But forget it, girl. Forget about sneaking outta bed tonight at Adele's, and doing something stupid on your own. You do that and it only really cheats the rest of us out of closure. Something all of us will regret."

"Yeah, forget that," Eleanor said, as if it were in truth a pronouncement.

Diego sat forward from the back seat and touched Jo's shoulder. "Hermana, por favor. Incluye nosotros."

Sister, please include us.

Suddenly, before her eyes, what was a latent thought dream memory appeared, flashing manifest sounds of its visulospacial past. And now Jo knew Raul had said those very words to Penny, when they'd talked about her escaping.

"But I'm pretty Penny, the monster's nightmare, that sexy sinister seducer in the House of Giral. I'm the sweetening trigger in all this. I'm the one to blame. it's me."

"No, you're not to blame. He is. We're all his external triggers," Raul said. "You and Carmen were easier to abuse because you were female. You're the ones who should, will and must escape."

Above as below. Everything changes. Nothing stays the same. Eternal Repetition.

"Not this time," Eleanor said. "This is fated. None of us will pay with our lives."

Jo hoped that Eleanor was right, that none of them would die this time around. But she had so often felt Penny's despair, had dreamt of her contemplating suicide so many different times, that she no longer felt certain, about much of anything at all.

So when they got back to Adele's, Jo asked Marina to do another reading. Her question was specific: would they all be free of the Giral life once he was held accountable?

Marina as instructed, fell back into her inner self and thought deeply about this. Setting her full concentration and continence upon this singular point, she let nothing save this enter or consume her mind.

I Ching.

Then she spread her cards out on the kitchen table, and looked at each of them. "To answer this as a collective group, I think each of you should in sequence select a card. Jo, you go first, since you're asking the question."

Jo passed her hand over the deck of Tarot cards without touching any of them. Then she drew back the one that spoke to her—fate or chance —she felt a destined compulsion. She picked it up. *Justice.*

"Well, that sure fits," Eleanor remarked, with a wry wide grin.

Marina nodded. "Once justice is served, will Jennifer be free of the influence of that Giral life? That's really *our* question. Okay, Eleanor. As Carmen Giral, the former mother figure of the family unit, it's your turn to choose and play."

Eleanor didn't hesitate. She chose a median card, right from the middle of the deck, turned it over. *The High Priestess.* "We'll know within a couple hours, days, weeks . . months. My sense is that we'll know within two days. "Diego. Want to give it a go?

He drew the Devil. "Shit, I don't like that card one bit. It's about fear, isn't it?"

"In this case, I think it's about the daemon in Young. He's the cunning devil we're dealing with," Marina replied. "Now its my turn." With the courage of confidence she drew the Eight of Wands. "We're going underground, to receive a message about what's next."

Adele had come into the room. She spied over the cards carefully, while her inner thoughts drifted off to Fuentes "I'll draw the last one," she said. And out came the *Star.*

"Wow, the second best card in the deck. That oddly shaped eight pointed Star, it heals; it signals and it signifies, new beginnings."

"How about the sixth card in this spread?" Jo asked. "The perfect resolution. Shall I? Many I? Have I inherited the right, to pick it?"

"Indeed," Marina replied. "No doubt about it. If not for you Jo, who else? She smiled a perfect smile. So in the darkest heart of that monstrous moment, Dr. Jennifer Hart knew what was always meant for her.

Get Back Jojo. Get back to where you once belonged.

Jo then confidently selected the Ten of Swords, which depicted a man facedown on the ground, ten swords sticking out of his back—not a hopeful card, unless of course the man turned out to be Albert Young. "Is it him? This temporal reincarnate of Pablo Giral? Is it this material apparition of which that the ten of swords speaks?

"Christ, I hope so," Diego said.

'FINGERPRINTING'

Before Fuentes got back to Lauderdale, he checked his email. Virtually buried under a gargantuan tumult of timely responses, Evan discerned this one important message.

It read:

FROM: lhouse.browardcountyhealth@hospital.com

TO: agentefuentes.forensicfeds@fbi.com
DATE: March 15, 2022

Agent Fuentes,

I am pleased to provide you what my authorities would in this matter deem ethically allowable correspondence. I have enclosed for your close review a copy of the original UDS requisition on Ms. Hart from her initial ER visit, dated March 10, 2022. As well, a follow up UDS requisition, highlighting all the detailed tests I ordered for purposes of clarification, during the days closely following her admission, along with follow-up correspondences I received from Broward County Hospital Laboratory Services.

With regard to specific inquiry about those two containers of sodium chloride and six bottles of Visine you found inside the medical suites of Dr. Albert Young, be well advised that even if I were Dr. Young's private personal physician, and this I am absolutely not, privy to medical case information and my sworn ethical duty as a Physician has me bound and bonded through repetition of our hippocratic oath, to the ways of written patient consent. Most regrettably without documentation of intent, I am unable to shed further light on Dr. Young, especially with reference to any definitive diagnosis.

For what my advice is worth, track down any medical visits Young may have had. Begin with the Ophthalmologists, for if this crafty jerk-off had not lost the totality of his mind already, conjunctivitis provides him a medically fit alibi—a perfectly valid reason for his use of Visine drops. No doubt this man is clever. You've checked his computer records? I'll bet you have. But did you find positive forensic links there to adulterant websites? If on first glance you didn't then I suggest you look a bit harder. I believe you'll find what your looking for buried somewhere amongst the vagrant images of expected porn.

Doubtless that Young had nicely disguised his hand but then an unconscious Freudian slip? Whom I ask save for God knows. A slight parapraxis of memory disclosed ever "unwittingly" to a psychologist? Perhaps something turns up— firmly linking motive to behavior — like salt water drops that show willful adulteration. Psychologists are well known to keep detailed documentation on their patients. Once served with a court subpoena, under the press of such an official document, this would force disclosure of his complete clinical record, opening up his most private confessions, for all to see and hear in open court.

Agent Fuentes, I beg of you, please understand. Know with absolute certainty this psychopathic bloke is well past clever enough to put you, I or anyone else at end. To this point, I most strongly encourage you to consider sodium chloride as a patent sign, a determinant force of prospect destiny. Christ asks that ye shall receive. I'd gladly give up Andy, in a heart beat. Be aware that here at Broward County Hospital, we've got collective will, expertise, and technical capacity. Enough to make a *tangible* difference. Just give me the word; you won't regret it.

Deep inside the heart and passion of Fuentes faint rustlings of Isabella Santo were heard. Quite suddenly, the image of Abuelita Adele Señora Cantera stood fully erect in front of him, reflected and refracted of many selves. His warm seeing heart and sensible mind seemed utterly compelled towards the gist, of what he instinctively knew would follow.

Salt is a known urine adulterant. Its concentration fixed and measurable. Narcotic addicts often add salt to their urine in rehab programs, adulterating its manifest, that is before they submit their sample. Salt and water mask and dilute all drugs in their system. Presto, but only if they are not caught, a clean, falsified officially negative UDS. Addicts are street smart. On the street is the place where they live, learn and play. Addicts learn quickly and efficiently how to maneuver, find ways around blockages, its a live game of cat and mouse, one side chasing the other, the head chasing the tail, whereas both parts of the brain, sides of the mind, passions of the spirit want to get themselves ahead. We have always had to be smarter in order to stay ahead of them.

Visine can be used to adulterate UDS, as its solvent contains a mixture of saltwater. However, with Visine there's more to say. Tetrahydrozoline HCl and Benzalkonium Cl, the active biochemical compounds in Visine work their ways of molecular magic to reduce redness and irritation, improving eye comfort, still they leave traces of them selves behind, easy enough for a detective mind to find. Biodetectable metabolites are the forensic signatures of their prior presence.

Agent Fuentes, your speculations are of great interest to me. They form a most logical and plausible sequence. Something else we both know: theories are not fact. Sad ideas, sordid feelings are speculative, they don't show proof of test but rather describe proof of detest. Your bloodhounds are done. They did their job and did it well. Their adaptive olfactory bulbs successfully sniffed out six 5 ml bottles of Visine. This was a great start, but I did some snooping around on my own, and found in Young's office garbage can the torn off remnants of a 2.5 oz package of Clean Shot, a well known UDS adulterant mix.

It stunk badly of rotten detest. Set from this detest of his, a new test of intuition was to begin in earnest. A journey to validation. The provision of positive empirical proof that Glutaraldehyde, the biologically active ingredient in Clean Shot, having no known bona fide medical purpose, had a greater purpose in masking substances. House rules at end.

UDS forensics for Dr. Young hold a dual prospect—detection and confirmation of his willful adulteration. His game still plays on, but now with odds crookedly bent like a old question mark, prospectively in our favor. Do not consider my refusal to disclose more specifically, either as a remiss or failure. I am in truth only disclosing what I can. I am not at legal liberty to discuss what lab markers were found, if at all, in Ms. Hart's UDS.

All third-party disclosures require expressly written authorization, which at Broward County Hospital, must be made in triplicate. Use USPS Priority Post. Address your requests to Dr. Raskin, our chief psychiatrist; Dr. Jack Gordon, our chief administrator; and Dr.

Proust, Broward County Hospital CEO. I wish you all the best luck, my friend. Kindly keep me in the loop.

LH

Attached to this email were copies of the lab tests House had ordered. In short, this email and the requisitions enclosed, provided tangible evidence, that even a jury could not ignore. Young had broken a number of laws—moral, ethical, and otherwise. Fuentes pumped his fist in the air. No one smiled or laughed. Not a soul or sound was heard.

Even when Young was miles from the old Giral neighborhood, he could see the thick billowing smoke from the Garcia place. Distantly, he heard sirens. He kept to the speed limit and debated to himself where to go. Not home. Not to the clinic. Maybe he would drop in on his ex. But first he really needed to eat. He was more than famished.

He pulled into a Denny's outside of Davie and hoped he looked local enough not to stand out. He ran his nimble fingers through his dark, greying hair, slapped at the bits of grass and dirt on his clothes. He unplugged his cell, pocketed it, and got out.

Apparently Denny's was a favorite stop for interstate truckers. A number of them were parked in the lot—moving trucks; trucks hauling goods for Target, Publix, Whole Foods; trucks loaded with new cars, wood, dirt, and sod. He saw two Amazon Prime vans. It made sense that they all stopped here. Denny's was quick and cheap, and good.

Young went inside, and the pretty young woman at the front counter asked, "How many in your party, sir?"

"Just me. May I sit by the window?"

"Sure."

She led him to the back of the restaurant, where a TV was tuned to a local news station, volume set on low. She seated him, dropped a menu on the table. "Your server will be over shortly."

"Thanks."

The air smelled delicious—bacon, eggs, coffee, toast, hash browns. His stomach grumbled in response. He couldn't remember the last time he'd eaten anything substantial, and he opened the menu with a kid's eagerness. *Vegetable omelet, hash browns, muffins, coffee, OJ. Perfect.* The server came over with a cup of dark brewed coffee, set it down in front of him, and he ordered.

He scrolled through his phone, sipping at his coffee, and felt almost normal. But only *almost.* In the back of his head, choppy frightful scenes kept popped in and out of his blank consciousness—snippets of the man he'd been. Pablo Giral. Young repeated the name in his head, and as he heard it play over and over again, it started to feel more familiar. More like him. He could see Giral's body, face, hair, eyes. This memory was plainly near.

Show me a really bad thing you did, Pablo.

Sure thing, Andy, you imposter.

And suddenly the inside of his head lit up and he—Giral—was beating Carmen for getting pregnant, with a *daughter.* He hated having sex with her, but one night he'd come home drunk and she'd seduced him, like he thought Penny often did. Two months later, she'd told him she was pregnant. She'd nearly lost the baby after he'd beat her to a pulp. A doctor had come out to the house several times a week, to see how Carmen was healing. During one of those visits, the doctor cornered him in the kitchen, sank his fist deep into Giral's gut, then kneed him hard in the groin.

"If you lay a hand on her again, I'll slice your balls off. Do you hear me?"

Yeah, he heard. The doc outweighed him, towered over him, was toned and muscular where Giral had gone soft and limp.

"Here you go, sir."

The server set the breakfast down in front of him, and when he saw he had toast rather than the muffins he'd ordered, he mistook her for Carmen and nearly grabbed her arm. "I ordered muffins, not toast," he snapped, then stabbed the toast with his fork and flung it off his plate onto the floor.

"That really wasn't necessary," the server said. "Once you pick it up, I'll be glad to bring you … your muffins."

He looked at her, enraged, felt like giving her a good smack accross the face. But he was too hungry for trouble. "Sure." He scooped up the toast, set the two pieces on a napkin, wrapped it up. "There we are. Happy?"

She scoffed and stormed off.

He scribbled away on his napkin, trying to estimate how long his money would last. He sketched because it calmed him. He ate because it calmed him. As he lifted the OJ glass to his lips, his eyes locked on the TV. A chopper video of the fire captured its utter fury and power. He was surprised at how rapidly it had spread to the trees and into the Everglades just beyond it. Under the picture ran a chyron: "Man responsible for the fire and explosion is Albert Young, MD. He is armed, wanted and dangerous. If you see him or have knowledge of his whereabouts, urgently call 888-477-8281."

His photo flashed briefly on the screen, and when he saw it he nearly choked on a bite of his omelet.

"Fuck."

Just then the server returned with a basket of biscuits. Terrified she would see the screen, he handed her a one-hundred-dollar bill. "Please, take this. Let it be my sincerest apology for the way I acted."

She looked at the bill, then at him. "That's okay." She took the bill and tucked it inside her bra. "I've had days like that too. Enjoy your muffins."

"I will. Thanks."

His photo had vanished from the screen.

Young picked the biscuits out of the basket, wrapped them in napkins, abandoned twenty more bucks on the table, and proceeded to leave.

They're after me.

He needed to find another car. Not his. He could use more cash but didn't care go to an ATM or use his credit cards. And he felt a pressing necessity to change his appearance.

Drug store first. For hair dye. And glasses. How else could he disguise himself?

But he kept driving south into Davie, the town of hitching posts, horses, and cowboys. *Perfect.* He would become a psychedelic urban millennial cowboy. First hair dye, and dark sunglasses, then for now, a cap with "Miami Heat" written in large glossy letters across the front, in bright catty yellow and black.

Young pulled into Walgreens. He slipped out his wallet and counted the cash he had on hand. When he got to 136 and still had a dollar left to count, his heart pounded into overdrive, as if he were running a world marathon.

Adrenaline coursed through him. *One fucking three shit fucking seven. How the hell did this happen* again?

He realized he shouldn't have given the server that hundred bucks.

He opened the glove compartment and rummaged through it, frantically searching for stray dollar bills. He finally found a twenty and let out a whoop of triumph. That brought the total to $157, which had had no fatal stigma, no psychotic history, attached. Young then tucked the twenty firmly into his wallet, and got out of the car.

Every Walgreens, every Home Depot, every Lowe's, every chain store in this country looks and smells exactly the same. The differences among them are small—the placement of products on the shelves, the locations of said shelves. Young easily found what he needed, leaving with chump change from the twenty.

His next stop was a gas station, where he used the bathroom to dye his hair. It was a mess, but so what. After all, he wouldn't have to clean the place.

Then onto an urban cowboy store. There were several in town, but he pulled into the lot of the first one he came to. Inside, even the employees were dressed like cowboys. Several of them wore visible holsters with weapons inside, along with John Wayne–type hats that they either tugged down low like hoodies over their faces or were nudged back farther on their heads. One guy in particular had a voice that sounded a lot like John Wayne's. Young pegged this urban cowboy as his kind of aspiring actor.

Young sifted through the racks of pants and shirts, tried on boots with spurs attached at the backs, and put on different-colored hats to see how or if they disguised him.

He made his final selections, carried everything up to the register, where a young millennial flashed him a thumbs-up.

"OMG, dude, did you find everything you need?" he asked.

"Yeah, this will do fine."

The cowboy began ringing up his purchases. "Looks like you'll be doing a serious kind of riding," the millennial quipped.

"Hope so, cowboy." Once each item had been rung up, all were all folded and neatly set aside. When the last item rang through, the clerk took out a large plastic bag, placing everything inside.

"That'll be ... one hundred thirty-seven, even. Whoa, that's big daddy dollars, sir."

Holy crap! Had this young urban buck actually said *that*?

"But I'll give you a thirty percent discount for the sale ... if you like, sir. That brings the total to one hundred and five, ninety."

This meant he had avoided karmic repetition and had $31.10 left in his wallet to boot. He still needed gas. At nearly five bucks a gallon, six would leave him with what? Loose change.

Christ.

Young placed two crisp bills, a 10 and a 100 on the counter, and tried to sound cheerful. "There you go man, keep as cool as you can."

The androgynous millennial cowboy slid him over a paltry $4.10 in change, followed by his bag of vagrant clothes. "Have a super great day, bronco. Enjoy your ride; your garbs will be a game changer for sure!"

Young walked back outside to his car, darkness spreading like a cancer inside.

Fuentes and Nelson were sitting in their offices at the bureau, writing up their reports on what had happened in the Giral neighborhood, when the landline rang. Fuentes snatched up the phone. "Agent Fuentes."

"Buenos tardes Agent Fuentes, Esta Carla. I work on the tips line in the Miami office. We just got a most interesting call. I'm going to put it right through to you."

"Thanks, Carla. Go ahead; put it through."

He made sure the speaker was on fairly loud so Nelson could also hear the call. "Hi, I'm Sharon Carter. I'm a server at the Denny's just north of Davie. Earlier today, I ... I waited on ... Dr. Albert Young. Shit, sorry, it slipped. I watched his photo come up on the news."

"Which Denny's?" Nelson asked.

She ticked off its address. Fuentes brought up a map on his phone and tapped it in. The place was maybe eight or ten miles tops from the home of Young's ex. "How did he act, Sharon?"

"Like a pure dick. He'd ordered biscuits, and when the prick saw he had been given hash browns, he threw an awful fit, stabbed the toast on his plate, and flung the bread to the floor. I told him I'd be happy to bring him *his* biscuits if *he* picked the toast off the floor. He wasn't a happy camper, but he eventually did comply."

Fuentes smiled like a rose at that. *A woman telling Young what to do, ha! That must hav pissed him off big time.*

"Then, when I went back with the biscuits, he apologized

and tipped me a hundred bucks. He seemed really uneasy. Anyway, his mind must have been a hot mess 'cuz he tried to take off before paying his bill, but I saw him about to leave, so I hurried after him, but I wasn't quick enough. He got into a gray Mazda SUV and took off down the road."

"Thanks much, Sharon. This is helpful," Fuentes said with genuine appreciation.

"Wait. There's more. I went back to his table to clean it off and found that he'd scribbled all over a napkin. Maybe there's some important stuff there. I can snap you a picture of it, if you like."

Fuentes gave her his cell number, and within a minute, two clear photos of the napkin came through. "This'll work fine, Sharon. Thank you."

Fuentes enlarged the image and texted it to Nelson. Numbers in all types of disorderly arrangement were half hazardly spread accross the napkin, scribbled additions and subtractions, each followed by the word "fuck" written, over and over again. But what the server had innocently called scribblings were actually neatly printed names, arranged in the form of a vertical pillar, obelisk, or monolith:

Albert Young—Pablo Giral
Carmen Collier—Margarita Garcia
Jennifer Hart—Penny Giral
Eleanor Raskin—Carmen Giral
Marina Bruce—Santiago Garcia
Diego Guzman—Raul Giral
Chris Laker—Circus Performer
Laurence House? Amy Young?

"Holy shit, Evan," Nelson burst out. "He knows what the fuck he's doing."

"Yes, it appears he exactly does." He emailed the photos to himself, then put out a statewide APB warning that Albert Young was presently headed to his ex-wife's house. He included the address, adding "We suspect he'll make his move as soon as it's dark. Be safe and for gods sake, make sure you're well hidden."

"We're on our way."

The call was answered by three Davie cops.

Jo, Marina, Eleanor, Diego, and Adele were all together, listening to the police radio for any updated news about Young. When the APB on Young came, they exchanged glances.

"Should we head over there too?" Marina asked.

Jo thought about it, but not for long. "That's what we've always done before - chased after Fuentes and tried to trap Young on our own. And things went south. My sense is that even if he goes to his ex-wife's, ultimately he'll return to the Giral home. And I think we should be waiting for him when he arrives."

"Interesting that Evan didn't call or text any of us," Eleanor said, already on her feet, checking her weapon.

Jo thought Fuentes saw them as byproducts of this drama. He needed immediate and definite proof that would convince a jury Albert Young was a fucking psychopath. It shouldn't matter to a jury *why* he was a psychopath. They wouldn't buy this past-life shit; that was the bottom line. Did he have that tangible proof yet? If so, he hadn't told them. That she understood.

But what he didn't understand was that they, the three of them, desperately needed closure. Otherwise, the rest of their lives would become a series of what ifs … For Marina, *what if* she hadn't flipped off Giral that day on her bike when he shot Santiago? For Diego, it was *what if* he'd intervened sooner? For Eleanor, it was *what if* she'd spoken up sooner as Penny's mother? And for her, it was *what if* she'd fought back sooner, blamed him and not herself?

And for Albert Young, it was *what if* he'd killed all of them earlier than he had?

"I'll drive," Jo said, a coy, dark smile on her face.

Chapter

17

It was March 14, 2022, the day before Good Friday. Young felt stuck in twilight time, a zone of in-between space with no definitive end, when he backed his car into Amy's driveway, parked alongside her Mercedes SUV. It probably had a full tank because she was usually obsessive about things like that: clean house, organics, health. She was the same way about the charge on her cell.

He glanced around, making sure no neighbors were about, got out of his car, and started casually strolling up the sidewalk. He now looked the authentic urban cowboy type to a tee, wearing a side holster that held his blackened Glock, set at crotch level down the right side to the tip of his the hip, of his historical Old West Emporium buffalo plaid pants. His stubbled moustache and dyed short black hair, decently slicked back under the wide-brimmed, high-crowned tan sugarloaf sombrero he wore, had him appear very much like Billy the Kid would have looked like himself. The dark tint of the glass perhaps a bit over the top, once the sun went down; but for right now, at the glaring reflected time of twilight, no doubt they did the trick. He could be some random guy walking up to her front door. The security cam wouldn't recognize him as anyone she knew, or knows. His eyes wildly stung in the painful glare up ahead.

Albert rang the doorbell. Amy answered it with the chain on, one slanted eye set, peering out of the open crack. Her pretty pert little nose, her round aqua blue green eyes, and especially her curly blond hair—all of it was so special and lovely. In actual fact, he found it practically seductive.

"Andy?" she snickered. "You going to a costume party or something?"

"Yeah, a fundraiser for a local urban millennial cowboy charity." He smiled,

"Jeez, what the hell do you want with me?"

"Mind opening the door, Amy?"

"Only if you've got on you at least some of the one million one hundred thirty-seven thousand you owe me."

"I do, indeed."

She shut the crack in the door, and he heard the clink of the chain as she removed it, inching the door until it was half-open. She looked him up and down before she burst out laughing. "You look entirely ridiculous, Andy."

Young was in no mood for small talk; he simply stepped inside as she shut the door, still snickering about the way he looked, the smirk plastered on the front of her face, this disappeared lightning fast, after Andy punched her flush in the face. Amy's hands flew up to stop her bloodied nose, as she stumbled awkwardly backward. Her eyes held their ground, firm and unyielding, absolutely wide and white with shock, as she tripped on the edge of the rug, and fell facedown flat on the floor. Young snapped the door lock shut and then slowly drew his weapon, pointing its barrel directly between her wildly stunned eyes.

"Listen up. Here's the real fucking deal. I need money. Now, follow my directions. Don't think you can trick me up. I've already seen your guilt laden ways. My conscience is clear and empty. I got no fear or guilt. You Amy got your whine house ass up some kinda wrong electrical socket. I was hung out bone dry right from the start. I knew ground zero would be my destiny. I felt its lash implode. Saw it flash upon my birth horizon as a double scorpio. I'm on to your skankly skinned masochistic bitch act. Am I to believe a snake's life like yours worthy of an afterlife? Go then my pretty Giral. But heed this fatal warning: don't try to fuck me up. Be the good girl you always were.

Amy scooted back on her ass, blood oozing through her fingers. "I ... I ... can't, Andy. What the fuck are you, actually—"

Whatever he is is no business of yours. My fierce battle's done. All here is gone dead and cold inside. As for my fair lady, open the hidden maple white hardwood gem safe you've stuck behind that god damn stinking portrait of Humberto Solás, that old mother fucker you've got hanging from your office wall. Then step away. Don't kid yourself, girl. I'll take whatever I want. Three hundred pounds of pure steely eyed professional protection, three quarter inch thickness from door to wall. You think this shit sways me away? He can't help you now, Madam Giral"

"I ... you ... broke my nose."

"Get up now, cowgirl," he demanded. Cowboy Young slowly brought the Glock 22 up, pressing it right against her forehead.

A hand fell, pale and trembling, away from her bloody nose, and she extended that elbow hard against the floor, struggling to push herself to her feet. Young politely held out his left hand to help her up, and she grabbed hold of it, raising herself up until her knee suddenly slammed into his groin. An excruciating sound of pain tore straight through him as he fell forward at the waist, and while he was busy flailing and clutching himself, he lost grip of the gun, which clattered against the floor with a resounding metallic clang. Her move was so sudden and unexpected that he was still leaning over, clutching his soon-to-be blue balls, as he pitched backward.

As Young slammed onto the floor, Amy came at him, screaming like a crazed banshee, blood pouring down from her broken nose, smearing her face a tint of sanguine.

She hurled an antique ceramic vase, worth maybe a grand or two, right at him. It missed by a wide margin, struck the bookcase beyond his shadow, shattering into sharp-edged pieces. His nuts still smarting Young rolled on the ground over to his side, grabbed the fallen gun, reached out, and fired it.

That shot missed. But his second, squarely hit the mark.

She gasped and gurgled, stumbled backward, hands flying to her chest. In one fell swoop she collapsed. Young bolted to his feet, ran over to her handbag, which was hanging over the coffee table. He dug out her wallet and pulled out a wad of bills—hundreds, fifties, twenties. He grabbed a full handful, didn't take the time to count.

Dr. Albert Young, now turned urban cowboy, had no idea whether neighbors were around or who might have heard the two gunshots. He stuffed the US bills into the side slit of his pants, pocketed her car keys, and hurried into her office, looking for her computer. Fortunately, it was fully booted up. And he didn't have to move her body much to get her fingerprints and a retina scan. First he erased the security footage. Next he eyed the wall safe. A kind of desperate hunger rose as he reckoned what might be kept hidden inside its square steel perimeter. But he hadn't time to figure its combination.

Pissed off at this fallen luck, he sloped outside into the deepening dusk of his darkish grey Chevrolet, grabbing his rifle and his pack of goodies from the back seat. Shots rang out, riddling the passenger side of his car with a swerve of holes.

Enemies. Fuck them. Fuck them all.

He twisted round with his rifle, returning a barrage of bullets. He was now on the move toward Amy's Mercedes. He threw the SUV passenger-side door open, tossed the pack inside, scrambled behind the steering wheel.

Off to the side and in front of him stood an angry group of them: dozens of cops in full mounted gear. What he saw was a virtual SWAT team moving rhythmically toward him.

An old-style guns-a-blazing shootout looked to be the inevitable conclusion to him, of this infamous Bonny and Clyde look-alike affair, save for the failed gas station robbery; the fact that this wasn't Texas, Oklahoma, New Mexico, or Missouri but Florida; and, moreover, the naked truth about Amy—that she was no kind of willing partner in crime.

Half a dozen or so cops peeled off to the right and left. More shots. The sound of the back passenger window as it blew, was bone shattering. If not, of course, taken literally.

Young was now firmly behind the wheel, tearing out of the driveway, headlights bright and blinding.

He swung wildly, veered to the left, and struck two cops—heard the sounds of their blunt bodies as they slid over top of the SUV. *A waste of good time eating flesh*, rang out inside his omnivorous desiring mind.

Then Young lowered the passenger-side window and began firing, aimlessly and blindly. Shots shattered parts of the rear window on the right, he gunned the accelerator and tore out of there, wind whistling through the shattered open windows, the accelerator needle brushing well past 130 mph. Behind and around him, sirens shrieked and wailed in the dimming darkness.

His mind raced on as he pulled onto I-95 heading due north. The red dot of his radar was dodging in and out of traffic as his eyes flicked from the rearview to the side mirrors and back. He turned off at Sunrise Boulevard, drove like a madman toward an industrial area of old warehouses and storage units. Finally he drew up in front of the unit Amy had rented after she'd moved out. Alas, he had helped her make that move. But she didn't know he had copied and kept a key because *he* paid the *goddamn* bills.

The headlights illuminated *numero, ciento treinta y siete*. It was 137 again.

"Fucked." This number compelled him, haunted him relentlessly. Was he, like Wolfgang Pauli, going to die? Was it all going to end in that godforsaken 137 place?

We'll just have to wait and see won't we, Young thought.

He walked over and unlocked it, raised the rusted metal gate, then drove inside. He turned off the engine, leaving the headlights on so he could see. Young then got out of his vehicle and flicked the inside wall switch on. He laughed when he saw a couple of lamps he thought had winked in unison at him.

His ego, still basically intact, was beginning to dissolve.

The storage unit was air-conditioned. *At least*, he reckoned, *I won't bake to death.* His mind seemed in the heat of a long drawn out final battle. He sat himself down on one of the half dozen chairs in the space, pale and sweating most profusely. The air was strangely calming as urban cowboy Young gradually removed the ridiculous spurs from his boots, pulling them *bare off* so his feet could yet again breathe.

"Jesus."

He noticed the storage room didn't have a shower. Why should it? There was just a plain toilet and a large utility sink. This satisfied him. Now he could wash up. He already had prepared a change of clothes in his pack, a towel, soap, a hairbrush and a grab bag of other indispensable toiletries.

He brought out the pocketed wad of cash he'd taken from Amy's wallet and counted it. $458. This wasn't much. But he wouldn't starve and could buy gas. Best of all he wouldn't have to use a credit or debit card, which could rather easily be traced.

Amy, bless her wicked heart, had a small fridge. In clear sight, it had been packed full of bottled water and snack-type foods. It didn't much surprise him. This was the woman, after all, who always had a full tank of gas and whose cell was always 100 percent charged.

Young snorted a kind of obscenity, killed off the SUV's headlights. He knew he would be safe here, at least for a night. The only people who knew about this storage unit were Amy, him, and their son. Young took in a deep, stale breath, clearing his mind of prospects.

Now he was ready. *Let fate come to me*, he thought, *be it as it may.*

When Fuentes, Nelson, a dozen or so other feds and local cops roared into the neighbor hood where Amy Young lived, little did they expect to find a bedlam of fire, ash, and dust at their feet. Two ashen cops lay prone in the street, apparently run over. Neighbors were out milling about, scattered and confused. Out front, two women were sobbing. A pair of Davie cops stood upright in an open doorway, preventing anyone with an inkling from entering inside. Tom Pearson's forensics van pulled up out front. Then he himself hopped out, marching straight up to the Davie cops, whose nods allowed his authoritative passage.

Fuentes was already parked on the front lawn. He and Nelson leaped from the grey unmarked vehicle, heading together for the door. Fuentes, aghast in the moment, still had the wherewithal to notice Young's car, parked alone in the driveway. Had he taken his ex-wife's vehicle? What kind of car did she drive? He couldn't quite remember.

The unstuck rest of the team spread themselves out, wanting to speak with each member of the throng of people gathered out front. But before they reached the front door, Pearson hurried out retching and gagging, leaned over the porch, railed, then promptly and forcefully vomited. Fuentes reached out to him, touching a bare hand to his seizing back.

"That bad, amigo?"

"Jesus God, we've got our hands full with a real live sicko here,"

Fuentes went inside and quickly understood why Pearson

had gotten sick. Amy Fuentes lay wasted on the living room floor, a torn Giral body left on its own, floating in a puddle of vomit and blood, shot straight through the chest, her once broken nose reset at an odd, disfiguring angle. Pearson came up alongside, popping papaya pills into his mouth. "Boy, this urban cowboy dude is on one serious rampage."

"Yeah. He's devolving. Can you get a couple people on your team to check over the car in the driveway? It's his."

"Sure thing."

Fuentes walked into the house, avoiding looking at Amy, and searched about for a computer. In an office at the back, he eyed the iMacBook Pro. As soon as he hit the first key, he recognized it was already booted up. Predictably, yesterday's most recent footage rose into clear view.

He checked the trash can on the Mac just to be sure, finding a single video file having today's date stamp. Apparently Young had been so rattled he'd overlooked emptying it.

He emailed the singularity to himself, forwarded it to Nelson, then he opened its contents to take a quick look. It showed Young stepping out of his car and into the house, dressed in cowboy clothes, holstered gun, John Wayne–like hat, and all. He let the video run on a bit further, watching the reenactment carefully. Young's ex wife was seen laughing as he crept his way into the house, where, in the blink of an eye her smile was replaced with a fist to the face. He then heard Young rant about the safe, watched the events play out, up to the last moments of Amy Young's life.

What Fuentes didn't know was that inside that steel and cement barricade lay video and auditory evidence, a virtual paper-trail manifesto— documentation of everything objective, from the instant he'd arrived, which had painstakingly taken place, in that living room. Irrefutable evidence a blind and deaf jury could not ignore, albeit under advisement of a high court judge. Even ordinary people who couldn't buy into past-life karma would likely find this evidence of homicide, more than compelling.

Fuentes seemed satisfied with this and closed the video. He then went through Amy Young's files and emails, meticulously searching for the make and model of her car. Finally, he found it. She drove a navy-blue 2021 Mercedes GLE350, a fancy name for an expensive SUV. He checked the DMV computer files on record, and there he found its license plate. He then phoned it into the Miami office, so as they could issue an updated APB.

He and Nelson then began talking with the neighbors to find out what they'd seen and heard. Pearson's team finished up around midnight. Between the late night darkness of March 14 and the dawn of Good Friday morning light, Amy Young's lifeless body was stuffed into the ambulance that would take her to the morgue. Though an updated APB had gone out and the media had picked up the story, all 888 lines at this moment were dead silent.

Jo felt dark and eerie. Good Friday was closing in, and the old House of Giral was dreary of light, except for the artificial illumination of their collective cell phones.

Together they gathered, united of purpose, undivided. All as one had agreed to take two-hour shift turns, as sentries at the downstairs window. It overlooked the entire front yard and part of the road so that if any car appeared, they would see its approach.

It was a tick past midnight. A new day had dawned upon the horizon.

What would it bring? Solitude, penitence, karma? A gang fated to synchronicity?

They had brought a cooler of food and bottled water with them, and Jo had pulled one of the chairs up to the window. So there she sat, munching at a peanut butter and jelly sandwich. But what she really could have used was a mug of strong Cuban coffee.

Jo heard a creaking noise somewhere about. She turned her head and sent a quick glance behind her, the cell's flashlight beaming out a line ahead. There Eleanor stood bare foot in the kitchen doorway, her jeans disheveled, her tee rumpled. "Anything come of it yet?" she asked.

"Nope. Just a couple of black bats flying round in circles." She brought an old wooden chair over to the window and sat down next to Jo. "It's so fucking weird being here at night, waiting for that monster to come."

"Yeah, I know."

"I just had a dream yesterday about the day he killed me. As Carmen."

"Jesus, Eleanor, I'm so sorry." Jo gave her hand a firm squeeze.

"It happened in *this* room." She turned slightly and pointed at the back wall. "He ... shot me as soon as he rushed through the door, where he'd been firing at the cops, who had arrived to arrest him for Santiago's murder. The first shot, it ... hit me in the leg." She touched her right knee. "Shattered my kneecap. I fell back dazed onto the couch."

She rolled up her pant leg, what was left of her patterned jeans, and brought the light from her cell towards what looked like a birth mark set on her skin just below her right knee.

"I'd always wondered 'bout this birth mark."

"So until you had this dream, you didn't have any memory of this?"

"No. In my regression with Carol all those years ago, she began at the very moment of my death. I didn't have a chance to see what had led up to it."

"Where were the sons?" Jo asked.

"Raul … tackled Pablo as soon as he shot me. Sebastian and Carlos came after him with baseball bats … at least I think that's what they had in their hands. He managed to shoot all three of them. I … I mean Carmen … was freaking out and trying to get off the couch and run, but it was impossible. He … he shot me through the chest and then … then I found myself floating somewhere above my body. I was … with my two sons. I mean … I, Carmen, her spirit rose." She rubbed her hands over her face, and when she spoke, her voice sounded choked. "I just can't keep identifying with that fucking life, Jojo."

"I know. I can't either. None of us can. That's why we're all here, together."

"Was your spirit still around when Pablo shot himself?"

"In the dream it was."

"What'd he do?"

"Raged … and bitterly complained that we'd done this to him. Made it necessary. Then he … I don't know. In the dream, he just … kind of vaporized."

"And the guys ... his cast of male characters? What became of them?"

"Same thing. But here's something weird. In the dream, there came a postscript—something about Carmen Collier, that homeless woman he murdered. She was Margarita Garcia."

"Santiago's mother, right."

Jo looked at Eleanor. "Oh my God, that makes so much sense to me now ... why they were living together in the old Garcia place."

"Wow, that's why he killed her, *there*."

Tears doused Eleanor's eyes as she slung her arm around Jo's shoulders. "If you hadn't been Baker Acted, if I hadn't met you and Marina and Diego, all this would have ... haunted me ... for the rest of my life."

Jo hugged her back. "That's why we're all going to get closure."

Just then, twin headlights appeared on the road.

Part 3

All Is Among Us

What makes psychopaths different from all the
others is the remarkable ease with which they
lie, the pervasiveness of their deception, and the
callousness with which they carry it out.
—Robert D. Hare

Chapter

18

As the headlights cut through the window of the room where Marina had been sound asleep, comfy and secure in her fleece sleeping bag, in a room that once had been Pablo Giral's office, Raskin, like a deer, bolted starkly awake. She grabbed her weapon off the top of her pack, slipped on her shoes, then ran downstairs to the front room.

The lights from the car spilled through the dusty window, illuminating Eleanor standing to one side of the casement, her weapon cocked and ready, Jo to the right of the front door.

"Any idea who's in the car, ladies?" she whispered.

"Not yet," Jo sighed back.

"I'll position myself to the right of the kitchen doorway."

"Where's Diego?" Eleanor asked.

"Right behind Marina," Diego replied. "I'll be to the left of the kitchen door."

"Is the back door locked?" Eleanor asked.

"I'll check," Diego said.

Whoever occupied the car took their sweet time getting out. And even when they did, they left the car's headlight beams fully on, making identification difficult. Then the man raised his arms and shouted, "Jo? You in there?"

"What the fuck," Marina muttered. "Chris Laker."

"Shit." Jo threw open the door and stepped out onto the porch. "What the hell are you doing here?"

Chris came toward her, arms held high in the air, making it clear he wasn't armed.

"I heard about the murder of Amy Young, that there's a warrant out for Young's arrest. I … I kinda knew you'd be here."

Marina marched through the door, and their eyes locked.

"You've got a hell of a lot of nerve, Christopher. Your time to show care and concern came the day Jo moved out of *your* house, and went with more than a dint of indifference. I saw your reptilian brain, litterally at work. I watched the change of proverbial color from grey white to bilious bean green. Nausea gripped my stomach hard and stench took hold of my mind, and the air turned so yellowy tight and cowardly, it took all I had not to puke my disgusted guts out and onto the floor in front of you." Her piercing fiery eyes fumed.

"You must've known I'd come some time Jo? Or have you forgotten who I am? " Chris asked.

Jo touched her arm. "It's okay, Marina."

Diego and Eleanor joined them on the porch. Diego pointed at Chris's car.

"Can you turn off your headlights, dude?"

"Sure can, dude." Laker aimed his keys at the car, it beeped twice, and the headlights went out. "Mind if I come in?"

"Yes, as a matter of fact I do," Jo replied. "Tell me your

real purpose Chris in coming to see me? He hesitated. Just answer my question."

"I remembered the circus."

"Holy shit," Diego whispered. "Tightrope walker."

"Apparently you forgot that night you degraded me to a circus performer."

Marina grabbed his arm. "Inside asshole. We all need to get inside, now."

They pulled another chair into the front room and everyone other than Chris sat down. At once, everyone started firing questions at the singled out non practicing Christian, who stood alone like the accused at the trial of his crossing: "What do you remember?" "How much do you recall?"

"They say, that time has come and passed, that all is destined, just let it go, Marina.

"I hate you Laker. Your a mean, willful, ill scheming narcissist, whose trickster days have passed. Your feeble rein of fucked up terror and misguided power, that had set its firm grips upon us, is over and done. In this god forsaken moment, dude, be real for once, exhort the dark demons that have for so long controlled your soul. " Lakers continence looked frosty cold, his eyes penetratingly ice blue, skin white and pale as a ghost.

"The proverbial beens, Chris. Start at the beginning. Tell nothing but the truth. Be inclusive and explicit. Leave nothing hanging. You subtle memory vault works like a sieve. Back then you knew us rather intimately. In that life doubtless you worked your magical mirror scheme to a tee, in the blinding black smoke and glare of the setting sun you willed Jenny into thinking all was fated: nothing to be done.

But you are not Estrogen, and this is not a Samuel Beckett play. If you believe this godforsaken life, to be insignificant and meaningless, illogical and uncertain, then this belief is itself a mirror to your soul.

Inside Laker laughed and his wry smile broadened. Words then spilled out.

"Your hero is unlikely. Mine is *LUCKY*. Yours won't wait. Mine will stay the course." "Shut your mouth, Christopher. We've heard quite enough of your raving psychobabble." Raskin shifted her body to the side until she was centered in the chair, now sitting tall and erect her image looked much larger, even omnipresent. On top of Eleanor's head, Marina and Jo thought they saw a gilded apparition, a crown of mother of pearls. Then she spoke.

"Like God we hover over the dark abyss and pray that we not be cast adrift. Unlike the man of constant sorrow, the megalomaniac visionary, the royal aristocratic herald, the autocratic depot and the plain religious fanatic, whose descent and emergency, time and again shows little of anything successfully realized, our end and means will not fail. We wail and wait with patients, likened to Job, as woman becomes man. But unlike man we shall receive an answer. We shan't be bullied and we won't take the blind plunge into that dark pit of endless sorrow, where all memory is ever lost and forgotten."

Jo foresaw in Chris's face, the image of a white cross and with his quivering lips tinged lifeless and cyanotic, Jo glanced round trying to envision that solemn place where a trickster like Laker might hide his last hours away. There, karma would take its revenge. Two sharp stakes would do, straight through his fat black heart, making the sign of a cross.

Where a trickster's fiendish laughs just echoes.

"Let us, Christopher, get straight to the point of the matter. Ethics forces disclosure. Tell us what you know and when you knew it. Who are we and how did you identify us?"

"Huh?" Chris patted the air with his hands. "Hold on for a moment, folks." He pointed first at Eleanor. "Carmen. I. . . I think you were Carmen Giral." He paused, eyed Diego. "You I think were Raul, my good friend, the youngest brother. We were shadow confidents. I was glad, no overjoyed to help your sister."

"And me?" Marina asked.

"Santiago. Your mother once read my cards. She was there at the circus when, what shall we call it, that incident happened." He closed his eyes, rapid saccades filled the space beneath his eyelids, motion that would track the whole picture. Yes, he remembered.

It was shortly before Penny fled." His eyes finally coming to rest on Jo. "Penny."

Jo reached deep into her bag and brought out Penny's diary. "Chris, you made a most curious entry in Penny's diary after she left the circus." She turned to the page, passing him the diary.

Christopher shone his cell flashlight square at the page. When he finally looked up again, tears brimmed over swelling eyes. "Yes," he whispered. I did write this, and it's true.

"Do you have details of what happened to her?" Jo asked. "After she left the circus?"

"The time frame is kind of hazy, but I think it was a few

years after she left the circus that she and Margarita Garcia together wrote *The House of Giral*."

"Margarita's name is the only one on the cover," Marina remarked.

"Penny didn't want her name on it. She didn't want anyone to know where or who she was, what she had became. Margarita at some point had located her. They somehow agreed to write a book, keeping her name out of it." Chris lowered his head as if in prayer.

"Why now, pray tell, Chris?" Eleanor pointedly asked. "For Gods sake, speak!"

"I had a Zoom session with Carol Bowman."

Eleanor tilted back, eyes wide, a zigzag of electric shock passing through her.

"Now *that's* a synchronicity," she said in a low soft voice, not to scream the obvious.

"You too?" Chris asked her.

Her twin ocular bulbs bobbed wildly up and down. "When her first book, *Children's Past Lives*, had just come out, I was in her home office in Pennsylvania. She began talking, something in her voice sounded familiar, whether form or content, it directly tapped into that Giral life."

"Yeah. That's exactly how it was, for me also." He looked at Jo. "You wanted to know which ex-girlfriend I was going to live with. Remember, Jo? I didn't have anywhere to go, so I checked into a motel and contacted Carol. Together, her and I, we did a virtual Zoom."

Jo felt nearly overwhelmed by all this sudden information. She sensed that she had lived most of her conscious adult life, at least this time, inside a giant invisible puzzle, which increasingly showed more and more missing and forgotten pieces. Now, abruptly, many of these pieces were slipping and sliding together. Her being Baker Acted had been a catalyst for effecting remembrance.

"I had a strong visceral reaction to Young when I first met him that day at the clinic." Chris stared at the wavy blue ocean breeze blowing through her green eyes, the beat of a summer sun on her brown tanned brow, idyllic golden dreams settled on a stilled heart.

"During the regression, I came to understand why. It was because he was Giral. Good ole fuckin' Pablo Giral. When I moved out, I was so freaked by everything, Jo. I … I just needed time … and space to get away, and think."

Jo realized Chris was apologizing to her. She reached for his hand, grasping tightly onto it. "Really I'm the one who owes *you*. If it hadn't been for the circus, he'd no doubt have killed me."

"But *House of Giral* would've never been written without your take on the story."

"I Dunno. When I heard that Young's ex had been murdered, and that a warrant had been issued for Young … well …" He raked his fingers back through his black hair and shook his head. "I just had … this feeling where you were and needed to go, Jo."

Get back. Get back. Get back Jojo. Get back to where you once belonged.

"We didn't know shit about his ex or the expectant warrant. We came here this afternoon because we all together felt confident Young would show up."

"Do you still think he will?" Chris asked.

Jo glanced at Eleanor, Diego, and Marina, and saw the

tense collective resolve on their faces. "Yeah, we do." She nodded. "Are we not Sumerian warriors?

"Then I'd like to stay. I have more weapons in my car, some explosives and—"

"Explosives?" Diego repeated. "Can we use them in the front yard? As protection?"

"We should be able to do just that. You know about explosives, Diego?"

"I know a little about a lot of things. And, I'm a quick learner."

"I can vouch for that," Jo exclaimed.

Marina and Eleanor echoed her sentiment.

"Okay, let's get to it." Chris glanced around at them. "Ladies, Diego and I have some work to accomplish out front."

"We'll join you," Jo said. "We're also quick learners."

Chris smiled. "Wow. We're in the same boat, all looking for closure."

"Yeah," Jo said. "Even Fuentes and Young."

"But no ship has yet to sail."

"I think what you really meant was 'sailed.' "

At that, all had a hearty laugh out loud.

And that was, for a time, all she wrote

Fuentes was asleep when the REM of his vision first began to stir inside his head.

And in the morning of wakening it will be stormy, for the sky today is red and threatening. As Fuentes's dreams lightened, they hurled him out of the dead of sleep, crashing him into full consciousness. They had been haunted by Amy Young and Carmen Collier, by Eleanor Raskin as Carmen Giral, the woman he had once truly known and loved; by Diego as Raul in the Giral life; by Marina as Santiago, fatally gunned down while on his bike; and by Jo, of course, as Penny.

It was minutes after 3:00 AM, as his wife slept on Fuentes burst up, unplugged the phone. The time flashed 3:14. *Pi. Not another sign.* He checked his text messages, emails, and voicemails. He'd texted Jo and the others before he'd fallen into bed four hours ago, he still hadn't heard anything back. He suspected that meant she and the others had gone out to the Giral place, as he knew they believed Young would show up there, eventually.

But Fuentes wasn't convinced of that. Young hadn't been seen or heard from since he escaped from his ex-wife's house the previous day. It seemed more likely he was headed out of state. Yet his ex's car had been badly damaged by gunfire: windows shattered, the body of her golden Mercedes riddled with bullet holes. Would he steal a car? Whose to choose? Which one?

He fixed himself a bowl of cereal loaded with fresh fruit, poured a mug of super-strong Cuban coffee, popped a piece of cranberry bread into the toaster. He badly needed a plan, an inner vision. Strange but his mind, just yesterday, seemed full of Stevie Wonder. *All's fair in love but love's a crazy game. Two people vow in love to stay as one they say. But all has changed with time the future none can see. For a losing side I'll play when all is put away.*

As he ate, Evan thought of Young and his next move, then texted Jo and her group: "Would all of you please let me know that you're not being held hostage?"

All's not fair in love and war . . . ain't that the sordid truth!

By the time he rinsed off his dishes and put them in the dishwasher, Jo had responded.

"We're at the Giral place. Chris Laker showed up. He bought weapons. We set some of his explosives up around the front yard, they've to be detonated by hand … by someone."

"Christ," Fuentes murmured and texted, "On my way."

He hurried into his office, put on a bulletproof vest, then unlocked the cabinet where he kept his weapons. He chose two handguns—AR15s with plenty of ammo. He had no idea what kind of explosives Laker might have brought, so he added some choices of his own.

Then he called Nelson, who didn't pick up. Fuentes left him a voicemail explaining all what was going on. He loaded everything into a large canvas bag, then headed out to his car.

It was now 3:30 AM on Good Friday. Traffic was negligible. The GPS said he was twenty minutes out. He texted his GPS to the group and immediately got a response from Jo: "Text me when you're on the road approaching the house. Leave your car. Bury it some where in the woods, I'll see you soon."

Young now walked around the dirty grey golden unmarked car, inspecting all the damage. If he drove this ruined heap of metallic rust anywhere in the daylight, he would doubtless be pulled over and sanctioned by the first cop he passed. *Shit.* He got his belongings out of the Mercedes, set them by the door, put on his lightweight jacket, tucked his weapon into the pocket, then off Albert went.

He hurried across the dimly lit parking lot to the main office.

What the hell are you doing now, Andy? His inner voice had become more and more persistent over the last few days—a nagging, demanding, devolving voice. He didn't know how, had no certain method in mind, to successfully shut it up.

He saw only one car parked out front—a red shiny Mazda SUV that he guessed was two or three years old. A light was on inside the office, with a sign on the office door that read: OPEN for business, so Young walked right in.

"Morning, sir," said the young man behind the desk, half a mug of stale coffee sitting in front of him. "What can I do for you today?"

"My car just broke down. I managed to pull it into my storage unit. Do you have cars to rent?"

His two brows in unison shot straight up like Vulcan ears. "Rent? No sir. But you can call an Uber; they'll take you to the airport. That's where all the major rentals are located."

But if Young chose smartly he could make a more expedient choice.

Be careful, Andy, warned that inner voice.

Whoever you are mind your own business dude and stay the fuck outta mine!

"Uh-huh." He pulled out his gun. "Or I can just shoot you and take your car."

The young man, whose name tag read Sammy, drew back, eyes wide with shock, terror cutting through his brain. "Listen, take my car, cowboy, It's all good." And with eyes never leaving his, Sammy ever so slowly laid his set of keys down upon the counter.

"Tie me up; it's okay. Gag me if you like; I can't do a thing. I wouldn't be stupid enough to hurt you. Please, man." He held out his wrists pressed together, shaking miserably. " Please, do me the honor."

"Is there a security cam here?"

"Not for the office. For the lot."

The lot didn't matter shit to Young. It was still dark outside, and getting foggy.

"Get me some masking tape. Be quick about it, Sammy."

"It's here in the drawer. I'm going to reach my hand inside, okay?"

Young brought the gun closer to his forehead. "Do it slowly, slow and steady."

"Yes ... yes sir."

And he did.

Young taped his wrists together then went behind the counter.

"Push your chair back."

Sammy did as ordered. Young proceeded to tape him flush to the chair, wrapping the tape around his shoulders and arms, tying him to the back, continuing around his waist and legs. Then, after taping his ankles together, he pressed the last of the tape across his mouth. "You still breathing?"

Sammy nodded and mumbled, unenthusiastically.

"Okay." Suddenly Young felt as if he should apologize to this guy. His only mistake was being in the wrong place at the wrong time. No karma with him. Nothing to resolve.

"Look, man, I'm sorry I'm doing this, but I'm a ... desperate urban cowboy."

Very very good, Andy, said the inner voice.

Sammy nodded, thick alarm in his eyes.

Young scooped up the car keys, cut the lights and lowered the window blinds. He turned the OPEN sign over to CLOSED. Then he stepped outside, walked over to the shiny brand spanking new red Mazda SUV that wasn't his, got in, turned the ignition, and hit the headlights. *Gas tank full.* The engine sounded as smooth as silk when it started.

"Outta here. I'm free. Going home."

But first, he needed to go back to number 137, get his stuff, and close up.

Shit. Again.

He drove across the lot and parked, leaving the engine running and the headlights on. He retrieved his belongings, killed the lights in the storage unit, and stepped outside, where he shut and locked the door. The coast was clear. His past was dead, long gone. Everything lay ahead of him.

He pulled out of the lot, sensing no one came after him—no cops, no sirens, no spinning red lights. No Sammy for sure, as he was sitting silently taped to the chair. Young got onto the interstate, hoping to God he wouldn't regret letting Sammy live. Maybe, just maybe, for the first time in this life, he had outwitted that fucking number 137.

No such luck. The 137 of the Giral place was still left to deal with.

Jo's phone vibrated. It was a message from Fuentes: "I just stashed my car in the woods."

Chris jumped to his feet, turned on the cell's flashlight. "I'll meet him out front."

"I'll come with you," Jo said.

"We've got you covered," Diego said with a comforting voice.

Jo and Chris walked out onto the broken-down splintered porch. He took her hand.

"We're a-okay with the explosives, right?"

Her hand in his felt oddly familiar, even comforting. It was the first time since he'd arrived that they'd been alone together. She realized she no longer loved him. Even though she surely understood what he had been going through, when he'd taken off like he had, he still should've talked to her—opened up and communicated something honest. But he wouldn't. His archetypal nature was too inauthentic, cunning, gamesman-like, phony.

"I'm sorry for what I did," he said suddenly, "leaving like I did, Jojo."

"I wish you'd said this back then, words about what you were feeling, to me."

He glanced at her. "I wish you'd done the same."

She brought his hand to her mouth and kissed one of the knuckles. "The problem is that at the time, I didn't know what I was feeling. I just felt *off*; that's the only way I can explain it."

The darkness was so silent and still that they most naturally whispered. "But what about all those nights you woke terrified, sometimes screaming or sobbing, and I asked you what was wrong, what you had dreamt, but you couldn't or wouldn't tell me?"

"I … I didn't know what to say, or how to say it. I didn't want to talk; I couldn't speak, but I dreamt a lot about it."

"Dreams about that fucked Giral life, right?" Chris held her hand closer.

She nodded, bit at her lower lip. "Images ... phantoms, mostly."

"Yet Giral tried to fuck us again this time around."

"Here's what makes me wonder. What happens to people like Young when they die? What happened to Hitler? To Pinochet? Stalin? Mussolini? What will happen to Putin? What becomes of all those evil autocrats?"

"Depends on who you ask, I guess. Catholics tell you they all go to hell. Atheists say that when you're dead, that's it. One time round is all you get. New Age future-thinking millennial types speculate that people like that get counseling on the other side, work with guides, and return to resolve their karma."

"I remember once speaking with Raskin about that." The face of Fuentes glowed.

"Jews have perpetually talked about this," she said. It had become widely accepted that the Kabbalah, a traditional term for Jewish mysticism—especially those forms which it assumed in the Middle Ages, from the twelfth century onward—was the esoteric part of the oral law given to Moses at Mount Sinai.

"According to the renound Jewish expert historian Gershom Scholem, Kabbalah represents the essence of consequence that identifies a people's history. 'Gilgul,' he writes, 'is that Hebrew term for reincarnation, metempsychosis or transmigration of souls'. No definite proof of doctrine, just testimonial: Josephus in Antiquities 18:1 and in Jewish Wars 2:8, in Gnostic sects, amongst Manichean Christians, and in Hindi and Platonic teachings. Isaac the Blind called it the secret of Ibbur, which referred to a soul's impregnation."

"Some believe it only as a rational excuse for injustice or

apparent lack of justice in this world, a pragmatic answer to a practical problem that postulates while the righteous have suffered, the wicked have prospered, providing the masses an inverted sense of hope."

"How did she say this gilgul thing worked?" Jo asked.

"The sinner in this life is paid back by gilgul in the next. Its karmic but with a darker twist. For instance, a man who sins against a woman in this life might become in his next life that same woman type. He learnt not this time round, failed to appreciate what it felt to be her, needs that knowledge of experience, so he as she gets a further iterative kick at the can, if you like. The book of Job interpreted under the light of gilgul brings out more sordid dynamics, so that the reading is a richer one. Franz Kafka's *Metamorphosis* is another case in point. And analogously, Flannery O'Conners *A Good Man Is Hard to Find* the analog in this case being a strict catholic woman's rather than a kabbalistic man's viewpoint.

"The thing about Gilgul is proportionality—the old adage that claims an eye for an eye and a tooth for a tooth. If you are evil in this life and won't learn your lessons, then your next life will be magnified, your trial that much more difficult. Don't be surprised if you end up like Gregor, the insect in Kafka's *Metamorphosis*. And don't forget this ungodly physical reptile has a human soul inside, a mind that thinks, reasons and believes. A hellish karma for a human to take, no?"

"Young has yet to resolve his karma. Seems to me he only potentiated it."

"Bingo. What doesn't kill you gives you the potential to be stronger. The question is WILL it? Kabbalah much like legal ethics says: if you knew, or ought to have known, and you willfully sin, this continuance of evil potentiates your perdition. Our psychopathic Young shall be in this case destined for transmigration into something like Gregor, who needs to learn life lessons from further back, those he forgot in this life, must be repeated over again. Why? Because he forgot what it was like not to be human. But in order to be human, he needs to remember what it felt like to be an animal, insect, fly, or ant.

"Gilgul works the sequence backward." Chris appeared relieved.

"Free will wins, I guess." Jo smiled.

"Yup." Having consequences on either side.

Her phone vibrated. Another synchronicity loomed ahead by way of text from Fuentes. He was soon coming out of the woods. All now seemed to be coming out of the woodwork. Jo then saw his cell's flashlight, and she and Chris hurried toward him. When they were face to face to face, Fuentes said, "Christ, Jo. You should've told me before."

"It is true? About his ex?"

"It is."

His eyes went to Chris. "What kind of explosives did you use?"

The two men traded info on explosives as they hurried back toward the house. Jo felt increasingly uncomfortable outside and kept glancing back and forth behind them.

"I feel like he's ... somewhere creepy close."

"We're ready for him," Fuentes said, patting the canvas bag slung over his shoulder.

Jo glanced at her watch. It was nearly 3:43 AM, but she wasn't tired, not even a bit.

Inside the house, they settled in the kitchen. Fuentes set

up his police radio, volume low but high enough for them to hear anything that came over it. He set down his thick canvas bag on top of the kitchen table and began removing hand grenades, explosives, and other weapons, including knives, rifles, and the pair of AR15s.

He laid out enough body armor for an army to share. Earplugs and mikes would connect them. It seemed like a Waco, Texas, do-over. But this time all are on the FEDS side.

Jo stood up and started putting on her body armor. The other three did the same. Fuentes checked them to make sure they'd put it on correctly.

The radio suddenly crackled. "510 Sunrise Boulevard, Jim's Storage. Guy named Sammy Wilton says his car was just stolen and he was restrained in a chair by Albert Young. He had storage unit 137. It was in his wife's name. Young's driving a red Mazda SUV. Armed and obviously dangerous. He's believed headed west to the old Giral neighborhood."

Six officers answered.

"Okay, we're on it, he's headed our way," Eleanor said. "We need to figure out who goes where."

"And exactly what we are to do," Diego added.

Fuentes shook his head. "No one can tell you *what* to do, Diego; we don't yet know the circumstances."

"So we just have to be ready for anything," Diego said.

Jo spoke up. "Follow your gut."

"May I have a couple of those grenades?" Marina asked.

"Everyone gets two," Fuentes said.

"I'd like to go outside," Jo said. I need a breath of fresh air.

Eleanor nodded. "Me too. Out in the breezy trees. We'll see him when he arrives, then alert the rest of you."

"I'll be on the right side of the house, ready to detonate explosives," Fuentes said. "Diego, you're my backup. Marina, you want to take the other side of the house? Be prepared to hurl grenades or to open fire—that is, if the explosives don't take him out first."

"Nothing would give me greater pleasure than to knock that fucker off, Evan."

"Lieutenant Nelson and a squad of his men will be coming shortly. I will text Nelson to go round the block, get himself into the Giral backyard. Let's all now take up our positions."

Chapter

19

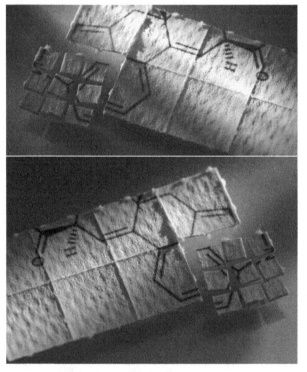

'LSD'

YOUNG LOVED SAMMY'S CAR. IT DROVE FAST AND SMOOTH, had a sunroof, and the sound system was nothing less than stellar. He liked the selection of sixties and seventies music too: old Dylan, Beatles, Rolling Stones, Jimi Hendrix, CSNY, Joan Baez, Carlos Santana, Grateful Dead.

Andy kept punching radio links, which sent him through fractured snippets and scenes of musical time. He heard the sounds of The Jazz Singer with Neil Diamond; the uncanny resound of Barbara Streisand's voice, in Funny Girl, belting out 'Don't you rain on my parade'; but for himself it was ever left to Hair, by McDermott, Ragni and Rado, that most strangely seized his inner nerve sheaths, and upset a fiery heart's most natural bodily rhythm. *Love on the rocks? Ain't no surprise. Just pour me a drink . . .*

And i'll tell you some lies.

To Young all this was nothing but random stuff, chance reflections, glare and soot spent off the surface of things. Meaning? He couldn't make heads or tails of it. Or wouldn't. It made no meaningful difference. Nothing made any difference. Still, a dominant sense of ambivalence, held passionless sway over his weaker pathetic Ego, as if it were, blinding and binding this sadistic El sicko, into a suspended state of perpetual indifference.

Familiar melodies transported Young accross the fifties, forties, thirties, twenties, until he heard it, "Farewell Blues," the song that played that one fateful night when he took his belt, his mouth and cock, unto Penny. His sons had all watched. Carmen had watched. Later that night, he heard them retching and puking their guts out. He felt fabulous.

His hand was tapping out the rhythm, against the steering wheel. He was hungry, thirsty, and tired, yet exhilarated to be driving this breathtaking car. He opened the sunroof and all that eerie dark Easter Morning air swept in. He cranked up the radio volume and sped on out into the distance, towards the west.

At one point, he saw a cop with a flashlight scanning on the other side of the road, he slowed down, muted the radio volume, then cruised straight on past, without suspicion of being stopped. That wouldn't have happened in Amy's ruined, shit ass, Mercedes. His ego was alive, sensory driven, a wildly exhilarating experience. His expanding mind was ready, prospects included. He had entered into his safe happy little cocoon.

He thought about setting fire to the Giral place—a final purge of that life. But first he wanted to see what it felt like to just be there, alone in the house, silently existing with the dark vaporous ghosts and demonic spirits from that life. Maybe he would bring some stuff from home and fix it up before the government levelled it, plowed the remnants under and hauled everything away. Or maybe he could buy it—buy the entire neighborhood. Yes, he would revive it; then it would; meaning the House of Giral would, live on … forever.

Uh-huh. Sure, Andy, challenged that voice of irony and sarcasm.

After all, with Amy out of the picture, he no longer owed her $1,137,000. That laundered money, and another million or so, still lay hidden in an account she hadn't been able to touch. She hadn't known about it. But he did. How much would the government take for the Giral neighborhood?

Andy, my stupid lost idiot child. Pay that unseen man behind the curtain no attention. The words you've heard, they are those of a raving wizard madman.

Even as he thought this, the voice silently prodded his

memory to come up with more, which it happily coughed up, in stark images of Amy, as he'd left her on the floor of their home, bleeding profusely from a chest wound.

The government won't sell you squat, Andy, whispered the voice. *You're a Federally wanted man. If you're smart now, you'll empty that crypto bank account, leave this sunny palm covered southern state of yours, and quickly get the fuck out of the country.*

Young violently hated, magnitudes more than anything else, this inhibitive dull-witted antagonistic voice, and wished he could silence it. But short of shooting himself, he hadn't figured yet how to do it. Maybe a PCP treatment. Or Ketamine. He had both with him, and other psychedelics as well.

He hadn't formulated any practical plan. Well, if nothing else, a self-administered psychedelic treatment, he thought, should surely reveal what his next step would, or could be. His final destiny.

Songs of sound, image and protest began to ebb and flow through his open mind. *Where do I go?* Follow the rainbow. *How do I go?* Follow the stars. *Will I find answers in children's faces? Shan't their eyes tell me why I live and die?*

Sounds of silence rose into witty laughter. Shades of a present life lit a path through his ears, inciting and inviting him, accross the universe. *Should I stay? or should I go?*

Jai guru deva om. Nothing's gonna change my world!

If he was advised to leave, where could he go? Might an LSD treatment show him? Would it be that specific?

At an intersection out west, he began to encounter traffic—commuters getting an early start, or night shift workers heading home from work. The ignorant asshole with the Air-pods in front of him wasn't paying close attention, and missed the yellow light. Young slammed his fist hard against the horn, letting the driver know he wasn't pleased. In fact he was irate. The driver opened his widow, thrust his arm out and up, flipping Young the bird. The red road raged its ravenous reflection right back.

A old deeply buried memory abruptly shot up to the surface of his mind, it was of Raul doing the same thing, when Pablo told him something he didn't particularly like. Young threw his car door open, took half a step out. He was ready and prepared to grab the other driver's hand, and without warning, snap it in half. But the green light arrow appeared, so he hopped back into his car, floored the gas, and sped on past. Through fierce steely red eyes he saw the amber flashes, the dead signs and the end warnings, that lay close ahead.

Fuck it. *Never look back.*

Raul. Where was Raul now?

Where were Sebastian? Carlos?

C'mon, Andy, you freak. You know the answers.

"I do not!" he snapped back.

Yeah, bro you do.

His fingers tightened on the wheel. "No, I ..."

And the voice tossed him an image of Diego Guzman, the janitor. Young realized he'd suspected, subconsciously all along, that Guzman was from that life, but something inside had blocked him of higher conscious knowledge. It was his gigantic fucked up bloated ego.

So *convenient now to forget, right, Andy? That Jo once was Penny, your daughter?*

Young violently shook his head, trying to rid himself of this persistent voice.

"No! No way, man. no fucking way!"

In response, he heard it emit a soft cackle, that of a lovely demoness witch. *Way!*

He was accelerating.

Hitchin' on a twilight train. Ain't nothin here I care to take along. Maybe a song.

Young was tuned into, getting close to free uninhibited, primal psychic capacity.

To sing when I want. I don't need to say please to no fucking woman tease.

Then he turned onto the dirt road that led into the Giral neighborhood. He was nearly home. It was 5:00 AM on the nose—very close to God frequency. He lowered the windows, and the familiar morning ocean air swept away the cobwebs from the car, carrying in the faint tinge and scent of smoke, from the Garcia house fire.

Gotcha feeling good as ever, boy.

As he first drove by the ruins of the Garcia place, Young felt enormous satisfaction that it was now obliterated. Gone were the vestiges of Santiago, Margarita, and Carmen Collier. *Hurrah!*

Tsk, tsk, Andy. You know what they were, and who we are. One and the same.

"You shut the fuck up.

Nope. Yo bitch dog.

Young slammed on the brakes, jumped out of the car, slapped himself across the face.

"You're lying, you slack sack of shit."

Yeah, to yourself bro.

The voice went silent, didn't seem to want to talk much after that. Young waited a moment, making sure it was really gone, then got back in the car. He unzipped his pack and brought out two brightly colored and patterned LSD blotters. He popped first the green stamp sail boat insignia, then the blue ocean wave into his mouth, swallowing them both at the same time, chased by a sip of bottled water.

There. Now, let the final ugly truth emerge.

Jo heard the car before she saw it—a slow grumbling prehistoric reptile that crept and seeped its way through the darkness — inching its way over moss, branch, mud and water toward them. Monster was back, but things would be different this time, they were ready.

Jenny texted everyone, pocketed her phone, tightening her grip on the gun. She had a grenade somewhere, in her jacket pocket. She paused just before the woods ended, and could just see him now, a dark shadow slowly and methodically, emerging from the car.

Jenny could see now a sharp outline of the millennial cowboy style, that of Andy's hat, clothes and military boots. A .22 handgun locked in his hip holster. An assault weapon slung over his right shoulder.

A 2022 ill tempered wild west version of John Wayne?

If it hadn't been so fucking pathetic, Jo'd have laughed out loud. Albert looked like an off beat character actor hired for a fifteen-second commercial, or that x-wannabe stand up comedian, whose walk-on routine had gone seriously south.

Jennifer Hart had a clear shot at the back of his skull, and longed to put a bullet straight through it. But that would be too easy a destiny for someone like Young. She wanted him to die a slow painful death with all his people, the eyes of each one his victims from the Giral life, all around and upon him. So when she fired, she shot out two Mazda's tires, then threw herself to the ground. A breath or two later, a barrage of bullets sprayed the air over and around her. Fire sliced across tree trunks, tore leaves off branches.

Albert scrambled back into the riddled SUV with the two flat tires as Eleanor raced out of the trees, firing her assault rifle all which ways, blowing out the last two tires. Young didn't leap out of the car and start firing right away. Instead he gunned the engine, but the Mazda only limped forward on its four flats, rubber slapping, metal scraping the road.

Jo ran over to Eleanor, spoke into the mike attached to her collar. "Four flats. But he's still moving, has an AK47 rifle and a handgun. Looks like a fucking rhinestone cowboy. Do you read me? Over and out."

Fuentes: "Got him in my sight. He's near the first explosive."

Diego: "Got you backed up, Jo."

Marina: "Gonna die, you motherfucker."

A grenade exploded several feet from Young's car, causing it to veer crazily down a steep hill toward a gully, even picking up speed on the descent. Suddenly a voice boomed over the loudspeaker; it was Diego's: "Hola, maricon. Es Raul. Me recuerdas?"

"Santiago tambien esta aqui," Marina multiplying the air, of collective sentiment.

The Mazda sped, spun hard then slammed into one of the trees, and a nearby explosive detonated, filing the ocean air with the stale smoke and stink of destruction.

The door of the SUV swung half open. Young stumbled

out, coughing, possibly wounded, firing the assault rifle repeatedly in all directions, throwing up a protective wall of bullets. Was it too little too late? His was a hard and shrewd, slickly tapered psychic hat—a thickened prefrontal cortex, whose genomic destiny had been preferentially chosen, to capture and enclose myelinated reptilian pathways—blind, closed, repetitive, uncal loops, those which would isolate a malefic familial will to power, singularize temporal motives, sequentially narrow and destroy access he had, to vitally adaptive human social pathways.

He stumbled forward, still firing shots at random, but the magazine was now empty. He dove low to reload. Jo and Eleanor ran toward him firing their assault rifles, one barrage hitting the SUV gas tank dead on. Zyklon blew cyanide blue fumes. A mushroom explosion brightly lit up the ebbing darkness. It threw Jenny and Eleanor right off their feet. Jo caught sight of Young, struggling to reach the trees, crawling and dragging one leg behind him, like some kind of artificial monster from a 1950s horror movie. Jennifer leaped up, and she and Eleanor tore after him, with Marina right up close behind.

Their unsub was devolving into a real bang on come to life shit show.

By this time dozens of police cruisers were roaring down the road and onto the property, blue lights a-blazing. Cops with search dogs, swarmed like wolf packs on a hunt, towards and into the smokey mossy wetland swamp.

Sirens, a howling moon, barking dogs, shouting, screaming, screeching noises—Young heard it all as he stumbled through the salt marsh, hunted by them whom hated Pablo Giral so deeply.

But why? Why did they hate me so much? What did I do to deserve this?

Really, Andy? Two hundred micrograms of lysergic acid diethylamide, is this not enough to show you?

"Shut up, motherfucker, whoever you are! I'll get you yet!"

Unplugged and ungrounded of censorship, Young stumbled upon something like an underwater root, tripped and pitched forward, landing facedown in the shallow water. He jerked his head around, twisted himself out of the water, gasping for air. *I … I can't breathe.*

Get up, asshole, get up.

His psyche, under the guise and press of strong dissociative intent, had gone far listless of living. With 200 mcgs of LSD having taken firm hold, ungodly otherworldly precepts, blackened with indifference, began to consume a wild untamable will to deceit. Ego crazed, wanton driven of ideological veracity, his malignant acid-laced mind thought it held fortune enough, to defiantly and delusively overpower death itself.

Big mistake, child boy.

Andy tried, really tried, to lift himself, thrusting his hands down into the water, his fingers squishing through the cool, misty mud, seeking anything solid to push up against. His nimble exploratory fingers finally to find solid ground under what seemed endless mud.

He pushed down hard, that enabled him, at least to get to his feet. He grabbed onto a low-hanging branch. His rifle was soaking wet, the other weapon in his holster, unusable.

Still yet they will supposedly fire, he thought.

He had two serrated knives of stainless steel, though he lacked the practical base to properly employ them, the way he could wield most competently a gun.

In a certain matter of speaking his mind was a hot mess. His drowned spirit had been caught like a mackerel out of water. A state of deathly panic began to wage relentless havoc upon his conscience, sensory confusion having long torn relevance and reality away, leaving an emergent vacant potentiality, that of a brand-new space in awake, *a tabula rasa*.

Young kept on sloshing through the mangroves, often stubbing and cutting his toes on their huge system of roots, his mind a panicked blankness, his hideous voice deathly silent. Lights burned a dark red orange beam, that shone through the singed glow of the trees, and as Albert glanced back, he saw three shadowy images pursuing him, three sets of eyes honed of intent, all with intense focus on one object, and they were getting closer. He knew who they were: Penny, Santiago, and Carmen, the three amigas.

The House of Giral, had meticulously selected a fearless faultless, waging warrior generational lineage, which shared a psychic immunity of the wild western sort, whose gunslinging cowboy ranch-house signature, and outcast outlaw system, bore a strong predisposition and potentiality, for psychopathic expression. This violent familial legacy and its phylogenetic determinant, would be passed down the line, given to Young at birth as a youthful malefic-majestic gift, of his singular inheritance.

Barred from entry, the gates to heaven closed, his

temperance thus fell east of Eden. What of his eternity? Where would he land, northwest of hell? Save for the likes of a distant few — Isiah, Joseph and Ezekiel; Tiberius, Confucius and Nostradamus — who knows?

Young's hardwired prefrontal and default mode genomics would have, under normal circumstances, been more than able to deke and dodge around this forthcoming onslaught of higher matters. But presently, under the hard persistent press of LSD, there were latent unconscious matters of accumulated evidence, lain down over years like tree trunk rings, layer upon layer of which had just begun to peel back. They had left a unique criminal signature, fingerprinting as it were, concentric rings that unwound and exposed an oddly shaped experimental mind, and familial lineage of an outcast criminal psychopath.

Andy scrambled onto dry land, landing on a hammock of thickly clustered man groves, struggling mightily, gasping just to catch his next to last breath. He pulled out his handgun, wiped it on the upper, dry part of his torn-up shirt, and, as Albert saw the three amigas inch closer and closer, he took dead aim at them, cocked his Glock, firing a round straight off at the middle one.

But his hand badly shook, so the shots flew wild. Now, in the half second it took for the sprayed bullets to pass through the mangroves, he was on the move again, sloshing through heaps of water, Lilly grass and pads, moss and dirt, until he reached another living hammock, another slice of dry earth.

His was a reflexive reptilian brain, set to sizzle upon automatic overdrive.

A female voice now spoke to Young. But whose was it? It seemed all too familiar.

"I know the bottom, it said. I know it with my great tap root. It is what you fear."

"Who the fuck are you talking to, girl?"

"I do not fear it. I have been there."

He paid no attention. It meant nothing to him. Nevertheless, it continued.

"Is it the sea you hear in me, its dissatisfactions?"

What does that even mean? Mind your own, bull shit business. Stay the fuck away!

You hear me right, don't ya girl.

"Or the voice of nothing, that was your madness?"

Fuck you, lady bitch. I couldn't care less. But then Andy heard the familiar ring,

that clear no nonsense tone of voice, which was none other than House.

"Angel dust is the street name for that infamous hallucinogen, ubiquitously sought by men and women alike to induce euphoria, sexual prowess, and social bravery— what otherwise amounts to the illusion of omnipotence. Under its most particular influence, crazed people often perform heroic acts of odd superhuman strength, some of these off tainted believers, have even attempted flight."

Rifle, Albert thought, and he swung it up, ready to shoot whoever or whatever appeared first. Then he saw something thick, moving below the water—something huge and spotted.

Fucker lizard. Andy fully realized it was a Burmese python. He gently backed away from it, hoping it hadn't sensed him, and when it raised its hideous head and hissed, he opened fire, shredding its long tapered body into small yellow-green fragmented pieces.

Nice, still got dead aim, he thought. *Magic's is working.*

Another male voice rose. This one he recognized as a memory of his own: "I call it angelic hog shit. Raskin says it's elephant dung. Our Broward County program hasn't used it for many years. These days we of course prefer ketamine—a PCP derivative that provides the same dissociative quality but with much less toxic potential for harm." He paused.

Some of us call it . . . *our peace pill.*" Ugh! Raskin thought.

Anticipating the return of gunfire, Albert threw himself to the ground, scrambling away from the python, scooting backwards upon his buttocks. Suddenly he heard the sound of choppers overhead, flying low, their powerful searchlights sweeping blue and white light in and across the mangrove, exposing him, a flaw in nature's design.

"Mother fucker," he spat, then dropped deep down underneath the water again.

More voices. The first one, clearly recognizable as House.

Not him again. I'll fuck that traitor up bad. Young still believed.

"Labeled by Parke Davis in the 1950s as an analgesic by trade, PCP was brought to market under the strange name Sernyl. By 1967, application for its use was restricted to animals. In 1978, the DEA placed it under the Controlled Substance Act, categorizing it as a schedule II drug — having high probability for abuse and a real potential for dependency. Use of Phencyclidine today, is strictly off label."

This time, Young held the assault rifle straight above his head. He tried to move on quickly toward the next hammock, but heard vocal shouts and barking dogs coming up close behind him, and off to his right. He slid over to his left, away from the taunts and barks. But the choppers kept relentlessly circling overhead, and when he dropped his head back, he could just make out one of them, about four hundred feet up and off to his right.

He raised his AK 47 assault rifle and opened fire. A eerily dark and familiar voice emerged. It would be her first proverbial kick at the bucket, with much more to come.

"You do not do. You do not do anymore black shoe, in which I've lived like a foot for thirty years, poor and white, barely daring to breathe or achoo. Daddy, I've had to kill you.

The voice of House now took hold.

"Phencyclidine accentuates a painless state of mind. Tack on, in cases of toxicity, delirium and agitation, jumbled thoughts, impaired judgement, and presto we've got a recipe ripe for disaster, not unlike what happened to Ms. Hart."

All lookalikes and soundalikes aren't always alike, Young thought, as the chopper exploded in midair above him. Burning chunks of laminates, thermoplastics, fiberglass amalgams, makrolon and kevlar, metallic fragments of aluminum and nickel, carbon and stainless steel descended, splintering through the trees, setting a swathe of them afire.

Young reached the closest hammock and scrambled onto it. Once his feet and body had better stabilized, he tore off through the trees, away from the choppers, the dogs, the shouts, the debris, and fire.

"CNS toxic effects are primarily and substantially alike, save for ones subjective impressions. They account for all the sensorimotor disturbances, autonomic stimulation, and a whole host of irregular, if not unwanted, behaviors. At first glance, users may well appear to be calm, cool and collected, nary a moment later becoming paranoid, agitated, irrational and aggressive. This tendency towards fluctuant symptomatology leaves them prone, to drunken and manic misinterpretations. Given a hefty enough dose, users will fall from awareness to unconsciousness, literally in the blink of an eye."

The falling sky appeared to be lightening. Young could see, or so he thought some brightness, here and there, colors of the rainbow zigzagging in-between fractal branches, refractions of light off the water's surface, reflected in shades and shadows off the trees.

Albert knew he had to stay low and flat, hidden amongst the mangroves, so he wouldn't be visible to the encroaching cops. But he was entirely visible to Penny Giral.

"Daddy, I've had to kill you. You died before I had time, marble-heavy, a bag full of God. Ghastly statue, with one gray toe, big as a Frisco seal."

You're one seductive bitch girl.

Young slipped back into the water again, and when he looked up, there they stood, the three of them: Penny and Carmen and Santiago, the three amigas.

"Game over." Penny shouted. "Drop the fucking rifle, daddy!"

"But a PCP delirium doesn't just stop there. Phencyclidine induced states of mind tend to variously vex and vacillate. Beneath closed lids, what seems to be most peaceful and relaxed, squirms haphazardly, up and down and halfway round. You've got to keep a high index of suspicion. It's tricky, sunny boy. Being, calm as a cucumber, on high alert."

Young was deathly bored.

"Listen, Andy. Show vigilance. Pay close attention. Be constantly on the look out, moreover heed to the signs.

Rotary nystagmus, if you haven't yet forgotten, is considered by most toxicology experts as a pathognomonic hallmark of PCP toxicity."

Who the hell cares? I sure don't. Young laughed. His ego was nearly impenetrable.

"Daddy, your head rests in the freakish Atlantic, where it pours bean green over blue. In the waters off beautiful Nauset, I used to pray to recover you. Ach, du. Ach du."

Calm and rather coolly Jo shot him clear through the shoulder. He stumbled back, lost his grip on the rifle, saw it slip and fall out of his hand, then watched helplessly as it disappeared into the deep dark water.

FUCK.

"Now the handgun, daddy-o, you shit cowardly bastard!"

"Okay." Andy patted the air with his hands. "It's in my holster. I'll reach down."

"We've got him! Over here. Come quick."

But a small voice, echoing of his past, had other thoughts.

"The name of the town is common. My Polack friend says there are a dozen or two. I never could tell where you put your foot, your root. Daddy, I never could talk to you."

Is that Carmen's voice? Young grabbed the handgun from his holster.

"You're a piece of shit!" he yelled. "Take this, you fucker bitch, whoever you are!"

But that voice, which rang so loud in his head now, was only his.

"What the fuck, House. This isn't rocket science. I am speaking to a forensics of human experience. Yes, subjectivity. That experiential place where all life forms live to consume, grow and evolve, otherwise starve to devolve, wither, and die."

Young was clearly on a roll. Yet neither House nor Raskin seemed interested.

"Replete of forgetfulness, autobiographical memory has riddled the human mind with historical inconsistency, a most fictionalized and biased perspective indeed. The all remarkable thing about current objective science, is the hardy insistent discontent it applies most equally, to all aspects of subjectivity."

Carmen just laughed, then abruptly shot him straight through the other shoulder, followed closely by Santiago, who fired his semi automatic weapon directly at the water in front of him, so that if Young moved but an inch . . . BINGO . . . he would be hit.

Nothing left to be done, old man. Your time has come, to an end.

The gun, where the hell is the gun?

"Kudos to you Dr. Young to think our scientific method needs to discount subjective knowledge, lest this be a karmic lesson, a reduced understanding of the human kind. Might it surprise you if this brought Ego a host of trouble? House never more insistent, insatiable and persistent, as he seemed right now. His entire body trembled with great excitement.

PCP is known to achieve its highest level of bodily concentration in fat tissue, this having become the ways and means of our human reptilian brain, the uncus having over eons acquired a high lipid content, and an ultra-efficient method of ion trapping."

What are these, House Rules? Does no one here know Giral rules? Young was puzzled.

"Our blood-brain barrier has phylogenetically subsumed a rise of levels ten times those measured in the blood. Impressive, huh? What this means is that brain detriments from drug toxicity persist, are very slowly washed out especially in chronic users, with accumulative toxicity, typically lasting up to seven days."

"Yeah, keep moving back," Santiago shouted at the shadowy unsub. "The gators behind you, they just love the scent of blood!"

Fucking Gators? Young twisted around, heard that cackling voice again, a demonic crack sound. *Karmic perversion. This predator gets eaten by a predator.* A cackle echoed.

It was getting darker, the darkness pressing, upon the deep. Young was dreaming, thrashing about in the wetland water. The LSD that he had taken just two hours ago, was presently at peak levels in his blood, expectantly, such a high concentration for the likes of Young, should make for tantalizing imagery. But all for the moment remained dead blank.

Suddenly, Albert saw the skeletal outline of a bare white hand, as pale and feminine as a ghost. From the deepest and darkest depths of the water it rose, thrusting its middle phalanx, as a gesture of pure irony, high up into the star scattered sky. The bitch was back.

"The tongue, it stuck in my jaw. It stuck in a barbed wire snare. Ich, ich, ich. I could hardly speak. I thought every German was you. And the language obscene. An engine, an engine chuffing me off like a Jew. A Jew to Dachau,

Auschwitz, Belsen. I began to talk like a Jew. I think I may well be a Jew."

There were not one but two gators now staring straight at him, each of them fifteen to twenty feet long. One was already in the water; the other was sliding off the bank, slowly but steadily, slinking its way under.

"Jesus God, shoot them!" Off to his right, a pair of police dogs barked furiously, as four cops held their guns trained upon him. "Shoot the gators, not me!" he screamed.

Carmen turned her back on him. Ditto Santiago. Leaving Penelope the last word.

"The snows of the Tyrol, the clear beer of Vienna, are not very pure or true. With my gypsy ancestress and my weird luck, and my Taroc pack, and my Tarot pack. I may be a bit of a Jew. I have always been scared of you, with your Luftwaffe, your gobbledygook. Your neat moustache and your Aryan eye, bright bright blue."

Albert was inching toward them, desperate arms splashing frantically in the water, the mud sucking at his shoes, the wide mouthed gators gaining on him. The dogs just kept barking, and the choppers kept circling. In the light of the crackling fire, in the red glow of the chopper headlights, with the dead sun rising over the eastern horizon, the largest of the two alligators quickly drew closer.

With a long powerful tail, it slammed into Young, hurling him with great force side ways into the twilight. Then the second gator sank its teeth deep into his right shoulder, shook him much like a dog shakes a bone. Agony exploded throughout his body, then he lost consciousness.

Young's ego moment brightened a bit, like that deer who

caught up in the headlights of oncoming traffic knows only right then, whether he's got the strength of will to survive.

"Toxic onset is insidiously and notoriously delayed. Moderate PCP intoxication might last two or three days. Severe intoxication, as measured by seizures, hyperthermia, renal failure, malignant hypertension or coma, on the other hand may last up to a week—even longer on rare occasions."

Suddenly, Young was hovering above his ruined body, watching as Carmen, Penny, Santiago, and three cops fired repeatedly at the two gators, killing them both.

"Panzer-man, panzer-man, O you, not God but a swastika, so black no sky could squeak through. Every woman adores a Fascist boot in the face, the brute, brute heart of a brute like you." Young heard nothing, saw nothing, of what or who it was or is.

"In the picture I have of you Daddy, you stand at the blackboard, a cleft in your chin instead of your foot, but no less a devil for that. No, not any less the black man who bit my pretty red heart in two."

Open hands of mercy helped Andy out of the water, got him onto a stretcher.

Medics now went to work, trying to stop the bleeding. They slapped an oxygen mask over Albert's face. But any simple peasant could see his injuries were fatal ones, the ligaments and muscles torn away, practically shredded, the various parts of his shoulder bones — the scapula and its spine, the clavicle, the acromion process and glenoid fossa, strewn and scattered in bits and pieces all about.

FUCKED. Young realized he'd lose both arms. At the minimum. Still there was more.

"Daddy, I was ten when they buried you. I tried to die and get back, back, back to you. At twenty, I thought the bones would do. But they pulled me out of the sack, and stuck me together with glue; then I knew just what to do."

"Continuous observation marks the order of the day. Early detection, subarachnoid and intracerebral hemorrhage prevention— emerging disasters that complicate and take months, if they ever do resolve. Worse is the permanent disability. Delayed PCP toxicity has become so infamously entwined with ICU admission, it rather seems a standard of practice."

Raskin had seen Young send his toxic glare at House many times before. She now saw traces of this propulsive stellar burn, the heat and singe that once pierced her scleral whites, again in his eyes and in the eyes of House.

"In a certain sense, one might consider rotary nystagmus as a nonverbal prospect sign, a gesture of things to come." Raskin remembered their meeting in her office. She had keyed "Spencer Kelly, Associate Professor of Psychology, Brain and Language Centre at Colgate University" into her iPad, clicking the first relevant article she saw, and listened.

"Nonverbal gestures make people hear, force them to pay more attention to the detailed acoustics of your speech. They are not merely add-ons, but fundamental parts of language. The addition of a gesture helps to access past memories. Adding gestures while speaking helps one talk quickly and see effectively, solidifying theirs and others' memories of what you say. Here at Colgate, we totally love fluid hand gestures. The smoother, the better. Jerky robotic like gestures feel and look unnatural, so they tend to be distracting." Raskin, with a flick of her wrist, closed her iPad.

"Pressure's dropping!" shouted the first medic.

"He's fucked. We need to get this sucker into the ambulance *now*."

"Daddy, I've had to make a model of you. A man in black with a *Mein Kampf* look and a love of the rack and the screw. And yes, I said I do, I do."

"It takes but one to five milligrams of PCP to fully inhibit neuronal reuptake of dopamine serotonin, and norepinephrine—a beautiful trifecta of emotional charge!"

Young was charged all right to hear but one voice—his.

"OMG, will you finally stop your pathetic ranting and raving, House? I know Jenny's got anxiety and depression; any increase we provide in available neurotransmitters should be of great benefit to her. Anyways, PCP is old-hat stuff; it hasn't been relevant for years."

"I'd beg to differ, Herr Doktor. In 1979 a general survey showed 13 percent of twelfth graders had used PCP within the past month. A recent report found that 25 percent of street marijuana samples tested positive for PCP. It might seem overly incredulous to you, but cigarette butts have resulted in more childhood cases of PCP toxicity and death than cannabis buds ever had in puppies. At least in a dog world we know they've an abundance of cannabinoid receptors; as to the human brain, it has not a single PCP receptor."

Young obviously hadn't a present wherewithal to anticipate House's next move, which would have, in differing circumstances, been highly predictable.

"Dr. Raskin, please pass over Ms. Hart's chart. I want to read you an excerpt.

It comes from her last admission. All four eyes made the saccade over to Young.

"Ms. Hart's irritability, thought and perceptual disturbances, not to mention her outlandish behaviors, have me concerned."

"Yes," Raskin interceded, "just like the great mimickers of old, tuberculosis and syphilis did a century ago, PCP has now become the new great copy mimicker of age."

"Yes, Daddy, I'm finally through. The black telephone's off at the root; the voices just can't worm through."

"Get the hell away from me. I've seen your act before."

The voice ignored his plea. "Back right off. Just listen. I'm not nearly done."

Young cringed, fell forward, cracking his back flush against the wheelchair.

"Jo's case was one of agitated delirium. Such a state could have been caused by drug toxicity. Cocaine, crystal meth, or PCP could have done the trick. As would have sepsis, meningitis, encephalitis, and a host of metabolic disturbances, like thyrotoxic storm or malignant neuroleptic syndrome." House was proud of his differential diagnostic skills.

Raskin's calm voice interceded. "Ms. Hart's temperature never rose. Her thyroid studies were normal. Her urinalysis report was clean. Blood cultures were negative."

House's voice continued to dominate. "Dissociative effects of PCP lead to poor decisions not remembered; bizarre, forgotten high-risk behaviors; disorganized thoughts whose imbedded nonsensical circumstances left not a single memory trace. Why punish yourself so hard for mistakes? Getting a reliable history with PCP on board might, my dear Albert, not even be possible. As for PCP ingested as an unsuspected adjunct, well ... patients in these circumstances would of course, be clueless to its source."

Raskin now couldn't resist putting into her two cents into play. "Precisely why *quantitative* identification meets the standard of care in our program—which drug and how much —why it's important in differential diagnosis of patients with altered mental status.

I'll have the lab run an HPLC. False negative EMITs are not at all unusual, and UDS tampering is commonplace amongst seasoned drug users." House smiled a broad smile.

"No identified etiology means a mental state yet to be determined. Right, Jo?"

"If I've killed one man, I've killed two; the vampire who said he was you and drank my blood for a year. Seven years, if you want to know, Daddy."

"We need forensics to check out Jo's living environment. See what's around. Speak with her family. Track down all potential sources of laced cannabis. With informed consent, our lab could test any and all items found for evidence of secondhand drug exposure."

You on it? Raskin asked House.

Motherfucker. Young thought.

Believe you me I'm on it. House replied.

Maybe so, but Jenny is an orphan. Young laughed and snickered out loud.

Albert awoke in the ambulance. One of the paramedics was at present attempting to resuscitate him, pounding on his chest. He knew at this point all was fruitless.

"Right, smart stuff, this angel dust. Question does two

mean, meant or minds? Benefit or bereft? Is two better than one? At certain times it is better. If put to the task, two can work better as one. If complementary, the effect proves magnitudes better—more than what each adds on its own. But might two be worse? How so?

Well, now let us see.

"PCP inhibits neuronal reuptake but at the same time increases production, so we get a double effect of addition. But angel dust is really super smart stuff, meanwhile it stimulates, a catalytic enzyme called tyrosine hydroxylase, in effect thrusting the whole chemical reaction into overdrive. Presto! A multiplication effect."

Albert's face had turned a deep red shade of purple.

PANIC in the air. He stopped breathing.

"There is a fine line between toxicity, illness, and death. Dosages as small as ten milligrams may induce an acute state of schizophrenia. Doubling the dosage to twenty milligrams is all that's necessary to result in deepening coma. PCP cuts a fine line.

Albert's eyes rolled up in his head and he was gone.

"One quarter to one half the dose causes behavior like that reported of Ms. Hart."

Young gasped. Did he have one last dying breath of life. His head spun round, paralyzed of thought and then collapsed, blood spattering as his head hit the floor.

Raskin and House helped Andy up and into a wheelchair. He remained unaware that his interrogation in earnest had just begun.

His heart gave up. For a few desperate moments, he was trapped inside a broken fracture body. Then he shot out of it, above it, directionless.

"Did you even check Jo's urine for myoglobin? Repeat her UDS?"

Albert's eyes dead and gone; body slumped on one side of the wheelchair.

"Wake up, Andy! Most deaths from PCP intoxication are not due to any direct drug effect, but are rather the result of a patients own violent behavior."

Albert's fiery eyes igniting his dark heart as he bolted out of the wheelchair.

"That's why Ms. Hart had to be restrained upon ER admission," Young screeched, to anyone around, who might hear. House saw a gigantic red glow of an ego gone golden.

"I tell you, Andy, be vigilant. Watch for self-inflicted trauma. Remain highly suspicious, of what seems like an accident. Prolonged PCP effects can outlast toxicity by months, even years. Once I watched a twenty something patient of mine, nine months post toxicity, walk starry-eyed straight into traffic. Saw another man jump smiling off the rooftop of a building, waving the whole way down. I've seen teenagers enucleate their own eyes.

PCP is recalcitrant and unremitting. Does any of this sound at all familiar, Andy?"

There was no Andy. He was long gone.

What now?

Isn't this when God himself is said to appear?

Where fate in the afterlife is sealed?

Young saw a bright light up ahead in the distance. More choppers? The rising sun? Albert realized the light he saw grew out of the ever brightening dawn. It was bone white, widening in size, until it seemed nearly as vast as the sky. He thought himself toward it, then stepped into it, and as he did, it swallowed him whole.

"Daddy, you can lie back now. There's a stake in your fat black heart. The villagers never liked you. They are dancing and stamping on you. They always *knew* it was you. Daddy, Daddy you bastard, I'm through."

Chapter
20

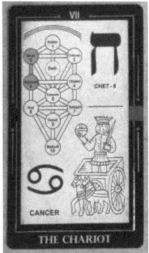

'137' Death Followed By The Chariot

THE LATE GOOD FRIDAY SKY OF MARCH 15, 2022 WAS A DEEP
Mediterranean blue color, the air unseasonably cool. As Jo
turned onto High Road, she spotted a mother hawk soaring
into that clear bitter blue with two smaller hawks. Her kids.

Jenny took it as a positive sign of things to come.

Jo stopped about half a mile from the Giral house, where
the area was cordoned off. She pulled in next to Marina's
car, surprised that everyone else had already arrived. Fuentes

stood with Marina, Eleanor, Diego, Chris, Adele, half a dozen cops and firemen, and four men, wearing hard hats.

Jo got out and joined them.

"Glad you made it," Fuentes smiled, put a hand on her shoulder.

"Got held up in traffic. Wouldn't miss this for the world."

A tall black guy in a hard hat said, "So Evan tells me y'all got some kind of connection to this old, decrepit place?"

Jo nodded.

"Is it, like, a family connection?"

Marina's laugh was quick. "Yeah, you might say that."

"Okay, here's what's going to happen. We've set up the explosives already. Once we get ready to detonate, you all should probably be farther back, especially since detonation might set off the other explosives—those Evan told me about. Have any of you ever seen a demolition before?"

"Not a controlled demolishment," Diego said.

"What do you do with all the rubble afterward?" Eleanor asked.

"Haul it off, recycle it."

"Good," Jo said. "How soon will the government start converting the area to parkland?"

"By May. Any more questions?"

"Yeah, I got one," Adele said. "Have you ever demolished a haunted house?"

"Haunted?" He laughed. "Well, actually, yeah, an old place once in South Miami. Urban myth says the place was haunted, but I never saw nothing. The day we brought it down, an elderly woman, a neighborhood watcher, she swore she saw spirits evaporating at the same time the place came tumbling down."

"Evaporating?" Fuentes looked at Adele. "What does that mean to a Santera, Adele?"

She answered without hesitation. "Souls are released from their karmic prisons."

"Sounds good," Chris remarked. "How far back do you want us?"

"A mile or so should do it."

Ten minutes later, they and their cars were a mile up the road from the old house. A team of hard hats walked quickly around the house, checking their explosives. Some black guy, wearing a cut off print shirt with I AM A RET ACTOR pasted accross his chest, swung into the realm of an earthmover, as his team retreated to tractors. Other earth retracting contractors, had parked behind Jo's group. The black man then made a signal for the cops and firemen to hold their position, wait upon his orders.

Once everyone was set a safe distance away, the black dude began a countdown that he broadcasted over a PA he had placed on the roof of a vehicle. "Ten … nine … eight …"

Jo hung on each number, and when the explosion occurred, the house of Giral which sat motionless on 137 High Street, all like Humpty Dumpty came tumbling down, as if it could no longer sustain the excess gravity that had held it there, intact for nearly a century.

Clouds of grey dust flew up around it, obscuring it from sight.

All happily joined hands, Adele chanting in Yoruba, the native language of Santeria, then in Spanish, "May you find solace and comfort in death and finally rest in peace."

But could she? In a dire need to hold the House of Giral

accountable, Jo had helped kill a man, her father. Would karma make her pay for that, in this or the next life?

Maybe. But if karma deemed it so, it was all worth it.

"I'm pulling a card." Marina reached for her bag and pulled out a tarot deck. She shuffled it, Held it out. "Pick one card, Jo."

Jennifer Hart took the deck into her hands, crouched and spread the cards against the ground. She held her hand low above the deck and moved where the energy drew her. She picked a card and turned it over.

Judgment.

Epilogue

"Silence flashed from the woodwork and the walls. It smote with an awful total power, as if generated by a vast mill. It rose from the floor, ascended from the torn grey wall to wall carpeting, unleashed itself from the tattered semi broken appliances in the kitchen. It smote from he dead machines, which hadn't worked, oozed out of the useless pole lamp in the living room, meshing with the empty wordless decent of itself, from the fly specked ceiling, as if it mean to supplant all things tangible. It not only assailed his ears but his eyes. As he stood by the inert TV set, K experienced this silence as visible. For this silence of the world, could not rein back its greed, not any longer, not when it had virtually won."

—Philip K. Dick 1968 Blade Runner

Blade Runner 2049, the American film version of Philip K. Dick's science fiction novel 'Do Androids Dream of Electric Sheep?' premiered under the astrological sign of Libra on 03/10/ 2017 in Los Angeles. Three days later in 2D, 3D and IMAX modes, it was released to a largerUS audience.

In 2049, 30 years following the events of Blade Runner, bioengineered humans known as replicants were left as slaves. K (short for his serial number, KD6-3.7), a Nexus-9 replicant, works for the LAPD as a 'blade runner' an officer who hunts and 'retires' as he 'kills' rogue replicants. As K retires Nexus-8 replicant Sapper Morton, K finds a box buried under a tree at Morton's protein farm. The box contains, the remains of a female replicant who died, during a caesarean section, ostensibly demonstrating that replicants can reproduce biologically, previously thought impossible.

K's superior, Lt. Joshi, fears this could lead to a war between the humans and replicants. She orders K to find and retire the replicant child, to hide the truth.

K visits the headquarters of the Wallace Corporation, successor to the defunct Tyrell Corporation, in the manufacture of replicants. Wallace staff members identify the deceased female from computer DNA archives as Rachael, an experimental replicant designed by Dr. Eldon Tyrell. K then learns of Rachael's deathly romantic ties with former blade runner Rick Deckard.

Meanwhile, Corporation CEO Niander Wallace wants to discover the hidden secret to replicant reproduction, in order to expand interstellar colonization. To this end he sends his replicant enforcer Luv to steal Rachael's remains and to follow K to Rachael's child.

At Morton's farm, K finds the numbers 6.10.21 carved into a tree trunk. This he now recognizes came from a forgotten childhood memory of a wooden toy horse. But because replicant memories are fictitious and artificial, K's holographic R.I.G.F

Joi, his girlfriend, believes this evidence that K was born, not created.

K incredulously searches the entire LAPD record data base only to discover identical twins born on that date, with identical DNA, save for the sex chromosome, but only the boy had been listed as alive. K then tracks this child to an orphanage, somewhere in ruined San Diego but the records from that year were oddly missing.

K recognizes this god forsaken place as his childhood orphanage. As the forgotten place where he once hid the toy horse.

In his classic, The Interpretation of Dreams, Sigmund Freud asks this question:What do sheep dream of? His quick witted answer, of course, was maize. Andy is an android blade runner. Would he, like Dr. Andy Young, dream of electric sheep?

REFERENCE

About Science Fiction Font Family https://www.myfonts.com/collections/science

Description: geometric sans-serif with clean, ordered, hi-tech, futuristic feeling.

Usage for texts, tiles, interfaces, logos, technical inscriptions, everything. .My Fonts by Monotype debuted on June 17, 2021 Designed by Alexander Bobrov,

Publisher, foundry and design ownership copyright from Indian Summer Studio.

Appendix

Exhibit "A"

DH1847, 13/05 FL HEALTH
Bureau of Public Health Laboratory

Laboratory Use Only

DR. LAURENCE HOUSE

BROWARD COUNTY HOSPITAL
ER CHIEF OF STAFF

Clinician/Practitioner Number	CPSO / Registration No.
AMA150959	299974

Clinician/Practitioner's Contact Number for Urgent Results

Service Date: YYYY / mm / dd

Health Number: FL 1 9 9 0 - 3 6 9 Version Sex M☐ F☐ Date of Birth: YYYY 1 9 9 0 mm 0 5 dd 1 4

Check [✓] one:
✓ FL Insured   ☐ Third Party / Uninsured   ☐ WSIB

Province: Other Provincial Registration Number   Patient's Telephone Contact Number

Additional Clinical Information (e.g. diagnosis)
DELERIUM

Patient's Last Name (as per OHIP Card)
HART

Patient's First & Middle Names (as per OHIP Card)
JENNIFER

Copy to: Clinician/Practitioner
Last Name   First Name
DR. YOUNG   ALBERT

Address
PSYCHIATRY

Patient's Address (including Postal Code)

Note: Separate requisitions are required for cytology, histology / pathology and tests performed by Public Health Laboratory

x	Biochemistry		x	Hematology	x	Viral Hepatitis (check one only)
	Glucose ☐ Random ☐ Fasting			CBC		Acute Hepatitis
	HbA1C			Prothrombin Time (INR)		Chronic Hepatitis
	Creatinine (eGFR)			Immunology		Immune Status / Previous Exposure
	Uric Acid			Pregnancy Test (Urine)		Specify ☐ Hepatitis A
	Sodium			Mononucleosis Screen		☐ Hepatitis B
	Potassium			Rubella		☐ Hepatitis C
	ALT			Prenatal: ABO, RhD, Antibody Screen (titre and ident. if positive)		or order individual hepatitis tests in the "Other Tests" section below
	Alk. Phosphatase			Repeat Prenatal Antibodies		Prostate Specific Antigen (PSA)
	Bilirubin					☐ Total PSA ☐ Free PSA
	Albumin			Microbiology ID & Sensitivities (if warranted)		Specify one below
	Lipid Assessment (includes Cholesterol, HDL-C, Triglycerides, calculated LDL-C & Chol/HDL-C ratio; individual lipid tests may be ordered in the "Other Tests" section of this form)			Cervical		Insured – FL Insured
				Vaginal		Uninsured – Screening: Patient responsible for payment
	Albumin / Creatinine Ratio, Urine			Vaginal / Rectal – Group B Strep		Vitamin D (25-Hydroxy)
	Urinalysis (Chemical)			Chlamydia (specify source)		Insured – FL Insured
	Neonatal Bilirubin			GC (specify source):		osteopenia, osteoporosis, rickets; renal disease, malabsorption syndromes; medications affecting vitamin D metabolism
	Child's Age days hours			Sputum		Uninsured – Patient responsible for payment
	Clinician/Practitioner's tel. no. ( )			Throat		Other Tests - one test per line
	Patient's 24 hr telephone no. ( )			Wound (specify source)		
	Therapeutic Drug Monitoring:			Urine		URINE Na, K, cl, pH,
	Name of Drug #1			Stool Culture		FINGER sg, temperature,
	Name of Drug #2			Stool Ova & Parasites		PRINTING creatinine.
	Time Collected #1 hr. #2 hr.			Other Swabs / Pus (specify source)		HPLC Opiates, PCP,
	Time of Last Dose #1 hr. #2 hr.					Cocaine, THC, Alcohol
	Time of Next Dose #1 hr. #2 hr.			Specimen Collection		Barbituites, Benzodiazepines
				Time Date		Nicotine, Cotinine

I hereby certify the tests ordered are not for registered in or out patients of a hospital.

Fecal Occult Blood Test (FOBT) (check one):
☐ FOBT (non CCC)   ☐ ColonCancerCheck FOBT (CCC) no other test can be ordered on this form

Taurine, Gluteraldehyde

Laboratory Use Only

X _____ (Admistration) 13 3 2022
_____ 13 3 2022
Clinician/Practitioner Signature   Date

4452-64 (2013/01) © Queen's Printer for Ontario, 2015   7530-4581

Exhibit 'B'

Printed in the United States
by Baker & Taylor Publisher Services